W9-CEH-649

CONFESSIONS OF AN ENGLISH OPIUM-EATER

broadview editions
series editor: L.W. Conolly

CONFESSIONS OF AN ENGLISH OPIUM-EATER
AND RELATED WRITINGS

Thomas De Quincey

edited by Joel Faflak

broadview editions

Library and Archives Canada Cataloguing in Publication

De Quincey, Thomas, 1785–1859

    Confessions of an English opium-eater / Thomas De Quincey ; editor, Joel Faflak.

Includes bibliographical references.

ISBN 978-1-55111-435-4

    1. De Quincey, Thomas, 1785–1859. 2. Drug addicts—Great Britain—Biography. 3. Authors, English—19th century—Biography. 4. Opium abuse—England. I. Faflak, Joel, 1959– II. Title.

PR4534.C6 2008   828'.809   C2008-908158-7

Broadview Editions

The Broadview Editions series represents the ever-changing canon of literature by bringing together texts long regarded as classics with valuable lesser-known works.

Advisory editor for this volume: Martin R. Boyne

Broadview Press is an independent, international publishing house, incorporated in 1985. Broadview believes in shared ownership, both with its employees and with the general public; since the year 2000 Broadview shares have traded publicly on the Toronto Venture Exchange under the symbol BDP.

We welcome comments and suggestions regarding any aspect of our publications—please feel free to contact us at the addresses below or at broadview@broadviewpress.com / www.broadviewpress.com.

North America
PO Box 1243, Peterborough, Ontario, Canada K9J 7H5
2215 Kenmore Ave., Buffalo, NY, USA 14207
Tel: (705) 743-8990; Fax: (705) 743-8353
email: customerservice@broadviewpress.com

UK, Ireland, and continental Europe
NBN International
Estover Road
Plymouth, UK PL6 7PY
Tel: 44 (0) 1752 202 300
Fax: 44 (0) 1752 202 330
email: enquiries@nbninternational.com

Australia and New Zealand
UNIREPS, University of New South Wales
Sydney, NSW, Australia 2052
Tel: 61 2 9664 0999; Fax: 61 2 9664 5420
email: info.press@unsw.edu.au

Broadview Press acknowledges the financial support of the Government of Canada through the Book Publishing Industry Development Program (BPIDP) for our publishing activities.

This book is printed on paper containing 100% post-consumer fibre.

PRINTED IN CANADA

Contents

Acknowledgements

I thank the Social Sciences and Humanities Research Council of Canada for its support of my research while I worked on this edition, the production of which has been rather De Quinceyesque. I say this by way of thanking Martin Boyne, Leonard Conolly, Julia Gaunce, Marjorie Mather, and the staff at Broadview Press for their assistance; and Haley Bordo, Ross Bullen, Lisa Butler, John Connolly, Amanda Irvine, and Sylvia Terzian, for theirs. *None* of them was dilatory. Nor was Michelle Faubert or Arnold Markley, who performed swift and always gracious turnarounds. I thank both Walter Zimmerman in the Weldon Library at the University of Western Ontario, and also the very helpful staff of the British Library. For their valuable feedback and suggestions, I thank the anonymous readers of my original proposal for this edition. To Tilottama Rajan and Ross Woodman I owe an incalculable debt of gratitude for all they have taught and continue to teach me. I owe an equal debt to Julia Wright, whose scholarly example and friendship remind me of what matters most in the academy. I thank David Clark for suggesting that I do this edition in the first place, and for his loyalty and support. Finally, I thank Norm, who would have had, and has, no patience for De Quincey—amen.

Introduction

> The mere understanding, however useful and indispensable, is the
> meanest faculty in the human mind and the most to be distrusted;
> and yet the great majority of people trust to nothing else; which
> may do for ordinary life, but not for philosophical purposes.

> —Thomas De Quincey,
> "On the Knocking at the Gate in *Macbeth*"

Thomas De Quincey's Life and Work

Since its first publication in 1821, *Confessions of an English Opium-Eater* has
often been fetishized as an occult production of the Romantic imagination, impossible to ignore, yet difficult to place within prevailing critical
ideologies about Romanticism. If one saw Romanticism as an anomaly
wedged between the eighteenth century and the Victorian period, and the
Romantics as Matthew Arnold saw them—"premature" and unable to
get out of their heads and back into action—*Confessions* exemplified the
worst aspects of Romantic solipsism. If one idealized the Romantic imagination as an engine of change, able to transcend historical, social, and
political vagaries in order to redeem a vision of the world empowered by
its own creative energies, *Confessions* was a pathology within
Romanticism's organic form. Usually, then, De Quincey was either an
appendix to Wordsworth or the Coleridgean side effect of a dangerous
Romantic inspiration. More to the point, the nineteenth century came to
see Wordsworth's and Coleridge's writings as culturally therapeutic. De
Quincey's were decidedly *not*, because his most notable effort was to
confess an addiction never overcome. And as much as he desired reparation, he also debunked its illusions. This ambivalence defines a more recent
view of the writer's achievement, from which the current introduction
and edition take their cue. The strategy herein is to focus on *Confessions*
as it is situated within what I will call De Quincey's larger confessional
project, which defines a matrix of interrelated issues through which to
examine the text's relationship to the culture it produced and in turn
helped to shape. De Quincey's personal and professional life reflect the
vagaries of a proto-Victorian public sphere increasingly consumed by a

utilitarian desire for material success, searching for domestic stability and for both personal and social success that would secure the myth of progress driving the Industrial Revolution and the building of Empire. The consumption of De Quincey's life and work by addiction is a comment on this culture's ideas of moral management, political economy, and increasingly zealous sense of imperial entitlement, all of which protected the nineteenth century from its own fears and appetites.

Thomas De Quincey, the fourth of eight children, was born in Manchester, England, on 15 August 1785, into what we would now call an upwardly mobile middle-class family. His father was Thomas Quincey, a successful textile merchant, and his mother was Elizabeth Penson, of higher social standing than her husband. Manchester was a centre for cotton manufacture and distribution, one of the engines driving the Industrial Revolution, which was by then in full swing. In 1791 the family relocated to a new country house christened "Greenhay," where life was quite comfortable. But in 1790 De Quincey's younger sister Jane had died, followed in 1792 by his older sister Elizabeth, two deaths that profoundly affected De Quincey's confessional writings. The following year Thomas Senior died, leaving the Quincey children to the care of their mother and four guardians, close friends appointed to manage the father's business affairs. At this they proved rather inept, and by 1796 Greenhay was sold for less than half its original cost, after which Elizabeth relocated the family to the fashionable city of Bath. Morally austere, Elizabeth carefully controlled her children's lives in order to optimize their social standing. At some point after the Bath move the aristocratic "De" was added to the family name, capitalizing upon a tradition that the family could trace its lineage to the De Quincis who followed William the Conqueror across the Channel in the twelfth century. Such was the mother's success at negotiating her son's future that by the age of 15, travelling with the young Lord Westport, son of the Irish peer Lord Altamount, Thomas met George III.

De Quincey was a preternaturally gifted adolescent, exceptional in Greek and Latin and possessed of a prodigious memory. But the ease of academic accomplishment also made him restless. His physical constitution wasn't the strongest, and from an early age he was prone to hypochondria. His time at school, therefore, was fitful and intermittent. By 1802, at 16, in order to assert autonomy from his mother, guardians, and institutional discipline, De Quincey ran away from Manchester Grammar School and wandered through Wales and London, an experience he recounts in "Preliminary Confessions." Reconciled with his mother and guardians the following year, he entered Worcester College, University of Oxford.

Worcester was one of the university's less prestigious colleges, but Oxford was still the right place for a middle-class son with scholarly aspirations. It was also where De Quincey started taking opium, at first to relieve a toothache, but mostly for recreational purposes, that is, "for the sake of creating an artificial state of pleasurable excitement." His confirmed addiction started around 1813 when a stomach "derangement," the chronic result of "extremities of hunger, suffered" while wandering in Wales and especially London, coupled with a "depression of spirits," "yielded to no remedies but opium." Past this point the "pleasures" and "pains" of opium intermixed to exert a sadomasochistic physical and mental influence that De Quincey never wholly subdued,[1] the tension between curbing addiction and its chronic return, forming the darkly creative matrix of his confessional project.

At first, however, opium merely strengthened the "great light of the majestic intellect" and thus sharpened De Quincey's passion, as he writes early on in *Confessions*, to lead "the life of a philosopher: from my birth I was made an intellectual creature." His intellectual heroes were the poet-philosopher Samuel Taylor Coleridge, and especially the philosopher Immanuel Kant and the political economist David Ricardo. But his desire for greatness was perhaps most powerfully fuelled by his idolization of William Wordsworth. By 1803 Wordsworth and Coleridge were part of a considerable cult of personality, and their joint effort, *Lyrical Ballads* (first published in 1798), was on its way to being canonized as one of the ur-texts of Romantic literature. De Quincey longed for some form of association with the Lake School that included Wordsworth, Coleridge, and Robert Southey. Besides, a literary career meant that he could earn his own way. He received an annuity of £150 when his father died, and £2,600 at his maturity at 21, in 1806. By that time he was £600 in debt, a situation that became chronic until the early 1840s when his eldest daughter Margaret took over the management of her father's household and finances. The decision to write a letter of introduction to Wordsworth in 1803, and Wordsworth's cautious yet flattered reply, were thus fortuitous for several reasons.[2] By August 1806 De Quincey had met Coleridge, and

---

[1]   *Confessions* is partly a case history of De Quincey's control of his opium intake. His dosage fluctuated wildly, from only several drops of laudanum per day to up to 8,000 drops (or so he claims in his 1822 Appendix to *Confessions*, included in Appendix A4 below) when his addiction was in full swing. Twenty-five drops of laudanum was the equivalent dosage of roughly one grain of opium, which, in apothecaries' weight, equalled approximately .002803 ounces in avoirdupois measure, or .0648 grams metric.

[2]   De Quincey's letter praises the "transcendency of [Wordsworth's] genius" and continues:

in November he finally met the Great Man. In May 1807 he abruptly left Oxford during final examinations, and that November moved to Grasmere, at first to live with the Wordsworths, and eventually in 1809 to lease Dove Cottage when the Wordsworths moved to larger quarters at Rydall Mount.

For some time De Quincey was very close to Wordsworth and his family, although Wordsworth, rather blinded by his own ego, was by times supportive of and diffident to his self-appointed protégé. It did not help that in 1816 De Quincey brought scandal close to the Wordsworth household by fathering an illegitimate child by Margaret Simpson, considered his social inferior, although they were married the following year. Moreover, the ensuing years were marked by De Quincey's illness and addiction, which strained his friendship with the poet, who was all too well acquainted with Coleridge's drug problems. Yet during the 1810s, at first through the introduction of John Wilson, his friend at Oxford and later editor of *Blackwood's Edinburgh Magazine*, De Quincey found an independent identity among intellectual and literary circles in Edinburgh. These included James Hogg, John Gibson Lockhart, William Hamilton, and eventually Thomas Carlyle, who with his wife Jane became one of De Quincey's lifelong supporters. In Edinburgh, Grevel Lindop writes, "[p]eople were impressed equally by [De Quincey's] learning and by his oddness," and he created "an aura about him which suggested that he ought to be famous for something" (213). Glasgow and Edinburgh had become centres of philosophical and medical learning during the Scottish Enlightenment, which profoundly influenced later thought in Britain and beyond. This influence was a distinctly non-English strain within the British intellectual hybrid symbolized by the 1707 Act of Union. De Quincey's decision in 1830 to move his family permanently to Scotland is therefore both symptomatic of his rabidly middle-class devotion to Britain's industrial and cultural expansion, and an odd dissociation from the hegemony of that nation's imperialism.

In 1818, just before the final demise of his friendship with Wordsworth, the poet, on the basis of De Quincey's first pamphlet, "Comments Upon a Straggling Speech," recommended De Quincey for his first professional

---

"to no man on earth except yourself and one other (a friend of yours [Coleridge]), would I thus lowly and suppliantly prostrate myself" (Wright 85–87). Wordsworth's reply was polite but distant: "My friendship is not in my power to give: this is a gift which no man can make, it is not in our power: a sound and healthy friendship is the growth of time and circumstance.... How many things are there in a man's character of which his writings however miscellaneous or voluminous will give no idea" (388–89).

job as editor of *The Westmorland Gazette*. "Comments" responded to the local Westmorland election, in which the Scots reformer Henry Brougham, future Lord Chancellor, attempted to break the Tory stranglehold of the Lowther family, headed by the Earl of Lonsdale. The pamphlet put De Quincey at the centre of the election's debates, and as *Gazette* editor he became embroiled in a bitter exchange with the Whig *Kendal Chronicle*. De Quincey's early journalism, his contemporary editors note, was "defensive, slightly hysterical," partly because of his ultra-Toryism, partly out of his desire to "impress his Westmorland peers" (*Works* 1:96).[1] This tension between principle and expediency defines much of De Quincey's subsequent writings, whether on politics, literature, political economy, rhetoric, history, or any of the numerous other subjects he tackles. The result is that one never quite knows where to place him as a writing subject,[2] complicated by the fact that much of his writing blurs the line between objective fact and authorial identity. *Confessions of an English Opium-Eater* is the blueprint for this approach, of course. De Quincey either lost or resigned from his post at the *Gazette* in 1819, but he began writing for *London Magazine* (1821–25), which published *Confessions* in two installments in 1821. Its immediate success led to the work's 1822 publication as a book by Taylor and Hessey. The work stages with disarming frankness "the spectacle of a human being obtruding on our notice his moral ulcers or scars, and tearing away that 'decent drapery,' which time, or indulgence to human frailty, may have drawn over them." De Quincey's confessional approach echoes what is considered to be the first Western autobiography, Augustine of Hippo's (St. Augustine's) *Confessions* (c. 397–98 CE), but most immediately echoes Jean-Jacques

---

[1]   I cite here and throughout from Grevel Lindop's 2000–04 *Works*, not to be confused with the 1871 Edinburgh edition, also entitled *Works*. See Bibliography for details.

[2]   In general De Quincey's writings reveal a deeply conservative, often stridently imperialist or paranoically isolationist, nature. Yet different venues brought out different voices. As Robert Morrison writes, the liberal *Tait's* "allowed [De Quincey] to explore the rebellious sides of his temperament, and to espouse the liberal features of his political ideology.... In *Blackwood's* he adhered closely to the magazine's firm Tory line, but in its rival he praised feminists, prophets, and radicals, acknowledged the need for reform, championed the working class and the newspaper press, and welcomed the legacy of the French Revolution, ... though De Quincey styled himself an 'uncompromising Tory'" (*Works* 9:304–05). In many ways De Quincey is the perfect embodiment of the often radically divided political temper of his time, deeply committed to, but often swept away by, the lure of progress, and deeply suspicious of its promises. Or as Morrison writes, De Quincey's "fascination with power is complicated by a profound sympathy with the underdog" (*Works* 8:224). De Quincey was no Reformist, although he was mindful of reform's humanity.

Rousseau's *Confessions* (1782), which galvanized the spirit of emotional and psychological introspection of that time. Rousseau begins *Confessions* by addressing his reader: "I am resolved on an undertaking that has no model and will have no imitator. I want to show my fellow-men in all the truth of nature; and this man is to be myself.... I have shown myself as I was, contemptible and vile when that is how I was, good, generous, sublime, when that is how I was; I have disclosed my innermost self as you alone know it to be" (5). Distinguishing De Quincey's approach, as we shall see in subsequent sections, was both its subject and its appearance in periodicals at a time when the working and middle classes, increasingly hungry for information and entertainment, were negotiating their stake in the political franchise.

Confessions canonized De Quincey as "the Opium-Eater," and for the remainder of his career he both capitalized upon and shrank from the notoriety of this identity. By the 1830s De Quincey undertook for *Tait's Edinburgh Magazine* a series of memoirs entitled "Sketches of Life and Manners from the Autobiography of an English Opium-Eater" (1834–41). The return to confessional writing "may have been," Lindop argues, "a psychological necessity," for by 1834 De Quincey's "health was ruined; his great works on philosophy and mathematics would never be written; he had a wife and seven children whom he could barely support. He had no leisure for scholarship, no prospect before him but hack-authorship" (313). Moreover, between 1832 and 1840 De Quincey was sued for debt numerous times, briefly imprisoned by his creditors on one occasion, and frequently fled for refuge to Holyrood.[1] And Margaret's

---

[1]   Lindop notes that De Quincey was, by Scottish law, "put to the horn" nine times: "This curious ritual arose from the fact that imprisonment for debt was technically not sanctioned by Scottish law. Attitudes to debtors being no more friendly in Scotland than elsewhere, a procedure had evolved whereby a debtor could be imprisoned under the legal fiction that he was guilty of a different offence. The creditor would apply to a court which had power to issue a letter commanding the debtor in the name of the monarch to pay his debt. If he still 'refused' to pay he was held to be disobeying a royal command, and an officer of the court would go to the market-place at Edinburgh and, with three blasts of a horn, publicly proclaim him a rebel. He could then be imprisoned" (302). The debtor's sanctuary of Holyrood Park adjoining Holyrood Palace, the current Royal residence, one mile from Edinburgh Castle, "offered a tolerable alternative to prison. To avail himself of the privilege of sanctuary, a debtor had to register with the Bailie—the officer who governed Holyrood—and pay a fee of two guineas, after which he could enjoy in peace the open space within the precincts ... Some were there for days or weeks, others for many years. They came from all walks of life, and at one time in the early nineteenth century they included three baronets" (310). The sanctuary was frequently home to De Quincey and various configurations of his immediate family.

chronic physical illness and depression, while understandable given the demands of wife- and motherhood at that time, left the family's domestic and financial management to De Quincey, a pressure that only increased after her death in 1837.

The *Tait's* pieces inaugurate a penultimate career phase during which, despite advancing age, "ruined" health, and misfortune, De Quincey was amazingly productive.[1] These sketches inspired a self-proclaimed 1845 sequel to *Confessions*, *Suspiria de Profundis*, published in four parts in *Blackwood's*. *Suspiria* was projected as a larger masterwork only partially realized through the 1849 *Blackwood's* publication of *The English Mail-Coach*. This productivity coincided with an 1843 move to Mavis Bush Cottage in Lasswade, seven miles outside Edinburgh, after which point De Quincey's domestic life achieved relative calm and happiness (he moved there to be with his family). By the end of the 1840s his career entered a final phase in which he re-fashioned his *oeuvre* for a Victorian audience. In 1851 the Boston publisher Ticknor, Reid, and Fields began publishing *De Quincey's Writings*, which extended to 20 volumes by 1859 and which republished both *Confessions* and *Suspiria de Profundis* as the apex of De Quincey's achievement. This American canonization inspired him to collect his works in a British edition, *Selections Grave and Gay, from Writings Published and Unpublished*, which he returned to Edinburgh to oversee. *Selections* opened with two volumes that re-collected his autobiographical sketches, a prelude to his substantial revision of the original *Confessions* for Volume Five, published in 1856. De Quincey intended to edit *Suspiria* as part of this larger effort, and thus to give definitive shape to the confessional project that had consumed his professional and personal life. However, having pirated much of *Suspiria* for Volumes One and Two, having lost much of its unpublished manuscript material, and being exhausted partly by the revision of *Confessions* and in general by his waning energies, this project went unrealized. De Quincey died in Edinburgh in 1859, one year before *Selections* was completed. By that time Wordsworth

---

[1] De Quincey wrote nearly 50 articles for *London Magazine* (1821–25), nearly 75 for *Tait's Edinburgh Magazine* (1833–51), and nearly 100 for *Blackwood's Edinburgh Magazine* (1821–45). This does not include his late contributions to *Hogg's Instructor* (1850–58), or his early journalism for the *Westmorland Gazette* (1818–20), the *Edinburgh Saturday Post* (1827–28), and the *Edinburgh Evening Post* (1828–29), as well as a host of other venues. He managed a novel *Klosterheim; or, The Masque* (1832); *Walladmor* (*London Magazine* 1825), De Quincey's translation of a "translated" (i.e., forged) 1824 Scott novel first published in Germany; the shorter narratives "The Household Wreck" and "The Avenger" (both for *Blackwood's* 1838); a substantial historical study, "The Caesars" (*Blackwood's* 1832–34); numerous translations of German texts; and the book-length *The Logic of Political Economy* (1844).

had been dead for nearly ten years. Indeed, most of the other figures of what we would now call High Romanticism—Coleridge, George Gordon Byron, Percy Shelley, John Keats, William Hazlitt, Charles Lamb—were long dead. The great irony is that De Quincey—the opium addict and "hack-writer" whose health and spirit were "broken" by personal and professional hardship and circumstance, who in so many ways went against the literary currents of his age—survived them all.

The Evolution and Reception of *Confessions*

Most of De Quincy's writings were published in periodicals and newspapers, whose publishing schedules were suited to De Quincey's fitful writing habits, formed by recurrent health, financial, and domestic problems, although serial publication imposed its own demands. The growth of periodicals from the early eighteenth century coincided with the expansion of print technologies and circulations, and with the emergence of a more diversified English reading audience whose identity the periodicals helped to shape. This development paralleled revolutions in taste and opinion leading up to events in France in 1789 and their impact on British reactions, both radical and conservative. The urban literary intelligentsia defined by Joseph Addison's *Spectator* (1711) or Samuel Johnson's *Rambler* (1759), or the more political articulation of an autonomous public opinion in the *English Review* (1783) or *Analytical Review* (1788), eventually gave way to publications whose professionalized critical practice ran parallel to the emergent modernity of a civil society sustained by a productive balance between commerce and state. Many of these journals originated in Edinburgh, centre of influence for the Scottish Enlightenment and its ideals of a rational, progressive society wherein political economy governs human interaction. Such quarterlies as the *Edinburgh Review* (1802) and *Quarterly Review* (1809), or the later *Westminster Review* (1824), depending on their political allegiances, either promulgated or critiqued such progress and so were battlegrounds for often acrimonious culture wars. Generally at stake, however, was the power to speak for the developing professional class of the new industrial age. These journals' critical function was no longer merely to purvey "literature" as the generic definition of all educated discourses but actively to identify and promote middle-class interests. The *New Monthly Magazine* (1814), *Blackwood's Edinburgh Magazine* (1817), and the *London Magazine* (1820) spoke to an audience eager to learn about the transformations taking place in their world, anxious about the market vagaries of mass production and mass culture, and thus ambivalent about the spirit of commercialism and consumerism that was coming to characterize the period.

In the early nineteenth century the literary essay and its attendant reconstruction of notions of authorship emerged to play a key role in defining this new cultural economy. The essay allowed critics to explore an eclectic range of topics from behind the cloak of anonymity, which protected them from public censure and meant their identities could emerge in distinct and rather partial ways.[1] Such avoidance, one can imagine, was especially helpful given De Quincey's rather sensational topic. The essay also helped to create a kind of scholarly prestige for the "hack" journalist, associated since the seventeenth century with the popular and gutter press of Grub Street. De Quincey became one such newly minted professional "author" of some ambition, which exposed his pretensions yet simultaneously abstracted him from the politics and commerce of his class. But as much as *Confessions* uses the circumstances of the writer's life to make Literature, it makes apparent that the author *has* to work. This tension is symptomatic of an uneasy negotiation between the working class and the middle class whose social aspirations attempt to distance it from the crass materialism of the labour upon which its success depends. Such a tension, as Margaret Russett suggests in *De Quincey's Romanticism,* marks out for De Quincey a marginal stance from which to view and critique his culture. This minority implicitly questions legitimate modes of public transmission as much as it longs for their validation. As much as De Quincey resigns himself to confession, then, he also mines its potential to speak for the self-made personality through the less prestigious but more widely accessible mass media. *Confessions* opened the door to this possibility, which in his later professional life began to look like a fortunate public and professional fall.

---

[1] One of the more notorious venues for such public performance was the monthly *Noctes Ambrosianae* series in *Blackwood's,* "purported to be the monthly record of conversation amongst a group of *Blackwood's* writers and their friends who met to dine, drink, play practical jokes and talk scandal at 'Ambrose's Tavern'" (Lindop 261). John Wilson, speaking as "Christopher North," orchestrated the series, which included Hogg, "The Ettrick Shepherd," and introduced "the Opium Eater" as one of its dramatis personae. De Quincey's anonymity was weakly disguised. In feigning that he does not know the identity of the author of *Confessions,* the reviewer for *The Monthly Review* (March 1823) says, "Yet we are quite as well assured that the English *Opium-Eater* is partly identified, in genius and social habits, with those whom Lord Byron rather uncourteously calls the *Naturals,* we mean *the Lake-school*" (296). Perhaps the most notorious case of critical abuse at this time is John Gibson Lockhart's scathing 1817 reviews in the Tory *Quarterly Review* of Keats's *Endymion,* which demonized the "Cockney School" of poets for their radical politics and class aspirations.

De Quincey published the two 1821 installments of *Confessions* in the liberal *London Magazine*, under the pseudonym "X.Y.Z." Because of the work's immediate notoriety, De Quincey published a December 1821 letter in the magazine (see Appendix A3), promising a third instalment, which he never wrote, an absence he explains at length in an Appendix that he included in the 1822 book publication of *Confessions* and reprinted in the December 1822 *London Magazine* (see Appendix A4). This third part would have addressed the related charges that the author was not real and not sufficiently critical of opium use. De Quincy claims to have "struggled against this fascinating enthralment with a religious zeal" and to have "untwisted, almost to its final links, the accursed chain which fettered me." Without the promised third instalment, however, that word "almost" troubled the work's reception thereafter. Early reviews (see Appendix B), while often favourable, question the work's authenticity and thus its "useful and instructive" value, as if to say the writer must have been high while writing. The *Sheffield Iris* wondered if the opium-eater "be real or imaginary," despite De Quincey's claim that he was, unlike much of the "*materia medica*" of his day, speaking from the "ground of a large and profound personal experience." The *Medico-Chirurgical Review* questioned the work's medical validity on the authority of the reviewer's own medicinal opium use. The *British Critic* said the text had "much genius, and fancy, and poetry, and metaphysics," but lacked "sober truths." The *British Review* called the work, despite "dazzling" qualities, "desultory and rambling," "without any intelligible drift or design," what in the early twentieth century Havelock Ellis would call its decadence (see Appendix D10). This temperament was linked to the opium-eater's "morbid existence," exacerbated by the metaphysical abstractions of Kant and Ricardo, creating an "abused intellect" that the reviewer hoped could be turned to some "useful" end. By the March 1823 *Monthly Review*, *Confessions* was already lodged in the popular imagination, and a call to resist its *fascination* began to inform the criticism. Just as the *Monthly* found the text not "very instructive or edifying to a large portion of society," *The Eclectic Review* feared its moral contagion, condemning its "strange production" as a "seductive picture ... too likely to tempt some of his readers to begin a practice" of opium-eating themselves. This effect was far-reaching, for *The North American Review* advocated quarantining the work's noxious effects from its audience.

The British public was unprepared for *Confessions*, so its strangeness, in a time that increasingly advocated the sober and productive life, seemed pathological. Such oddness made the work famous, then immediately problematic *because of* its fame, then notorious because its famous strangeness meant that the text would not go away. By the time De Quincey began to collect his works, he seemed anxious to fit himself into the mainstream. To accomplish this, he disengaged his writings from the marketplace. The 1853 general Preface to *Selections Grave and Gay* (see Appendix A5) organizes De Quincey's works into three classes of writings, *Confessions* and *Suspiria* being not only the highest class but the "highest modes of impassioned prose ranging under no precedents that [De Quincey is] aware of in any literature." In 1856 he revised *Confessions* for Volume Five of his collected works, adding a Prefatory Notice to justify why he revisited the 1821 text (see Appendix A7), and dividing the work neatly into three sections. He expanded "Preliminary Confessions" fourfold, expanded the opening of "The Pains of Opium," and appended "The Daughter of Lebanon," originally intended for *Suspiria de Profundis*, in which the Daughter's confession of her sins to her father-confessor the Evangelist, and subsequent death, somehow redeem the earlier loss of Ann, which De Quincey associates with his unsuccessful drug rehabilitation. Overall, the 1856 revision shifts the text from confession to an illumination of the well-told life. De Quincey's *Tait's* Sketches begin this process by forming the nucleus of his formal Autobiography, which frames his early life in order to justify and forestall the psychological chaos of his later addiction. Including biographical as well as autobiographical sketches, and thus taking confession in a more outwardly sociological direction, these recollections, as Vincent de Luca writes, are "carefully edited and arranged to form a narrative continuum, ... a kind of anthology of [De Quincey's] previous autobiographical writings" (118–20).[1] Keen to capitalize on ongoing interest in his confessions, yet careful to ameliorate this notoriety for his Victorian audience, De Quincey used his Autobiography to manage future receptions of his work. The Autobiography confirms his status as a Man of Letters, like Wordsworth or Carlyle, and so redeems his moral character. It separates public persona from private addictions and shows a Victorian ability to transform inner demons by giving the chronic need *to* confess an acute shape.

De Quincey's renewed reputation was also the impetus for his "sequel"

---

[1] The biographical sketches focus primarily on Coleridge, Wordsworth, Southey, and Lamb, and the autobiographical on De Quincey's life up to Westmorland and the Lake District. The first two volumes of *Selections Grave and Gay* re-organize these writings as "Autobiographic Sketches" and "Autobiographic Sketches, with Recollections of the Lakes" respectively, a rubric that prepared the way for De Quincey's 1856 expansion of "Preliminary Confessions" in Volume Five of the edition.

to *Confessions, Suspiria de Profundis.* The work begins with an "Introductory Notice" that argues that *Suspiria* will pick up where *Confessions* left off by "reveal[ing] something of the grandeur which belongs *potentially* to human dreams." Following the pattern set by *Confessions*, Part 1 continues with "The Affliction of Childhood," which, like the account of Anne's disappearance in *Confessions*, focuses on the death of De Quincey's sister Elizabeth and the dreams and visions that result from his grief. The work continues with a series of "impassioned prose" episodes in the spirit of De Quincey's opium dreams in *Confessions* and then returns to autobiography, what was later called "The Vision of Life," which fragments, leaving *Suspiria* itself unfinished. *Suspiria* turns the largely narrative structure of *Confessions* into a hybrid of narrative and multiple versions of the self and its unconscious, wherein autobiography becomes a struggle between narrative closure and psychological proliferation. These repetitions serve to explain what De Quincey calls the dreaming "machinery," but they also reflect the recurrence of his addiction. By 1845 he admits to a "third prostration before the dark idol" as a "final stage" that "differ[s] in something more than degree" from his previous two attempts, which by the 1856 revision has grown to *four* attempts. By 1845, then, De Quincey was clearly less concerned with managing addiction than he was with understanding its psychological effects. As with the narrator of "Kubla Khan," the "sensual pleasure" of opium suspends the common sense of De Quincey's reason in a "fascinating enthralment," just as the narrator of Wordsworth's Arab dream is convinced that "Of such a madness, reason did lie couched" (see Appendix A10). If, as Goya pronounced, "the sleep of reason breeds monsters," in *Suspiria* De Quincey seems disposed to meet those monsters head on.

The confrontation fell short, for as De Quincey explains in the 1856 Prefatory Notice to *Confessions* (see Appendix A7), he lost what was to have been the "crowning grace" of his confessional project, "a succession of some twenty or twenty-five dreams and noon-day visions, which had arisen under the latter stages of opium influence." A manuscript list provided by Alexander H. Japp, one of De Quincey's late Victorian editors, gives some sense of *Suspiria*'s projected shape.[1] Apart from

---

[1]   Of the thirty-two sections provided in the list, only fourteen are known to exist. Contemporary editors debate the list's authenticity because it no longer exists, if it ever did ("Japp the Ripper" was a notoriously capricious editor), and transcribe a modest version from De Quincey's manuscripts. See Frederick Burwick's transcription of this list in *Works* (15:567). Nonetheless, I provide Japp's list because of its metaphorical evocativeness, very much in the spirit of De Quincey's ambition for *Suspiria* (see Appendix A9).

"Daughter," the most significant continuation of *Suspiria* was *The English Mail-Coach*. Like *Confessions* and *Suspiria*, *Mail-Coach* explores how the circumstances of De Quincey's life both generate and are in turn re-fashioned by his dreams, which serve to expose the unconscious of everyday life. Because in *Mail-Coach* these circumstances are more broadly political, it becomes a sometimes disturbing exposure of the two earlier texts' political unconscious. Following De Quincey's 1853 Preface, however, later nineteenth-century editors and reviewers, by projecting *Mail-Coach* as merely an extension of *Suspiria*, sidestep its political content. David Masson, who edited the fourteen-volume *The Collected Writings of Thomas De Quincey* (1889–90), found De Quincey's redemption in both texts' "impassioned prose," which speaks in the highest voice of poetry, the spiritual and philosophical message of which the Victorians valorized over the novel's more prosaic socio-political concerns. This view neglects history in favour of aesthetics and downplays the empiricism of De Quincey's confessional writings in favour of their almost mystical calling, as De Quincey argues in the Notice to the 1856 *Confessions*, to "communicate the Incommunicable." Masson suggests that De Quincey was bound by what an 1863 *British Quarterly Review* claimed he lacked: a sense of "Duty." By addressing in *Suspiria* the "powers in man which suffer by this too intense life of the *social* instinct," De Quincey demonstrated a profound concern for Victorian well-being. Rather than threatening an epidemic of addicted behaviours among the English, De Quincey's opium writings, especially *Suspiria* and *Mail-Coach*, were what Japp calls "Prose-poems," "deeply philosophical" works "presenting under the guise of phantasy the profoundest laws of the working of the human spirit in its most terrible disciplines" (2). Japp's view characterizes De Quincey's writings less in terms of their relationship to history than according to the universality of spirit informing history. This De Quincey, the Victorian Genius as St. Augustine rather than Rousseau, harnesses the creative energy of an otherwise wayward dream life for public and cultural service, turning addiction and moral irresolution into a cautionary tale.

De Quincey's writings, especially *Confessions*, *Suspiria*, and *The English Mail-Coach*, were thus made to fit the Victorian idea of Great Literature and its myth of national greatness that transcended politics—although, ironically, De Quincey's fervent patriotism helped to promote such myths in the first place. Yet De Quincey's resurrection as an eminent Victorian remained only partial. For one thing, his 1830s sketches for *Tait's* were also sublimely gossipy and irreverent accounts of their subjects, especially Wordsworth and Coleridge. Written at a crucial time in the reevaluation of the legacy of Romanticism for a Victorian audience, they did little to memorialize the spirit of the age and make De Quincey's later attempts to redeem himself seem ingenuous. George Gilfillan (see Appendix B8) typifies a mid-nineteenth-century view of De Quincey as "one of the master spirits of the age," now "[n]eglected and left alone as a corpse in the shroud of his own genius," whose works are "towers of Babel." Thinking about collecting the "prodigal profusion" of De Quincey's texts, Gilfillan quotes the author as saying, "Sir, the thing is absolutely, insuperably and for ever impossible." Reducing the symptomatic power of such statements to mere quaintness, Gilfillan gives De Quincey's mind considerable authority, while subsequently defusing its power to influence the future, except insofar as "De Quincey has never ceased to believe in Christianity." The *Quarterly* disavowed even this distinction. De Quincey, while a "fine, brilliant, and unusual talent," was not a genius, famous only for being "THE ENGLISH OPIUM-EATER." Like Tennyson's Ulysses, he is just a name, both the paradigm and victim of the Victorian public sphere's worst impulses. His "decadent" appeal to a late Victorian aestheticism would invite the same criticism.

But perhaps the final portrait here of the artist as a disengaged, ruined genius comes from the author himself in 1821:

> ... I had devoted the labour of my whole life, and had dedicated my intellect, blossoms and fruits, to the slow and elaborate toil of constructing one single work, to which I had presumed to give the title of an unfinished work of Spinosa's; viz. *De emendatione humani intellectûs*. This was now lying locked up, as by frost, like any Spanish bridge or aqueduct, begun upon too great a scale for the resources of the architect; and, instead of surviving me as a monument of wishes at least, and aspirations, and a life of labour dedicated to the exaltation of human nature in that way in which God had best fitted me to promote so great an object, it was likely to stand a memorial to my children of hopes defeated, of baffled efforts, of materials uselessly accumulated, of foundations laid that were never to support a superstructure,—of the grief and the ruin of the architect....

De Quincey's competition for this role was Coleridge, whose own canonization was by the 1850s well underway (Gilfillan continues that they both "were great in spite of their habits"). In his second 1834 *Tait's* installment on Coleridge, published rather indiscreetly close after the poet's death, De Quincey writes:

[Coleridge] began the use of opium, not as a relief from any bodily pains or nervous irritations, ... but as a source of luxurious sensations. It is a great misfortune, at least it is a great peril, to have tasted the enchanted cup of youthful rapture incident to the poetic temperament. That standard of high-wrought sensibility once made known experimentally, it is rare to see a submission afterwards to the sobrieties of daily life. Coleridge ... wanted better bread than was made of wheat; and when youthful blood no longer sustained the riot of his animal spirits, he endeavoured to excite them by artificial stimulants. (*Works* 10:318)

Confessions had alluded to the poet's addiction, which Coleridge then denied. De Quincey found this not a little hurtful, at the very least unempathic, and the essay wrests Coleridge's addiction back from the grip of fate and drops it squarely in his lap: "The fine saying of Addison is familiar to most readers,—that Babylon in ruins is not so affecting a spectacle, or as solemn, as a mind overthrown by lunacy. How much more awful, then, and more magnificent a wreck, when a mind so regal as that of Coleridge is overthrown or threatened with overthrow, not by a visitation of Providence, but by the treachery of his own will" (10:304).

The comparison didn't end there. An 1859 obituary in *The Athenæum* (see Appendix B12) tries to dissociate Coleridge from De Quincey. De Quincey had the "habit of diseased introspection ... so tolerant of its own deformities as to lose all sensitiveness about them," the sign of a "most unhealthy and abnormal mind to be found amongst modern writers." Coleridge shared De Quincey's "intellectual sympathies," but possessed a "philosophic breadth and genuine Christian goodness" that allowed him to show proper "remorse" for his "moral infirmities," about which De Quincey remained unapologetic. De Quincey was thus an "egotist," "guilty of betraying confidences that, as a man of honour, he ought to have held sacred," whereas Coleridge was selfless—i.e., the model of the perfectly disinterested (in the Arnoldian sense) Victorian gentleman.

Such statements, both pathetically sincere and sensationally ironic, make the modern reader wonder to what extent De Quincey ever trusted, or took seriously, whatever myths of greatness he might have courted or was criticized for not fulfilling. They also show a De Quincey already keenly aware of the future effect his works might have.

The Opium Question: History and Politics

Confessions and its related writings are anything but apolitical texts, however. As perhaps the first work on drug addiction, *Confessions* galvanizes the political history of opium (see the writings in Appendix C, discussed below) both before and after its publication, a history that intersects crucially with the development of medical and psychological knowledge about opium, which we will examine in the next section. Influenced by early travel accounts of Eastern opium customs, British attitudes to opium were subsequently determined by the Empire's expanding involvement in the opium trade (as John Francis Davis writes in his 1838 *The Chinese: A General Description of The Empire of China and Its Inhabitants,* between 1821 and 1832 British opium imports into China grew nearly fivefold). These attitudes in turn affected a domestic response to opium practice that, using the example of the East, was at once fascinated and cautious about the drug's effect on English minds and bodies. The 1821 publication of *Confessions* marks a pivotal moment in the shaping of this political consciousness, especially as England became increasingly occupied with the minds and bodies of its colonized subjects. That is to say, *Confessions,* helping to shape a broader ideology about the benefits and perils of opium, in turn became part of *and* helped to read the political *unconscious* of Britain's colonizing efforts, particularly in India and China. Indeed, opium's history, filtered through *Confessions* and its related writings, reads like a political allegory of the idealisms and dangers of British imperialist expansion.

Opium was produced primarily in India under the control of the East India Company[1] and was imported to China in exchange for tea and other commodities such as porcelain. As Nigel Leask notes, "This formed a delicately balanced trade triangle: the Chinese had to pay for Indian opium, Britain's Indian subjects had to pay for the privilege of British rule, and the British consumer had to pay for Chinese tea. These

---

[1] Founded in 1600 by a royal charter that gave it exclusive control over England's trade with Asia, the company was a commercial venture capitalized (in an innovation that was eventually to revolutionize global commerce) by joint stockholders. By the latter half of the eighteenth century, especially by the time of the East India Act of 1784 (although this was a result of the Company's corporate and military volatility in the region), the Company's administrative role in the East was more than financial, and by this time it had become a central mechanism through which Britain exerted the political and military influence of its colonial rule. By the early nineteenth century the Company's influence had begun to wane, but its success in extending Britain's cultural power had taken on an autonomous life in the form of the Empire's self-appointed civilizing mission around the globe.

outstanding claims were cancelled one against the other, to the benefit of Britain's worldwide trade" (217). The Company's networks of influence, akin to the modern multinational corporate franchise, evoked the fraught compromise between state and business, increasingly fuelled in the nineteenth century by the religious zeal of the Empire's "civilizing mission" in far-flung parts of the world. As Algernon S. Thelwall writes in *The Inequities of the Opium Trade with China* (1839), the British "hold our Eastern Empire by *moral power*, and not by *physical* strength." Thelwall advocates eliminating the opium trade's immoral practice (but not the trade itself), which would provide Christian access to Chinese souls, simultaneously converting Chinese currency to pounds and granting access to their untapped markets. While its influence eventually waned in the nineteenth century, the Company exemplified the Empire's use of this mission to justify the conduct of *its* business.

Confessions reminds us that more than tea made it back to England, where opium became readily available for English consumption, ostensibly for medicinal use, although, as we shall see, it held other, more troubling, attractions. Travel literature had made opium part of the English popular imagination for some time. Jean-Baptiste Tavernier, Sir John Chardin, and William Marsden's later *History of Sumatra* (1783), which was in its third edition by 1811, all show how the East was imagined by the West in order to educate its audience about worlds unknown (see Appendix C1–3). These accounts use opium as one way of marking the East's otherness, often claiming to be startled by this difference in order to demonstrate how a Western imagination might assimilate it (Marsden's "enlightened" response to misconceptions about Eastern practice demonstrates this process). Such writings are "orientalist" in Edward Said's famous sense of the term. They constitute a body of scholarly knowledge, however misrepresentative, about the East that evokes the West's desire to understand worlds beyond its ken. At the same time, they "orientalize" other cultures *as other*. This imagining of the East was more than rhetorical, for it rendered the other capable of assimilation in order to alleviate Western anxieties, and was thus a potent weapon of Western colonialism. Opium both stimulates and menaces this process. Texts such as Coleridge's "Kubla Khan," the product of a trance induced by the combination of taking opium with the reading of Samuel Purchas's *Purchas his Pilgrimage* (first published in 1613), indicate a Romanticism high on other cultures yet equally wary of their seductive properties, represented in Coleridge's text as the veiled Abyssinian's siren call (see Appendix A2). De Quincey's opium writings exemplify how by 1821 England's dreams of Empire were very much byproducts of the West's orientalist imagination. That neither Thelwall nor De Quincey ever visited the East indicates how profoundly this imagination shaped Western attitudes as fantasies about the East, or what Nigel Leask and John Barrell have explored as this imagination's cultural psychopathology.

By the time of Marsden's *History* or Samuel Crumpe's *An Inquiry Into the Nature and Properties of Opium* (1793), the distinction between controlled British habits and Eastern barbarism had taken hold in opium rhetoric. By then Britain's industrial expansion was well under way, bringing home commodities that materialized Britain's ability to "domesticate" the world. But these were also "foreign" intrusions into an English sanctuary. Fears of invasion had haunted England since the Norman Conquest, most recently with the French Revolution and Napoleon's ascension, and until Napoleon's defeat at Waterloo—about which De Quincey obsesses so much in *The English Mail-Coach*—such European threats were roadblocks to Britain's global interests. Ironically, it was this very expansion of British industry that at the same time made Britain vulnerable to external political and economic competition. By 1838 the threat was China and its response to Britain's growing export of opium to its mainland, where the drug was contraband. Suspicious of British opium exports and thus of British influence, Chinese authorities confiscated an opium shipment in Canton. Not surprisingly, the British government declared the seizure of its property and subjects illegal, and home response, while by no means unanimous, was largely indignant (see De Quincey's "The Opium and the China Question" in Appendix C11). The British navy's subsequent attack on Canton and seizure of Hong Kong produced the Treaty of Nanking in 1842, which opened China to Western trade.

The Opium Wars (there was a second crisis in the early 1850s), like the 1857 Indian Mutiny, galvanized Britain's view of the colonies, very much by entrenching the imperialist mission's sound morality. Largely this view proceeded by both a metaphorical and a literal view of the East as an opiated body politic. The West feared foreign populations whose armies, fuelled by opium's artificial but supernatural physical effects, posed a kind of uncontrollable and thus invincible threat. Such fears were crystallized through the trope of the drugged foreign warrior immune to reason. Crumpe notes that "the Turks, and other nations, swallow [opium] in large quantities, when marching to battle, or under any other circumstances, which require a mind void of depressing fears, and inspired with fortitude." For Marsden, whom Crumpe echoes, such "desperate acts of indiscriminate murder" have only to do with natives' "unruly passions," which made the enemy at once harmless and fearful. For Samuel Morewood the Malay warrior is a caged animal whose courage is "artificial" and whose inability to bear "misfortune or disappointment" makes him that much more capable of wreaking havoc. Both "native and slave," he also threatens class boundaries. But the transgression went both ways. Morewood describes a visit to a "Mahometan prince," an "inveterate opium-taker" who appears dead from opium abuse but who is brought back to life with each new dose. This image of power dead on the throne was a potent cautionary tale for a Britain scared that things might "run amuck" at home, from both the top down and the bottom up.

De Quincey's account in *Confessions* of a Malay's appearance in 1816 at Dove Cottage is one of the most powerful contributions to this cultural imaginary of opium recklessness. The passage contrasts the Malay's dark skin against white complexions, and the cottage's dark mahogany against his white robe, a figural miscegenation that plays out fears of other intermixings, what *The English Mail-Coach* calls the "horrid inoculation upon each other of inviolable natures." Such breakdowns reflect fears of possession: the colonized Malay by the colonizer De Quincey; the servant girl by her "master"; the Malay's potentially fatal possession of/by the drug that De Quincey possesses and bequeaths in turn to the East; the legacy of imperial possession that comes home to visit De Quincey himself in the form of his own addiction, which he would pawn off on this oriental other. The Malay's sudden appearance as a guest on foreign soil, and the way in which he just as "suddenly" downs the opium offered by his domestic host, creates a sense of crisis, a terrorist incursion that in turn calls for desperate measures; the passage thus pointedly Easternizes the irrationalities of chance in order to justify the author's Western response. As Leask notes, by 1816 "Britain had just emerged from the Congress of Vienna laden with the spoils of a second empire—in stimulating a crisis-ridden and enervated national culture into what De Quincey represents as a condition of organic integration" (213). That the Malay swallows De Quincey's parting "gift," "enough to kill three dragoons and their horses," signals Britain's genocidal designs upon the East as a projection of fears about its own asthenic state. By the 1856 revision of *Confessions*, when anxieties were even higher, the amount changed to "enough to kill some half-dozen dragoons together with their horses," playing out the irony that "the opium war had forcibly opened up the Chinese markets to the biggest narcotics consumption in history" (Leask 214), thus completing the East's habituation by the West.

Also haunting this passage, then, is the spectre of Britain's displacement by the East. Later, in "The Pains of Opium," De Quincey describes himself transplanted to "Chinese houses, with cane tables, & c." and "[a]ll the feet of the tables, sophas, &c. soon became instinct with life." The dream stages as nightmarish phantasmagoria the domestic space of the middle-class English living room, increasingly filled with "orientalizing" commodities either imported from the East or reflecting Eastern tastes, which begin to take on an uncontrollable life of their own. He becomes lost in the "great *officina gentium*" ("workshop of the world") of "southern Asia," which "has been for thousands of years, the part of the earth most swarming with human life," where "Man is a weed." De Quincey is the most paranoid of orientalists: "I am terrified by the modes of life, by the manners, and the barrier of utter abhorrence, and want of sympathy, placed between us by feelings deeper than I can analyse. I could sooner live with lunatics, or brute animals." The Chinese are a sub-species whose "abominable head" and "leering eyes" are "multiplied into a thousand repetitions," signifying a Chinese rapaciousness that leaves him "loathing and fascinated." As Thelwall writes, between her "Heathen and Mohammedan subjects" and those of India, Queen Victoria maintains power over 230,000,000 people—a frighteningly divergent population that, as De Quincey argues in "The Opium and the China Question," is "inorganic" and without internal organs, a claim that ignores its vital differences in order to justify the need to discipline this mass. Moreover, De Quincey seems painfully aware that its civilization has existed among "immemorial tracts of time" at a time when historiography and mythography, like the emergence of sciences increasingly influenced by evolutionary rather than metaphysical principles, were challenging Britain's myths of origin and thus its cultural and historical pre-eminence.

De Quincey's and Thelwall's descriptions reflect anxieties about a globalism beyond control, and thus about an Empire divided between conservative and liberal versions of itself, between expansion and isolationism. In *An Essay on the Principle of Population* (first published in 1798; see Appendix C4), Thomas Malthus argues that the "germs of existence contained in this spot of earth, with ample food, and ample room to expand in, would fill millions of worlds." Profligate in generating but not in sustaining life, Nature thus curtails society's perfectibility. Luckily, "Necessity, that imperious all pervading law of nature, restrains [Nature] within the prescribed bounds," a "great restrictive law" of starvation, death, misery, and vice. Malthus raises such fears in order to argue for sustainability. But the spectre of an "imperious" nature enlisted in the cause of other imperialisms should disturb us here. De Quincey likewise worries about how "this spot of earth" (read: England) might "fill millions of worlds" (read: the globe) when so much of the world's workshop has an excessive life of its own beyond the Empire's sobrieties, an instinct for growth that threatens to swallow up rather than fuel England's expansion. If Malthus's approach suggests how populations could be de-humanized, treated as organic masses prone to their own biological necessities, David Ricardo's political economy appeals to De Quincey because it de-humanizes via a kind of philosophical abstraction of these necessities. Ricardo argues for the "rapid accumulation" of Western capital (ironically anything but sober) to rationalize progress: "the labouring classes should have a taste for comforts and enjoyments, and ... should be stimulated by all legal means in their exertions to procure them. There cannot be a better security against a superabundant population."[1] Ricardo's economics regulates nature's consumptive desires by, paradoxically, fuelling them, which in turn alleviates a growing problem of class dissension (see Appendix C5).

The English Mail-Coach, published between the two Opium Wars, is most saturated by opium's political history. In "Going Down with Victory" (a reference to coaches "going down" from London to the rest of the nation with news of its politics), the text plays out anxieties about England's political past, particularly 1790s Jacobinism as it transmogrified into Napoleonic imperialism and its global competition with Britain. Whereas Confessions focuses on the addict's deracinated body, in Mail-Coach power and progress threaten the body politic. The text stages a globally industrial present whose increasingly complex networks of communication and power, what the first section calls "The Glory of Motion," bind the nation but also bring it into a relentless and often perilous confrontation with itself. "The Vision of Sudden Death" figures this encounter as England's catastrophic meeting with its irrevocable yet all too insistent past and future. Here we find leadership (the "slumbering coachman," like the opiated "Mahometan" prince in Morewood's account) asleep at the reins, driven by "maniacal horses." The author "pretend[s] to no presence of mind, ... miserably

---

[1] An equally telling fantasy here is of a deracinated Chinese population. John Awsiter's 1767 *An Essay on the Effects of Opium* (see Appendix D3) worries that addiction will, in the "Eastern countries," depopulate the "Flower of their Youth." W.H. Medhurst's *China: Its State and Prospects* (1838; see Appendix C9), published on the eve of the first Opium War, sounds a more ominous note about the effect of a "demoralizing and destructive traffic" in opium on a "superabundant populace."

and shamefully deficient in ... action," so that "[t]he palsy of doubt and distraction hangs like some guilty weight of dark unfathomed remembrances upon [his] energies." Such paralysis amidst ceaseless progress informs the mail-coach's murderous contact with the smaller carriage, specifically with the woman traveller whose sacrifice in silent despair reflects no hope for change except to accept change itself. This vision repeats the earlier loss of Fanny on the Bath Road, and the irrevocable losses of Anne in *Confessions* and Elizabeth in *Suspiria*, and transforms most fearfully in *Mail-Coach* into a contest with "unfathomable remembrances" that are at once progressive and degenerative.

Throughout De Quincey's writing, women, at once ideals and victims, both suffer for and redeem a masculinist imperial vision often unable to confront its own flaws and losses. This projection translates also into the vision of an emasculating East that threatens the virility and finer sensibilities of the Empire's civilizing mission. Perhaps most disturbingly, in its final section, "Dream-Fugue," the text explodes to reveal a "racist psychosis in which De Quincey allowed full rein to the vengefulness of the repressed 'natural Jacobinism' of his own heart": "The anxieties which the dreams rehearse and repeat in fugues of spiralling prose represent ... the 'progressive' nature of western civilization as merely repetition, evolution as degeneration, mastery as disintegration" (Leask 216–17). The mail-coach uncannily repeats throughout the domestic space of England anxieties of power multiplying beyond its borders. As if unable to stop this threat, the text stages a full-blown imperialist paranoia born from the nation's habituation to power, a habit very much fuelled by the opium trade. Here what in *Confessions* De Quincey calls the "unutterable abortions and monsters" of the addict's dreams merge nightmarishly with the nation's dreams of imperial domination.

The Opium Question: Medicine and Psychology

How the political history of opium came home to roost on British soil was largely a question of understanding at first its medical but increasingly its psychological effects on English bodies and minds. It thus induced, separate from the colonial project abroad, a different—but in its own way equally coercive—set of social controls by the British body politic. These controls, reflected in the various excerpts in Appendix D, took shape primarily by distinguishing proper from improper—that is, socially unacceptable—opium practices and behaviours. De Quincey's medicinal use of opium was accepted practice; its recreational use was not. Ideas about opium as both cure and addiction were by 1821 part of cultural parlance, as was, more urgently, the careful moral delineation of one against the other. Opium was available, as De Quincey notes, from the local apothecary, sold in the form of pills measured in grains, which before they reached British soil had been extracted from the juice of poppy seeds and dried into a brown granular powder. It was also commonly dispensed as the tincture of opium called laudanum, a liquid mixture of opium in alcohol that De Quincey calls "ruby-coloured" because of its hue.

Medical knowledge about opium as both anodyne and stimulant extends well into ancient times. John Jones's *The Mysteries of Opium Reveal'd* (1700) inaugurated roughly the period of modern debate about opium and drug culture in general. To resolve the contradiction between opium's beneficial and noxious effects, its pleasures and pains, Jones was the first to advocate moderation and common sense. Ironically, he was an addict himself, and the book, posing as a medical tract, is rather misleading about the drug's addictive properties. Such misinformation affected public opinion and practice for some time thereafter, an influence we can read in the excerpts from George Young (1753), John Awsiter (1767), and Samuel Crumpe (1793), who are increasingly anxious to distinguish opium's medicinal uses from its "poisonous" physiological and, especially by the end of the eighteenth century, psychological effects. This latter shift reflects a rising concern with the body as a dynamic rather than static entity. This nervous or sensible body was perhaps most influentially outlined in John Brown's *Elements of Medicine* (first published in Latin as *Elementa Medicinae* in 1780). The Brunonian system explained bodily health as the balanced excitability of the body's nervous tissue, its proper nervous sensitivity to the environment. This body, prone to internal and external stimulation, was more complexly situated between the physical and the social, a relationship explored elsewhere in the eighteenth century via the concepts of sentiment, sensibility, and sympathy, which concerned themselves with how bodily constitutions related 'sensibly' to one another. Such concerns are reflected in Brown's treatment of opium as a preternatural remedy for numerous physical or nervous complaints, from hysteria and hangovers to insomnia, indigestion, typhus, venereal disease, cancer, rheumatism, and cholera.

Opium was also a dangerous drug, however, because of its ability to produce altered states of mind and body beyond society's control. Drug intoxication was increasingly demonized through an emergent temperance movement.[1] Thomas Trotter's *An Essay, Medical, Philosophical, and Chemical, on Drunkenness* (1803), cautioning against Brown's optimism, is the first significant medical treatise also to warn against the use of stimulants. Drug habituation in England's industrial centres such as Sheffield, Birmingham, or Manchester, as De Quincey notes in "The Pleasures of Opium," was of special concern. De Quincey's own sense of urgency about England's opium crisis speaks to the need for health and social reform to teach and empower the labouring classes, at the same that it reflects anxieties about this enfranchisement: "happiness might now be bought for a penny, and carried in the waistcoat pocket: portable ecstacies might be had corked up in a pint bottle: and peace of mind could be sent down in gallons by the mail coach." Unlike Marsden's Sumatra, an affluent England makes opium's "luxury" easily available to everyone. De Quincey's tone here is seemingly indignant, fomenting concern about opium's ready effect on the disenfranchised, especially as elsewhere he is ready to out its use among the professional classes. But the statement's equally ironic, even celebratory, tone tells two other conflicting stories. On one hand, De Quincey implies that workers can't handle (i.e., shouldn't have access to) such "luxuries." On the other, that workers were drunk or stoned on Saturday evening suggested that they were otherwise productive during the week, a necessary evil for larger economic payoff. And such pastimes diverted them from other forms of political congregation. Keeping bodies sedated was a way of habituating the working population to other forms of social sedation. Essentially this meant treating the working class like children,[2]

---

[1] Mounting public concern about intemperance in the eighteenth century was eventually taken up as part of a broader push toward social reform in the nineteenth century. According to the *Encylopædia Britannica* (11th ed., 25:579; 15th ed., 11:622), although churches and religious groups had earlier shouldered the burden of promoting abstinence, the origins of a formal temperance movement are American, as early as 1808 in New York, the American Temperance Society being founded in 1826. In Europe the first such organization was in Ireland, the Ulster Temperance Society (1829), after which the movement quickly spread to Scotland and Britain, where the British and Foreign Temperance Society was founded in London in 1831. Temperance took its most extreme, one might say fundamentalist, form as teetotalism, "from 'tee-total,' a local intensive for 'total'" (25:579). An early promoter was Joseph Livesey (1794-1884), philanthropist, who started a temperance movement in Preston and who demanded a pledge of total abstinence from his members.

[2] Ironically, as with modern debates about using drugs to monitor children's unruly behaviour, the nineteenth century became concerned that opium was a common ingredient of various children's prescriptions, such as Batley's Sedative Solution, Mother Bailey's Quieting Syrup, and especially Godfrey's Cordial (a mixture of opium, treacle, water, and spices), which were used to "quiet" children. These were earlier forms of patent medicines,

at which point we need to remember that De Quincey was himself a Tory member of the middle class.

The text's ambivalence about the fraught relationship between class, commerce, and addiction points to a larger concern about the nation's health that takes its cue from a perceived difference between Eastern (uncivilized) and Western (civilized) practices. Crumpe demonizes opium use as a "foreign" threat to Christian habits. This distinction rests partly on the fact that "Mahometans" take opium because their religion denies them wine and liquor. De Quincey and Morewood exploit this difference in order to separate ordinary (read: curable or manageable) inebriations from opium's more intoxicating powers. Rampant Eastern opium use is more damaging than Western habits. "Mahometans" transgress state and religious law to take opium, and are thus punished by an addiction that undermines cultural and religious values. But Britons, thankfully devoid of such weakness, can innoculate themselves against the contagion of Eastern custom and thus better superintend their habits. Such Victorian notions of moral management (an 1853 *Blackwood's* article terms opium indulgence "criminal") were already prevalent by De Quincey's time.[1] Trotter's earlier *A View of the Nervous Temperament* (1807) warns against the dissipating effects of a "nervous malady" (a term it borrows from George Cheyne's earlier 1733 *The English Malady*) resulting from a society "enervated by luxury and refinement." Trotter writes:

---

referring to "letters patent" granted by the English crown, pre-packaged or "commercial" medicines sold without doctor's prescriptions. Often little more than quack remedies, they were nonetheless affordable cures among the working classes. Opium was a significant cause of infant mortality because it suppressed hunger, but therefore caused malnutrition (Wohl 34-35).

[1] De Quincey contributes to the temperance debates in his 1845 *Tait's* article, "On the Temperance Movement of Modern Times," by offering nine strategies for temperate behaviour, drawn from his own opium experience. In the end, he sees temperance as a necessary check to the "greatest era by far of human expansion," and thus suggests that opium was itself an inevitable, although dangerous, respite from the effects of this expansion: "Two vast movements are hurrying into action by velocities continually accelerated— the great revolutionary movement from political causes concurring with the great physical movement in locomotion and social intercourse, from the gigantic (though still infant) powers of steam. No such Titan resources for modifying each other were ever before dreamed of by nations: and the next hundred years will have changed the face of the world. At the opening of such a crisis, had no third movement arisen of resistance to intemperate habits, there would have been ground for despondency as to the amelioration of the human race" (*Works* 15:259). In his 1845 *Suspiria*, De Quincey also reads the capacity to dream as a necessary remedy against the effects of expansion, which he so clearly describes in *The English Mail-Coach*. The conflation of dreams and opium, both of which replicate as much as they remedy these effects, makes this call for "temperance" rather ironic.

"the temperate man is observed to bear sickness with more patience and resignation, than those accustomed to indulgence" (see Appendix D6). Moderation restores bodily vitality to the body politic by managing its habits. Trotter's work reflects a modernity at once unable and unwilling to overcome its own indulgences. In his 1798 *Anthropology from a Pragmatic Point of View*, like Trotter's text a primer for the general reading public, Immanuel Kant valorizes an autonomous pragmatic anthropology, or "what man makes, can, or should make of himself as a freely acting being," over physiological anthropology, "what Nature makes of man" (3) (the material determinisms of biology, memory, addiction, etc.). This regulation of human practice reflects a rationalized world increasingly dependent on its own habits as survival techniques, a common sense that feeds on its own excessive desires.[1] The fact that so much of De Quincey's response to his addiction is fuelled by the psychosomatics of his own hypochondria points to a breakdown between the physiological and the pragmatic that Kant would maintain.

The account of opium's supernatural strength in *Confessions* makes clear that "intoxication" was different from drunkenness. Robert Macnish's *The Anatomy of Drunkenness* (1827) entertains this prospect head on: "there is more poetry in [opium's] visions, more mental aggrandizement, more range of imagination." Writing that "Wine robs a man of his self-possession" while "opium greatly invigorates it," De Quincey invokes a by-then typical comparison between wine and opium that Macnish echoes (see Appendix D7). Ironically, by arguing for self-possession, De Quincey turns a proto-Victorian moralist stance against drug use against itself. He further extols opium's almost mystical properties: "whereas wine disorders the mental faculties, opium, on the contrary (if taken in a proper manner), introduces amongst them the most exquisite order, legislation, and harmony." The parenthetical clause is crucial. Apart from De

---

[1]   Kant's idea in *The Critique of Judgement* (1790) of a *sensus communis* that binds all humans as a community of like-minded beings is the model here. For De Quincey, as we have seen, this model both fascinates and repels because of its foreign intrusions—the Malay, the Chinese population—that comprise the human race as "one people" under the Empire's banner. In a somewhat different but related vein, Lindop, writing on the 1803 diary that De Quincey kept for the period of his wanderings in Wales and London, notes that by then the "practice of keeping a fussy watch over the details of his health was already well established" (107), and that for most of his life "[h]e was prone to obsessive, repetitious thought carried to the point of mental fatigue. His life had been lived in a continual climate of anxiety palliated by ambition and private fantasy" (223). See Paul Youngquist and David Clark in particular for the broader connection between obsessively worrying about the body's habits and the habitual nature of these practices.

Quincey's own self-justifications, and apart from the fact that, like Macnish, he documents addiction's less intellectual properties, he wants it both ways. Drug use had its negative effects; yet in controlled situations, its recreational use tapped into the powers of the human imagination, and at a time nearly obsessed with imagination, De Quincey is most openly tempted by its intoxicating relationship to opium. Coleridge's paradigmatic definition of imagination in *Biographia Literaria* (1817), influenced by the German idealism of Kant, Fichte, and Schelling, argues for the mind's secondary ability to "idealize and to unify" (1:304) its primary perceptions. These two modes offer a powerful model of self-regulation, suggesting a naturally organized social body in which the mind and nature, individuals and society, cohere as part of an organic whole bound and energized by the imagination's creative capacities. This desire for unity reflected both a post-Revolutionary hope for democracy and a conservative backlash against radicalism's threat to social order. The spectre here was not chaos but other collectives that menaced the balance of power between classes, sexes, races, and nations, as well as between private and public, individual and state, commerce and state.

Opium thus became, throughout the nineteenth century, a powerfully ambivalent metaphor for the dangers of imagination and its (re)organizations of minds, bodies, and even power itself, as we can see in Mordecai C. Cooke's at times hysterical (and often hysterically funny) High Victorian drug compendium *The Seven Sisters of Sleep* (1860; see Appendix D9) or, from the same year, Charles Baudelaire's *Les Paradis Artificiel*, a kind of cautionary hymn to the enticements of hashish. If how man "possessed" himself was of paramount concern to temperance debates of the time, however, where the possession was psychological, as in the world of imagination and especially of dreams, this placed him entirely, and thus most disturbingly, beyond society's purview. If opium is the "hero" of De Quincey's text, dreams are this hero's weapons of mass deconstruction. A 1797 *Encyclopædia Britannica* article traces an earlier view of dreams as expressions of prophetic or occult states (as in Andrew Baxter's 1737 *An Enquiry into the Nature of the Human Soul*), to their later reflection of nervous excitability (via Brunonian theory), to a subsequent emphasis on dream psychology. De Quincey contributes powerfully to this evolution by reading dreams as comments upon the consciousness of waking life and its behaviours. He defines consciousness as a continuum or series of various stages from dreams and nightmares to waking dreams and semi-conscious reveries. "The Pains of Opium" offers a brief interpretation of dreams in the form of four facts particular to his own dream life. The opening section of *Suspiria* then organizes these disparate facts into a larger theory of the psychological and sociological benefits of dreams. Here they are a palliative for the pressures of modern sociability; moreover, they provide access to states of being essential to understanding existence. But these states remain beyond our grasp.

For De Quincey, as for Freud, dreams repeat existence in a finer but stranger tone, uncannily reflecting what waking experience forgets about itself. But they also mark a rupture between consciousness and the unconscious and thus signify an impossible union with ourselves, those parts absolutely constitutive of our being yet lost forever to our comprehension. De Quincey states that his loss of Anne "shaped, moulded and remoulded, composed and decomposed—the great body of opium dreams." In *Suspiria* Elizabeth's death "remoulded itself continually" in De Quincey's "Oxford dreams." Dreams signify a free-associating imagination that, like De Quincey's fears about political others, endlessly reproduces itself through the "lost features" of Anne's face or of any of the "*myriad*" associations of his unconscious through which his identity becomes a series of characters in search of an author.

De Quincey's interpretation of dreams confronts this multiple personality without apparent judgement at the same time that fears of an absent governing ego, as in the coachman asleep at the reins in *Mail-Coach*, produces a reactionary swerve toward imperialism. Reflecting the fateful sway of De Quincey's waking life, *Suspiria* stands outside the everyday to imagine a dreaming apparatus through which the subject is self-analysed by the doubles, shadows, and phantasms of his psychic interiority. After "The Affliction of Childhood," the text proceeds through a series of metaphors for understanding the mind's states. These metaphors figure history both personally and transpersonally, individually and culturally. The first is the palimpsest, which describes the psychic apparatus as successive layerings of experience not unlike the Freudian unconscious, an archive or archaeological dig that also models how we might read the mind as cultural archive. "Savannah-la-Mar" depicts this archive as a ruined city glimpsed dimly at the bottom of the ocean, the cultural dimensions of which can be potentially read, yet only through the distortions of history and memory. In "The Dark Interpreter" (intended for *Suspiria* yet not included in its original publication; see Appendix A8), the impact of the external world's accumulated impressions becomes the "mightier agency" of "suffering," imagined as the mind's dark self-reflection of its own experience, a radical interpretation that is at once instructive and inaccessible to reason. "The Affliction of Childhood" describes this process as "phantasmagorical," like the child's ability to conjure apparitions, but equally to lose power over this visitation, as in De Quincey's church visions during his sister Elizabeth's funeral. "The Apparition of the Brocken" stages and constitutes the subject through his self-manifestations at the same time that these "*umbras* and *penumbras*," to borrow a phrase from "The Dark Interpreter," haunt his waking life. "Levana and Our Ladies of Sorrow" invokes a present and future always drawn back to the past, each figure a "mighty phantom" that stages experience as a site of interminable grief. The text's governing trope of *suspiria de profundis*, or "sighs from the depths," figures this repeated return to the past through dreams as an experience of both unavoidable suffering and necessary significance. Dreams stage a traumatic history *of* trauma, a past that we understand only through its future traumatic repetitions. Whereas *Confessions* suggests that addiction, despite its disturbing unconscious effects, can be potentially overcome, *Suspiria*, like *The English Mail-Coach*, suggests that these effects, *because* they are traumatic, are imaginatively constitutive.

Yet the text's Romantic claim that dreams alleviate the demands of sociability doesn't promise a better world. Whereas an earlier view saw sympathy for one's fellow beings as a means to progress, De Quincey's faith in the social potential of dreams is limited by their equally nightmarish qualities. Dreams collapse boundaries between inside and outside, subject and world, reason and unreason, and make expansion compulsively repetitious, degenerative, consumptive. In the Explanatory Notice to Volume Four of *Selections Grave and Gay* (see Appendix A6), De Quincey writes that dreams have their own "law of association" (xiii), which makes them, not the dreamer, the "responsible party" (xiv). This makes dreams the real hero of De Quincey's confessional writings but also displaces the burden of proof (partly a way of displacing the author's own moral responsibility). Dreams suggest other, less tractable forms of "association." Matthew Arnold feared Romantic solipsism because it might cripple his own time's ability to act decisively. Yet the obsession with self-analysis has proven Arnold's fears in ways he might not have anticipated. At the beginning of *Confessions* De Quincey writes, "I have indulged in [opium-eating] to an excess, not yet *recorded* of any other man." Later in "Introduction to the Pains of Opium," he asks, "why confess at all?" In "The Pains of Opium" De Quincey wonders if he is "too confidential and communicative of my own history." Knowing that he is by no means the first to talk about himself in such detail, even if his subject matter is unique, one might ask what such sensationalizing gestures mean. For by making a spectacle of the Romantic pursuit of self-understanding, *Confessions* manufactures a public craving for more talk, for further displays of the "egotism" for which De Quincey's texts were often criticized. De Quincey's life is by no means unremarkable, nor are the erudition and encyclopaedic range of the scholarship that inform his writings. *Confessions* and its related texts are an imposing pastiche of classical, biblical, and contemporary sources, standard for a man of learning in the early nineteenth century. Yet the context of confession also turns this knowledge into fodder for modernity's compulsion to reflect endlessly upon itself. *Confessions* also helps to usher in what we might now call the "cult of celebrity"; De Quincey becomes famous for the sake of being famous, not because of *what* he knows, but for the fact *that* he knows.

This is perhaps the most powerful psychological legacy of *Confessions*: its need *to* confess defines how subjects were to be treated in the modern public sphere. In "Pains" De Quincey also writes: "my way of writing is rather to think aloud, and follow my own humours, than much to consider who is listening to me." This marks one of the origins of psychiatry and of the free association of Freud's talking cure. Psychiatry emerged parallel to modern medical science in the eighteenth century, born partly from a desire to expose the mind to analysis in order to distinguish its normalities from its pathologies. A rather disturbing paradox emerges here, however. To effect the cure of troubled souls, such distinctions depend, as De Quincey notes, on not caring who is listening—that is, on resisting any social judgement of the speaker's innermost thoughts. That De Quincey seems equally concerned about what his audience thinks of him, however, suggests that he is more than passingly aware of how such free association remains subject to outside surveillance and control. The emergence in Romanticism of a psychiatric mentality suggests the desire to communicate and to make oneself understood to others, the basis by which productive social collectives cohere. Yet this mentality also reflects a desire to manage wayward minds and bodies. As Michel Foucault writes, in the confession of sex in the emerging bourgeois order of the nineteenth century, "one had to speak of [sex] as of a thing to be not simply condemned or tolerated but managed, inserted into systems of utility, regulated for the greater good of all, made to function according to an optimum" (24). Making sense of things, not just sex, by talking about them means making something of one's life for a public sphere that functions by reproducing classifications of its citizens so as to make them "fit" within its social order.

On several levels, then, De Quincey's confessional writings raise the spectre that one's life is never one's own. By both reflecting and capitalizing upon the period's burgeoning psychiatric disposition, they suggest a confession of thoughts that, because it can go on interminably without producing a cure, is inevitably somewhat pointless. But this pointlessness is precisely the point. *What* one says gets displaced by the fact that one is talking, an endless communication that, paradoxically, preempts the possibility of genuine individual and collective action. De Quincey seems all too aware of how opium suspends individual and collective wills. In turn, however, his confessional texts suggest that opium's effect on the popular imagination is related directly to society's ability to control this imagination, to its concerns about improperly "nervous" bodies. He both crystallizes and generates fears about subjects and subjectivities beyond society's control, about bodily desires and mental imaginings immune to social discipline. Excessive or wayward conditions—madness, hysteria, melancholy, addiction—threatened the ability of society to function efficiently, productively, and, in the increasingly dominant model of political economy in the late eighteenth century and beyond, profitably. Perhaps the most telling psychological paradox of De Quincey's texts is how they both resist and participate in this mode of cultural profitability.

The Impact of *Confessions*

De Quincey's confessional writings are perhaps all too relevant to today's audience. Certainly we can recognize debates about opium in more recent arguments about the medicinal versus the recreational use of drugs, or about drug habituation as a problem that originates "elsewhere" than at home. But its influence is more broad-reaching than this. De Quincey's writings heighten one's sense that his often conservative convictions about his time were also those of a subject distinctly aware that his time was in need of change, even when he seemed committed to setting that time right, often far to the right. *Confessions* puts its finger on the pulse of a country and empire, coming to a profound realization of the effects of their own habituated practices on the individuals and world. This self-realization is rooted in De Quincey's own experience as an object lesson in what is at stake in realizing one's dreams—the post-industrial dream that it is possible to always get what one wants—when one ends up also having to deal with the surfeit of pleasure that such satisfaction inevitably brings. Just as there seems something excessive and redundant about De

Quincey's talents, he becomes one of our first thinkers about the productive and regressive value of excess. The age's concern with utilitarianism and political economy became a way of managing this excess according to the pleasure principle of a society that always profits from its labours—material, intellectual, sexual, or otherwise. But De Quincey's dreams constitute a body of "excess, not yet recorded" that reproduces itself through a psychic determinism from which he cannot free himself. So, when in *Confessions* he asks us to imagine him poised between a "quart of ruby-coloured laudanum" and a "book of German metaphysics," the clash between philosophy's sense-making rationality and opium's sense-altering properties is meant to give pause. For Kant, intoxication is both narcotic and stimulus to the imagination, which is for him at once the most profound and most troubling aspect of Reason, even though he worries about its "unnatural and artificial" element of the body's otherwise natural or normal functioning. For, as both David Clark and Paul Youngquist have asked, what happens when philosophy's dependence on system gets linked to other dependencies that suspend the human capacity to make sense of oneself and the world?

De Quincey turns to Ricardo's Kantian abstraction of economic principles because of the vagaries of his own material existence. Addiction ruined the organically architectural growth of his imagination, but if De Quincey's life was a series of missed opportunities and encounters, the resultant ruin became this life's generative matrix. It is thus ultimately their evocation of ruin as a kind of proto-Freudian cultural death drive that makes De Quincey's confessional writings so compelling. John Whale argues that De Quincey is fascinated in Ricardo by "deterioration and chaos; his aestheticising of an alien system as a sublime structure riddled with ruination" is a counterpoint to his Tory reaction to shoring the Empire against the threat of radical economics and politics. De Quincey was "clearly intellectually excited by the 'system' and the abstraction of the new economics, by the idea of a secret process and set of principles at work in the historical process." Ricardo's theories are thus for De Quincey like the sublime itself, in which he takes "aesthetic pleasure" (*Works* 15:187). And Whale concludes that, against Ricardo and Adam Smith before Ricardo, De Quincey was a "proponent of the consumer whose human desire has the power to transform value" and thus of a Romantic subject whose thoughts and actions matter in the world.

Yet De Quincey seems ambivalent about this transformation and its positive effects. Obsessed with his desires and desperate to escape them,

De Quincey must master a place for himself in a world that values only self-contained subjects who willingly submit themselves to cultural administration, to living by the illusion of a world of checks and balances, of a political and moral economy in which the subject's labour is productive and does not disrupt this economy's efficient functioning. The struggle to fit the realm of personal feelings, practices, and actions within the larger social sphere are at the heart of De Quincey's confessional project. As an early reviewer of *Selections Grave and Gay* writes (see Appendix B10), De Quincey's writings constitute an "irregular autobiography": "He is everywhere—not as if protruded by conceit—but as if he were a necessary part of every spectacle. In a nature so peculiar as his, egotism ceases to be egotism, and assumes a certain catholic air; you feel you cannot spare a single I—since each personal pronoun is an algebraic symbol of great and general truths." Yet De Quincey is everywhere by being nowhere at all, or rather by being profoundly both in and out of sync both with himself and with the world around him. If Wordsworth believed that the mind of man was exquisitely fitted to the world around it, De Quincey's mind seemed eminently out of kilter. In fact De Quincey makes this the starting point of his writing life, defined by a sense of being a pariah in a world that shunned the difference of exceptional natures—that shunned difference itself, in fact. His interest in alternate or Pariah Worlds (as he intended to call the uncompleted fourth part of *Suspiria*) is thus both a fascination with and repulsion by difference, which is what makes his encounter with Anne in *Confessions* so profoundly moving and *The English Mail-Coach's* elision of difference so disturbing.

Such paradoxes make De Quincey's confessional writings his still most compelling works. The 1822 publication of *Confessions* in book form made it a work of "literature" rather than "hack-journalism" but at the same time canonized it as a work that, because of its controversial content, did not belong in the canon. That it subsequently took on a life of its own through so many editions and reprints only heightens its already powerful impression of a confessional subject irrevocably determined by private demons and autonomous psychosomatic impulses that fashion him against his will. Its morally ambiguous confession of addiction, irrevocably entrenched in the popular imagination, left it prone to misinterpretation and misrepresentation. Like the mass-circulated broadsheet that sensationalizes the criminal life of Caleb Williams in Godwin's 1793 novel, the autonomous life of *Confessions* plays out fears about the circulation of texts and ideas both within and beyond the purview of state and cultural sanction. As much as the work was praised for raising awareness about drug abuse (as in Macnish and Morewood), and thus followed in the moral vein of Charles Lamb's 1813 "Confessions of a Drunkard" (see Appendix A1), it was reviled for promulgating such abuses. Aesthetes such as Charles Baudelaire, who translated De Quincey's *Confessions* into French and provided one of the most extensive commentaries on it and the related *Suspiria* in the nineteenth century, read De Quincey's addiction as part of the exquisite beauty of a life lived too exquisitely, a dangerous literary existence suffused with an "incurable melancholy" (158). But we can see in such "French" praise of De Quincey the kind of degenerate example the *British Quarterly* feared his text might set.

Such fears defined the text's reception into the twentieth century.[1] Ellis's classification of De Quincey's writings (along with Baudelaire's) as decadent, a post-Freudian classification of literature as psychological disorder, replays Victorian anxieties about moral management. That De Quincey poised himself between laudanum and German metaphysics, both foreign intrusions into the safe space of an anglophone critical mind that dictated how British literature was taught and analysed well into the twentieth century, didn't help. He too openly admitted that his mind and life—transient, debt-ridden, addictive—were in ruins, their energies

---

[1] This reception was often rooted in decisions about which text, the 1821 or 1856, was more representative of De Quincey's achievement. Sackville-West's 1950 edition calls the 1821 text a "considerable work of art," the 1856 "hardly that" (xvi) because it is digressive, even superfluous. Van Doren Stern's 1939 and Jordan's 1960 editions favoured 1856 as a less fragmentary work reflecting the author's final intentions, a preference replayed in the criticism. As Vincent de Luca wrote in his 1980 *The Prose of Vision*, the "new material becomes a kind of commentary on the old" (122) and brings to a manifest conclusion meanings that were only latent in the original text. Most recent editions have favoured 1821 because of its proximity to the impulse behind De Quincey's creative vision for the work, and until the recently published *Works of Thomas De Quincey*, the 1856 text languished in the background. For reasons of space, I also set aside 1856, yet I readily admit that, especially because of its expansion of "Preliminary Confessions," the text is quite tedious. In an 1855 letter to his daughter Emily, De Quincey himself expressed dissatisfaction with the new text's more "finished" state (see Appendix B11). Nonetheless, it makes some compelling additions. The added footnote on Rhabdomancy, or the added anecdotes of the Whispering Gallery of St. Paul's Cathedral or the tidal Bore on the River Dee (see *Works* 2:152n, 155–57, 162–66), provide crucial metaphors for the autonomous power of the mind's powers and thus compound the kinds of acute psychological insight that De Quincey was able to draw so brilliantly from his confrontation with addiction. Moreover, the text overall evokes a kind of interminable analysis of the past to find the secret of his future strife, and thus to cure the profound melancholy that attends his almost insurmountable sense of grief.

diverted with compulsive repetitiveness. Yet those qualities for which De Quincey was previously set aside—irretrievable loss, unabundant recompense, the fragmented literary achievement—have become at the end of the twentieth century his most valuable assets. De Quincey's critical fortunes have risen dramatically, with at least ten book-length studies of his writings having appeared since the 1980s.[1] These studies are rooted in a hermeneutics of suspicion about texts and authors and relocate literature within the conflicted sociohistorical context of its making in order to see how ideologies transformed and were transformed by literature. They explore De Quincey's marginality as a powerful tool for understanding the ambivalence of Romantic and post-Romantic culture. This critical resurgence coincides with the first major editing of De Quincey's works since Masson's effort, long considered the standard edition. The 21-volume *Works of Thomas De Quincey*, edited by Grevel Lindop and his colleagues, assembles for the first time all known published, and a host of previously unpublished, De Quincey writings. Far from consolidating his critical identity, *Works* confronts the reader with the profoundly indeterminate nature of this identity, and the fact that most of the studies mentioned above appeared in advance of the publication of *Works* suggests that De Quincey's re-evaluation has barely begun.

When in *Confessions* De Quincey divides his opium experience into "pleasures" and "pains," the former never quite subduing the latter, his addiction remaining "almost" overcome, the division materializes a recurrent symptom in the body of De Quincey's writings. The inability to (re)collect his various "crazy bodies"—physiological, psychological, editorial, political, philosophical—returns each time De Quincey himself returns to his confessional project as a way of "thinking" his approach to writing and experience. Delineating his works in 1853 according to two modes of intellectual being, "gravity" and "pleasure," itself a gesture of Victorian scholarly propriety, is just the start of De Quincey's giving his various bodies organic shape. Yet this distinction also signifies how these bodies are at once riven and sustained by their own conflicting energies and states of being. Organizing such an unwieldy body only exacerbates its exceedingly *un*collectable nature. As Paul Youngquist argues, accounts of De Quincey frequently pathologize his "crazy body" because of his intellect's inability to call this body to order, which is why in his 1822 Appendix to *Confessions* he bequeaths his own body to science so that it

---

[1]   See Barrell, Baxter (1990), Burwick (2001), Clej, McDonagh, Roberts, Russett (1997), Rzepka (1995), Schneider, and Whale (1984).

might make some sense of things. De Quincey's body "has a mind of its own" that De Quincey, unlike Kant, decides to feed with opium and dreams. The "kind of life [this body] affirms," its "physiological aesthetics" (356–57), makes *Confessions* and its related writings, which launched De Quincey's writing career with spectacular aplomb, part of our ongoing seduction by the mind and body as the template for our explorations of human nature and the nature of being human. De Quincey's confessional project externalizes Romanticism as a kind of multiple personality in search of itself. We read through this work's palimpsest for the political unconscious of a culture at once found and lost to itself. De Quincey is the hybrid Man of Letters-as-journalist who negotiates culture as both a vital matrix and atavistic harbinger of public energies. Discontinuously periodical, De Quincey's writings, whatever the author's intentions, comprise a shifting and serial commentary upon, as much as an aesthetic abstraction of, Romantic culture. As a pathology "unfit" within the organic whole of Romanticism, he is one of its most presciently ambivalent figures. He both monumentalizes and demolishes Romantic shibboleths, confessing addiction as a symptom of nineteenth-century culture's larger traumas. Which is what makes him such a compelling figure for us now.

Thomas De Quincey: A Brief Chronology

1785   Born 15 August in Manchester, England, to Thomas
        Quincey and Elizabeth Penson
1790   Sister Jane dies
1792   Sister Elizabeth dies
1793   Father dies
1796   Enters Bath Grammar School; stays until 1799
1799   Brother William dies; first reads William Wordsworth's
        poetry; enters Spencer's Academy, Winkfield, Wiltshire;
        stays until 1800
1800   Enters Manchester Grammar School
1802   Runs away from Manchester Grammar School to Wales
        and London, an experience which forms the basis of
        Confessions
1803   March: reconciled with guardians; May: sends first letter to
        Wordsworth, which begins a four-year correspondence;
        December: enters Worcester College, Oxford
1804–08 Student at Oxford
1804   First tries opium
1806   Reaches age of majority and receives inheritance
1807   August: first meets Samuel Taylor Coleridge; November:
        first meets Wordsworth
1808   May: abruptly leaves Oxford during examinations;
        November: moves in with Wordsworth and his family at
        Allan Bank, Grasmere
1809   February: leaves for London to oversee publication of
        Wordsworth's pamphlet, *The Convention of Cintra;*
        October: returns to Grasmere and leases Dove Cottage
1812   March: enters the Middle Temple in London to study law
1812–13 Periods of illness and convalescence
1813   Becomes a confirmed opium addict
1813–15 Periods of intense addiction and worsening finances
1816   November: birth of son, William Penson, by Margaret
        Simpson
1817   February: marries Margaret Simpson
1818   June: birth of daughter, Margaret; becomes editor of *The
        Westmorland Gazette*

1819	Dismissed (resigned?) from editorship of *The Westmorland Gazette*
1821	January: publishes first magazine article for *Blackwood's Edinburgh Magazine*, a translation of Schiller's "*Spiel des Schicksals*" (1789) as "The Sport of Fortune. A Fragment"; publishes *The Confessions of an English Opium-Eater* (anonymously) in September and October installments of *The London Magazine*; publishes "Letter from the English Opium Eater" in *The London Magazine*
1821–24	Frequent contributor to *The London Magazine* under the pseudonyms "The Opium-Eater" and "XYZ"
1822	October: publishes *Confessions* in book form with Taylor and Hessey; December: publishes "Appendix" in *The London Magazine*
1823	Publishes "Letters to a Young Man Whose Education has Been Neglected" and "On the Knocking at the Gate in *Macbeth*" in *The London Magazine*
1824	Translates (and heavily revises) the German novel *Walladmor*, by Ewald Hering, later known as Willibald Alexis, a German forger of novels in the style of Walter Scott; begins long association with *Blackwood's Edinburgh Magazine*
1827–28	Frequent contributor of political articles to the *Edinburgh Saturday Post*
1830	De Quincey and family move to Edinburgh
1832	Publishes *Klosterheim; or the Masque* in *Blackwood's*; son Julius dies (age 3)
1832–33	Worsening financial distress; beginning of numerous prosecutions (and brief imprisonments) for debt
1834	Begins publishing autobiographical sketches, as well as personal recollections of literary acquaintances, including Wordsworth and Coleridge, in *Tait's Magazine*; eldest son, William, dies (age 18)
1837	Death of wife, Margaret; publishes articles in the *Encyclopædia Britannica* on Goethe, Pope, Schiller, and Shakespeare; De Quincey's family moves to Mavis Bush, Lasswade, south of Edinburgh
1841–43	De Quincey moves to Glasgow
1842	Son Horace (age 22) dies in China
1843	Moves to Mavis Bush to live with family

1844   Publishes *The Logic of Political Economy*
1845   Publishes "Coleridge and Opium-Eating" and *Suspiria de Profundis* in *Blackwood's*
1849   Publishes "The English Mail-Coach" in *Blackwood's*
1851   Ticknor, Reed, and Fields of Boston begin publication of *De Quincey's Writings* (20 volumes; completed in 1856)
1853   James Hogg of Edinburgh begins publication of *Selections Grave and Gay, from Writings Published and Unpublished* (14 volumes; completed in 1860)
1854   Moves to Edinburgh to oversee the editing/publication of *Selections*
1856   Volume 5 of *Selections* published, containing a much-revised and expanded *Confessions*
1859   Dies in Edinburgh (age 74), December 8

A Note on the Text

The copy text for this edition is the original publication of De Quincey's work in periodicals. The copy text for *Confessions of an English Opium-Eater* is *London Magazine* (September, October 1821), vol. 4, pp. 293–312 and 353–79; the copy text for *Suspiria de Profundis* is *Blackwood's Edinburgh Magazine* (March, April, June, July 1845), vol. 57, pp. 269–85, 489–502, 739–51, and vol. 58, 43–55; the copy text for *The English Mail-Coach, or the Glory of Motion* is *Blackwood's Edinburgh Magazine* (October 1849), vol. 66, pp. 485–500. These transcriptions were checked against the now authoritative edition, *Works of Thomas De Quincey* (London: Pickering and Chatto, 2000–05). Where I encountered minor divergences (as in De Quincey's use of italics), I treated the original publication as the authoritative source. I have silently corrected superficial inconsistencies, and standardized the use of double quotations (more often than not the usage in the original publication anyway, if not in *Works*) throughout. When he revised the original *Confessions* in 1856, for *Selections Grave and Gay*, De Quincey was especially anxious about the fact that the composition, typesetting, and publication of the original 1821 text had been a rushed affair. But then, due to the various personal and professional exigencies of De Quincey's life, all of his publications were tortuous affairs in this regard, an anxiety that becomes intrinsic to his reflections on the act of composition.

The copy texts for materials related to the writing and publication of *Confessions* in Appendix A were taken from various sources, all indicated in the head-notes to each entry. These were also checked against *Works*. Divergences are given in the footnotes to Appendix A. All of De Quincey's footnotes and Editor's notices are taken from the original publication.

Author's original notes have been retained in the text and are identified by asterisks. Where necessary, editorial explanations of the Author's notes are included in square brackets immediately following the note.

CONFESSIONS OF AN ENGLISH OPIUM-EATER:

BEING AN EXTRACT FROM THE LIFE OF A SCHOLAR.

deQuincy wants to become the drug, addict you to his book (he was addicted to books)..

TO THE READER.—I here present you, courteous reader, with the record of a remarkable period in my life: according to my application of it, I trust that it will prove, not merely an interesting record, but, in a considerable degree, useful and instructive. In *that* hope it is, that I have drawn it up: and *that* must be my apology for breaking through that delicate and honourable reserve, which, for the most part, restrains us from the public exposure of our own errors and infirmities. Nothing, indeed, is more revolting to English feelings, than the spectacle of a human being obtruding on our notice his moral ulcers or scars, and tearing away that "decent drapery,"[1] which time, or indulgence to human frailty, may have drawn over them: accordingly, the greater part of *our* confessions (that is, spontaneous and extra-judicial confessions) proceed from demireps,[2] adventurers, or swindlers: and for any such acts of gratuitous self-humiliation from those who can be supposed in sympathy with the decent and self-respecting part of society, we must look to French literature,[3] or to that part of the German,[4] which is tainted with the spurious and defective sensibility of the French. All this I feel so forcibly, and so nervously am I alive to reproach of this tendency, that I have for many months hesitated about the propriety of allowing this, or any part of my narrative, to come before the public eye, until after my death (when, for many reasons, the whole will be published): and it is not

---

[1] Edmund Burke (1729–97), Irish statesman, writer, orator, author of *Reflections on the Revolution in France* (1790). Burke writes of the (for him) catastrophic social and political effects of the Revolution: "But now all is to be changed. All the pleasing illusions, which made power gentle and obedience liberal, which harmonized the different shades of life, and which, by a bland assimilation, incorporated into politics the sentiments which beautify and soften private society, are to be dissolved by this new conquering empire of light and reason. All the decent drapery of life is to be rudely torn off. All the superadded ideas, furnished from the wardrobe of a moral imagination, which the heart owns, and the understanding ratifies, as necessary to cover the defects of our naked, shivering nature, and to raise it to dignity in our own estimation, are to be exploded as a ridiculous, absurd, and antiquated fashion."

[2] "A woman whose character is only half reputable; a woman of doubtful reputation or suspected chastity" (*OED*).

[3] Perhaps *Confessions* (1782), by Jean-Jacques Rousseau (1712–78), French autobiographer, novelist, and political philosopher.

[4] Perhaps the autobiography of Johann Wolfgang von Goethe (1749–1832), *Dichtung und Wahrheit* ("Poetry and Truth"), the first fifteen books of which were published in 1811–14 (completed in 1831); or Goethe's semi-autobiographical *The Sorrows of Young Werther* (1774).

without an anxious review of the reasons, for and against this step, that I have, at last, concluded on taking it.

Guilt and misery shrink, by a natural instinct, from public notice: they court privacy and solitude: and, even in their choice of a grave, will sometimes sequester themselves from the general population of the church-yard, as if declining to claim fellowship with the great family of man, and wishing (in the affecting language of Mr. Wordsworth)

———Humbly to express
A penitential loneliness.[1]

It is well, upon the whole, and for the interest of us all, that it should be so: nor would I willingly, in my own person, manifest a disregard of such salutary feelings; nor in act or word do anything to weaken them. But, on the one hand, as my self-accusation does not amount to a confession of guilt, so, on the other, it is possible that, if it *did*, the bene-fit resulting to others, from the record of an experience purchased at so heavy a price, might compensate, by a vast overbalance, for any violence done to the feelings I have noticed, and justify a breach of the general rule. Infirmity and misery do not, of necessity, imply guilt. They approach, or recede from, the shades of that dark alliance, in proportion to the probable motives and prospects of the offender, and the pallia-tions, known or secret, of the offence: in proportion as the temptations to it were potent from the first, and the resistance to it, in act or in effort, was earnest to the last. For my own part, without breach of truth or modesty, I may affirm, that my life has been, on the whole, the life of a philosopher: from my birth I was made an intellectual creature: and intellectual in the highest sense my pursuits and pleasure have been, even from my school-boy days. If opium-eating be a sensual pleasure, and if I am bound to confess I have indulged in it to an excess, not yet *recorded*★ of any other man, it is no less true, that I have struggled against

---

★ 'Not yet *recorded*,' I say: for there is one celebrated man [Samuel Taylor Coleridge (1772–1834), poet, philosopher, known opium user] of the present day, who, if all be true which is reported of him, has greatly exceeded me in quantity.

---

[1] "The White Doe of Rylstone." At this point in the text the White Doe is sitting "in peace, and lovingly" (147) in a church graveyard on "a solitary mound" (170), a "sabbath couch" (169) that evokes for the Narrator "pride / Or melancholy's sickly mood, / Still shy of human neighbourhood; / Or guilt, that humbly would express / A penitential lone-liness" (173–77).

this fascinating enthralment with a religious zeal, and have, at length, accomplished what I never yet heard attributed to any other man— have untwisted, almost to its final links, the accursed chain which fettered me. Such a self-conquest may reasonably be set off in counter-balance to any kind or degree of self-indulgence. Not to insist, that in my case, the self-conquest was unquestionable, the self-indulgence open to doubts of casuistry, according as that name shall be extended to acts aiming at the bare relief of pain, or shall be restricted to such as aim at the excitement of positive pleasure.

Guilt, therefore, I do not acknowledge: and, if I did, it is possible that I might still resolve on the present act of confession, in consideration of the service which I may thereby render to the whole class of opium-eaters. But who are they? Reader, I am sorry to say, a very numerous class indeed. Of this I became convinced some years ago, by computing, at that time, the number of those in one small class of English society (the class of men distinguished for talents, or of eminent station), who were known to me, directly or indirectly, as opium-eaters; such for instance, as the eloquent and benevolent ——, the late dean of ——; Lord ——; Mr. ——, the philosopher; a late under-secretary of state (who described to me the sensation which first drove him to the use of opium, in the very same words as the dean of ——, viz. "that he felt as though rats were gnawing and abrading the coats of his stomach"); Mr. ——; and many others, hardly less known, whom it would be tedious to mention.[1] Now, if one class, comparatively so limited, could furnish so many scores of cases (and *that* within the knowledge of one single inquirer), it was a natural inference, that the entire population of England would furnish a propor-tionable number. The soundness of this inference, however, I doubted, until some facts became known to me, which satisfied me, that it was not incorrect. I will mention two: 1. Three respectable London druggists, in widely remote quarters of London, from whom I happened lately to be purchasing small quantities of opium, assured me, that the number of *amateur* opium-eaters (as I may term them) was, at this time, immense; and that the difficulty of distinguishing these persons, to whom habit had

---

[1] The 1856 *Confessions* supplies full names, in order: 1) William Wilberforce (1759-1833), leader of the movement against the slave trade in Parliament; 2) Isaac Milner (1750-1820), Dean of Carlisle and head of Queen's College, Cambridge; 3) Thomas, first Baron Erskine (1750-1823), lawyer, politician, and in 1806, Lord Chancellor of England; 4) Mr. Dash? "Who is Mr. Dash, the philosopher? Really I have forgot," writes De Quincey in a note to the 1856 text; 5) Henry Addington (1790-1870), Permanent Under-Secretary for Foreign Affairs; 6) Charles Lloyd (1775-1839), poet; De Quincey forgets Lloyd and misidentifies the last person on the list as Coleridge (*Works* 2:96-97).

rendered opium necessary, from such as were purchasing it with a view to suicide, occasioned them daily trouble and disputes. This evidence respected London only. But, 2. (which will possibly surprise the reader more,) some years ago, on passing through Manchester, I was informed by several cotton-manufacturers, that their work-people were rapidly getting into the practice of opium-eating; so much so, that on a Saturday afternoon the counters of the druggists were strewed with pills of one, two, or three grains, in preparation for the known demand of the evening. The immediate occasion of this practice was the lowness of wages, which, at that time, would not allow them to indulge in ale or spirits: and, wages rising, it may be thought that this practice would cease: but, as I do not readily believe that any man, having once tasted the divine luxuries of opium, will afterwards descend to the gross and mortal enjoyments of alcohol, I take it for granted,

> That those eat now, who never ate before;
> And those who always ate, now eat the more.[1]

Indeed the fascinating powers of opium are admitted, even by medical writers, who are its greatest enemies: thus, for instance, Awsiter,[2] apothecary to Greenwich-hospital, in his "Essay on the Effects of Opium" (published in the year 1763), when attempting to explain, why Mead[3] had not been sufficiently explicit on the properties, counteragents, &c. of this drug, expresses himself in the following mysterious terms (Φωναντα συνετοισι):[4] "perhaps he thought the subject of too delicate a nature to be made common; and as many people might then indiscriminately use it, it would take from that necessary fear and caution, which should prevent their experiencing the extensive power of this drug: *for there are many properties in it, if universally known, that would habituate the use, and make it more in request with us than the Turks themselves*: the result of which knowledge," he adds, "must prove a general misfortune." In the necessity of this conclusion I do not altogether concur: but upon that point I shall have occasion to speak at the close of my confessions, where I shall present the reader with the *moral* of my narrative.

---

[1]   A parody of "The Vigil of Venus" (ll. 1–2) by Thomas Parnell (1679–1718).

[2]   John Awsiter, author of *An Essay on the Effects of Opium, Considered as a Poison, with the most rational method of cure, deduced from experience* (1763); see Appendix D3.

[3]   Richard Mead (1673–1754), physician at St. Thomas's Hospital; published *A Mechanical Account of Poisons* (1702), which includes a chapter on opium.

[4]   "Speaking to the wise."

PRELIMINARY CONFESSIONS

These preliminary confessions, or introductory narrative of the youthful adventures which laid the foundation of the writer's habit of opium-eating in after-life, it has been judged proper to premise, for three several reasons:

1. As forestalling that question, and giving it a satisfactory answer, which else would painfully obtrude itself in the course of the Opium-Confessions—"How came any reasonable being to subject himself to such a yoke of misery, voluntarily to incur a captivity so servile, and knowingly to fetter himself with such a seven-fold chain?"—a question which, if not somewhere plausibly resolved, could hardly fail, by the indignation which it would be apt to raise as against an act of wanton folly, to interfere with that degree of sympathy which is necessary in any case to an author's purposes.

2. As furnishing a key to some parts of that tremendous scenery which afterwards peopled the dreams of the Opium-eater.

3. As creating some previous interest of a personal sort in the confessing subject, apart from the matter of the confessions, which cannot fail to render the confessions themselves more interesting. If a man "whose talk is of oxen,"[1] should become an Opium-eater, the probability is, that (if he is not too dull to dream at all)—he will dream about oxen: whereas, in the case before him, the reader will find that the Opium-eater boasteth himself to be a philosopher; and accordingly, that the phantasmagoria of *his* dreams (waking or sleeping, day-dreams or night-dreams) is suitable to one who in that character,

Humani nihil a se alienum putat.[2]

For amongst the conditions which he deems indispensable to the sustaining of any claim to the title of philosopher, is not merely the possession of a superb intellect in its *analytic* functions (in which part of the pretension, however, England can for some generation show but few claimants; at least, he is not aware of any known candidate for this honour who can be styled emphatically *a subtle thinker*, with the exception of

---

[1]   De Quincey misquotes from Ecclesiasticus, one of the Apocrypha: "How can one become wise who follows the plough, / whose pride is in wielding the goad, / who is absorbed in the task of driving oxen, / whose talk is all about cattle?" (38:25).

[2]   "He believes nothing human to be alien to him"; adapted from Terence, *Heauton Timoroumenos* (77).

Samuel Taylor Coleridge, and in a narrower department of thought, with the recent illustrious exception* of *David Ricardo*)[1]—but also on such a constitution of the *moral* faculties, as shall give him an inner eye and power of intuition for the vision and the mysteries of our human nature: *that* constitution of faculties, in short, which (amongst all the generations of men that from the beginning of time have deployed into life, as it were, upon this planet) our English poets have possessed in the highest degree—and Scottish** Professors[2] in the lowest.

I have often been asked, how I first came to be a regular opium-eater; and have suffered, very unjustly, in the opinion of my acquaintance, from being reputed to have brought upon myself all the sufferings which I shall have to record, by a long course of indulgence in this practice purely for the sake of creating an artificial state of pleasurable excitement. This, however, is a misrepresentation of my case. True it is, that for nearly ten years I did occasionally take opium, for the sake of the exquisite pleasure it gave me: but, so long as I took it with this view, I was effectually protected from all material bad consequences, by the necessity of interposing long intervals between the several acts of indulgence, in order to renew the

---

* A third exception might perhaps have been added: and my reason for not adding that exception is chiefly because it was only in his juvenile efforts that the writer whom I allude to, expressly addressed himself to philosophical themes; his riper powers having been all dedicated (on very excusable and very intelligible grounds, under the present direction of the popular mind in England) to criticism and the Fine Arts. This reason apart, however, I doubt whether he is not rather to be considered an acute thinker than a subtle one. It is, besides, a great drawback on his mastery over philosophical subjects, that he has obviously not had the advantage of a regular scholastic education: he has not read Plato in his youth (which most likely was only his misfortune); but neither has he read Kant in his manhood (which is his fault). [De Quincey likely means William Hazlitt (1778–1830), art and literary critic, essayist, author of *Essay on the Principles of Human Action* (1805).]

** I disclaim any allusion to *existing* professors, of whom indeed I know only one. [De Quincey knew John Wilson (1785–1854), critic, poet, professor, regular contributor to *Blackwood's Magazine* under the pseudonym "Christopher North" (*Works* 2:330).]

---

1   David Ricardo (1772–1823), political economist and politician, author of *Principles of Political Economy and Taxation* (1817).

2   De Quincey points to the influence of the Scottish Enlightenment on British thought, such as Adam Smith (1723–90), professor of logic and moral philosophy at Glasgow, author of *Theory of Moral Sentiments* (1759) and *The Wealth of Nations* (1776); and James Beattie (1735–1803), professor of moral philosophy and logic at Marischal College, Aberdeen. De Quincey is perhaps debunking the Common Sense philosophy of Thomas Reid (1710–96), who succeeded Smith at Glasgow, and Reid's disciple Dugald Stewart, professor of mathematics and moral philosophy at Edinburgh. Reid published *An Enquiry into the Human Mind on the Principles of Common Sense* (1764), *Essays on the Intellectual Powers of Man* (1785), and *Essays on the Active Powers of Man* (1788).

pleasurable sensations. It was not for the purpose of creating pleasure, but of mitigating pain in the severest degree, that I first began to use opium as an article of daily diet. In the twenty-eighth year of my age, a most painful affection of the stomach, which I had first experienced about ten years before, attacked me in great strength. This affection had originally been caused by extremities of hunger, suffered in my boyish days. During the season of hope and redundant happiness which succeeded (that is, from eighteen to twenty-four) it had slumbered: for the three following years it had revived at intervals: and now, under unfavourable circumstances, from depression of spirits, it attacked me with a violence that yielded to no remedies but opium. As the youthful sufferings, which first produced this derangement of the stomach, were interesting in themselves, and in the circumstances that attended them, I shall here briefly retrace them.

My father died, when I was about seven years old, and left me to the care of four guardians. I was sent to various schools, great and small; and was very early distinguished for my classical attainments, especially for my knowledge of Greek. At thirteen, I wrote Greek with ease; and at fifteen my command of that language was so great, that I not only composed Greek verses in lyric metres, but could converse in Greek fluently, and without embarrassment—an accomplishment which I have not since met with in any scholar of my times, and which, in my case, was owing to the practice of daily reading off the newspapers into the best Greek that I could furnish *extempore*: for the necessity of ransacking my memory and invention, for all sorts and combinations of periphrastic expressions, as equivalents for modern ideas, images, relations of things, &c. gave me a compass of diction which would never have been called out by a dull translation of moral essays, &c. "That boy," said one of my masters,[1] pointing the attention of a stranger to me, "that boy could harangue an Athenian mob, better than you or I could address an English one." He who honoured me with this eulogy, was a scholar, "and a ripe and good one:" and of all my tutors, was the only one whom I loved or reverenced. Unfortunately for me (and, as I afterwards learned, to this worthy man's great indignation), I was transferred to the care, first of a blockhead, who was in a perpetual panic, lest I should expose his ignorance; and finally, to that of a respectable scholar,[2] at

---

[1]   Mr. Morgan, headmaster of Bath Grammar School, which De Quincey attended from 1796 to 1799 (*Works* 2:330).

[2]   The "blockhead" was Rev. Edward Spencer, headmaster of Spencer's Academy, Winkfield, Wiltshire, which De Quincey attended from 1799 to 1800; the "respectable scholar" was Dr. Charles Lawson, headmaster of Manchester Grammar School, which De Quincey entered in 1800 (*Works* 2:330).

the head of a great school on an ancient foundation. This man had been appointed to his situation by —— College, Oxford;[1] and was a sound, well-built scholar, but (like most men, whom I have known from that college) coarse, clumsy, and inelegant. A miserable contrast he presented, in my eyes, to the Etonian brilliancy of my favourite master: and besides, he could not disguise from my hourly notice, the poverty and meagerness of his understanding. It is a bad thing for a boy to be, and to know himself, far beyond his tutors, whether in knowledge or in power of mind. This was the case, so far as regarded knowledge at least, not with myself only: for the two boys, who jointly with myself composed the first form, were better Grecians than the head-master, though not more elegant scholars, nor at all more accustomed to sacrifice to the graces. When I first entered, I remember that we read Sophocles; and it was a constant matter of triumph to us, the learned triumvirate of the first form, to see our "Archididascalus"[2] (as he loved to be called) conning our lesson before we went up, and laying a regular train, with lexicon and grammar, for blowing up and blasting (as it were) any difficulties he found in the choruses; whilst *we* never condescended to open our books, until the moment of going up, and were generally employed in writing epigrams upon his wig, or some such important matter. My two class-fellows were poor, and dependant for their future prospects at the university, on the recommendation of the head-master: but I, who had a small patrimonial property, the income at which was sufficient to support me at college, wished to be sent thither immediately. I made earnest representations on the subject to my guardians, but all to no purpose. One, who was more reasonable, and had more knowledge of the world than the rest, lived at a distance: two of the other three resigned all their authority into the hands of the fourth;[3] and this fourth with whom I had to negotiate, was a worthy man, in his way, but haughty, obstinate, and intolerant of all opposition to his will. After a certain number of letters and personal interviews, I found that I had nothing to hope for, not even a compromise of the matter, from my guardian: unconditional submission was what he demanded: and I prepared myself, therefore, for other measures. Summer was now coming on with hasty steps, and my seventeenth birthday was fast approaching; after which day I had worn within myself, that I would no longer be numbered amongst school-boys. Money being what I chiefly wanted, I wrote to a woman of high rank,[4] who, though young herself, had

---

[1] Brasenose College.
[2] Headmaster.
[3] Henry Gee, Thomas Belcher, James Entwhistle, and Rev. Samuel Hall (*Works* 2:330).
[4] Lady Susan Carbery, friend of De Quincey's family.

known me from a child, and had latterly treated me with great distinction, requesting that she would "lend" me five guineas. For upwards of a week no answer came; and I was beginning to despond, when, at length, a servant put into my hands a double letter, with a coronet on the seal. The letter was kind and obliging: the fair writer was on the sea-coast, and in that way the delay had arisen: she inclosed double of what I had asked, and good-naturedly hinted, that if I should *never* repay her, it would not absolutely ruin her. Now then, I was prepared for my scheme: ten guineas, added to about two which I had remaining from my pocket money, seemed to me sufficient for an indefinite length of time: and at that happy age, if no *definite* boundary can be assigned to one's power, the spirit of hope and pleasure makes it virtually infinite.

It is a just remark of Dr. Johnson's (and what cannot often be said of his remarks, it is a very feeling one), that we never do any thing consciously for the last time (of things, that is, which we have long been in the habit of doing) without sadness of heart.[1] This truth I felt deeply, when I came to leave ——, a place which I did not love, and where I had not been happy. On the evening before I left ——[2] for ever, I grieved when the ancient and lofty school-room resounded with the evening service, performed for the last time in my hearing; and at night, when the muster-roll of names was called over, and mine (as usual) was called first, I stepped forward, and, passing the head-master, who was standing by, I bowed to him, and looked earnestly in his face, thinking to myself, "He is old and infirm, and in this world I shall not see him again." I was right: I never *did* see him again, nor ever shall. He looked at me complacently, smiled goodnaturedly, returned my salutation (or rather, my valediction), and we parted (though he knew it not) for ever. I could not reverence him intellectually: but he had been uniformly kind to me, and had allowed me many indulgencies: and I grieved at the thought of the mortification I should inflict upon him.

The morning came, which was to launch me into the world, and from which my whole succeeding life has, in many important points, taken its colouring. I lodged in the head-master's house, and had been allowed, from my first entrance, the indulgence of a private room, which I used both as

---

[1]   Samuel Johnson (1709–84), critic, poet, lexicographer, author of *A Dictionary of the English Language* (1755), writes in *The Idler*, No. 103, 5 April 1760: "There are few things not purely evil, of which we can say, without some emotion of uneasiness, 'this is the last.' ... of a place which has been frequently visited, tho' without pleasure, the last look is taken with heaviness of heart."

[2]   Manchester Grammar School.

a sleeping room and as a study. At half after three I rose, and gazed with deep emotion at the ancient towers of———,[1] "drest in earliest light,"[2] and beginning to crimson with the radiant luster of a cloudless July morning. I was firm and immoveable in my purpose: but yet agitated by anticipation of uncertain danger and troubles; and, if I could have foreseen the hurricane, and perfect hail-storm of affliction which soon fell upon me, well might I have been agitated. To this agitation the deep peace of the morning presented an affecting contrast, and in some degree a medicine. The silence was more profound than that of midnight: and to me the silence of a summer morning is more touching than all other silence, because, the light being broad and strong, as that of noon-day at other seasons of the year, it seems to differ from perfect day, chiefly because man is not yet abroad; and thus, the peace of nature, and of the innocent creatures of God, seems to be secure and deep, only so long as the presence of man, and his restless and unquiet spirit, are not there to trouble its sanctity. I dressed myself, took my hat and gloves, and lingered a little in the room. For the last year and a half this room had been my "pensive citadel:"[3] here I had read and studied through all the hours of night: and, though true it was, that for the latter part of this time I, who was framed for love and gentle affections, had lost my gaiety and happiness, during the strife and fever of contention with my guardian; yet, on the other hand, as a boy, so passionately fond of books, and dedicated to intellectual pursuits, I could not fail to have enjoyed many happy hours in the midst of general dejection. I wept as I looked round on the chair, hearth, writing-table, and other familiar objects, knowing too certainly, that I looked upon them for the last time. Whilst I write this, it is eighteen years ago: and yet, at this moment, I see distinctly as if it were yesterday, the lineaments and expression of the object on which I fixed my parting gaze: it

---

[1]   Manchester Cathedral, then the Collegiate Church of St. Mary.

[2]   Percy Shelley (1792-1822), *The Revolt of Islam* (1818); Shelley is describing a "sacred Festival, / A rite to attest the equality of all who live" (5.37.2047-48): "To the great Pyramid I came: its stair / With female choirs was thronged: the loveliest / Among the free, grouped with its sculptures rare; / As I approached, the morning's golden mist, / Which now the wonder-stricken breezes kissed / With their cold lips, fled, and the summit shone, / Like Athos seen from Samothracia, dressed / In earliest light" (5.43.2098-104). Mount Athos, named in Greek mythology for the Thracian giant who fought Poseidon; in Christian mythography, a holy site associated with the Virgin Mary; Samothracia (Samothraki), island in the Aegean sea off the coast of Thracia.

[3]   Wordsworth, "Nuns fret not at their convent's narrow room" l.3. Wordsworth argues that his "Sonnet's scanty ground" (11) offers, like the "prison" (8,9) "brief solace" (14) for those "Who have felt the weight of too much liberty" (13).

was a picture of the lovely ——— ,[1] which hung over the mantle-piece; the eyes and mouth of which were so beautiful, and the whole countenance so radiant with benignity, and divine tranquility, that I had a thousand times laid down my pen, or my book, to gather consolation from it, as a devotee from his patron saint. Whilst I was yet gazing upon it, the deep tones of ——— clock proclaimed that it was four o'clock. I went up to the picture, kissed it, and then gently walked out, and closed the door forever!

So blended and intertwisted in this life are occasions of laughter and of tears, that I cannot yet recal, without smiling, an incident which occurred at that time, and which had nearly put a stop to the immediate execution of my plan. I had a trunk of immense weight; for, besides my clothes, it contained nearly all my library. The difficulty was to get this removed to a carrier's: my room was at an aërial elevation in the house, and (what was worse) the stair-case, which communicated with this angle of the building, was accessible only by a gallery, which passed the head-master's chamber-door. I was a favourite with all the servants; and, knowing that any of them would screen me, and act confidentially, I communicated my embarrassment to a groom of the head-master's. The groom swore he would do any thing I wished; and, when the time arrived, went up stairs to bring the trunk down. This I feared was beyond the strength of any one man: however, the groom was a man—

Of Atlantean shoulders, fit to bear
The weight of mightiest monarchies;[2]

and had a back as spacious as Salisbury plain. Accordingly he persisted in bringing down the trunk alone, whilst I stood waiting at the foot of the last flight, in anxiety for the event. For some time I heard him descending with slow and firm steps: but, unfortunately, from his trepidation, as he drew near the dangerous quarter, within a few steps of the gallery, his foot slipped; and the mighty burden falling from his shoulders, gained

---

[1] In an 1856 note, De Quincey writes that the portrait was a seventeenth-century copy from the Flemish painter Anthony van Dyck (1599-1641), of the Duchess of Somerset, a benefactor of Manchester Grammar School and Brasenose College (*Works* 2:157).

[2] John Milton (1608–74), *Paradise Lost* (1667). Milton is describing Satan, whose "face yet shone / Majestic though in ruin; sage he stood / With *Atlantean* shoulders fit to bear / The weight of mightiest Monarchies" (2.304–07).

such increase of impetus at each step of the descent, that, on reaching the bottom, it trundled, or rather leaped, right across, with the noise of twenty devils, against the very bed–room door of the archididascalus. My first thought was, that all was lost; and that my only chance for executing a retreat was to sacrifice my baggage. However, on reflection, I determined to abide the issue. The groom was in the utmost alarm, both on his own account and on mine: but, in spite of this, so irresistibly had the sense of the ludicrous, in this unhappy *contretemps*,[1] taken possession of his fancy, that he sang out a long, loud, and canorous peal of laughter, that might have wakened the Seven Sleepers.[2] At the sound of this resonant merriment, within the very ears of insulted authority, I could not myself forbear joining in it: subdued to this, not so much by the unhappy *étourderie*[3] of the trunk, as by the effect it had upon the groom. We both expected, as a matter of course, that Dr. —— would sally out of his room: for, in general, if but a mouse stirred, he sprang out like a mastiff from his kennel. Strange to say, however, on this occasion, when the noise of laughter had ceased, no sound, or rustling even, was to be heard in the bed-room. Dr. —— had a painful complaint, which, sometimes keeping him awake, made his sleep, perhaps, when it *did* come, the deeper. Gathering courage from the silence, the groom hoisted his burden again, and accomplished the remainder of his descent without accident. I waited until I saw the trunk placed on a wheel-barrow, and on its road to the carrier's: then, "with Providence my guide,"[4] I set off on foot,—carrying a small parcel, with some articles of dress, under my arm; a favourite English poet in one pocket; and a small 12mo. volume,[5] containing about nine plays of Euripides, in the other.[6]

---

[1] "An inopportune occurrence; an untoward accident; an unexpected mishap or hitch" (*OED*).

[2] Legend of early Christians who escaped from Roman persecution in a cave, where they slept for several hundred years; see Mordecai C. Cooke, *The Seven Sisters of Sleep*, in Appendix D9.

[3] "Thoughtlessness, carelessness, blundering" (*OED*).

[4] Paraphrase of Milton, *Paradise Lost* (12.647).

[5] 12mo. stands for "duodecimo" or "twelvemo," which indicates "the number of leaves into which a sheet of the paper on which the book is printed has been folded" (*OED*).

[6] De Quincey's revisions for the 1856 edition of *Confessions* identifies the volume as "Canter's 'Euripides'" (*Works* 2:158), likely referring to Wilhelm Canter (1542-75), Dutch humanist, textual scholar, and translator. The editors of *Works* cite De Quincey's addition in MS B of *Confessions*, a copy of *Confessions of an English Opium-Eater and Suspiria de Profundis* (Boston: Tichnor, Reed, and Fields), which contains the author's 1854 holograph revisions. Their note reads: "De Quincey's addition in MS B identifies this as an odd volume of Wilhelm Canter's edition of Euripides, published at Heidelberg in 1597 (and therefore not, as he claims in MS B, '250 years old')" (2:331).

It had been my intention originally to proceed to Westmoreland, both from the love I bore to that country, and on other personal accounts. Accident, however, gave a different direction to my wanderings, and I bent my steps towards North Wales.

After wandering about for some time in Denbighshire, Merionethshire, and Caernarvonshire, I took lodgings in a small neat house in B——. Here I might have staid with great comfort for many weeks; for, provisions were cheap at B——,[1] from the scarcity of other markets for the surplus produce of a wide agricultural district. An accident, however, in which, perhaps, no offence was designed, drove me out to wander again. I know not whether my reader may have remarked, but *I* have often remarked, that the proudest class of people in England (or at any rate, the class whose pride is most apparent) are the families of bishops. Nobleman, and their children, carry about with them, in their very titles, a sufficient notification of their rank. Nay, their very names (and this applies also to the children of many untitled houses) are often, to the English ear, adequate exponents of high birth, or descent. Sackville, Manners, Fitzroy, Paulet, Cavendish, and scores of others, tell their own tale. Such persons, therefore, find every where a due sense of their claims already established, except among those who are ignorant of the world, by virtue of their own obscurity: "Not to know *them*, argues one's self unknown."[2] Their manners take a suitable tone and colouring; and, for once that they find it necessary to impress a sense of their consequence upon others, they meet with a thousand occasions for moderating and tempering this sense by acts of courteous condescension. With the families of bishops it is otherwise: with them it is all up-hill work, to make known their pretensions: for the proportion of the episcopal bench, taken from noble families, is not at any time very large; and the succession to these dignities so rapid, that the public ear seldom has time to become familiar with them, unless where they are connected with some literary reputation. Hence it is, that the children of bishops carry about with them an austere and repulsive air, indicative of claims not generally acknowledged, a sort of *noli me tangere*[3] manner, nervously apprehensive of too familiar approach, and shrinking with the sensitiveness of a gouty man, from all contact with the ὁι πολλοι.[4] Doubtless, a powerful understanding, or unusual goodness of nature, will preserve a

---

[1]   Bangor.
[2]   Paraphrase of Milton, *Paradise Lost* (4.830).
[3]   "Touch me not."
[4]   "The many," or "the common people."

man from such weakness: but, in general, the truth of my representation will be acknowledged: pride, if not of deeper root in such families, appears, at least, more upon the surface of their manners. This spirit of manners naturally communicates itself to their domestics, and other dependants. Now, my landlady had been a lady's maid, or a nurse, in the family of the Bishop of ——;[1] and had but lately married away and "settled" (as such people express it) for life. In a little town like B——, merely to have lived in the bishop's family, conferred some distinction: and my good landlady had rather more than her share of the pride I have noticed on that score. What "my lord" said, and what "my lord" did, how useful he was in parliament, and how indispensable at Oxford, formed the daily burden of her talk. All this I bore very well: for I was too good-natured to laugh in any body's face, and I could make an ample allowance for the garrulity of an old servant. Of necessity, however, I must have appeared in her eyes very inadequately impressed with the bishop's importance: and, perhaps, to punish me for my indifference, or possibly by accident, she one day repeated to me a conversation in which I was indirectly a party concerned. She had been to the palace to pay her respects to the family; and, dinner being over, was summoned into the dining-room. In giving an account of her household economy, she happened to mention, that she had let her apartments. Thereupon the good bishop (it seemed) had taken occasion to caution her as to her selection of inmates: "for," said he, "you must recollect, Betty, that this place is in the high road to the Head;[2] so that multitudes of Irish swindlers, running away from their debts into England—and of English swindlers, running away from their debts to the Isle of Man, are likely to take this place in their route." This advice was certainly not without reasonable grounds: but rather fitted to be stored up for Mrs. Betty's private meditations, than specially reported to me. What followed, however, was somewhat worse:—"Oh, my lord," answered my landlady (according to her own representation of the matter), "I really don't think this young gentleman is a swindler; because—:" "You don't *think* me a swindler?" said I, interrupting her, in a tumult of indignation: "for the future I shall spare you the trouble of thinking about it." And without delay I prepared for my departure. Some concessions the good woman seemed disposed to make: but a harsh and contemptuous expression,

---

[1]   Dr. William Cleaver (1742–1815), Bishop of Bangor, master of Brasenose College (*Works* 2:331).

[2]   Holyhead, central port for travel to Ireland.

which I feared that I applied to the learned dignitary himself, roused *her* indignation in turn: and reconciliation then became impossible. I was, indeed, greatly irritated at the bishop's having suggested any grounds of suspicion, however remotely, against a person whom he had never seen: and I thought of letting him know my mind in Greek: which, at the same time that it would furnish some presumption that I was no swindler, would also (I hoped) compel the bishop to reply in the same language; in which case, I doubted not to make it appear, that if I was not so rich as his lordship, I was a far better Grecian. Calmer thoughts, however, drove this boyish design out of my mind: for I considered, that the bishop was in the right to counsel an old servant; that he could not have designed that his advice should be reported to me; and that the same coarseness of mind, which had led Mrs. Betty to repeat the advice at all, might have coloured it in a way more agreeable to her own style of thinking, than to the actual expressions of the worthy bishop.

I left the lodgings the very same hour; and this turned out a very unfortunate occurrence for me: because, living henceforward at inns, I was drained of my money very rapidly. In a fortnight I was reduced to short allowance; that is, I could allow myself only one meal a-day. From the keen appetite produced by constant exercise, and mountain air, acting on a youthful stomach, I soon began to suffer greatly on this slen-der regimen; for the single meal, which I could venture to order, was coffee or tea. Even this, however, was at length withdrawn: and after-wards, so long as I remained in Wales, I subsisted either on blackber-ries, hips, haws, &c. or on the casual hospitalities which I now and then received, in return for such little services as I had an opportunity of rendering. Sometimes I wrote letters of business for cottagers, who happened to have relatives in Liverpool, or in London: more often I wrote love-letters to their sweethearts for young women who had lived as servants in Shrewsbury, or other towns on the English border. On all such occasions I gave great satisfaction to my humble friends, and was generally treated with hospitality: and once, in particular, near the village of Llan-y-styndw (or some such name),[1] in a sequestered part of Merionethshire, I was entertained for upwards of three days by a family of young people, with an affectionate and fraternal kindness that left an impression upon my heart not yet impaired. The family consisted, at that time, of four sisters, and three brothers, all grown up, and all remarkable for elegance and delicacy of manners. So much beauty, and

---

[1]   Llanstumdwy.

so much native good-breeding and refinement, I do not remember to have seen before or since in any cottage, except once or twice in Westmorland and Devonshire. They spoke English: an accomplishment not often met with in so many members of one family, especially in villages remote from the high-road. Here I wrote, on my first intro-duction, a letter about prize-money,[1] for one of the brothers, who had served on board an English man of war; and more privately, two love-letters for two of the sisters. They were both interesting looking girls, and one of uncommon loveliness. In the midst of their confusion and blushes, whilst dictating, or rather giving me general instructions, it did not require any great penetration to discover that what they wished was, that their letters should be as kind as was consistent with proper maidenly pride. I contrived so to temper my expressions, as to recon-cile the gratification of both feelings: and they were as much pleased with the way in which I had expressed their thoughts, as (in their simplicity) they were astonished at my having so readily discovered them. The reception one meets with from the women of a family, generally determines the tenor of one's whole entertainment. In this case, I had discharged my confidential duties as secretary, so much to the general satisfaction, perhaps also amusing them with my conversa-tion, that I was pressed to stay with a cordiality which I had little incli-nation to resist. I slept with the brothers, the only unoccupied bed standing in the apartment of the young women: but in all other points, they treated me with a respect not usually paid to purses as light as mine; as if my scholarship were sufficient evidence, that I was of "gentle blood." Thus I lived with them for three days, and great part of a fourth: and, from the undiminished kindness which they continued to show me, I believe that I might have staid with them up to this time, if their power had corresponded with their wishes. On the last morning, however, I perceived upon their countenances, as they sate at breakfast, the expression of some unpleasant communication which was at hand; and soon after one of the brothers explained to me, that their parents had gone, the day before my arrival, to an annual meeting of Methodists,[2] held at Caernarvon, and were that day expected to return; "and if they should not be so civil as they ought to be," he begged, on the part of all the young people, that I would not take it amiss. The

---

[1]   Value of an enemy ship divided among crew members of the capturing warship.
[2]   Evangelical revivalists, led by John and Charles Wesley and George Whitefield; the group formed around 1738 and broke from the Church of England in 1795.

parents returned, with churlish faces, and "*Dym Sassenach*" (*no English*), in answer to all my addresses. I saw how matters stood; and so, taking an affectionate leave of my kind and interesting young hosts, I went my way. For, though they spoke warmly to their parents in my behalf, and often excused the manner of the old people, by saying, that it was "only their way," yet I easily understood that my talent for writing love-letters would do as little to recommend me, with two grave sexagenarian Welsh Methodists, as my Greek Sapphics or Alcaics:[1] and what had been hospitality, when offered to me with the gracious courtesy of my young friends, would become charity, when connected with the harsh demeanour of these old people. Certainly, Mr. Shelley is right in his notions about old age:[2] unless powerfully counteracted by all sorts of opposite agencies, it is a miserable corrupter and blighter to the genial charities of the human heart.

Soon after this, I contrived, by means which I must omit for want of room, to transfer myself to London. And now began the latter and fiercer stage of my long-sufferings; without using a disproportionate expression I might say, of my agony. For I now suffered, for upwards of sixteen weeks, the physical anguish of hunger in various degrees of intensity; but as bitter, perhaps, as ever any human being can have suffered who has survived it. I would not needlessly harass my reader's feelings, by a detail of all that I endured: for extremities such as these, under any circumstances of heaviest misconduct or guilt, cannot be contemplated, even in description, without a rueful pity that is painful to the natural goodness of the human heart. Let it suffice, at least on this occasion, to say, that a few fragments of bread from the breakfast-table of one individual (who supposed me to be ill, but did not know of my being in utter want), and these at uncertain intervals, constituted my whole support. During the former part of my sufferings (that is, generally in Wales, and always for the first two months in London) I was houseless, and very seldom slept under a roof. To this constant exposure to the open air I ascribe it mainly, that I did not sink under my torments. Latterly, however, when colder and more inclement weather came on, and when, from the length of my sufferings, I had begun to sink into a more languishing condition, it was, no doubt, fortunate for me, that the same person to whose breakfast-table I had

---

[1] Sapphics and Alcaics are metres in Greek verse.

[2] Shelley, *The Revolt of Islam*: "[old age] is ... cold and cruel, and is made / The careless slave of that dark power which brings / Evil, like blight, on man, who, still betrayed, / Laughs o'er the grave in which his living hopes are laid" (2.33.960–63).

access, allowed me to sleep in a large unoccupied house, of which he was tenant. Unoccupied, I call it, for there was no household or establishment in it; nor any furniture, indeed, except a table, and a few chairs. But I found, on taking possession of my new quarters, that the house already contained one single inmate, a poor friendless child, apparently ten years old; but she seemed hunger-bitten; and sufferings of that sort often make children look older than they are. From this forlorn child I learned, that she had slept and lived there alone, for some time before I came: and great joy the poor creature expressed, when she found that I was, in future, to be her companion through the hours of darkness. The house was large; and, from the want of furniture, the noise of the rats made a prodigious echoing on the spacious stair-case and hall; and, amidst the real fleshly ills of the cold, and, I fear, hunger, the forsaken child had found leisure to suffer still more (it appeared) from the self-created one of ghosts. I promised her protection against all ghosts whatsoever: but, alas! I could offer her no other assistance. We lay upon the floor, with a bundle of cursed law papers for a pillow: but with no other covering than a sort of large horseman's cloak: afterwards, however, we discovered, in a garret, an old sopha-cover, a small piece of rug, and some fragments of other articles, which added a little to our warmth. The poor child crept close to me for warmth, and for security against her ghostly enemies. When I was not more than usually ill, I took her into my arms, so that, in general, she was tolerably warm, and often slept when I could not: for, during the last two months of my sufferings, I slept much in the day-time, and was apt to fall into transient dozings at all hours. But my sleep distressed me more than my watching: for, besides the tumultuousness of my dreams (which were only not so awful as those which I shall have to describe hereafter as produced by opium), my sleep was never more than what is called *dog-sleep*; so that I could hear myself moaning, and was often, as it seemed to me, wakened suddenly by my own voice; and, about this time, a hideous sensation began to haunt me as soon as I fell into a slumber, which has since returned upon me, at different periods of my life, viz. a sort of twitching (I know not where, but apparently about the region of the stomach), which compelled me violently to throw out my feet for the sake of relieving it. This sensation coming on as soon as I began to sleep, and the effort to relieve it constantly awaking me, at length I slept only from exhaustion; and from increasing weakness (as I said before) I was constantly feeling asleep, and constantly awaking. Meantime, the master of the house sometimes came in upon us suddenly, and very early, sometimes not till ten o'clock, sometimes not at all. He was in constant fear of bailiffs: improving on the plan of Cromwell,[1] every night he slept in a different quarter of London; and I observed that he never failed to examine, through a private window, the appearance of those who knocked at the door, before he would allow it to be opened. He breakfasted alone: indeed, his tea equipage would hardly have admitted of his hazarding an invitation to a second person—any more than the quantity of esculent *matériel*, which for the most part, was little more than a roll, or a few biscuits, which he had bought on his road from the place where he had slept. Or, if he *had* asked a party, as I once learnedly and facetiously observed to him—the several members of it must have *stood* in the relation to each other (not *sate* in any relation whatever) of succession, as the metaphysicians have it, and not of co-existence; in the relation of the parts of time, and not of the parts of space. During his breakfast, I generally contrived a reason for lounging in; and, with an air of as much indifference as I could assume, took up such fragments as he had left—sometimes, indeed, there were none at all. In doing this, I committed no robbery except upon the man himself, who was thus obliged (I believe) now and then to send out at noon for an extra biscuit; for, as to the poor child, *she* was never admitted into his study (if I may give that name to his chief depository of parchments, law writings, &c.); that room was to her the Blue-beard room[2] of the house, being regularly locked on his departure to dinner, about six o'clock, which usually was his final departure for the night. Whether this child were an illegitimate daughter of Mr. ——,[3] or only a servant, I could not ascertain; she did not herself know; but certainly she was treated altogether as a menial servant. No sooner did Mr. —— make his appearance, than she went below stairs, brushed his shoes, coat, &c.; and, except when she was summoned to run an errand, she never emerged from the dismal Tartarus[4] of the kitchens, &c. to the upper air, until my welcome knock at night called up her little trembling footsteps to the front door. Of her life during the day-time, however, I knew little but

---

1   Oliver Cromwell (1599–1658), parliamentary reformer, leader of the English Civil War and Lord Protector from 1653–58 after the execution of Charles I, avoided assassination by repeatedly changing where he slept.

2   In the fairy tale by Charles Perrault (1628–1703), Bluebeard keeps his murdered wives in a room to which his current wife does not have access.

3   In the 1856 *Confessions* De Quincey writes that the attorney "called himself, on most days of the week, by the name of Brunell, but occasionally ... by the more common name of Brown" (*Works* 2:195).

4   In Greek mythology, the lowest region of the world.

what I gathered from her own account at night; for, as soon as the hours of business commenced, I saw that my absence would be acceptable; and, in general, therefore, I went off and sate in the parks, or elsewhere, until night-fall.

But who, and what, meantime, was the master of the house himself? Reader, he was one of those anomalous practitioners in lower departments of the law, who—what shall I say?—who, on prudential reasons, or from necessity, deny themselves all indulgence in the luxury of too delicate a conscience: (a periphrasis which might be abridged considerably, but *that* I leave to the reader's taste:) in many walks of life, a conscience is a more expensive incumbrance, than a wife or a carriage; and just as people talk of "laying down" their carriages, so I suppose my friend, Mr. —— had "laid down" his conscience for a time; meaning, doubtless, to resume it as soon as he could afford it. The inner economy of such a man's daily life would present a most strange picture, if I could allow myself to amuse the reader at his expense. Even with my limited opportunities for observing what went on, I saw many scenes of London intrigues, and complex chicanery, "cycle and epicycle, orb in orb,"[1] at which I sometimes smile to this day—and at which I smiled then, in spite of my misery. My situation, however, at that time, gave me little experience, in my own person, of any qualities in Mr. ——'s character but such as did him honour; and of his whole strange composition, I must forget every thing but that towards me he was obliging, and, to the extent of his power, generous.

That power was not, indeed, very extensive; however, in common with the rats, I sate rent free; and, as Dr. Johnson has recorded, that he never but once in his life had as much wall-fruit as he could eat, so let me be grateful, that on that single occasion I had as large a choice of apartments in a London mansion as I could possibly desire. Except the Blue-beard room, which the poor child believed to be haunted, all others, from the attics to the cellars, were at our service; "the world was all before us;"[2] and we pitched our tent for the night in any spot we chose. This house I have already described as a large one; it stands in a conspicuous situation, and in a well-known part of London. Many of my readers will have passed it, I doubt not, within a few hours of reading this. For myself, I never fail to visit it when business draws me to London; about ten o'clock, this very night, August 15, 1821, being my birth-day—I turned aside from my

---

[1] Milton, *Paradise Lost* (8.84).
[2] Paraphrase of Milton, *Paradise Lost* (12.646).

evening walk, down Oxford-street, purposely to take a glance at it: it is now occupied by a respectable family; and, by the lights in the front drawing-room, I observed a domestic party, assembled perhaps at tea, and apparently cheerful and gay. Marvellous contrast in my eyes to the darkness—cold—silence—and desolation of that same house eighteen years ago, when its nightly occupants were one famishing scholar, and a neglected child.—Her, by the bye, in after years, I vainly endeavoured to trace. Apart from her situation, she was not what would be called an interesting child: she was neither pretty, nor quick in understanding, nor remarkably pleasing in manners. But, thank God! even in those years I needed not the embellishments of novel-accessories to conciliate my affections; plain human nature, in its humblest and most homely apparel, was enough for me: and I loved the child because she was my partner in wretchedness. If she is now living, she is probably a mother, with children of her own; but, as I have said, I could never trace her.

This I regret, but another person there was at that time, whom I have since sought to trace with far deeper earnestness, and with far deeper sorrow at my failure. This person was a young woman, and one of that unhappy class who subsist upon the wages of prostitution. I feel no shame, nor have any reason to feel it, in avowing, that I was then on familiar and friendly terms with many women in that unfortunate condition. The reader needs neither smile at this avowal, nor frown. For, not to remind my classical readers of the old Latin proverb—"*Sine Cerere*,"[1] &c., it may well be supposed that in the existing state of my purse, my connexion with such women could not have been an impure one. But the truth is, that at no time of my life have I been a person to hold myself polluted by the touch or approach of any creature that wore a human shape: on the contrary, from my very earliest youth it has been my pride to converse familiarly, *more Socratico*,[2] with all human beings, man, woman, and child, that chance might fling in my way: a practice which is friendly to the knowledge of human nature, to good feelings, and to that frankness of address which becomes a man who would be thought a philosopher. For a philosopher should not see with the eyes of the poor limitary creature calling himself a man of the world, and filled with narrow and self-regarding prejudices of birth and education, but should look upon himself as a Catholic creature, and as standing in an equal relation to high and low—to educated and uneducated, to the

---

[1] "*Sine Cerere et Libero [or Baccho] friget Venus*," or "Without bread and wine love turns cold."
[2] "In the Socratic manner."

guilty and the innocent. Being myself at that time of necessity a peri-
patetic, or a walker of the streets, I naturally fell in more frequently with
those female peripatetics who are technically called Street-walkers. Many
of these women had occasionally taken my part against watchmen who
wished to drive me off the steps of houses where I was sitting. But one
amongst them, the one on whose account I have at all introduced this
subject—yet no! let me not class thee, Oh noble minded Ann—, with
that order of women; let me find, if it be possible, some gentler name to
designate the condition of her to whose bounty and compassion, ministering to my necessities when all the world had forsaken me, I owe it
that I am at this time alive.——For many weeks I had walked at nights
with this poor friendless girl up and down Oxford Street, or had rested
with her on steps and under the shelter of porticos. She could not be so
old as myself: she told me, indeed, that she had not completed her
sixteenth year. By such questions as my interest about her prompted, I
had gradually drawn forth her simple history. Her's was a case of ordinary occurrence (as I have since had reason to think), and one in which,
if London beneficence had better adapted its arrangements to meet it,
the power of the law might oftener be interposed to protect, and to
avenge. But the stream of London charity flows in a channel which,
though deep and mighty, is yet noiseless and underground; not obvious
or readily accessible to poor houseless wanderers: and it cannot be denied
that the outside air and frame-work of London society is harsh, cruel,
and repulsive. In any case, however, I saw that part of her injuries might
easily have been redressed: and I urged her often and earnestly to lay her
complaint before a magistrate: friendless as she was, I assured her that she
would meet with immediate attention; and that English justice, which
was no respecter of persons, would speedily and amply avenge her on
the brutal ruffian who had plundered her little property. She promised
me often that she would; but she delayed taking the steps I pointed out
from time to time: for she was timid and dejected to a degree which
showed how deeply sorrow had taken hold of her young heart: and
perhaps she thought justly that the most upright judge, and the most
righteous tribunals, could do nothing to repair her heaviest wrongs.
Something, however, would perhaps have been done: for it had been
settled between us at length, but unhappily on the very last time but one
that I was ever to see her, that in a day or two we should go together
before a magistrate, and that I should speak on her behalf. This little service it was destined, however, that I should never realize. Meantime, that
which she rendered to me, and which was greater than I could ever have

repaid her, was this:—One night, when we were pacing slowly along Oxford Street, and after a day when I had felt more than usually ill and faint, I requested her to turn off with me into Soho Square: thither we went: and we sate down on the steps of a house, which, to this hour, I never pass without a pang of grief, and an inner act of homage to the spirit of that unhappy girl, in memory of the noble action which she there performed. Suddenly, as we sate, I grew much worse: I had been leaning my head against her bosom; and all at once I sank from her arms and fell backwards on the steps. From the sensations I then had, I felt an inner conviction of the liveliest kind that without some powerful and reviving stimulus, I should either have died on the spot—or should at least have sunk to a point of exhaustion from which all reäscent under my friendless circumstances would soon have become hopeless. Then it was, at this crisis of my fate, that my poor orphan companion—who had herself met with little but injuries in this world—stretched out a saving hand to me. Uttering a cry of terror, but without a moment's delay, she ran off into Oxford Street, and in less time than could be imagined, returned to me with a glass of port wine and spices, that acted upon my empty stomach (which at that time would have rejected all solid food) with an instantaneous power of restoration: and for this glass the gener-ous girl without a murmur paid out of her own humble purse at a time—be it remembered!—when she had scarcely wherewithal to purchase the bare necessaries of life, and when she could have no reason to expect that I should ever be able to reimburse her. Oh! youthful bene-factress! how often in succeeding years, standing in solitary places, and thinking of thee with grief of heart and perfect love, how often have I wished that, as in ancient times the curse of a father was believed to have a supernatural power, and to pursue its object with a fatal necessity of self-fulfilment,—even so the benediction of a heart oppressed with grat-itude, might have a like prerogative; might have power given to it from above to chace—to haunt—to way-lay—to overtake—to pursue thee into the central darkness of a London brothel, or (if it were possible) into the darkness of the grave—there to awaken thee with an authentic message of peace and forgiveness, and of final reconciliation!

I do not often weep: for not only do my thoughts on subjects connected with the chief interests of man daily, nay hourly, descend a thousand fathoms "too deep for tears;"[1] not only does the sternness of my habits of thought present an antagonism to the feelings which

---

[1] Wordsworth, "Ode: Intimations of Immortality" (207).

prompt tears—wanting of necessity to those who, being protected usually by their levity from any tendency to meditative sorrow, would by that same levity be made incapable of resisting it on any casual access of such feelings:—but also, I believe that all minds which have contemplated such objects as deeply as I have done, must, for their own protection from utter despondency, have early encouraged and cherished some tranquilizing belief as to the future balances and the hieroglyphic meanings of human sufferings. On these accounts, I am cheerful to this hour: and, as I have said, I do not often weep. Yet some feelings, though not deeper or more passionate, are more tender than others: and often, when I walk at this time in Oxford Street by dreamy lamp-light, and hear those airs played on a barrel-organ which years ago solaced me and my dear companion (as I must always call her) I shed tears, and muse with myself at the mysterious dispensation which so suddenly and so critically separated us for ever. How it happened, the reader will understand from what remains of this introductory narration.

Soon after the period of the last incident I have recorded, I met, in Albemarle Street, a gentleman of his late Majesty's household. This gentleman had received hospitalities, on different occasions, from my family: and he challenged me upon the strength of my family likeness. I did not attempt any disguise: I answered his questions ingenuously,— and, on his pledging his word of honor that he would not betray me to my guardians, I gave him an address to my friend the Attorney's. The next day I received from him a 10*l.*[1] Bank-note. The letter inclosing it was delivered with other letters of business to the Attorney: but, though his look and manner informed me that he suspected its contents, he gave it up to me honorably and without demur.

This present, from the particular service to which it was applied, leads me naturally to speak of the purpose which had allured me up to London, and which I had been (to use a forensic word) *soliciting* from the first day of my arrival in London, to that of my final departure.

In so mighty a world as London, it will surprise my readers that I should not have found some means of staving off the last extremities of penury: and it will strike them that two resources at least must have been open to me,—viz. either to seek assistance from the friends of my family, or to turn my youthful talents and attainments into some channel of pecuniary emolument. As to the first course, I may observe, generally, that what I dreaded beyond all other evils was the chance of being reclaimed

---

[1]   The abbreviation "*l.*" stands for British pounds sterling.

by my guardians; not doubting that whatever power the law gave them would have been enforced against me to the utmost; that is, to the extremity of forcibly restoring me to the school which I had quitted: a restoration which as it would in my eyes have been a dishonor, even if submitted to voluntarily, could not fail, when extorted from me in contempt and defiance of my known wishes and efforts, to have been a humiliation worse to me than death, and which would indeed have terminated in death. I was, therefore, shy enough of applying for assistance even in those quarters where I was sure of receiving it—at the risk of furnishing my guardians with any clue for recovering me. But, as to London in particular, though, doubtless, my father had in his life-time had many friends there, yet (as ten years had passed since his death) I remembered few of them even by name: and never having seen London before, except once for a few hours, I knew not the address of even those few. To this mode of gaining help, therefore, in part the difficulty, but much more the paramount fear which I have mentioned, habitually indisposed me. In regard to the other mode, I now feel half inclined to join my reader in wondering that I should have overlooked it. As a corrector of Greek proofs (if in no other way), I might doubtless have gained enough for my slender wants. Such an office as this I could have discharged with an exemplary and punctual accuracy that would soon have gained me the confidence of my employers. But it must not be forgotten that, even for such an office as this, it was necessary that I should first of all have an introduction to some respectable publisher: and this I had no means of obtaining. To say the truth, however, it had never once occurred to me to think of literary labours as a source of profit. No mode sufficiently speedy of obtaining money had ever occurred to me, but that of borrowing it on the strength of my future claims and expectations. This mode I sought by every avenue to compass: and amongst other persons I applied to a Jew named D ——.*

---

*   To this same Jew, by the way, some eighteen months afterwards, I applied again on the same business; and, dating at that time from a respectable college, I was fortunate enough to gain his serious attention to my proposals. My necessities had not arisen from any extravagance, or youthful levities (these my habits and the nature of my pleasures raised me far above), but simply from the vindictive malice of my guardian, who, when he found himself no longer able to prevent me from going to the university, had, as a parting token of his good nature, refused to sign an order for granting me a shilling beyond the allowance made to me at school—viz. 100*l.* per ann. Upon this sum it was, in my time, barely possible to have lived in college; and not possible to a man who, though above the paltry affectation of ostentatious disregard for money, and without any expensive tastes, confided nevertheless rather too much in servants, and did not delight in the petty details of minute economy.

To this Jew, and to other advertising money-lenders (some of whom were, I believe, also Jews), I had introduced myself with an account of my expectation; which account, on examining my father's will at Doctor's Commons,[1] they had ascertained to be correct. The person there mentioned as the second son of ———,[2] was found to have all the claims (or more than all) that I had stated: but one question still remained, which the faces of the Jews pretty significantly suggested,— was *I* that person? This doubt had never occurred to me as a possible one: I had rather feared, whenever my Jewish friends scrutinized me keenly, that I might be too well known to be that person—and that some scheme might be passing in their minds for entrapping me and selling me to my guardians. It was strange to me to find my own self, *materialiter* considered (so I expressed it, for I doated on logical accuracy of distinctions), accused, or at least suspected, of counterfeiting my own self, *formaliter*[3] considered. However, to satisfy their scruples, I took the only course in my power. Whilst I was in Wales, I had received various letters from young friends: these I produced: for I carried them constantly in my pocket—being, indeed, by this time, almost the only relics of my personal incumbrances (excepting the clothes I wore) which I had not in one way or other disposed of. Most of these letters were from the Earl of ———, who was at that time my chief (or rather only) confidential friend. These letters were dated from Eton. I had also some from the Marquis of ———,[4] his father, who, though absorbed in

---

I soon, therefore, became embarrassed: and at length, after a most voluminous negotiation with the Jew, (some parts of which, if I had leisure to rehearse them, would greatly amuse my readers), I was put in possession of the sum I asked for—on the "regular" terms of paying the Jew seventeen and a half per cent. by way of annuity on all the money furnished; Israel, on his part, graciously resuming no more than about ninety guineas of the said money, on account of an Attorney's bill, (for what services, to whom rendered, and when, whether at the siege of Jerusalem—at the building of the Second Temple—or on some earlier occasion, I have not yet been able to discover). How many perches this bill measured I really forget: but I still keep it in a cabinet of natural curiosities; and sometime or other I believe I shall present it to the British Museum. [In a note to the 1856 *Confessions*, De Quincey gives the name of the Jew as Dell. He adds, "Like all other Jews with whom I have had negotiations, he was frank and honourable in his mode of conducting business. What he promised, he performed; and if his terms were high, as naturally they could not *but* be, to cover his risks, he avowed them from the first" (*Works* 2:206).]

---

1   College for the study and practice of civil law.
2   Thomas Quincey.
3   "*materialiter*": "materially"; ... "*formaliter*": "formally."
4   The Earl of Altamont, whom De Quincey had met while in school in Bath, was the son of the Marquis of Sligo. De Quincey had visited their estate in Ireland in the summer of 1800.

agricultural pursuits, yet having been an Etonian himself, and as good a scholar as a nobleman needs to be—still retained an affection for classical studies, and for youthful scholars. He had, accordingly, from the time that I was fifteen, corresponded with me; sometimes upon the great improvements which he had made, or was meditating, in the counties of M —— and Sl ——[1] since I had been there; sometimes upon the merits of a Latin poet; at other times, suggesting subjects to me on which he wished me to write verses.

On reading the letters, one of my Jewish friends agreed to furnish two or three hundred pounds on my personal security—provided I could persuade the young Earl, who was, by the way, not older than myself, to guarantee the payment on our coming of age: the Jew's final object being, as I now suppose, not the trifling profit he could expect to make by me, but the prospect of establishing a connection with my noble friend, whose immense expectations were well known to him. In pursuance of this proposal on the part of the Jew, about eight or nine days after I had received the 10l., I prepared to go down to Eton. Nearly 3l. of the money I had given to my money-lending friend, on his alleging that the stamps must be bought, in order that the writings might be preparing whilst I was away from London. I thought in my heart that he was lying; but I did not wish to give him any excuse for charging his own delays upon me. A smaller sum I had given to my friend the attorney (who was connected with the money-lenders as their lawyer), to which, indeed, he was entitled for his unfurnished lodgings. About fifteen shillings I had employed in re-establishing (though in a very humble way) my dress. Of the remainder I gave one quarter to Ann, meaning on my return to have divided with her whatever might remain. These arrangements made,—soon after six o'clock, on a dark winter evening, I set off, accompanied by Ann, towards Piccadilly; for it was my intention to go down as far as Salt-hill on the Bath or Bristol Mail. Our course lay through a part of the town which has now all disappeared, so that I can no longer retrace its ancient boundaries: Swallow-street, I think it was called. Having time enough before us, however, we bore away to the left until we came into Golden-square: there, near the corner of Sherrard-street, we sat down; not wishing to part in the tumult and blaze of Piccadilly. I had told her of my plans some time before: and I now assured her again that she should share in my good fortune, if I met with any; and that I would never forsake her, as soon as I had power to

_____

[1]   Mayo and Sligo.

protect her. This I fully intended, as much from inclination as from a sense of duty: for, setting aside gratitude, which in any case must have made me her debtor for life, I loved her as affectionately as if she had been my sister: and at this moment, with seven-fold tenderness, from pity at witnessing her extreme dejection. I had, apparently, most reason for dejection, because I was leaving the saviour of my life: yet I, considering the shock my health had received, was cheerful and full of hope. She, on the contrary, who was parting with one who had had little means of serving her, except by kindness and brotherly treatment, was overcome by sorrow; so that, when I kissed her at our final farewell, she put her arms about my neck, and wept without speaking a word. I hoped to return in a week at farthest, and I agreed with her that on the fifth night from that, and every night afterwards, she should wait for me at six o'clock, near the bottom of Great Titchfield-street, which had been our customary haven, as it were, of rendezvous, to prevent our missing each other in the great Mediterranean of Oxford-street. This, and other measures of precaution I took: one only I forgot. She had either never told me, or (as a matter of no great interest) I had forgotten, her surname. It is a general practice, indeed, with girls of humble rank in her unhappy condition, not (as novel-reading women of higher pretensions) to style themselves—*Miss Douglass, Miss Montague,* &c. but simply by their Christian names, *Mary, Jane, Frances,* &c. Her surname, as the surest means of tracing her hereafter, I ought now to have inquired: but the truth is, having no reason to think that our meeting could, in consequence of a short interruption, be more difficult or uncertain than it had been for so many weeks, I had scarcely for a moment adverted to it as necessary, or placed it amongst my memoranda against this parting interview: and, my final anxieties being spent in comforting her with hopes, and in pressing upon her the necessity of getting some medicines for a violent cough and hoarseness with which she was troubled, I wholly forgot it until it was too late to recal her.

It was past eight o'clock when I reached the Gloucester Coffee-house: and, the Bristol Mail being on the point of going off, I mounted on the outside. The fine fluent motion* of this Mail soon laid me to asleep: it is somewhat remarkable, that the first easy or refreshing sleep which I had enjoyed for some months, was on the outside of a Mail-coach—a bed which, at this day, I find rather an uneasy one. Connected with this sleep

---

*   The Bristol Mail is the best appointed in the kingdom—owing to the double advantage of an unusually good road, and of an extra sum for expences subscribed by the Bristol merchants.

was a little incident, which served, as hundreds of others did at that time, to convince me how easily a man who has never been in any great distress, may pass through life without knowing, in his own person at least, anything of the possible goodness of the human heart—or, as I must add with as sigh, of its possible vileness. So thick a curtain of *manners* is drawn over the features and expression of men's *natures*, that to the ordinary observer, the two extremities, and the infinite field of varieties which lie between them, are all confounded—the vast and multitudinous compass of their several harmonies reduced to the meagre outline of differences expressed in the gamut or alphabet of elementary sounds. The case was this: for the first four or five miles from London, I annoyed my fellow passenger on the roof by occasionally falling against him when the coach gave a lurch to his side; and indeed, if the road had been less smooth and level than it is, I should have fallen off from weakness. Of this annoyance, · he complained heavily, as perhaps, in the same circumstances most people would; he expressed his complaint, however, more morosely than the occasion seemed to warrant; and, if I had parted with him at that moment, I should have thought of him (if I had considered it worth while to think of him at all) as a surly and almost brutal fellow. However, I was conscious that I had given him some cause for complaint: and, therefore, I apologized to him, and assured him I would do what I could to avoid falling asleep for the future; and, at the same time, in as few words as possible, I explained to him that I was ill and in a weak state from long suffering; and that I could not afford at that time to take an inside place. The man's manner changed, upon hearing this explanation, in an instant: and when I next woke for a minute from the noise and lights of Hounslow (for in spite of my wishes and efforts I had fallen asleep again within two minutes from the time I had spoken to him) I found that he had put his arm round me to protect me from falling off: and for the rest of my journey he behaved to me with the gentleness of a woman, so that, at length, I almost lay in his arms: and this was the more kind, as he could not have known that I was not going the whole way to Bath or Bristol. Unfortunately, indeed, I *did* go rather farther than I intended: for so genial and refreshing was my sleep, that the next time, after leaving Hounslow that I fully awoke, was upon the sudden pulling up of the Mail (possibly at a Post-office); and, on inquiry, I found that we had reached Maidenhead—six or seven miles, I think, a-head of Salt-hill. Here I alighted: and for the half minute that the Mail stopped, I was entreated by my friendly companion (who, from the transient glimpse I had had of him in Piccadilly, seemed to me to be a gentleman's butler—or person of that rank) to go to bed without delay. This I promised, though with no intention of doing so: and in fact, I immediately set forward, or rather backward, on foot. It must then have been nearly midnight: but so slowly did I creep along, that I heard a clock in a cottage strike four before I turned down the lane from Slough to Eton. The air and the sleep had both refreshed me; but I was weary nevertheless. I remember a thought (obvious enough, and which has been prettily expressed by a Roman poet) which gave me some consolation at that moment under my poverty. There had been some time before a murder committed on or near Hounslow-heath. I think I cannot be mistaken when I say that the name of the murdered person was *Steele*, and that he was the owner of a lavender plantation in that neighbourhood. Every step of my progress was bringing me nearer to the Heath: and it naturally occurred to me that I and the accursed murderer, if he were that night abroad, might at every instant be unconsciously approaching each other through the darkness: in which case, said I,—supposing I, instead of being (as indeed I am) little better than an outcast, —

Lord of my learning and no land beside,[1]

were, like my friend, Lord ——,[2] heir by general repute to 70,000*l*. per. ann., what a panic should I be under at this moment about my throat!— indeed, it was not likely that Lord —— should ever be in my situation. But nevertheless, the spirit of the remark remains true—that vast power and possessions make a man shamefully afraid of dying: and I am convinced that many of the most intrepid adventurers, who, by fortunately being poor, enjoy the full use of their natural courage, would, if at the very instant of going into action news were brought to them that they had unexpectedly succeeded to an estate in England of 50,000*l*. a year, feel their dislike to bullets considerably sharpened★—and their efforts at perfect equanimity and self-possession proportionably difficult. So true it is, in the language of a wise man whose own experience had made him acquainted with both fortunes, that riches are better fitted—

★ It will be objected that many men, of the highest rank and wealth, have in our own day, as well as throughout our history, been amongst the foremost in courting danger in battle. True: but this is not the case supposed: long familiarity with power has to them deadened its effect and its attractions.

---

[1] Source unknown.
[2] Lord Altamont.

To slacken virtue, and abate her edge,
Than tempt her to do aught may merit praise. *Parad. Regained.*[1]

I dally with my subject because, to myself, the remembrance of these times is profoundly interesting. But my reader shall not have any further cause to complain: for I now hasten to its close.—In the road between Slough and Eton, I fell asleep: and, just as the morning began to dawn, I was awakened by the voice of a man standing over me and surveying me. I know not what he was: he was an ill-looking fellow—but not therefore of necessity an ill-meaning fellow: or, if he were, I suppose he thought that no person sleeping out-of-doors in winter could be worth robbing. In which conclusion, however, as it regarded myself, I beg to assure him, if he should be among my readers, that he was mistaken. After a slight remark he passed on: and I was not sorry at his disturbance, as it enabled me to pass through Eton before people were generally up. The night had been heavy and lowering: but towards the morning it had changed to a slight frost: and the ground and the trees were now covered with rime. I slipped through Eton unobserved; washed myself, and, as far as possible, adjusted my dress at a little public-house in Windsor; and about eight, o'clock went down towards Pote's.[2] On my road I met some junior boys of whom I made enquiries: an Etonian is always a gentleman; and, in spite of my shabby habiliments, they answered me civilly. My friend, Lord ——, was gone to the University of ——. "Ibi omnis effusus labor!"[3] I had, however, other friends at Eton: but it is not to all who wear that name in prosperity that a man is willing to present himself in distress. On recollecting myself, however, I asked for the Earl of D ——,[4] to whom, (though my acquaintance with him was not so intimate as with some others) I should not have shrunk from presenting myself under any circumstances. He was still at Eton, though I believe on the wing for Cambridge. I called, was received kindly, and asked to breakfast.

Here let me stop for a moment to check my reader from any erroneous conclusions: because I have had occasion incidentally to speak of various patrician friends, it must not be supposed that I have myself any pretensions to rank or high blood. I thank God that I have not:—I am

---

[1]   Milton, *Paradise Regained* (2.455–56).
[2]   A bookseller in High Street, Eton.
[3]   "Here all labour vanished," from the *Georgics* (4.491–92) by Virgil (70–19 BCE), Roman poet and author of *The Aeneid*.
[4]   The Earl of Dorset.

the son of a plain English merchant, esteemed during his life for his great integrity, and strongly attached to literary pursuits (indeed, he was himself, anonymously, an author): if he had lived, it was expected that he would have been very rich; but, dying prematurely, he left no more than 30,000*l*. amongst seven different claimants. My mother I may mention with honour, as still more highly gifted. For, though unpretending to the name and honours of a *literary* woman, I shall presume to call her (what many literary women are not) an *intellectual* woman: and I believe that if ever her letters should be collected and published, they would be thought generally to exhibit as much strong and masculine sense, delivered in as pure "mother English," racy and fresh with idiomatic graces, as any in our language—hardly excepting those of lady M.W. Montague.[1]—These are my honours of descent: I have no others: and I have thanked God sincerely that I have not, because, in my judgment, a station which raises a man too eminently above the level of his fellow-creatures is not the most favourable to moral, or to intellectual qualities.

Lord D —— placed before me a most magnificent breakfast. It was really so; but in my eyes it seemed trebly magnificent—from being the first regular meal, the first "good man's table,"[2] that I had sate down to for months. Strange to say, however, I could scarcely eat any thing. On the day when I first received my 10*l*. bank-note, I had gone to a baker's shop and bought a couple of rolls: this very shop I had two months or six weeks before surveyed with an eagerness of desire which it was almost humiliating to me to recollect. I remembered the story about Otway;[3] and feared that there might be danger in eating too rapidly. But I had no need for alarm, my appetite was quite sunk, and I became sick before I had eaten half of what I had bought. This effect from eating what approached to a meal, I continued to feel for weeks: or, when I did not experience any nausea, part of what I ate was rejected, sometimes with acidity, sometimes immediately, and without any acidity. On the present occasion, at lord D ——'s table, I found myself not at all better than usual: and, in the midst of luxuries, I had no appetite. I had, however, unfortunately at all times a craving for wine: I explained my situation, therefore, to lord D ——, and gave him a short account of my late sufferings, at which he expressed great compassion, and called

---

[1]   Lady Mary Wortley Montague (1689–1762), famous for her letters, especially *The Turkish Embassy Letters* (first published in 1763); also a poet.

[2]   A paraphrase of Shakespeare's "good man's feast," *As You Like It* (2.7.115, .122).

[3]   Thomas Otway (1651–85), dramatist; supposedly Otway, hiding from creditors, received money from a stranger to buy food and choked to death when he took his first bite.

for wine. This gave me a momentary relief and pleasure; and on all occasions when I had an opportunity, I never failed to drink wine— which I worshipped then as I have since worshipped opium. I am convinced, however, that this indulgence in wine contributed to strengthen my malady; for the tone of my stomach was apparently quite sunk; but by a better regimen it might sooner, and perhaps effectually, have been revived. I hope that it was not from this love of wine that I lingered in the neighbourhood of my Eton friends: I persuaded myself *then* that it was from reluctance to ask of Lord D ——, on whom I was conscious I had not sufficient claims, the particular service in quest of which I had come down to Eton. I was, however, unwilling to lose my journey, and—I asked it. Lord D ——, whose good nature was unbounded, and which, in regard to myself, had been measured rather by his compassion perhaps for my condition, and his knowledge of my intimacy with some of his relatives, than by an over-rigorous inquiry into the extent of my own direct claims, faultered, nevertheless, at this request. He acknowledged that he did not like to have any dealings with money-lenders, and feared lest such a transaction might come to the ears of his connexions. Moreover, he doubted whether *his* signature, whose expectations were so much more bounded than those of ——, would avail with my unchristian friends. However, he did not wish, as it seemed, to mortify me by an absolute refusal: for after a little consideration, he promised, under certain conditions which he pointed out, to give his security. Lord D —— was at this time not eighteen years of age: but I have often doubted, on recollecting since the good sense and prudence which on this occasion he mingled with so much urbanity of manner (an urbanity which in him wore the grace of youthful sincerity), whether any statesman—the oldest and the most accomplished in diplomacy—could have acquitted himself better under the same circumstances. Most people, indeed, cannot be addressed on such a business, without surveying you with looks as austere and unpropitious as those of a Saracen's head.

Recomforted by this promise, which was not quite equal to the best, but far above the worst that I had pictured to myself as possible, I returned in a Windsor coach to London three days after I had quitted it. And now I come to the end of my story:—the Jews did not approve of Lord D ——'s terms; whether they would in the end have acceded to them, and were only seeking time for making due enquiries, I know not; but many delays were made—time passed on—the small fragment of my bank note had just melted away; and before any conclusion could have been put to the business, I must have relapsed into my former state of wretchedness. Suddenly, however, at this crisis, an opening was made, almost by accident, for reconciliation with my friends. I quitted London, in haste, for a remote part of England: after some time, I proceeded to the university; and it was not until many months had passed away, that I had it in my power again to re-visit the ground which had become so interesting to me, and to this day remains so, as the chief scene of my youthful sufferings.

Meantime, what had become of poor Anne?[1] For her I have reserved my concluding words: according to our agreement, I sought her daily, and waited for her every night, so long as I staid in London, at the corner of Titchfield-street. I inquired for her of every one who was likely to know her; and, during the last hours of my stay in London, I put into activity every means of tracing her that my knowledge of London suggested, and the limited extent of my power made possible. The street where she had lodged I knew, but not the house; and I remembered at last some account which she had given me of ill treat-ment from her landlord, which made it probable that she had quitted those lodgings before we parted. She had few acquaintance; most people, besides, thought that the earnestness of my inquiries arose from motives which moved their laughter, or their slight regard; and others, thinking I was in chase of a girl who had robbed me of some trifles, were naturally and excusably indisposed to give me any clue to her, if, indeed, they had any to give. Finally, as my despairing resource, on the day I left London I put into the hands of the only person who (I was sure) must know Anne by sight, from having been in company with us once or twice, an address to ——— in ——— shire,[2] at that time the resi-dence of my family. But, to this hour, I have never heard a syllable about her. This, amongst such troubles as most men meet with in this life, had been my heaviest affliction.—If she lived, doubtless we must have been sometimes in search of each other, at the very same moment, through the mighty labyrinths of London; perhaps, even within a few feet of each other—a barrier no wider in a London street, often amounting in the end to a separation for eternity! During some years, I hoped that she *did* live; and I suppose that, in the literal and unrhetorical use of the word *myriad*, I may say that on my different visits to London, I have

---

[1] De Quincey spells Anne both with and without the 'e' in his original *Confessions*.
[2] St. John's Priory, Cheshire.

looked into many, many myriads of female faces, in the hope of meeting her. I should know her again amongst a thousand, if I saw her for a moment; for, though not handsome, she had a sweet expression of countenance, and a peculiar and graceful carriage of the head.—I sought her, I have said, in hope. So it was for years; but now I should fear to see her; and her cough, which grieved me when I parted with her, is now my consolation. I now wish to see her no longer; but think of her, more gladly, as one long since laid in the grave; in the grave, I would hope, of a Magdalen;[1] taken away, before injuries and cruelty had blotted out and transfigured her ingenuous nature, or the brutalities of ruffians had completed the ruin they had begun.

[*The remainder of this very interesting Article will be given in the next Number. ED.*]

NOTICE TO THE READER:—The incidents recorded in the Preliminary Confessions already published, lie within a period of which the earlier extreme is now rather more, and the latter extreme less, than nineteen years ago: consequently, in a popular way of computing dates, many of the incidents might be indifferently referred to a distance of eighteen or of nineteen years; and, as the notes and memoranda for this narrative were drawn up originally about last Christmas, it seemed most natural in all cases to prefer the former date. In the hurry of composing the narrative, though some months had then elapsed, this date was every where retained: and, in many cases, perhaps, it leads to no error, or to none of importance. But in one instance, viz. where the author speaks of his own birth-day, this adoption of one uniform date has led to a positive inaccuracy of an entire year: for, during the very time of composition, the *nineteenth* year from the earlier term of the whole period revolved to its close. It is, therefore, judged proper to mention, that the period of that narrative lies between the early part of July, 1802, and the beginning or middle of March, 1803.

---

[1] Reference to Mary Magdalene as reformed prostitute.

PART II

So then, Oxford-street, stony-hearted step-mother! thou that listenest to the sighs of orphans, and drinkest the tears of children, at length I was dismissed from thee: the time was come at last that I no more should pace in anguish thy never-ending terraces; no more should dream, and wake in captivity to the pangs of hunger. Successors, too many, to myself and Ann, have, doubtless, since then trodden in our footsteps—inheritors of our calamities: other orphans than Ann have sighed: tears have been shed by other children: and thou, Oxford-street, hast since, doubtless, echoed to the groans of innumerable hearts. For myself, however, the storm which I had outlived seemed to have been the pledge of a long fair-weather; the premature sufferings which I had paid down, to have been accepted as a ransom for many years to come, as a price of long immunity from sorrow: and if again I walked in London, a solitary and contemplative man (as oftentimes I did), I walked for the most part in serenity and peace of mind. And, although it is true that the calamities of my noviciate in London had struck root so deeply in my bodily constitution that afterwards they shot up and flourished afresh, and grew into a noxious umbrage that has overshadowed and darkened my latter years, yet these second assaults of suffering were met with a fortitude more confirmed, with the resources of a maturer intellect, and with alleviations from sympathising affection—how deep and tender!

Thus, however, with whatsoever alleviations, years that were far asunder were bound together by subtle links of suffering derived from a common root. And herein I notice an instance of the short-sightedness of human desires, that oftentimes on moonlight nights, during my first mournful abode in London, my consolation was (if such it could be thought) to gaze from Oxford-street up every avenue in succession which pierces through the heart of Marylebone to the fields and the woods; for *that*, said I, travelling with my eyes up the long vistas which lay part in light and part in shade, "*that* is the road to the North, and therefore to ——,[1] and if I had the wings of a dove,[2] *that* way I would fly for comfort." Thus I said, and thus I wished, in my blindness; yet, even in that very northern region it was, even in that very valley, nay, in that very house to which my erroneous wishes pointed, that this

---

[1] Dove Cottage, Wordsworth's residence at the time; De Quincey took over residence in 1809.

[2] "Fear and trembling assail me and my whole frame shudders. / I say: 'Oh that I had the wings of a dove to fly away and find rest!'" (Psalms 55:6).

second birth of my sufferings began; and that they again threatened to besiege the citadel of life and hope. There it was, that for years I was persecuted by visions as ugly, and as ghastly phantoms that ever haunted the couch of an Orestes:[1] and in this unhappier than he, that sleep, which comes to all as a respite and a restoration, and to him especially, as a blessed★ balm for his wounded heart and his haunted brain, visited me as my bitterest scourge. Thus blind was I in my desires; yet, if a veil interposes between the dim-sightedness of man and his future calamities, the same veil hides from him their alleviations; and a grief which had not been feared is met by consolations which had not been hoped. I, therefore, who participated, as it were, in the troubles of Orestes (excepting only in his agitated conscience), participated no less in all his supports: my Eumenides, like his, were at my bed-feet, and stared in upon me through the curtains: but, watching by my pillow, or defrauding herself of sleep to bear me company through the heavy watches of the night, sate my Electra: for thou, beloved M.,[2] dear companion of my later years, thou wast my Electra! and neither in nobility of mind nor in long-suffering affection, wouldst permit that a Grecian sister should excel an English wife. For thou thoughtst not much to stoop to humble offices of kindness, and to servile★★ ministrations of tenderest affection;—to wipe away for years the unwholesome dews upon the forehead, or to refresh the lips when parched and baked with fever; nor, even when thy own peaceful slumbers had by long sympathy become infected with the spectacle of my dread contest with phantoms and shadowy enemies that oftentimes bade me "sleep no more!"[3]—not even then, didst thou utter a complaint or any murmur, nor withdraw thy angelic smiles, nor shrink from thy service of love more than Electra did of old. For she too, though she was a Grecian woman, and the

---

★   φίλον ὕπνου θελγήτρον ἐπίχον νόσου ["Dear spell of sleep, assuager of disease": Euripides, *Orestes* (211).]

★★ ἡδὺ δύλευμα. *Eurip. Orest.* |"Sweet slavery," paraphrase of Euripides, *Orestes* (221).|

---

1   Reference to *Orestes* by Euripides (485–406 BCE), author of over ninety plays, nineteen of which survive; Clytemnestra, Orestes's mother, has murdered his father, Agamemnon; Orestes avenges the murder and kills his mother, but is punished by the Eumenides, or Furies, avenging spirits who torment him.

2   Margaret, De Quincey's wife.

3   Shakespeare, *Macbeth*; after murdering Duncan in his sleep, Macbeth says to Lady Macbeth, "Methought I heard a voice cry 'Sleep no more, / Macbeth does murder sleep'" (2.2.33–34).

daughter of the king* of men, yet wept sometimes, and hid her face**
in her robe.

But these troubles are past: and thou wilt read these records of a period
so dolorous to us both as the legend of some hideous dream that can return
no more. Meantime, I am again in London: and again I pace the terraces
of Oxford-street by night: and oftentimes, when I am oppressed by anxieties that demand all my philosophy and the comfort of thy presence to
support, and yet remember that I am separated from thee by three hundred
miles, and the length of three dreary months,—I look up the streets that
run northwards from Oxford-street, upon moonlight nights, and recollect
my youthful ejaculation of anguish;—and remembering that thou art sitting
alone in that same valley, and mistress of that very house to which my heart
turned in its blindness nineteen years ago, I think that, though blind indeed,
and scattered to the winds of late, the promptings of my heart may yet have
had reference to a remoter time, and may be justified if read in another
meaning:—and, if I could allow myself to descend again to the impotent
wishes of childhood, I should again say to myself, as I look to the north,
"Oh, that I had the wings of a dove—" and with how just a confidence in
thy good and gracious nature might I add the other half of my early ejaculation—"And *that* way I would fly for comfort."

THE PLEASURES OF OPIUM

It is so long since I first took opium, that if it had been a trifling incident
in my life, I might have forgotten its date: but cardinal events are not to be
forgotten; and from circumstances connected with it, I remember that it
must be referred to the autumn of 1804. During that season I was in
London, having come thither for the first time since my entrance at college.
And my introduction to opium arose in the following way. From an early
age I had been accustomed to wash my head in cold water at least once
a day: being suddenly seized with tooth-ache, I attributed it to some

---

* ἄναξ ἄνδρων Ἀγαμεμνων ["Agamemnon, King of Men."]
** ὄμμα θεισ᾽ ἐιοω πεπλων. The scholar will know that throughout this passage I refer to the
   early scenes of the Orestes; one of the most beautiful exhibitions of the domestic affections which even the dramas of Euripides can furnish. To the English reader, it may be
   necessary to say, that the situation at the opening of the drama is that of a brother attended
   only by his sister during the demoniacal possession of a suffering conscience (or, in the
   mythology of the play, haunted by the furies), and in circumstances of immediate danger
   from enemies, and of desertion or cold regard from nominal friends.

relaxation caused by an accidental intermission of that practice; jumped out of bed; plunged my head into a basin of cold water; and with hair thus wetted went to sleep. The next morning, as I need hardly say, I awoke with excruciating rheumatic pains of the head and face, from which I had hardly any respite for about twenty days. On the twenty-first day, I think it was, and on a Sunday, that I went out into the streets; rather to run away, if possible, from my torments, than with any distinct purpose. By accident I met a college acquaintance who recommended opium. Opium! dread agent of unimaginable pleasure and pain! I had heard of it as I had of manna or of Ambrosia,[1] but no further: how unmeaning a sound was it at that time! what solemn chords does it now strike upon my heart! what heart-quaking vibrations of sad and happy remembrances! Reverting for a moment to these, I feel a mystic importance attached to the minutest circumstances connected with the place and the time, and the man (if man he was) that first laid open to me the Paradise of Opium-eaters. It was a Sunday afternoon, wet and cheerless: and a duller spectacle this earth of ours has not to show than a rainy Sunday in London. My road homewards lay through Oxford-street; and near "the *stately* Pantheon,"[2] (as Mr. Wordsworth has obligingly called it) I saw a druggist's shop. The druggist—unconscious minister of celestial pleasures!—as if in sympathy with the rainy Sunday, looked dull and stupid, just as any mortal druggist might be expected to look on a Sunday: and, when I asked for the tincture of opium,[3] he gave it to me as any other man might do: and furthermore, out of my shilling, returned to me what seemed to be real copper halfpence, taken out of a real wooden drawer. Nevertheless, in spite of such indications of humanity, he has ever since existed in my mind as the beatific vision of an immortal druggist, sent down to earth on a special mission to myself. And it confirms me in this way considering him, that, when I next came up to London, I sought him near the stately Pantheon, and found him not: and thus to me, who knew not his name (if indeed he had one) he seemed rather to have vanished from Oxford-street than to have removed in any bodily fashion. The reader may choose to think of him as, possibly, no more

---

[1] Manna, or "miraculous food," which God gave to the Israelites starving in the wilderness of Sin after their exodus from Egypt (see Exodus 16:1–16); Ambrosia was the food of the Greek gods.

[2] Wordsworth, "The Power of Music" (3); "A large building (now no longer in existence) in Oxford Street, London, with a dome likened to that of the Pantheon in Rome, and used in the late 18th and early 19th centuries for public entertainments such as balls, masquerades, and plays" (*OED*).

[3] Laudanum, or opium mixed with alcohol.

than a sublunary druggist: it may be so: but my faith is better: I believe him to have evanesced,* or evaporated. So unwillingly would I connect any mortal remembrances with that hour, and place, and creature, that first brought me acquainted with the celestial drug.

Arrived at my lodgings, it may be supposed that I lost not a moment in taking the quantity prescribed. I was necessarily ignorant of the whole art and mystery of opium-taking: and, what I took, I took under every disadvantage. But I took it:—and in an hour, oh! Heavens! what a revulsion! what an upheaving, from its lowest depths, of the inner spirit! what an apocalypse of the world within me! That my pains had vanished, was now a trifle in my eyes:—this negative effect was swallowed up in the immensity of those positive effects which had opened before me—in the abyss of divine enjoyment thus suddenly revealed. Here was a panacea—a ψαρμαχον νήπενθες[1] for all human woes: here was the secret of happiness, about which philosophers had disputed for so many ages, at once discovered: happiness might now be bought for a penny, and carried in the waistcoat pocket: portable ecstacies might be had corked up in a pint bottle: and peace of mind could be sent down in gallons by the mail coach. But, if I talk in this way, the reader will think I am laughing: and I can assure him, that nobody will laugh long who deals much with opium: its pleasures even are of a grave and solemn complexion; and in his happiest state, the opium-eater cannot present himself in the character of *l'Allegro*: even then, he speaks and thinks as becomes *Il Penseroso*.[2] Nevertheless, I have a very reprehensible way of jesting at

---

* *Evanesced*:—this way of going off the stage of life appears to have been well known in the 17th century, but at that time to have been considered a peculiar privilege of blood-royal, and by no means to be allowed to druggists. For about the year 1686, a poet of rather ominous name (and who, by the bye, did ample justice to his name), viz. Mr. *Flat-man*, in speaking of the death of Charles II. expresses his surprise that any prince should commit so absurd an act as dying; because, says he,

    Kings should disdain to die, and only *disappear*.

They should *abscond*, that is, into the other world. [Thomas Flatman (1637–88) writes, in "On the much Lamented Death of Our Late Sovereign Lord King Charles II": "Princes ... should be free / From Death's Unbounded Tyranny, / And when their Godlike Race is run, / And nothing glorious left undone, / Never submit to Fate, but only Disappear" (21–25).]

[1] From Homer's *Odyssey*; Helen gives Telemachus and his men, who have visited Sparta on their journey to find Telemachus's father, Odysseus, a drug to ease their grief: "Into the wine of which they were drinking she cast a medicine of heartsease, free of gall, to make one forget all sorrows, and whoever had drunk it down ... for the day that he drank it would have no tear roll down his face" (4.220–23).

[2] Milton's poems "The Happy Man" (*l'Allegro*) and "The Pensive Man" (*Il Penseroso*).

times in the midst of my own misery: and, unless when I am checked by some more powerful feelings, I am afraid that I shall be guilty of this indecent practice even in these annals of suffering or enjoyment. The reader must allow a little to my infirm nature in this respect; and with a few indulgences of that sort, I shall endeavour to be as grave, if not drowsy, as fits a theme like opium, so anti-mercurial as it really is, and so drowsy as it is falsely reputed.

And, first, one word with respect to its bodily effects: for upon all that has been hitherto written on the subject of opium, whether by travellers in Turkey (who may plead their privilege of lying as an old immemorial right), or by professors of medicine, writing *ex cathedra*,[1]—I have but one emphatic criticism to pronounce—Lies! lies! lies! I remember once, in passing a book-stall, to have caught these words from a page from some satiric author:—"By this time I became convinced that the London newspapers spoke truth at least twice a week, viz. on Tuesday and Saturday, and might safely be depended upon for —— the list of bank-rupts."[2] In like manner, I do by no means deny that some truths have been delivered to the world in regard to opium: thus it has been repeat-edly affirmed by the learned, that opium is a dusky brown in colour; and this, take notice, I grant: secondly, that it is rather dear; which also I grant: for in my time, East-India opium has been three guineas a pound, and Turkey eight: and, thirdly, that if you eat a good deal of it, most probably you must —— do what is particularly disagreeable to any man of regu-lar habits, viz. die.* These weighty propositions are, all and singular, true:

---

* Of this, however, the learned appear latterly to have doubted: for in a pirated edition of Buchan's *Domestic Medicine*, which I once saw in the hands of a farmer's wife who was study-ing it for the benefit of her health, the Doctor was made to say—"Be particularly careful never to take above five-and-twenty *ounces* of laudanum at once:" the true reading being probably five and twenty *drops*, which are held equal to one grain of crude opium.[William Buchan (1729–1805) was the author of *Domestic Medicine; or the Family Physician* (orig. published 1769), a book of medical advice for the lay public which remained popular throughout the nineteenth century. In a later edition, subtitled *A Treatise on the Prevention and Cure of Diseases by Regime and Simple Medicines. With an Appendix, containing a Dispensatory for the Use of Private Practitioners* (Glasgow: S. and A. Gardner, D. Shaw, and J. Struthers, 1806), Buchan writes in the Appendix, under "Tincture of Opium, or Liquid Laudanum": "Take of crude opium, two ounces; spiritous aromatic water, and mountain wine, of each ten ounces. Dissolve the opium, sliced, in the wine, with a gentle heat, frequently stirring it; afterward add the spirit, and strain off the tincture. As twenty-five drops of this tincture contain about a grain of opium, the common dose may be from twenty to thirty drops" (605).]

---

[1] "'From the chair,' i.e., in the manner of one speaking from the seat of office or professo-rial chair, with authority" (*OED*).

[2] Source unknown.

I cannot gainsay them: and truth ever was, and will be, commendable. But in these three theorems, I believe we have exhausted the stock of knowledge as yet accumulated by man on the subject of opium. And therefore, worthy doctors, as there seems to be room for further discoveries, stand aside, and allow me to come forward and lecture on this matter.

First, then, it is not so much affirmed as taken for granted, by all who ever mention opium, formally or incidentally, that it does, or can, produce intoxication. Now, reader, assure yourself, *meo periculo*,[1] that no quantity of opium ever did, or could intoxicate. As to the tincture of opium (commonly called laudanum) *that* might certainly intoxicate if a man could bear to take enough of it; but why? because it contains so much proof spirit, and not because it contains so much opium. But crude opium, I affirm peremptorily, is incapable of producing any state of body at all resembling that which is produced by alcohol. And not in *degree* only incapable, but even in *kind*: it is not in the quantity of its effects merely, but in the quality, that it differs altogether. The pleasure given by wine is always mounting, and tending to a crisis, after which it declines: that from opium, when once generated, is stationary for eight or ten hours: the first, to borrow a technical distinction from medicine, is a case of acute—the second, of chronic pleasure: the one is a flame, the other a steady and equable glow. But the main distinction lies in this, that whereas wine disorders the mental faculties, opium, on the contrary (if taken in a proper manner), introduces amongst them the most exquisite order, legislation, and harmony. Wine robs a man of his self-possession: opium greatly invigorates it. Wine unsettles and clouds the judgment, and gives a preternatural brightness, and a vivid exaltation to the contempts and the admirations, the loves and the hatreds, of the drinker: opium, on the contrary, communicates serenity and equipoise to all the faculties, active or passive: and with respect to the temper and moral feelings in general, it gives simply that sort of vital warmth which is approved by the judgment, and which would probably always accompany a bodily constitution of primeval or antediluvian health. Thus, for instance, opium, like wine, gives an expansion to the heart and the benevolent affections: but then, with this remarkable difference, that in the sudden development of kind-heartedness which accompanies inebriation, there is always more or less of a maudlin character, which exposes it to the contempt of the bystander. Men shake hands, swear eternal friendship, and shed tears—no mortal knows why: and the sensual creature is clearly uppermost. But the expan-

---

[1] "At my own risk."

sion of the benigner feelings, incident to opium, is no febrile access, but a healthy restoration to that state which the mind would naturally recover upon the removal of any deep-seated irritation of pain that had disturbed and quarrelled with the impulses of a heart originally just and good. True it is, that even wine, up to a certain point, and with certain men, rather tends to exalt and to steady the intellect: I myself, who have never been a great wine-drinker, used to find that half a dozen glasses of wine advantageously affected the faculties—brightened and intensified the consciousness—and gave to the mind a feeling of being "ponderibus liberata suis:"[1] and certainly it is most absurdly said, in popular language, of any man, that he is *disguised* in liquor: for, on the contrary, most men are disguised by sobriety; and it is when they are drinking (as some old gentleman says in Athenaeus),[2] that men ἑαυτοὺς ἐμφανίζουσιν οἵτινες εἰσίν—display themselves in their true complexion of character; which surely is not disguising themselves. But still, wine constantly leads a man to the brink of absurdity and extravagance; and, beyond a certain point, it is sure to volatilize and to disperse the intellectual energies: whereas opium always seems to compose what had been agitated, and to concentrate what had been distracted. In short, to sum up all in one word, a man who is inebriated, or tending to inebriation, is, and feels that he is, in a condition which calls up into supremacy the merely human, too often the brutal, part of his nature: but the opium-eater (I speak of him who is not suffering from any disease, or other remote effects of opium) feels that the diviner part of his nature is paramount; that is, the moral affections are in a state of cloudless serenity; and over all is the great light of the majestic intellect.

This is the doctrine of the true church on the subject of opium: of which church I acknowledge myself to be the only member—the alpha and the omega: but then it is to be recollected, that I speak from the ground of a large and profound personal experience: whereas most of the unscientific★ authors who have at all treated of opium, and even of

---

★ Amongst the great herd of travellers, &c. who show sufficiently by their stupidity that they never held any intercourse with opium, I must caution my reader specially against the brilliant author of "*Anastasius.*" This gentleman, whose wit would lead one to presume him an opium-eater, has made it impossible to consider him in that character from the grievous misrepresentation which he gives of its effects, at p. 215–17, of vol. 1.—Upon consideration, it must appear such to the author himself: for, waiving the errors I have insisted on in the text, which (and others) are adopted in the fullest manner, he will himself admit, that an old gentleman "with a snow-white beard," who

---

[1]   "Poised by its own balance," Ovid, *Metamorphoses* (1.13).
[2]   Author of *The Deipnosophists*, or "Masters of the Art of Dining" (c. 200 CE).

those who have written expressly on the materia medica,[1] make it evident, from the horror they express of it, that their experimental knowledge of its action is none at all. I will, however, candidly acknowledge that I have met with one person who bore evidence to its intoxicating power, such as staggered my own incredulity: for he was a surgeon,[2] and had himself taken opium largely. I happened to say to him, that his enemies (as I had heard) charged him with talking nonsense on politics, and that his friends apologized for him, by suggesting that he was constantly in a state of intoxication from opium. Now the accusation, said I, is not *primâ facie*,[3] and of necessity, an absurd one: but the defence *is*. To my surprise, however, he insisted that both his enemies and his friends were in the right: "I will maintain," said he, "that I *do* talk nonsense; and secondly, I will maintain that I do not talk nonsense upon principle, or with any view to profit, but solely and simply, said he, solely and simply,—solely and simply (repeating it three times over), because I am drunk with opium; and *that* daily." I replied that, as to the allegation of his enemies, as it seemed to be established

---

eats "ample doses of opium," and is yet able to deliver what is meant and received as very weighty counsel on the bad effects of that practice, is but an indifferent evidence that opium either kills people prematurely, or sends them into a madhouse. But, for my part, I see into this old gentleman and his motives: the fact is, he was enamoured of "the little golden receptacle of the pernicious drug" which Anastasius carried about him; and no way of obtaining it so safe and so feasible occurred, as that of frightening its owner out of his wits (which, by the bye, are none of the strongest). This commentary throws a new light upon the case, and greatly improves it as a story: for the old gentleman's speech, considered as a lecture on pharmacy, is highly absurd: but, considered as a hoax on Anastasius, it reads excellently. [*Anastasius, or, Memoirs of a Greek, written at the close of the eighteenth century* (1819) was a novel by Thomas Hope (1770?–1831).]

[1]   Literally, "medical material" (Latin); medical science that deals with the sources, properties, and uses of drugs.

[2]   Probably John Abernethy (1764–1831), St. Bartholomew's Hospital, London. In the 1856 *Confessions*, De Quincey expands by saying:"[H]e was a surgeon, and had himself taken opium largely for a most miserable affection (past all hope of cure), seated in one particular organ. This affection was a subtle inflammation, not acute, but chronic; and with this he fought for more (I believe) than twenty years; fought victoriously, if victory it were, to make life supportable for himself, and during all that time to maintain in respectability a wife and a family of children altogether dependent on him." In a note to this passage, he continues: "This surgeon it was who first made me aware of the dangerous variability in opium as to strength under the shifting proportions of its combination with alien impurities. Naturally, as a man professionally alive to the danger of creating any artificial need of opium beyond what the anguish of his malady at any rate demanded, trembling every hour on behalf of his poor children, lest, by any indiscretion of his own, he should precipitate the crisis of his disorder, he saw the necessity of reducing the daily dose to a *minimum*" (*Works* 2:221).

[3]   "At first sight."

upon such respectable testimony, seeing that the three parties concerned all agreed in it, it did not become me to question it; but the defence set up I must demure to. He proceeded to discuss the matter, and to lay down his reasons: but it seemed to me so impolite to pursue an argument which must have presumed a man mistaken in a point belonging to his own profession, that I did not press him even when his course of argument seemed open to objection: not to mention that a man who talks nonsense, even though "with no view to profit," is not altogether the most agreeable partner in a dispute, whether as opponent or respondent. I confess, however, that the authority of a surgeon, and one who was reputed a good one, may seem a weighty one to my prejudice: but still I must plead my experience, which was greater than his greatest by 7000 drops a day; and, though it was not possible to suppose a medical man unacquainted with the characteristic symptoms of vinous intoxication, it yet struck me that he might proceed on a logical error of using the word intoxication with too great latitude, and extending it generically to all modes of nervous excitement, instead of restricting it as the expression for a specific sort of excitement, connected with certain diagnostics. Some people have maintained, in my hearing, that they had been drunk upon green tea: and a medical student in London, for whose knowledge in his profession I have reason to feel great respect, assured me, the other day, that a patient, in recovering from an illness, had got drunk on a beef-steak.

Having dwelt so much on this first and leading error, in respect to opium, I shall notice very briefly a second and a third; which are, that the elevation of spirits produced by opium is necessarily followed by a proportionate depression, and that the natural and even immediate consequence of opium is torpor and stagnation, animal and mental. The first of these errors I shall content myself with simply denying; assuring my reader, that for ten years, during which I took opium at intervals, the day succeeding to that on which I allowed myself this luxury was always a day of unusually good spirits.

With respect to the torpor supposed to follow, or rather (if we were to credit the numerous pictures of Turkish opium-eaters) to accompany the practice of opium-eating, I deny that also. Certainly, opium is classed under the head of narcotics; and some such effect it may produce in the end: but the primary effects of opium are always, and in the highest degree, to excite and stimulate the system: this first stage of its action always lasted with me, during my noviciate, for upwards of eight hours; so that it must be the fault of the opium-eater himself if he does not so time his exhibition of the dose (to speak medically) as that the whole weight of its narcotic influence may descend upon his sleep. Turkish opium-eaters, it seems, are absurd enough to sit, like so many equestrian statues, on logs of wood as stupid as themselves. But that the reader may judge of the degree in which opium is likely to stupify the faculties of an Englishman, I shall (by way of treating the question illustratively, rather than argumentatively) describe the way in which I myself often passed an opium evening in London, during the period between 1804–1812. It will be seen, that at least opium did not move me to seek solitude, and much less to seek inactivity, or the torpid state of self-involution ascribed to the Turks. I give this account at the risk of being pronounced a crazy enthusiast or visionary: but I regard *that* little: I must desire my reader to bear in mind, that I was a hard student, and at severe studies for all the rest of my time: and certainly I had a right occasionally to relaxations as well as other people: these, however, I allowed myself but seldom.

The late Duke of ———[1] used to say, "Next Friday, by the blessing of Heaven, I purpose to be drunk:" and in like manner I used to fix before-hand how often, within a given time, and when, I would commit a debauch of opium. This was seldom more than once in three weeks: for at that time I could not have ventured to call every day (as I did afterwards) for "*a glass of laudanum negus,*[2] *warm, and without sugar.*" No: as I have said, I seldom drank laudanum, at that time, more than once in three weeks: this was usually on a Tuesday or a Saturday night; my reason for which was this. In those days Grassini[3] sang at the Opera: and her voice was delightful to me beyond all that I had ever heard. I know not what may be the state of the Opera-house now, having never been within its walls for seven or eight years, but at that time it was by much the most pleasant place of public resort in London for passing an evening. Five shillings admitted one to the gallery, which was subject to far less annoyance than the pit of the theatres: the orchestra was distinguished by its sweet and melodious grandeur from all English orchestras, the composition of which, I confess, is not acceptable to my ear, from the predominance of the clangorous instruments, and the absolute tyranny of the violin. The choruses were divine to hear: and when Grassini appeared in some interlude, as she

---

[1]   Charles Howard, 11th Duke of Norfolk (1746–1815).

[2]   De Quincey's variation of negus, or wine and hot water with lemon juice, sugar, and other spices.

[3]   Josephina Grassini (1773–1850), Italian contralto, noted for her singing, acting, and beauty; sang in London 1804–06 and again in 1814; alleged to be the mistress of Wellington and Napoleon, for whom she was court singer.

often did, and poured forth her passionate soul as Andromache, at the tomb of Hector, &c. I question whether any Turk, of all that ever entered the Paradise of opium-eaters, can have had half the pleasure I had. But, indeed, I honour the Barbarians too much by supposing them capable of any pleasures approaching to the intellectual ones of an Englishman. For music is an intellectual or a sensual pleasure, according to the temperament of him who hears it. And, by the bye, with the exception of the fine extravaganza on that subject in Twelfth Night,[1] I do not recollect more than one thing said adequately on the subject of music in all literature: it is a passage in the *Religio Medici*★ of Sir T. Brown;[2] and, though chiefly remarkable for its sublimity, has also a philosophic value, inasmuch as it points to the true theory of musical effects. The mistake of most people is to suppose that it is by the ear they communicate with music, and, therefore, that they are purely passive to its effects. But this is not so: it is by the re-action of the mind upon the notices of the ear, (the *matter* coming by the senses, the *form* from the mind) that the pleasure is constructed: and therefore it is that people of equally good ear differ so much in this point from one another. Now opium, by greatly increasing the activity of the mind generally, increases, of necessity, that particular mode of its activity by which we are able to construct out of the raw material of organic sound an elaborate intellectual pleasure. But, says a friend, a succession of musical sounds is to me like a collection of Arabic characters: I can attach no ideas to them. Ideas! my good sir? there is no occasion for them: all that class of ideas, which can be available in such a case, has a language of representative feelings. But this is a subject foreign to my present purposes: it is sufficient to say, that a chorus, &c. of elaborate harmony, displayed before me, as in a piece of arras work, the whole of my past life—not, as if recalled by an act of memory, but as if present and incarnated in the music: no

---

★ I have not the book at this moment to consult: but I think the passage begins—"And even that tavern music, which makes one man merry, another mad, in me strikes a deep fit of devotion," &c.

---

[1] Shakespeare, *Twelfth Night*: "If music be the food of love, play on, / Give me excess of it, that, surfeiting, / The appetite may sicken, and so die" (1.1.1–3).

[2] Sir Thomas Browne (1605–82), *Religio Medici* (1643): "Whatsoever is harmonically composed delights in harmony ... for even that vulgar and tavern-musick which makes one man merry, another mad, strikes in me a deep fit of devotion, and a profound contemplation of the first composer. There is something in it of divinity more than the ear discovers: it is an hieroglyphical and shadowed lesson of the whole world, and creatures of God,—such a melody to the ear, as the whole world, well understood, would afford the understanding. In brief, it is a sensible fit of that harmony which intellectually sounds in the ears of God" (Part 2, Section 9).

longer painful to dwell upon: but the detail of its incidents removed, or blended in some hazy abstraction; and its passions exalted, spiritualized, and sublimed. All this was to be had for five shillings. And over and above the music of the stage and the orchestra, I had all around me, in the intervals of the performance, the music of the Italian language talked by Italian women: for the gallery was usually crowded with Italians: and I listened with a pleasure such as that with which Weld[1] the traveler lay and listened, in Canada, to the sweet laughter of Indian women; for the less you understand of a language, the more sensible you are to the melody or harshness of its sounds: for such a purpose, therefore, it was an advantage to me that I was a poor Italian scholar, reading it but little, and not speaking it at all, nor understanding a tenth part of what I heard spoken.

These were my Opera pleasures: but another pleasure I had which, as it could be had only on a Saturday night, occasionally struggled with my love of the Opera; for, at that time, Tuesday and Saturday were the regular Opera nights. On this subject I am afraid I shall be rather obscure, but, I can assure the reader, not at all more so than Marinus in his life of Proclus,[2] or many other biographers and auto-biographers of fair reputation. This pleasure, I have said, was to be had only on a Saturday night. What then was Saturday night to me more than any other night? I had no labours that I rested from; no wages to receive: what needed I to care for Saturday night, more than as it was a summons to hear Grassini? True, most logical reader: what you say is unanswerable. And yet so it was and is, that, whereas different men throw their feelings into different channels, and most are apt to show their interest in the concerns of the poor, chiefly by sympathy, expressed in some shape or other, with their distresses and sorrows, I, at that time, was disposed to express my interest by sympathising with their pleasures. The pains of poverty I had lately seen too much of; more than I wished to remember: but the pleasures of the poor, their consolations of spirit, and their reposes from bodily toil, can never become oppressive to contemplate. Now Saturday night is the season for the chief, regular, and periodic return of rest to the poor: in this point the most hostile sects unite, and acknowledge a common link of brother-

---

[1] Isaac Weld Jr. (1774–1856), *Travels Through the States of North America, and the Provinces of Upper and Lower Canada, During the Years 1795, 1796, and 1797* (1799): "[Native American women] speak with the utmost ease, and the language, as pronounced by them, appears as soft as the Italian. They have ... the most delicate harmonious voices I ever heard ... I have oftentimes sat amongst a group of them for an hour or two together, merely for the pleasure of listening to their conversation, on account of its wonderful softness and delicacy" (411–12).

[2] Marinus, disciple of Proclus (412–85 CE), Neoplatonist philosopher.

hood: almost all Christendom rests from its labours. It is a rest introductory to another rest: and divided by a whole day and two nights from the renewal of toil. On this account I feel always, on a Saturday night, as though I also were released from some yoke of labour, had some wages to receive, and some luxury of repose to enjoy. For the sake, therefore, of witnessing, upon as large a scale as possible, a spectacle with which my sympathy was so entire, I used often, on Saturday nights, after I had taken opium, to wander forth, without much regarding the direction or the distance, to all the markets, and other parts of London, to which the poor resort on a Saturday night, for laying out their wages. Many a family party, consisting of a man, his wife, and sometimes one or two of his children, have I listened to, as they stood consulting on their ways and means, or the strength of their exchequer, or the price of household articles. Gradually I became familiar with their wishes, their difficulties, and their opinions. Sometimes there might be heard murmurs of discontent: but far oftener expressions on the countenance, or uttered in words, of patience, hope, or tranquillity. And taken generally, I must say, that, in this point at least, the poor are far more philosophic than the rich—that they show a more ready and cheerful submission to what they consider as irremediable evils, or irreparable losses. Whenever I saw occasion, or could do it without appearing to be intrusive, I joined their parties; and gave my opinion upon the matter in discussion, which, if not always judicious, was always received indulgently. If wages were a little higher, or expected to be so, or the quartern loaf a little lower, or it was reported that onions and butter were expected to fall, I was glad: yet, if the contrary were true, I drew from opium some means of consoling myself. For opium (like the bee, that extracts its materials indiscriminately from roses and from the soot of chimneys) can overrule all feelings into a compliance with the master key. Some of these rambles led me to great distances: for an opium-eater is too happy to observe the motion of time. And sometimes in my attempts to steer homewards, upon nautical principles, by fixing my eye in the pole-star, and seeking ambitiously for a north-west passage, instead of circumnavigating all the capes and headlands I had doubled in my outward voyage, I came suddenly upon such knotty problems of alleys, such enigmatical entries, and such sphynx's riddles of streets without thoroughfares, as must, I conceive, baffle the audacity of porters, and confound the intellects of hackney-coachmen. I could almost have believed, at times, that I must be the first discoverer of some of these *terrae incognitae*,[1]

---

[1]   "Unknown territories."

and doubted, whether they had yet been laid down in the modern charts of London. For all this, however, I paid a heavy price in distant years, when the human face tyrannized over my dreams, and the perplexities of my steps in London came back and haunted my sleep, with the feeling of perplexities moral or intellectual, that brought confusion to the reason, or anguish and remorse to the conscience.

Thus I have shown that opium does not, of necessity, produce inactivity or torpor; but that, on the contrary, it often led me into markets and theatres. Yet, in candour, I will admit that markets and theatres are not the appropriate haunts of the opium-eater, when in the divinest state incident to his enjoyment. In that state, crowds become an oppression to him; music even, too sensual and gross. He naturally seeks solitude and silence, as indispensable conditions of those trances, or profoundest reveries, which are the crown and consummation of what opium can do for human nature. I, whose disease it was to mediate too much, and to observe too little, and who, upon my first entrance at college, was nearly falling into a deep melancholy, from brooding too much on the sufferings which I had witnessed in London, was sufficiently aware of the tendencies of my own thoughts to do all I could to counteract them.— I was, indeed, like a person who, according to the old legend, had entered the cave of Trophonius:[1] and the remedies I sought were to force myself into society, and to keep my understanding in continual activity upon matters of science. But for these remedies, I should certainly have become hypochondriacally melancholy. In after years, however, when my cheerfulness was more fully re-established, I yielded to my natural inclination for a solitary life. And, at that time, I often fell into these reveries upon taking opium; and more than once it has happened to me, on a summer-night, when I have been at an open window, in a room from which I could overlook the sea at a mile below me, and could command a view of the great town of L——,[2] at about the same distance, that I have sate, from sun-set to sun-rise, motionless, and without wishing to move.

I shall be charged with mysticism, Behmenism, quietism,[3] &c. but *that* shall not alarm me. Sir H. Vane,[4] the younger, was one of our wisest men: and let my readers see if he, in his philosophical works, be half as

[1] Site of oracle at Lebadea in Boeotia where, according to legend, the Greek architect Trophonius, builder of the temple of Apollo at Delphi, was swallowed up by the earth.

[2] Liverpool.

[3] Behmenism: following the thought of Jakob Boehme (1575–1624), German mystic; quietism: passive contemplation of the mystical.

[4] Sir Henry Vale (1613–62), Puritan and Parliamentarian during the English Civil War, wrote mystical works influenced by Boehme.

unmystical as I am.—I say, then, that it has often struck me that the scene itself was somewhat typical of what took place in such a reverie. The town of L—— represented the earth, with its sorrows and its graves left behind, yet not out of sight, nor wholly forgotten. The ocean, in everlasting but gentle agitation, and brooded over by a dove-like calm, might not unfitly typify the mind and the mood which then swayed it. For it seemed to me as if then first I stood at a distance, and aloof from the uproar of life; as if the tumult, the fever, and the strife, were suspended; a respite granted from the secret burthens of the heart; a sabbath of repose; a resting from human labours. Here were the hopes which blossom in the paths of life, reconciled with the peace which is in the grave; motions of the intellect as unwearied as the heavens, yet for all anxieties a halcyon calm: a tranquillity that seemed no product of inertia, but as if resulting from mighty and equal antagonisms; infinite activities, infinite repose.

Oh! just, subtle, and mighty opium![1] that to the hearts of poor and rich alike, for the wounds that will never heal, and for "the pangs that tempt the spirit to rebel,"[2] bringest an assuaging balm; eloquent opium! that with thy potent rhetoric stealest away the purposes of wrath; and to the guilty man, for one night givest back the hopes of his youth, and hands washed pure from blood; and to the proud man, a brief oblivion for

Wrongs unredress'd, and insults unavenged;[3]

that summonest to the chancery of dreams, for the triumphs of suffering innocence, false witnesses; and confoundest perjury; and dost reverse the sentences of unrighteous judges:—thou buildest upon the bosom of darkness, out of the fantastic imagery of the brain, cities and temples, beyond the art of Phidias and Praxiteles[4]—beyond the splendour of Babylon and Hekatómpylos:[5] and "from the anarchy of dreaming sleep,"[6] callest into sunny light the faces of long-buried beauties, and

---

[1] Paraphrase of apostrophe on the last page of *History of the World* (1614) by Sir Walter Ralegh (c. 1554–1618): "O eloquent, just and mightie Death!."

[2] Wordsworth, Dedication to "The White Doe of Rylstone" (36).

[3] Wordsworth, *The Excursion* (3.374).

[4] Classical Greek sculptors: Phidias (c. 490–430 BCE), purported to have designed the Parthenon frieze; Praxiteles (370–330 BCE); that is, beyond the architectural ideal of beauty and form.

[5] Babylon, famous for its Hanging Gardens, one of the seven Ancient Wonders of the World; Hekatómpylos ("hundred-gated"), ancient Egyptian city of Thebes, as opposed to the Greek Thebes, city of seven gates.

[6] Wordsworth, *The Excursion* (4.87).

the blessed household countenances, cleansed from the "dishonours of the grave."[1] Thou only givest these gifts to man; and thou hast the keys of Paradise, oh, just, subtle, and mighty opium!

INTRODUCTION TO THE PAINS OF OPIUM

Courteous, and, I hope, indulgent reader (for all *my* readers must be indulgent ones, or else, I fear, I shall shock them too much to count on their courtesy), having accompanied me thus far, now let me request you to move onwards, for about eight years; that is to say, from 1804 (when I have said that my acquaintance with opium first began) to 1812. The years of academic life are now over and gone—almost forgotten:—the student's cap no longer presses my temples; if my cap exist at all, it presses those of some youthful scholar, I trust, as happy as myself, and as passionate a lover of knowledge. My gown is, by this time, I dare to say, in the same condition with many thousands of excellent books in the Bodleian,[2] viz. diligently perused by certain studious moths and worms: or departed, however (which is all that I know of its fate), to that great reservoir of *somewhere*, to which all the tea-cups, tea-caddies, tea-pots, tea-kettles, &c. have departed (not to speak of still frailer vessels, such as glasses, decanters, bed-makers, &c.) which occasional resemblances in the present generation of tea-cups, &c. remind me of having once possessed, but of whose departure and final fate I, in common with most gownsmen of either university, could give, I suspect, but an obscure and conjectural history. The persecutions of the chapel-bell, sounding its unwelcome summons to six o'clock matins, interrupts my slumbers no longer: the porter who rang it, upon whose beautiful nose (bronze, inlaid with copper) I wrote, in retaliation, so many Greek epigrams, whilst I was dressing, is dead, and has ceased to disturb any body: and I, and many others, who suffered much from his tintinnabulous[3] propensities, have now agreed to overlook his errors, and have forgiven him. Even with the bell I am now in charity: it rings, I suppose, as formerly, thrice a-day: and cruelly annoys, I doubt not, many worthy gentlemen, and disturbs their peace of mind: but as to me, in this year 1812, I regard its treacherous voice no longer (treacherous, I call it, for, by some refinement of malice, it spoke in as

---

[1]   Thomas Aird, *A Summer Day*: "Noon"; Thomas Flatman, "On the Death of the Truly Valiant George Duke of Buckingham"; and I Corinthians 15:43 are possible sources (*Works* 2:335).

[2]   Library of the University of Oxford.

[3]   "Characterized by or pertaining to bell-ringing" (*OED*).

sweet and silvery tones as if it had been inviting one to a party): its tones have no longer, indeed, power to reach me, let the wind sit as favourable as the malice of the bell itself could wish: for I am 250 miles away from it, and buried in the depth of mountains. And what am I doing amongst the mountains? Taking opium. Yes, but what else? Why, reader, in 1812, the year we are now arrived at, as well as for some years previous, I have been chiefly studying German metaphysics, in the writings of Kant, Fichte, Schelling, &c.[1] And how, and in what manner, do I live? in short, what class or description of men do I belong to? I am at this period, viz. in 1812, living in a cottage; and with a single female servant (honi soit qui mal y pense),[2] who, amongst my neighbours, passes by the name of my "house-keeper." And, as a scholar and a man of learned education, and in that sense a gentleman, I may presume to class myself as an unworthy member of that indefinite body called *gentlemen*. Partly on the ground I have assigned, perhaps; partly because, from my having no visible calling or business, it is rightly judged that I must be living on my private fortune; I am so classed by my neighbours: and, by the courtesy of modern England, I am usually addressed on letters, &c. *esquire*, though having, I fear, in the rigorous construction of heralds, but slender pretensions to that distinguished honour: yes, in popular estimation, I am X.Y.Z.,[3] esquire, but not Justice of the Peace, nor Custos Rotulorum.[4] Am I married? Not yet. And I still take opium? On Saturday nights. And, perhaps, have taken it unblushingly ever since "the rainy Sunday," and "the stately Pantheon," and "the beatific druggist" of 1804?—Even so. And how do I find my health after all this opium-eating? in short, how do I do? Why, pretty well, I thank you, reader: in the phrase of ladies in the straw,[5] "as well as can be expected." In fact, if I dared to say the real and simple truth, though, to satisfy the theories of medical men, I *ought* to be ill, I never was better in my life than in the spring of 1812; and I hope sincerely, that the quantity of claret, port, or "particular Madeira," which, in all probability, you, good reader, have taken, and design to take, for every term of eight years, during your natural life, may as little

---

[1]   Immanuel Kant (1724–1804), Professor of Logic and Metaphysics at Königsberg, Germany, philosopher of the Critical Philosophy; Johann Gottlieb Fichte (1762–1814) and Wilhelm Joseph von Schelling (1775–1854), followers of Kant and developers of German idealism, specifically of transcendental philosophy.

[2]   "Shame on him who thinks evil"; motto of the Order of the Garter.

[3]   De Quincey's pseudonym when writing for *London Magazine*.

[4]   "Keeper of the Rolls," the literal name of the chief Justice of the Peace in the country who kept the rolls or record of the Court of Quarter Sessions.

[5]   Women in childbirth.

disorder your health as mine was disordered by the opium I had taken for the eight years, between 1804 and 1812. Hence you may see again the danger of taking any medical advice from *Anastasius*; in divinity, for aught I know, or law, he may be a safe counselor; but not in medicine. No: it is far better to consult Dr. Buchan; as I did: for I never forgot that worthy man's excellent suggestion: and I was "particularly careful not to take above five-and-twenty ounces of laudanum." To this moderation and temperate use of the article, I may ascribe it, I suppose, that as yet, at least, (*i.e.* in 1812,) I am ignorant and unsuspicious of the avenging terrors which opium has in store for those who abuse its lenity. At the same time, it must not be forgotten, that hitherto I have been only a dilettante eater of opium: eight years' practice even, with the single precaution of allowing sufficient intervals between every indulgence, has not been sufficient to make opium necessary to me as an article of daily diet. But now comes a different era. Move on, if you please, reader, to 1813. In the summer of the year we have just quitted, I had suffered much in bodily health from distress of mind connected with a very melancholy event.[1] This event, being no ways related to the subject now before me, further than through the bodily illness which it produced, I need not more particularly notice. Whether this illness of 1812 had any share in that of 1813, I know not: but so it was, that in the latter year, I was attacked by a most appalling irritation of the stomach, in all respects the same as that which had caused me so much suffering in youth, and accompanied by a revival of all the old dreams. This is the point of my narrative on which, as respects my own self-justification, the whole of what follows may be said to hinge. And here I find myself in a perplexing dilemma:—Either, on the one hand, I must exhaust the reader's patience, by such a detail of my malady, and of my struggles with it, as might suffice to establish the fact of my inability to wrestle any longer with irritation and constant suffering: or, on the other hand, by passing lightly over this critical part of my story, I must forego the benefit of a stronger impression left on the mind of the reader, and must lay myself open to the misconstruction of having slipped by the easy and gradual steps of self-indulging persons, from the first to the final stage of opium-eating (a misconstruction to which there will be a lurking predisposition in most readers, from my previous acknowledgements.) This is the dilemma: the first horn of which would be sufficient to toss and gore any column of patient readers, though drawn up

---

[1]   The death of Catherine Wordsworth (1808–12), Wordsworth's youngest daughter, very close to De Quincey.

sixteen deep and constantly relieved by fresh men: consequently *that* is not to be thought of. It remains then, that I *postulate* so much as is necessary for my purpose. And let me take as full credit for what I postulate as if I had demonstrated it, good reader, at the expense of your patience and my own. Be not so ungenerous as to let me suffer in your good opinion through my own forbearance and regard for your comfort. No: believe all that I ask of you, viz. that I could resist no longer, believe it liberally, and as an act of grace: or else in mere prudence: for, if not, then in the next edition of my Opium Confessions revised and enlarged, I will make you believe and tremble: and *à force d'ennuyer,*[1] by mere dint of pandiculation[2] I will terrify all readers of mine from ever again questioning any postulate that I shall think fit to make.

This then, let me repeat, I postulate—that, at the time I began to take opium daily, I could not have done otherwise. Whether, indeed, afterwards I might not have succeeded in breaking off the habit, even when it seemed to me that all efforts would be unavailing, and whether many of the innumerable efforts which I *did* make, might not have been carried much further, and my gradual reconquests of ground lost might not have been followed up much more energetically—these are questions which I must decline. Perhaps I might make out a case of palliation; but, shall I speak ingenuously? I confess it, as a besetting infirmity of mine, that I am too much of an Eudaemonist:[3] I hanker too much after a state of happiness, both for myself and others: I cannot face misery, whether my own or not, with an eye of sufficient firmness: and am little capable of encountering present pain for the sake of any reversionary benefit. On some other matters, I can agree with the gentlemen in the cotton trade★ at Manchester in affecting the Stoic philosophy: but not in this. Here I take the liberty of an Eclectic philosopher, and I look out for some courteous and considerate sect

---

★ A handsome news-room, of which I was very politely made free in passing through Manchester by several gentlemen of that place, is called, I think, *The Porch*: whence I, who am a stranger in Manchester, inferred that the subscribers meant to profess themselves followers of Zeno. But I have been since assured that this is a mistake. [*The Porch*: "The Portico Library, a private subscription library founded in 1806, still exists in Mosley Street, Manchester" (*Works* 2:336); Zeno of Cittium (334–264 BCE): founder of Stoic philosophy, which argues that the will can overcome and control the passions, lectured from the Stoa (porch) in Athens.]

---

[1] "By utter boredom."
[2] "The act of stretching (extending the limbs and neck), as a manifestation of weariness, a sign of disease, etc. In later use also: yawning (*rare*)" (*OED*).
[3] One who believes that happiness is the highest good.

that will condescend more to the infirm condition of an opium-eater; that are "sweet men," as Chaucer says, "to give absolution,"[1] and will show some conscience in the penances they inflict, and the efforts of abstinence they exact, from poor sinners like myself. An inhuman moralist I can no more endure in my nervous state than opium that has not been boiled. At any rate, he, who summons me to send out a large freight of self-denial and mortification upon any cruising voyage of moral improvement, must make it clear to my understanding that the concern is a hopeful one. At my time of life (six and thirty years of age) it cannot be supposed that I have much energy to spare: in fact, I find it all little enough for the intellectual labours I have on my hands: and, therefore, let no man expect to frighten me by a few hard words into embarking any part of it upon desperate adventures of morality.

Whether desperate or not, however, the issue of the struggle in 1813 was what I have mentioned; and from this date, the reader is to consider me as a regular and confirmed opium-eater, of whom to ask whether on any particular day he had or had not taken opium, would be to ask whether his lungs had performed respiration, or the heart fulfilled its functions.—You understand now, reader, what I am: and you are by this time aware, that no old gentleman, "with a snow-white beard," will have any chance of persuading me to surrender "the little golden receptacle of the pernicious drug." No: I give notice to all, whether moralist or surgeons, that, whatever be their pretensions and skill in their respective lines of practice, they must not hope for any countenance from me, if they think to begin by any savage proposition for a Lent or Ramadan[2] of abstinence from opium. This then being all fully understood between us, we shall in future sail before the wind. Now then, reader, from 1813, where all this time we have been sitting down and loitering—rise up, if you please, and walk forward about three years more. Now draw up the curtain, and you shall see me in a new character.

If any man, poor or rich, were to say that he would tell us what had been the happiest day in his life, and the why, and the wherefore, I suppose that we should all cry out—Hear him! Hear him!—As to the happiest *day*, that must be very difficult for any wise man to name: because any event, that could occupy so distinguished a place in a man's retrospect of his life, or be entitled to have shed a special felicity on any one day, ought

---

[1] Paraphrase of Geoffrey Chaucer (c. 1343–1400), General Prologue to *Canterbury Tales* (1387–94), the Friar's Portrait: "Ful swetely herde he confessioun, / And plesaunt was his absolucioun" (221–22).

[2] Christian and Muslim fasting days.

to be of such an enduring character, as that (accidents apart) it should have continued to shed the same felicity, or one not distinguishably less, on many years together. To the happiest *lustrum*,[1] however, or even to the happiest *year*, it may be allowed to any man to point without discountenance from wisdom. This year, in my case, reader, was the one which we have now reached; though it stood, I confess, as a parenthesis between years of a gloomier character. It was a year of brilliant water[2] (to speak after the manner of jewellers), set as it were, and insulated, in the gloom and cloudy melancholy of opium. Strange as it may sound, I had a little before this time descended suddenly, and without any considerable effort, from 320 grains of opium (i.e. eight* thousand drops of laudanum) per day, to forty grains, or one eighth part. Instantaneously, and as if by magic, the cloud of profoundest melancholy which rested upon my brain, like some black vapours that I have seen roll away from the summits of mountains, drew off in one day (νυχθημερον);[3] passed off with its murky banners as simultaneously as a ship that has been stranded, and is floated off by a spring tide—

That moveth altogether, if it move at all.[4]

Now, then, I was again happy: I now took only 1000 drops of laudanum per day: and what was that? A latter spring had come to close up the season of youth: my brain performed its functions as healthily as ever before: I read Kant again; and again I understood him, or fancied that I did. Again my feelings of pleasure expanded themselves to all around me: and if any man from Oxford or Cambridge, or from neither had been announced to me in my unpretending cottage, I should have welcomed him with as sumptuous a reception as so poor a man could

---

* I here reckon twenty-five drops of laudanum as equivalent to one grain of opium, which, I believe, is the common estimate. However, as both may be considered variable quantities (the crude opium varying much in strength, and the tincture still more), I suppose that no infinitesimal accuracy can be had in such a calculation. Tea-spoons vary as much in size as opium in strength. Small ones hold about 100 drops: so that 8000 drops are about eighty times a teaspoonful. The reader sees how much I kept within Dr. Buchan's indulgent allowance.

---

1   Period of five years.
2   Lustre or clarity of a precious gem.
3   Twenty-four hours.
4   Wordsworth, "Resolution and Independence"; the narrator is describing the Leech-Gatherer he has just met: "as I drew near with gentle pace, / Upon the margin of that moorish flood / Motionless as a cloud the old Man stood, / That heareth not the loud winds when they call; / And moveth all together, if it move at all" (73–77).

offer. Whatever else was wanting to a wise man's happiness,—of laudanum I would have given him as much as he wished, and in a golden cup. And, by the way, now that I speak of giving laudanum away, I remember, about this time, a little incident, which I mention, because, trifling as it was, the reader will soon meet it again in my dreams, which it influenced more fearfully than could be imagined. One day a Malay knocked at my door. What business a Malay could have to transact amongst English mountains, I cannot conjecture: but possibly he was on his road to a sea-port about forty miles distant.

The servant who opened the door to him was a young girl born and bred amongst the mountains, who had never seen an Asiatic dress of any sort: his turban, therefore, confounded her not a little: and, as it turned out, that his attainments in English were exactly of the same extent as hers in the Malay, there seemed to be an impassable gulph fixed between all communication of ideas, if either party had happened to possess any. In this dilemma, the girl, recollecting the reputed learning of her master (and, doubtless, giving me credit for a knowledge of all the languages of the earth, besides, perhaps, a few of the lunar ones), came and gave me to understand that there was a sort of demon below, whom she clearly imagined that my art could exorcise from the house. I did not immediately go down: but, when I did, the group which presented itself, arranged as it was by accident, though not very elaborate, took hold of my fancy and my eye in a way that none of the statuesque attitudes exhibited in the ballets at the Opera House, though so ostentatiously complex, had ever done. In a cottage kitchen, but panelled on the wall with dark wood that from age and rubbing resembled oak, and looking more like a rustic hall of entrance than a kitchen, stood the Malay—his turban and loose trowsers of dingy white relieved upon the dark panelling: he had placed himself nearer to the girl than she seemed to relish; though her native spirit of mountain intrepidity contended with the feeling of simple awe which her countenance expressed as she gazed upon the tiger-cat before her. And a more striking picture there could not be imagined, than the beautiful English face of the girl, and its exquisite fairness, together with her erect and independent attitude, contrasted with the sallow and bilious skin of the Malay, enamelled or veneered with mahogany, by marine air, his small, fierce, restless eyes, thin lips, slavish gestures and adorations. Half-hidden by the ferocious looking Malay, was a little child from a neighbouring cottage who had crept in after him, and was now in the act of reverting its head, and gazing upwards at the turban and the fiery eyes beneath it, whilst with one hand he caught at the dress of the young woman for protection. My knowledge of the Oriental tongues is not remarkably extensive, being indeed confined to two words—the Arabic word for barley, and the Turkish for opium (madjoon), which I have learnt from Anastasius. And, as I had neither a Malay dictionary, nor even Adelung's *Mithridates*,[1] which might have helped me to a few words, I addressed him in some lines from the Iliad; considering that, of such languages as I possessed, Greek, in point of longitude, came geographically nearest to an Oriental one. He worshipped me in a most devout manner, and replied in what I suppose was Malay. In this way I saved my reputation with my neighbours: for the Malay had no means of betraying the secret: He lay down upon the floor for about an hour, and then pursued his journey. On his departure, I presented him with a piece of opium. To him, as an Orientalist, I concluded that opium must be familiar: and the expression of his face convinced me that it was. Nevertheless, I was struck with some little consternation when I saw him suddenly raise his hand to his mouth, and (in the school-boy phrase) bolt the whole, divided into three pieces at one mouthful. The quantity was enough to kill three dragoons and their horses: and I felt some alarm for the poor creature: but what could be done? I had given him the opium in compassion for his solitary life, on recollecting that if he had travelled on foot from London, it must be nearly three weeks since he could have exchanged a thought with any human being. I could not think of violating the laws of hospitality, by having him seized and drenched with an emetic, and thus frightening him into a notion that we were going to sacrifice him to some English idol. No: there was clearly no help for it:— he took his leave: and for some days I felt anxious: but as I never heard of any Malay being found dead, I became convinced that he was used★ to opium: and that I must have done him the service I designed, by giving him one night of respite from the pains of wandering.

★ This, however, is not a necessary conclusion: the varieties of effect produced by opium on different constitutions are infinite. A London Magistrate (Harriott's *Struggles through Life*, vol. iii. p. 391, Third Edition), has recorded that, on the first occasion of his trying laudanum for the gout, he took *forty* drops, the next night *sixty*, and on the fifth night *eighty*, without any effect whatever: and this at an advanced age. I have an anecdote from a country surgeon, however, which sinks Mr. Harriott's case into a trifle; and in my projected medical treatise on opium, which I will publish, provided the College of Surgeons will pay me for enlightening their benighted understandings upon this subject, I will relate it: but it is far too good a story to be published gratis.

---

[1] Johann Christoph Adelung (1732–1806), German grammarian and philologist, author of *Mithridate, or the Universal Table of Languages with the Lord's Prayer in 500 Dialects* (1806).

This incident I have digressed to mention, because this Malay (partly from the picturesque exhibition he assisted to frame, partly from the anxiety I connected with his image for some days) fastened afterwards upon my dreams, and brought other Malays with him worse than himself, that ran "a-muck"* at me, and led me into a world of troubles.—But to quit this episode, and to return to my intercalary year[1] of happiness. I have said already, that on a subject so important to us all as happiness, we should listen with pleasure to any man's experience or experiments, even though he were but a plough-boy, who cannot be supposed to have ploughed very deep into such an intractable soil as that of human pains and pleasures, or to have conducted his researches upon any very enlightened principles. But I, who have taken happiness, both in a solid and a liquid shape, both boiled and unboiled, both East India and Turkey—who have conducted my experiments upon this interesting subject with a sort of galvanic battery—and have, for the general benefit of the world, inoculated myself, as it were, with the poison of 8000 drops of laudanum per day (just, for the same reason, as a French surgeon inoculated himself lately with cancer—an English one, twenty years ago, with plague—and a third, I know not of what nation, with hydrophobia),[2]—I (it will be admitted) must surely know what happiness is, if any body does. And, therefore, I will here lay down an analysis of happiness; and as the most interesting mode of communicating it, I will give it, not didactically, but wrapt up and involved in a picture of one evening, as I spent every evening during the intercalary year when laudanum, though taken daily, was to me no more than the elixir of pleasure. This done, I shall quit the subject of happiness altogether, and pass to a very different one—the *pains of opium*.

Let there be a cottage, standing in a valley, 18 miles from any town— no spacious valley, but about two miles long, by three quarters of a mile in average width; the benefit of which provision is, that all the families resident within its circuit will compose, as it were, one larger household personally familiar to your eye, and more or less interesting to your affections. Let the mountains be real mountains, between 3 and 4000 feet high;

---

* See the common accounts in any Eastern traveller or voyager of the frantic excesses committed by Malays who have taken opium, or are reduced to desperation by ill luck at gambling.

---

[1] A day inserted to make a year correspond to the solar year; for De Quincey a pleasurable break or reprieve between two more painful parts.

[2] The 1856 *Confessions* says the third surgeon was a doctor in Brighton, but does not identify him; hydrophobia: rabies (*Works* 2:236).

and the cottage, a real cottage; not (as a witty author has it) "a cottage with a double coach-house:"[1] let it be, in fact (for I must abide by the actual scene), a white cottage, embowered with flowering shrubs, so chosen as to unfold a succession of flowers upon the walls, and clustering round the windows through all the months of spring, summer, and autumn—beginning, in fact, with May roses, and ending with jasmine. Let it, however, *not* be spring, nor summer, nor autumn—but winter, in his sternest shape. This is a most important point in the science of happiness. And I am surprised to see people overlook it, and think it matter of congratulation that winter is going; or, if coming, is not likely to be a severe one. On the contrary, I put up a petition annually, for as much snow, hail, frost, or storm, of one kind or other, as the skies can possibly afford us. Surely every body is aware of the divine pleasures which attend a winter fire-side: candles at four o'clock, warm hearth-rugs, tea, a fair tea-maker, shutters closed, curtains flowing in ample draperies on the floor, whilst the wind and rain are raging audibly without,

And at the doors and windows seem to call,
As heav'n and earth they would together mell;
Yet the least entrance find they none at all;
Whence sweeter grows our rest secure in massy hall.
    —*Castle of Indolence.*[2]

All these are items in the description of a winter evening, which must surely be familiar to every body born in a high latitude. And it is evident, that most of these delicacies, like ice-cream, require a very low temperature of the atmosphere to produce them: they are fruits which cannot be ripened without stormy weather or inclement, in some way or other. I am not "*particular*," as people say, whether it be snow, or black frost, or wind so strong, that (as Mr. —— says)[3] "you may lean your back against it like a post." I can put up even with rain, provided it rains cats and dogs: but something of the sort I must have: and, if I have it not, I think myself in a manner ill-used: for why am I called on to pay so heavily for winter, in coals, and candles, and various privations that will occur even to gentlemen, if I am not to have the article good of its kind? No: a Canadian winter for my money: or a Russian one, where every man is but a co-proprietor with the

---

[1]   Coleridge, "The Devil's Thoughts" (21).
[2]   James Thomson (1700–48), *The Castle of Indolence* (1748), 1.43.6–9.
[3]   The 1856 *Confessions* identifies this as Thomas Clarkson (1760–1846), anti-slavery campaigner (*Works* 2:238).

north wind in the fee-simple[1] of his own ears. Indeed, so great an epicure am I in this matter, that I cannot relish a winter night fully if it be much past St. Thomas's day,[2] and have degenerated into disgusting tendencies to vernal appearances: no: it must be divided by a thick wall of dark nights from all return of light and sunshine.——From the latter weeks of October to Christmas-eve, therefore, is the period during which happiness is in season, which, in my judgment, enters the room with the tea-tray: for tea, though ridiculed by those who are naturally of coarse nerves, or are become so from wine-drinking, and are not susceptible of influence from so refined a stimulant, will always be the favourite beverage of the intellectual: and, for my part, I would have joined Dr. Johnson in a *bellum internecinum* against Jonas Hanway,[3] or any other impious person, who should presume to disparage it.——But here, to save myself the trouble of too much verbal description, I will introduce a painter; and give him directions for the rest of the picture. Painters do not like white cottages, unless a good deal weather-stained: but as the reader now understands that it is a winter night, his services will not be required, except for the inside of the house.

Paint me, then, a room seventeen feet by twelve, and not more than seven and a half feet high. This, reader, is somewhat ambitiously styled, in my family, the drawing-room: but, being contrived "a double debt to pay,"[4] it is also, and more justly, termed the library; for it happens that books are the only article of property in which I am richer than my neighbours. Of these, I have about five thousand, collected gradually since my eighteenth year. Therefore, painter, put as many as you can into this room. Make it populous with books: and, furthermore, paint me a good fire; and furniture, plain and modest, befitting the unpretending cottage of a scholar. And, near the fire, paint me a tea-table; and (as it is clear that no creature can come to see one such a stormy night,) place only two cups and saucers on the tea-tray: and, if you know how to paint such a thing symbolically, or otherwise, paint me an eternal tea-pot—eternal *à parte ante*, and *à parte post*;[5] for I usually drink tea from eight o'clock at night to four o'clock in the morning. And, as it is very unpleasant to make

---

1   Complete ownership.
2   December 21, the longest night of the year.
3   "Samuel Johnson, 'a hardened and shameless tea-drinker,' criticized Jonas Hanway's *Essay on Tea* in *The Literary Magazine* II (1757), xiii. Hanway had attacked tea for its damaging effects on health" [*Works* 2:337]; *bellum internecinum* means "civil war."
4   Oliver Goldsmith (1730?–74), *The Deserted Village* (1770): "The chest contrived a double debt to pay, / A bed by night, a chest of drawers by day" (229–30).
5   "Beforehand" and "afterward."

tea, or to pour it out for oneself, paint me a lovely young woman, sitting at the table. Paint her arms like Aurora's, and her smiles like Hebe's:[1]— But no, dear M., not even in jest let me insinuate that thy power to illuminate my cottage rests upon a tenure so perishable as mere personal beauty; or that the witchcraft of angelic smiles lies within the empire of any earthly pencil. Pass, then, my good painter, to something more within its power: and the next article brought forward should naturally be myself—a picture of the Opium-eater, with his "little golden receptacle of the pernicious drug," lying beside him on the table. As to the opium, I have no objection to see a picture of *that,* though I would rather see the original: you may paint it, if you choose; but I apprize you, that no "little" receptacle would, even in 1816, answer *my* purpose, who was at a distance from the "stately Pantheon," and all druggists (mortal or otherwise). No: you may as well paint the real receptacle, which was not of gold, but of glass, and as much like a wine-decanter as possible. Into this you may put a quart of ruby-coloured laudanum: that, and a book of German metaphysics placed by its side, will sufficiently attest my being in the neighbourhood; but, as to myself,—there I demur. I admit that, naturally, I ought to occupy the foreground of the picture; that being the hero of the piece, or (if you choose) the criminal at the bar, my body should be had into court. This seems reasonable: but why should I confess, on this point, to a painter? or why confess at all? If the public (into whose private ear I am confidentially whispering my confessions, and not into any painter's) should chance to have framed some agreeable picture for itself, of the Opium-eater's exterior,—should have ascribed to him, romantically, an elegant person, or a handsome face, why should I barbarously tear from it so pleasing a delusion—pleasing both to the public and to me? No: paint me, if at all, according to your own fancy: and, as a painter's fancy should teem with beautiful creations, I cannot fail, in that way, to be a gainer. And now, reader, we have run through all the ten categories of my condition, as it stood about 1816–17: up to the middle of which latter year I judge myself to have been a happy man: and the elements of that happiness I have endeavoured to place before you, in the above sketch of the interior of a scholar's library, in a cottage among the mountains, on a stormy winter evening.

But now farewell—a long farewell to happiness—winter or summer! farewell to smiles and laughter! farewell to peace of mind! farewell to hope and to tranquil dreams, and to the blessed consolations of sleep!

---

[1] Aurora, Roman goddess of dawn; Hebe, cupbearer to the Greek gods.

for more than three years and a half I am summoned away from these: I am now arrived at an Iliad of woes: for I have now to record

THE PAINS OF OPIUM

————as when some great painter dips
His pencil in the gloom of earthquake and eclipse.
                                    —*Shelley's Revolt of Islam.*[1]

Reader, who have thus far accompanied me, I must request your attention to a brief explanatory note on three points:

1. For several reasons, I have not been able to compose the notes for this part of my narrative into any regular and connected shape. I give the notes disjointed as I find them, or have now drawn them up from memory. Some of them point to their own date; some I have dated; and some are undated. Whenever it could answer my purpose to transplant them from the natural or chronological order, I have not scrupled to do so. Sometimes I speak in the present, sometimes in the past tense. Few of the notes, perhaps, were written exactly at the period of time to which they relate; but this can little affect their accuracy; as the impressions were such that they can never fade from my mind. Much has been omitted. I could not, without effort, constrain myself to the task of either recalling, or constructing into a regular narrative, the whole burthen of horrors which lies upon my brain. This feeling partly I plead in excuse, and partly that I am now in London, and am a helpless sort of person, who cannot even arrange his own papers without assistance; and I am separated from the hands which are wont to perform for me the offices of an amanuensis.

2. You will think, perhaps, that I am too confidential and communicative of my own private history. It may be so. But my way of writing is rather to think aloud, and follow my own humours, than much to consider who is listening to me; and, if I stop to consider what is proper to be said to this or that person, I shall soon come to doubt whether any part at all is proper. The fact is, I place myself at a distance of fifteen or twenty years ahead of this time, and suppose myself writing to those

---

[1] Shelley, *The Revolt of Islam*: "the King, with gathered brow, and lips / Wreathed by long scorn, did inly sneer and frown / With hue like that when some great painter dips / His pencil in the gloom of earthquake and eclipse" (5.23.1923–26).

who will be interested about me hereafter; and wishing to have some record of a time, the entire history of which no one can know but myself, I do it as fully as I am able with the efforts I am now capable of making, because I know not whether I can ever find time to do it again.

3. It will occur to you often to ask, why did I not release myself from the horrors of opium, by leaving it off, or diminishing it? To this I must answer briefly: it might be supposed that I yielded to the fascinations of opium too easily; it cannot be supposed that any man can be charmed by its terrors. The reader may be sure, therefore, that I made attempts innumerable to reduce the quantity. I add, that those who witnessed the agonies of those attempts, and not myself, were the first to beg me to desist. But could not I have reduced it a drop a day, or by adding water, have bisected or trisected a drop? A thousand drops bisected would thus have taken nearly six years to reduce; and that way would certainly not have answered. But this is a common mistake of those who know nothing of opium experimentally; I appeal to those who do, whether it is not always found that down to a certain point it can be reduced with ease and even pleasure, but that, after that point, further reduction causes intense suffering. Yes, say many thoughtless persons, who know not what they are talking of, you will suffer a little low spirits and dejection for a few days. I answer, no; there is nothing like low spirits; on the contrary, the mere animal spirits are uncommonly raised: the pulse is improved: the health is better. It is not there that the suffering lies. It has no resemblance to the sufferings caused by renouncing wine. It is a state of unutterable irritation of stomach (which surely is not much like dejection), accompanied by intense perspirations, and feelings such as I shall not attempt to describe without more space at my command.

I shall now enter "*in medias res*,"[1] and shall anticipate, from a time when my opium pains might be said to be at their *acmé*,[2] an account of their palsying effects on the intellectual faculties.

My studies have now been long interrupted. I cannot read to myself with any pleasure, hardly with a moment's endurance. Yet I read aloud sometimes for the pleasure of others; because, reading is an accomplishment of mine; and, in the slang use of the word *accomplishment* as a superficial

---

[1]   Literally, "in the middle of things" or into the middle of the story.
[2]   "Pinnacle" or "climax."

and ornamental attainment, almost the only one I possess: and formerly, if I had any vanity at all connected with any endowment or attainment of mine, it was with this; for I had observed that no accomplishment was so rare. Players are the worst readers of all: —— reads vilely: and Mrs. ——, who is so celebrated,[1] can read nothing well but dramatic composi- tions: Milton she cannot read sufferably. People in general either read poetry without any passion at all, or else overstep the modesty of nature, and read not like scholars. Of late, if I have felt moved by any thing in books, it has been by the grand lamentations of Sampson Agonistes, or the great harmonies of the Satanic speeches in Paradise Regained, when read aloud by myself. A young lady sometimes comes and drinks tea with us: at her request and M.'s I now and then read W——'s poems[2] to them. (W. by the bye, is the only poet I ever met who could read his own verses: often indeed he reads admirably.)

For nearly two years I believe that I read no book but one: and I owe it to the author, in discharge of a great debt of gratitude, to mention what that was. The sublimer and more passionate poets I still read, as I have said, by snatches, and occasionally. But my proper vocation, as I well knew, was the exercise of the analytic understanding. Now, for the most part, analytic studies are continuous, and not to be pursued by fits and starts, or frag- mentary efforts. Mathematics, for instance, intellectual philosophy, &c. were all become insupportable to me; I shrunk from them with a sense of power- less and infantine feebleness that gave me an anguish the greater from remembering the time when I grappled with them to my own hourly delight; and for this further reason, because I had devoted the labour of my whole life, and had dedicated my intellect, blossoms and fruits, to the slow and elaborate toil of constructing one single work, to which I had presumed to give the title of an unfinished work of Spinosa's; viz. *De emendatione humani intellectûs*.[3] This was now lying locked up, as by frost, like any Spanish bridge or aqueduct, begun upon too great a scale for the resources of the architect; and, instead of surviving me as a monument of wishes at least, and aspirations, and a life of labour dedicated to the exaltation of human nature in that way in which God had best fitted me to promote so great an object, it was likely to stand a memorial to my children of hopes defeated, of baffled efforts, of materials uselessly accumulated, of

---

[1]   The 1856 *Confessions* identifies the actor John Kemble (1757-1823) and his sister, the actor Sarah Siddons (1755-1831) (*Works* 2:252).
[2]   Wordsworth's.
[3]   The unfinished *Tractatus de Intellectus Emendatione* ("Treatise on the Improvement of the Understanding") by Dutch-Jewish philosopher Baruch Spinoza (1632–77).

foundations laid that were never to support a superstructure,—of the grief and the ruin of the architect. In this state of imbecility, I had, for amusement, turned my attention to political economy; my understanding, which formerly had been as active and restless as a hyena, could not, I suppose (so long as I lived at all) sink into utter lethargy; and political economy offers this advantage to a person in my state, that though it is eminently an organic science (no part, that is to say, but what acts on the whole, as the whole again re-acts on each part), yet the several parts may be detached and contemplated singly. Great as was the prostration of my powers at this time, yet I could not forget my knowledge; and my understanding had been for too many years intimate with severe thinkers, with logic, and the great masters of knowledge, not to be aware of the utter feebleness of the main herd of modern economists. I had been led in 1811 to look into loads of books and pamphlets on many branches of economy; and, at my desire, M. sometimes read to me chapters from more recent works, or parts of parliamentary debates. I saw that these were generally the very dregs and rinsings of the human intellect; and that any man of sound head, and practiced in wielding logic with a scholastic adroitness, might take up the whole academy of modern economists, and throttle them between heaven and earth with his finger and thumb, or bray their fungus heads to powder with a lady's fan. At length, in 1819, a friend in Edinburgh sent me down Mr. Ricardo's book:[1] and recurring to my own prophetic anticipation of the advent of some legislator for this science, I said, before I had finished the first chapter, "Thou art the man!" Wonder and curiosity were emotions that had long been dead in me. Yet I wondered once more: I wondered at myself that I could once again be stimulated to the effort of reading: and much more I wondered at the book. Had this profound work been really written in England during the nineteenth century? Was it possible? I supposed thinking[*] had been extinct in England. Could it be that an Englishman, and he not in academic bowers, but oppressed by

---

[*] The reader must remember what I here mean by *thinking:* because, else this would be a very presumptuous expression. England, of late, has been rich to excess in fine thinkers, in the departments of creative and combining thought; but there is a sad dearth of masculine thinkers in any analytic path. A Scotchman of eminent name has lately told us, that he is obliged to quit even mathematics, for want of encouragement. *Works* identifies the "Scotchman" as: Sir John Leslie (1766–1832). "The Preface to his *Elements of Geometry, and Plane Trigonometry* (1820) explains his abandonment of a plan for a five-volume mathematical work on the grounds that there is 'very little incitement to the publication of abstract works in this country'" (*Works* 2:337).]

---

[1] See p. 55, n. 1 above; sent to De Quincey by John Wilson, editor at *Blackwood's*, for review.

mercantile and senatorial cares, had accomplished what all the universities of Europe, and a century of thought, had failed even to advance by one hair's breadth? All other writers had been crushed and overlaid by the enormous weight of facts and documents; Mr. Ricardo had deduced *à priori*,[1] from the understanding itself, laws which first gave a ray of light into the unwieldy chaos of materials, and had constructed what had been but a collection of tentative discussions into a science of regular proportions, now first standing on an eternal basis.

Thus did one single work of a profound understanding avail to give me a pleasure and an activity which I had not known for years:—it roused me even to write, or, at least, to dictate, what M. wrote for me. It seemed to me, that some important truths had escaped even "the inevitable eye" of Mr. Ricardo: and, as these were, for the most part, of such a nature that I could express or illustrate them more briefly and elegantly by algebraic symbols than in the usual clumsy and loitering diction of economists, the whole would not have filled a pocket-book; and being so brief, with M. for my amanuensis, even at this time, incapable as I was of all general exertion, I drew up my *Prolegomena to all future Systems of Political Economy.*[2] I hope it will not be found redolent of opium; though, indeed, to most people, the subject itself is a sufficient opiate.

This exertion, however, was but a temporary flash; as the sequel showed—for I designed to publish my work: arrangements were made at a provincial press, about eighteen miles distant, for printing it. An additional compositor was retained, for some days, on this account. The work was even twice advertised: and I was, in a manner, pledged to the fulfilment of my intention. But I had a preface to write; and a dedication, which I wished to make a splendid one, to Mr. Ricardo. I found myself quite unable to accomplish all this. The arrangements were countermanded: the compositor dismissed: and my "Prolegomena" rested peacefully by the side of its elder and more dignified brother.

I have thus described and illustrated my intellectual torpor, in terms that apply, more or less, to every part of the four years during which I was under the Circean spells[3] of opium. But for misery and suffering, I might, indeed, be said to have existed in a dormant state. I seldom could

---

[1] Literally "from the former"; deduction from self-evident propositions or first principles.

[2] Adapted from Kant's *Prolegomena to all Future Metaphysics* (1783); "Prolegomena": prefatory remarks; De Quincey finally published *The Logic of Political Economy* in 1844.

[3] In Greek myth, when men drink from the sorceress Circe's magic cup, they are turned into animals and imprisoned; she thus imprisons Odysseus's men in Aeaea; Hermes gave Odysseus a herb to resist her potion, after which she frees his men.

prevail on myself to write a letter; an answer of a few words, to any that I received, was the utmost that I could accomplish; and often *that* not until the letter had lain weeks, or even months, on my writing table. Without the aid of M. all records of bills paid, or *to be* paid, must have perished: and my whole domestic economy, whatever became of Political Economy, must have gone into irretrievable confusion.—I shall not afterwards allude to this part of the case: it is one, however, which the opium-eater will find, in the end, as oppressive and tormenting as any other, from the sense of incapacity and feebleness, from the direct embarrassments incident to the neglect or procrastination of each day's appropriate duties, and from the remorse which must often exasperate the stings of these evils to a reflective and conscientious mind. The opium-eater loses none of his moral sensibilities, or aspirations: he wishes and longs, as earnestly as ever, to realize what he believes possible, and feels to be exacted by duty; but his intellectual apprehension of what is possible infinitely outruns his power, not of execution only, but even of power to attempt. He lies under the weight of incubus and night-mare: he lies in sight of all that he would fain perform, just as a man forcibly confined to his bed by the mortal languor of a relaxing disease, who is compelled to witness injury or outrage offered to some object of his tenderest love:—he curses the spells which chain him down from motion:—he would lay down his life if he might but get up and walk; but he is powerless as an infant, and cannot even attempt to rise.

I now pass to what is the main subject of these latter confessions, to the history and journal of what took place in my dreams; for these were the immediate and proximate cause of my acutest suffering.

The first notice I had of any important change going on in this part of my physical economy, was from the re-awakening of a state of eye generally incident to childhood, or exalted states of irritability. I know not whether my reader is aware that many children, perhaps most, have a power of painting, as it were, upon the darkness, all sorts of phantoms; in some, that power is simply a mechanic affection of the eye; others have a voluntary, or a semi-voluntary power to dismiss or to summon them; or, as a child once said to me when I questioned him on this matter, "I can tell them to go, and they go; but sometimes they come, when I don't tell them to come." Whereupon I told him that he had almost as unlimited a command over apparitions, as a Roman centurion over his soldiers.—In the middle of 1817, I think it was, that this faculty became positively distressing to me: at night, when I lay awake in bed, vast processions passed along in mournful pomp; friezes of never-ending stories, that to my feelings were as sad and solemn as if they were stories drawn from times before Oedipus or Priam—before Tyre—before Memphis.[1] And, at the same time, a corresponding change took place in my dreams; a theatre seemed suddenly opened and lighted up within my brain, which presented nightly spectacles of more than earthly splendour. And the four following facts may be mentioned, as noticeable at this time:

1. That, as the creative state of the eye increased, a sympathy seemed to arise between the waking and the dreaming states of the brain in one point—that whatsoever I happened to call up and to trace by a voluntary act upon the darkness was very apt to transfer itself to my dreams; so that I feared to exercise this faculty; for, as Midas turned all things to gold, that yet baffled his hopes and defrauded his human desires, so whatsoever things capable of being visually represented I did but think of in the darkness, immediately shaped themselves into phantoms of the eye; and, by a process apparently no less inevitable, when thus once traced in faint and visionary colours, like writings in sympathetic ink, they were drawn out by the fierce chemistry of my dreams, into insufferable splendour that fretted my heart.

2. For this, and all other changes in my dreams, were accompanied by deep-seated anxiety and gloomy melancholy, such as are wholly incommunicable by words. I seemed every night to descend, not metaphorically, but literally to descend, into chasms and sunless abysses, depths below depths, from which it seemed hopeless that I could ever re-ascend. Nor did I, by waking, feel that I *had* re-ascended. This I do not dwell upon; because the state of gloom which attended these gorgeous spectacles, amounting at last to utter darkness, as of some suicidal despondency, cannot be approached by words.

3. The sense of space, and in the end, the sense of time, were both powerfully affected. Buildings, landscapes, &c. were exhibited in proportions so vast as the bodily eye is not fitted to receive. Space swelled, and was amplified to an extent of unutterable infinity. This, however, did not disturb me so much as the vast expansion of time; I sometimes seemed to have lived for 70 or 100 years in one night; nay, sometimes had feelings representative of a millennium passed in that time, or, however, of a duration far beyond the limits of any human experience.

---

[1]   Oedipus, legendary king of Thebes; Priam, legendary king of Troy; Tyre was a Phoenician seaport dating from the third millennium BCE, Memphis an Egyptian city from before that time.

4. The minutest incidents of childhood, or forgotten scenes of later years, were often revived: I could not be said to recollect them; for if I had been told of them when waking, I should not have been able to acknowledge them as parts of my past experience. But placed as they were before me, in dreams like intuitions, and clothed in all their evanescent circumstances and accompanying feelings, I *recognized* them instantaneously. I was once told by a near relative[1] of mine, that having in her childhood fallen into a river, and being on the very verge of death but for the critical assistance which reached her, she saw in a moment her whole life, in its minutest incidents, arrayed before her simultaneously as in a mirror; and she had a faculty developed as suddenly for comprehending the whole and every part. This, from some opium experiences of mine, I can believe; I have, indeed, seen the same thing asserted twice in modern books, and accompanied by a remark which I am convinced is true; viz. that the dread book of account,[2] which the Scriptures speak of, is, in fact, the mind itself of each individual. Of this at least, I feel assured, that there is no such thing as *forgetting* possible to the mind; a thousand accidents may, and will interpose a veil between our present consciousness and the secret inscriptions on the mind; accidents of the same sort will also rend away this veil; but alike, whether veiled or unveiled, the inscription remains for ever; just as the stars seem to withdraw before the common light of day, whereas, in fact, we all know that it is the light which is drawn over them as a veil—and that they are waiting to be revealed when the obscuring daylight shall have withdrawn.

Having noticed these four facts as memorably distinguishing my dreams from those of health, I shall now cite a case illustrative of the first fact; and shall then cite any others that I remember, either in their chronological order, or any other that may give them more effect as pictures to the reader.

I had been in youth, and even since, for occasional amusement, a great reader of Livy,[3] whom, I confess, that I prefer, both for style and matter, to any other of the Roman historians: and I had often felt as most solemn and appalling sounds, and most emphatically representative of the majesty

---

[1]   De Quincey's mother.

[2]   De Quincey likely means Revelation: "I saw a great, white throne, and the One who sits upon it. From his presence earth and heaven fled away, and there was no room for them any more. I saw the dead, great and small, standing before the throne; and books were opened. Then another book, the book of life, was opened. The dead were judged by what they had done, as recorded in these books" (20:11–12).

[3]   Titus Livy (59 BCE–17 CE), Roman historian, author of *Ab Urbe Condita* ("From the Founding of the City"), a history of Rome.

of the Roman people, the two words so often recurring in Livy—*Consul Romanus*; especially when the consul is introduced in his military character. I mean to say, that the words king—sultan—regent, &c. or any other titles of those who embody in their own persons the collective majesty of a great people, had less power over my reverential feelings. I had also, though no great reader of history, made myself minutely and critically familiar with one period of English history, viz. the period of the Parliamentary War, having been attracted by the moral grandeur of some who figured in that day, and by the many interesting memoirs which survive those unquiet times. Both these parts of my lighter reading, having furnished me often with matter of reflection, now furnished me with matter for my dreams. Often I used to see, after painting upon the blank darkness a sort of rehearsal whilst waking, a crowd of ladies, and perhaps a festival, and dances. And I heard it said, or I said to myself, "these are English ladies from the unhappy times of Charles I. These are the wives and the daughters of those who met in peace, and sate at the same tables, and were allied by marriage or by blood; and yet, after a certain day in August, 1642, never smiled upon each other again, nor met but in the field of battle; and at Marston Moor, at Newbury, or at Naseby,[1] cut asunder all ties of love by the cruel sabre, and washed away in blood the memory of ancient friendship."—The ladies danced, and looked as lovely as the court of George IV. Yet I knew, even in my dream, that they had been in the grave for nearly two centuries.—This pageant would suddenly dissolve: and, at a clapping of hands, would be heard the heart-quaking sound of *Consul Romanus*: and immediately came "sweeping by," in gorgeous paludaments, Paulus or Marius, girt round by a company of centurions, with the crimson tunic hoisted on a spear, and followed by the *alalagmos* of the Roman legions.[2]

Many years ago, when I was looking over Piranesi's *Antiquities of Rome*,[3] Mr. Coleridge, who was standing by, described to me a set of

---

[1]   Battles fought in the English Civil War (1642–45).

[2]   Paludaments: Roman military cloaks; Paulus, general at the Battle of Cannae (216 BC); Marius, Consul who led the Romans in the conquest of Numidia; the 1856 *Confessions* says the crimson tunic is "The signal which announced a day of battle" and "*alalagmos*" is "A word expressing collectively the gathering of the Roman war-cries—*Alála, alála!*" (*Works* 2:258n).

[3]   Giovanni Battista Piranesi (1720–78), Italian architectural engraver. *Antiquities of Rome* depicts Ancient Rome via a series of colossal, dreamlike streetscapes. De Quincey's reference to *Dreams* is actually to Piranesi's *Carceri d'Invenzione* ("Imaginary Prisons"), which depicts seemingly infinite carceral spaces, gothic in their dimensions and impression, if not properly Gothic architecturally.

plates by that artist, called his *Dreams,* and which record the scenery of
his own visions during the delirium of a fever. Some of them (I describe
only from memory of Mr. Coleridge's account) represented vast Gothic
halls: on the floor of which stood all sorts of engines and machinery,
wheels, cables, pulleys, levers, catapults, &c. &c. expressive of enormous
power put forth, and resistance overcome. Creeping along the sides of
the walls, you perceived a staircase; and upon it, groping his way
upwards, was Piranesi himself: follow the stairs a little further, and you
perceive it come to a sudden abrupt termination, without any balustrade,
and allowing no step onwards to him who had reached the extremity,
except into the depths below. Whatever is to become of poor Piranesi,
you suppose, at least, that his labours must in some way terminate here.
But raise your eyes, and behold a second flight of stairs still higher: on
which again Piranesi is perceived, but this time standing on the very
brink of the abyss. Again elevate your eye, and a still more aerial flight
of stairs is beheld: and again is poor Piranesi busy on his aspiring
labours: and so on, until the unfinished stairs and Piranesi both are lost
in the upper gloom of the hall.—With the same power of endless
growth and self-reproduction did my architecture proceed in dreams.
In the early stage of my malady, the splendours of my dreams were
indeed chiefly architectural: and I beheld such pomp of cities and
palaces as was never yet beheld by the waking eye, unless in the clouds.
From a great modern poet I cite part of a passage which describes, as
an appearance actually beheld in the clouds, what in many of its circumstances I saw frequently in sleep:

> The appearance, instantaneously disclosed,
> Was of a mighty city—boldly say
> A wilderness of building, sinking far
> And self-withdrawn into a wondrous depth,
> Far sinking into splendour—without end!
> Fabric it seem'd of diamond, and of gold,
> With alabaster domes, and silver spires,
> And blazing terrace upon terrace, high
> Uplifted; here, serene pavilions bright
> In avenues disposed; there towers begirt
> With battlements that on their restless fronts
> Bore stars—illumination of all gems!
> By earthly nature had the effect been wrought
> Upon the dark materials of the storm

Now pacified; on them, and on the coves,
And mountain-steeps and summits, whereunto
The vapours had receded,—taking there
Their station under a cerulean sky. &c. &c.[1]

The sublime circumstance—"battlements that on their *restless* fronts
bore stars,"—might have been copied from my architectural dreams, for
it often occurred.—We hear it reported of Dryden, and of Fuseli in
modern times, that they thought proper to eat raw meat for the sake of
obtaining splendid dreams: how much better for such a purpose to have
eaten opium, which yet I do not remember that any poet is recorded to
have done, except the dramatist Shadwell:[2] and in ancient days, Homer
is, I think, rightly reputed to have known the virtues of opium.[3]

To my architecture succeeded dreams of lakes—and silvery expanses of
water:—these haunted me so much, that I feared (though possibly it will
appear ludicrous to a medical man) that some dropsical state or tendency
of the brain might thus be making itself (to use a metaphysical word) *objective*; and the sentient organ *project* itself as its own object.—For two months
I suffered greatly in my head,—a part of my bodily structure which had
hitherto been so clear from all touch or taint of weakness (physically, I
mean), that I used to say of it, as the last Lord Orford[4] said of his stomach,
that it seemed likely to survive the rest of my person.—Till now I had
never felt a head-ache even, or any the slightest pain, except rheumatic
pains caused by my own folly. However, I got over this attack, though it
must have been verging on something very dangerous.

The waters now changed their character,—from translucent lakes,
shining like mirrors, they now became seas and oceans. And now came
a tremendous change, which, unfolding itself slowly like a scroll,
through many months, promised an abiding torment; and, in fact, it

---

[1]   Wordsworth, *The Excursion* (2.834–51). This passage is from Book Two, "The Solitary."
      The Solitary sees through the "blind vapour" (831) of mist a waking vision of the New
      Jerusalem that leaves him questioning his everyday reality: "That which I *saw* was the
      revealed abode / Of Spirits in beautitude: my heart / Swelled in my breast.—'I have been
      dead,' I cried, / And now I live! Oh! wherefore *do* I live?' / And with that pang I prayed
      to be no more!" (873–77).

[2]   John Dryden (1631–1700), poet, dramatist and essayist; Henry Fuseli (1741–1825), painter
      of nightmarish scenes; Thomas Shadwell (1642–92), poet and dramatist.

[3]   See p. 89, n. 1 above.

[4]   Horace Walpole (1717–97), fourth Earl of Orford, author of *The Castle of Otranto* (1764), often
      considered the first Gothic novel, and builder of Strawberry Hill, Twickenham, his "little
      Gothic castle"; perhaps best known for his voluminous, autobiographical correspondence.

never left me until the winding up of my case. Hitherto the human face had mixed often in my dreams, but not despotically, nor with any special power of tormenting. But now that which I have called the tyranny of the human face began to unfold itself. Perhaps some part of my London life might be answerable for this. Be that as it may, now it was that upon the rocking waters of the ocean the human face began to appear: the sea appeared paved with innumerable faces, upturned to the heavens: faces, imploring, wrathful, despairing, surged upwards by thousands, by myriads, by generations, by centuries:—my agitation was infinite,—my mind tossed—and surged with the ocean.

May, 1818.

The Malay has been a fearful enemy for months. I have been every night, through his means, transported into Asiatic scenes. I know not whether others share in my feelings on this point; but I have often thought that if I were compelled to forego England, and to live in China, and among Chinese manners and modes of life and scenery, I should go mad. The causes of my horror lie deep; and some of them must be common to others. Southern Asia, in general, is the seat of awful images and associations. As the cradle of the human race, it would alone have a dim and reverential feeling connected with it. But there are other reasons. No man can pretend that the wild, barbarous, and capricious superstitions of Africa, or of savage tribes elsewhere, affect him in the way that he is affected by the ancient, monumental, cruel, and elaborate religions of Indostan, &c. The mere antiquity of Asiatic things, of their institutions, histories, modes of faith, &c. is so impressive, that to me the vast age of the race and name overpowers the sense of youth in the individual. A young Chinese seems to me an antediluvian man renewed. Even Englishmen, thought not bred in any knowledge of such institutions, cannot but shudder at the mystic sublimity of *castes*[1] that have flowed apart, and refused to mix, through such immemorial tracts of time; nor can any man fail to be awed by the names of the Ganges, or the Euphrates. It contributes much to these feelings, that southern Asia is, and has been for thousands of years, the part of the earth most swarming with human life; the great *officina gentium*.[2] Man is a weed

---

[1]   Hindu class system and social stratification based on strict rules of heredity, privilege, profession, or occupation.
[2]   "Workshop of the world."

in those regions. The vast empires also, into which the enormous population of Asia has always been cast, give a further sublimity to the feelings associated with all oriental names or images. In China, over and above what it has in common with the rest of southern Asia, I am terrified by the modes of life, by the manners, and the barrier of utter abhorrence, and want of sympathy, placed between us by feelings deeper than I can analyze. I could sooner live with lunatics, or brute animals. All this, and much more than I can say, or have time to say, the reader must enter into before he can comprehend the unimaginable horror which these dreams of oriental imagery, and mythological tortures, impressed upon me. Under the connecting feeling of tropical heat and vertical sun-lights, I brought together all creatures, birds, beasts, reptiles, all trees and plants, usages and appearances, that are found in all tropical regions, and assembled them together in China or Indostan. From kindred feelings, I soon brought Egypt and all her gods under the same law. I was stared at, hooted at, grinned at, chattered at, by monkeys, by paroquets, by cockatoos. I ran into pagodas: and was fixed, for centuries, at the summit, or in secret rooms; I was the idol; I was the priest; I was worshipped; I was sacrificed. I fled from the wrath of Brama through all the forests of Asia:Vishnu hated me: Seeva laid wait for me. I came suddenly upon Isis and Osiris:[1] I had done a deed, they said, which the ibis and the crocodile trembled at. I was buried, for a thousand years, in stone coffins, with mummies and sphynxes, in narrow chambers at the heart of eternal pyramids. I was kissed, with cancerous kisses, by crocodiles; and laid, confounded with all unutterable slimy things, amongst reeds and Nilotic mud.

I thus give the reader some slight abstraction of my oriental dreams, which always filled me with such amazement at the monstrous scenery, that horror seemed absorbed, for a while, in sheer astonishment. Sooner or later, came a reflux of feeling that swallowed up the astonishment, and left me, not so much in terror, as in hatred and abomination of what I saw. Over every form, and threat, and punishment, and dim sightless incarceration, brooded a sense of eternity and infinity that drove me into an oppression as of madness. Into these dreams only, it was, with one or two slight exceptions, that any circumstances of physical horror entered. All before had been moral and spiritual terrors. But here the main agents were ugly birds, or snakes, or crocodiles; especially the last. The cursed

---

[1]   Brama (or Brahma, god of creation),Vishnu (god of preservation), and Seeva (or Siva, god of destruction and regeneration) form the sacred triad of Hinduism; Isis (Egyptian nature goddess) is the wife and sister of Osiris (god of the underworld) in Egyptian mythology. Here they evoke a tormenting return to the fundamental or primal nature of existence.

crocodile became to me the object of more horror than almost all the rest. I was compelled to live with him; and (as was always the case almost in my dreams) for centuries. I escaped sometimes, and found myself in Chinese houses, with cane tables, &c. All the feet of the tables, sophas, &c. soon became instinct with life: the abominable head of the crocodile, and his leering eyes, looked out at me, multiplied into a thousand repetitions: and I stood loathing and fascinated. And so often did this hideous reptile haunt my dreams, that many times the very same dream was broken up in the very same way: I heard gentle voices speaking to me (I hear every thing when I am sleeping); and instantly I awoke: it was broad noon; and my children were standing, hand in hand, at my bed-side; come to show me their coloured shoes, or new frocks, or to let me see them dressed for going out. I protest that so awful was the transition from the damned crocodile, and the other unutterable monsters and abortions of my dreams, to the sight of innocent *human* natures and of infancy, that, in the mighty and sudden revulsion of mind, I wept, and could not forbear it, as I kissed their faces.

June, 1819.

I have had occasion to remark, at various periods of my life, that the deaths of those whom we love, and indeed the contemplation of death generally, is (*caeteris paribus*)[1] more affecting in summer than in any other season of the year. And the reasons are these three, I think: first, that the visible heavens in summer appear far higher, more distant, and (if such a solecism may be excused) more infinite; the clouds, by which chiefly the eye expounds the distance of the blue pavilion stretched over our heads, are in summer more voluminous, massed, and accumulated in far grander and more towering piles: secondly, the light and the appearances of the declining and setting sun are much more fitted to be types and characters of the Infinite: and, thirdly, (which is the main reason) the exuberant and riotous prodigality of life naturally forces the mind more powerfully upon the antagonist thought of death, and the wintry sterility of the grave. For it may be observed, generally, that wherever two thoughts stand related to each other by a law of antagonism, and exist, as it were, by mutual repulsion, they are apt to suggest each other. On these accounts it is that I find it impossible to banish the thought

---

[1] "Other things being equal."

of death when I am walking alone in the endless days of summer; and any particular death, if not more affecting, at least haunts my mind more obstinately and besiegingly in that season. Perhaps this cause, and a slight incident which I omit, might have been the immediate occasions of the following dream; to which, however, a predisposition must always have existed in my mind; but having been once roused, it never left me, and split into a thousand fantastic varieties, which often suddenly reunited, and composed again the original dream.

I thought that it was a Sunday morning in May, that it was Easter Sunday, and as yet very early in the morning. I was standing, as it seemed to me, at the door of my own cottage. Right before me lay the very scene which could really be commanded from that situation, but exalted, as was usual, and solemnized by the power of dreams. There were the same mountains, and the same lovely valley at their feet; but the mountains were raised to more than Alpine height, and there was interspace far larger between them of meadows and forest lawns; the hedges were rich with white roses; and no living creature was to be seen, excepting that in the green church-yard there were cattle tranquilly reposing upon the verdant graves, and particularly round about the grave of a child[1] whom I had tenderly loved, just as I had really beheld them, a little before sun-rise in the same summer, when that child died. I gazed upon the well-known scene, and I said aloud (as I thought) to myself, "it yet wants much of sun-rise; and it is Easter Sunday; and that is the day on which they celebrate the first fruits of resurrection. I will walk abroad; old griefs shall be forgotten to-day; for the air is cool and still, and the hills are high, and stretch away to Heaven; and the forest-glades are as quiet as the church-yard; and, with the dew, I can wash the fever from my forehead, and then I shall be unhappy no longer." And I turned, as if to open my garden gate; and immediately I saw upon the left a scene far different; but which yet the power of dreams had reconciled into harmony with the other. The scene was an oriental one; and there also it was Easter Sunday, and very early in the morning. And at a vast distance were visible, as a stain upon the horizon, the domes and cupolas of a great city—an image or faint abstraction, caught perhaps in childhood from some picture of Jerusalem. And not a bow-shot from me, upon a stone, and shaded by Judean plants, there sat a woman; and I looked; and it was—Ann! She fixed her eyes upon me earnestly; and I said to her at length: "So then I have found you at last." I waited: but she

---

[1]   Catherine Wordsworth; see p. 103, n. 1 above.

answered me not a word. Her face was the same as when I saw it last, and yet again how different! Seventeen years ago, when the lamp-light fell upon her face, as for the last time I kissed her lips (lips, Ann, that to me were not polluted), her eyes were streaming with tears: the tears were now wiped away; she seemed more beautiful than she was at that time, but in all other points the same, and not older. Her looks were tranquil, but with unusual solemnity of expression; and I now gazed upon her with some awe, but suddenly her countenance grew dim, and, turning to the mountains, I perceived vapours rolling between us; in a moment, all had vanished; a thick darkness came on; and, in the twinkling of an eye, I was far away from mountains, and by lamp-light in Oxford-street, walking again with Ann—just as we walked seventeen years before, when we were both children.

As a final specimen, I cite one of a different character, from 1820.

The dream commenced with a music which now I often heard in dreams—a music of preparation and of awakening suspense; a music like the opening of the Coronation Anthem,[1] and which, like *that* gave the feeling of a vast march—of infinite cavalcades filing off—and the tread of innumerable armies. The morning was come of a mighty day—a day of crisis and of final hope for human nature, then suffering some mysterious eclipse, and labouring in some dread extremity. Somewhere, I knew not where—somehow, I knew not how—by some beings, I knew not whom—a battle, a strife, an agony, was conducting,—was evolving like a great drama, or piece of music; with which my sympathy was the more insupportable from my confusion as to its place, its cause, its nature, and its possible issue. I, as is usual in dreams (where, of necessity, we make ourselves central to every movement), had the power, and yet had not the power, to decide it. I had the power, if I could raise myself, to will it; and yet again had not the power, for the weight of twenty Atlantics was upon me, or the oppression of inexpiable guilt. "Deeper than ever plummet sounded,"[2] I lay inactive. Then, like a chorus, the passion deepened. Some greater interest was at stake; some mightier cause than ever yet the sword had pleaded, or trumpet had proclaimed. Then came sudden alarms: hurryings to and fro: trepidations of innumerable fugitives, I knew not

---

[1] Composed by George Friedrich Handel (1685–1759), Saxon composer best known for his operas and oratorios, for the coronation of George II in 1727.

[2] Shakespeare, *The Tempest* (3.3.101). Shipwrecked on Prospero's island, Alonso, King of Naples, is desperate to find his supposedly drowned son, Ferdinand: "my son i' th' ooze is bedded; and / I'll seek him deeper than e'er plummet sounded, / And with him there lie mudded" (100–102).

whether from the good cause or the bad: darkness and lights: tempest and human faces; and at last, with the sense that all was lost, female forms, and the features that were worth all the world to me, and but a moment allowed,—and clasped hands, and heart-breaking partings, and then—everlasting farewells! and with a sigh, such as the caves of hell sighed when the incestuous mother uttered the abhorred name of death,[1] the sound was reverberated—everlasting farewells! and again, and yet again reverberated—everlasting farewells!

And I awoke in struggles, and cried aloud—"I will sleep no more!"

But I am now called upon to wind up a narrative which has already extended to an unreasonable length. Within more spacious limits, the materials which I have used might have been better unfolded; and much which I have not used might have been added with effect. Perhaps, however, enough has been given. It now remains that I should say something of the way in which this conflict of horrors was finally brought to its crisis. The reader is already aware (from a passage near the beginning of the introduction to the first part) that the opium-eater has, in some way or other, "unwound, almost to its final links, the accursed chain which bound him."[2] By what means? To have narrated this, according to the original intention, would have far exceeded the space which can now be allowed. It is fortunate, as such a cogent reason exists for abridging it, that I should, on a maturer view of the case, have been exceedingly unwilling to injure, by any such unaffecting details, the impression of the history itself, as an appeal to the prudence and the conscience of the yet unconfirmed opium-eater—or even (though a very inferior consideration) to injure its effect as a composition. The interest of the judicious reader will not attach itself chiefly to the subject of the fascinating spells, but to the fascinating power. Not the opium-eater, but the opium, is the true hero of the tale; and the legitimate centre on which the interest revolves. The object was to display the marvellous agency of opium, whether for pleasure or for pain: if that is done, the action of the piece has closed.

However, as some people, in spite of all laws to the contrary, will persist in asking what became of the opium-eater, and in what state he

---

[1]   Milton, *Paradise Lost* (10.602); Satan gives birth to Sin, his daughter, and with her begets Death, her son and brother; their unholy alliance forms a demonic inversion of the Holy Trinity.

[2]   Here De Quincey misquotes in the third person the moral he implicitly promises at the opening of *Confessions*: "[I] have untwisted, almost to its final links, the accursed chain which fettered me."

now is, I answer for him thus: The reader is aware that opium had long ceased to found its empire on spells of pleasure; it was solely by the tortures connected with the attempt to abjure it, that it kept its hold. Yet, as other tortures, no less it may be thought, attended the non-abjuration of such a tyrant, a choice only of evils was left; and *that* might as well have been adopted, which, however terrific in itself, held out a prospect of final restoration to happiness. This appears true; but good logic gave the author no strength to act upon it. However, a crisis arrived for the author's life, and a crisis for other objects still dearer to him—and which will always be far dearer to him than his life, even now that it is again a happy one.—I saw that I must die if I continued the opium: I determined, therefore, if that should be required, to die in throwing it off. How much I was at that time taking I cannot say; for the opium which I used had been purchased for me by a friend who afterwards refused to let me pay him; so that I could not ascertain even what quantity I had used within the year. I apprehend, however, that I took it very irregularly: and that I varied from about fifty or sixty grains, to 150 a-day. My first task was to reduce it to forty, to thirty, and, as fast as I could, to twelve grains.

I triumphed: but think not, reader, that therefore my sufferings were ended; nor think of me as of one sitting in a *dejected* state. Think of me as of one, even when four months had passed, still agitated, writhing, throbbing, palpitating, shattered; and much, perhaps, in the situation of him who has been racked, as I collect the torments of that state from the affecting account of them left by a most innocent sufferer★ (of the times of James I.). Meantime, I derived no benefit from any medicine, except one prescribed to me by an Edinburgh surgeon of great eminence, viz. ammoniated tincture of Valerian.[1] Medical account, therefore, of my emancipation I have not much to give: and even that little, as managed by a man so ignorant of medicine as myself, would probably tend only to mislead. At all events, it would be misplaced in

---

★   William Lithgow: his book (Travels, &c.) is ill and pedantically written: but the account of his own sufferings on the rack at Malaga is overpoweringly affecting. [William Lithgow (1582–1645?), poet, traveller, author of *Discourse of a Peregrination in Europe, Asia and Affricke* (1614).]

---

[1]   "George Bell (1777–1832), a noted Edinburgh doctor who treated De Quincey in 1820. His prescription, ammoniated tincture of valerian, was a standard remedy for 'debility of the nervous system'" [*Works* 2:338].

this situation. The moral of the narrative is addressed to the opium-eater; and therefore, of necessity, limited in its application. If he is taught to fear and tremble, enough has been effected. But he may say, that the issue of my case is at least a proof that opium, after a seventeen years' use, and an eight years' abuse of its powers, may still be renounced: and that *he* may chance to bring to the task greater energy than I did, or that with a stronger constitution than mine he may obtain the same results with less. This may be true: I would not presume to measure the efforts of other men by my own: I heartily wish him more energy: I wish him the same success. Nevertheless, I had motives external to myself which he may unfortunately want: and these supplied me with conscientious supports which mere personal interests might fail to supply to a mind debilitated by opium.

Jeremy Taylor conjectures that it may be as painful to be born as to die:[1] I think it probable: and, during the whole period of diminishing the opium, I had the torments of a man passing out of one mode of existence into another. The issue was not death, but a sort of physical regeneration: and I may add, that ever since, at intervals, I have had a restoration of more than youthful spirits, though under the pressure of difficulties, which, in a less happy state of mind, I should have called misfortunes.

One memorial of my former condition still remains: my dreams are not yet perfectly calm: the dread swell and agitation of the storm have not wholly subsided: the legions that encamped in them are drawing off, but not all departed: my sleep is still tumultuous, and, like the gates of Paradise to our first parents when looking back from afar, it is still (in the tremendous line of Milton)—

With dreadful faces throng'd and fiery arms.[2]

---

[1] In a note to the 1856 *Confessions* De Quincey corrects the reference to the "Essay on Death" by Francis Bacon (1561–1626), and quotes the essay: "'It is as natural to die as to be born; and to a little infant perhaps the one is as painful as the other'" (*Works* 2:266).

[2] Milton, *Paradise Lost*; Adam and Eve have been banished from the Garden of Eden: "They looking back, all th' Eastern side beheld / Of Paradise, so late their happy seat, Wav'd over by that flaming Brand, the Gate / With dreadful Faces throng'd and fiery Arms" (12.641–44).

SUSPIRIA DE PROFUNDIS:

BEING A SEQUEL TO THE CONFESSIONS OF AN ENGLISH OPIUM-EATER.

INTRODUCTORY NOTICE

In 1821, as a contribution to a periodical work—in 1822, as a separate volume—appeared the "Confessions of an English Opium-Eater." The object of that work was to reveal something of the grandeur which belongs *potentially* to human dreams. Whatever may be the number of those in whom this faculty of dreaming splendidly can be supposed to lurk, there are not perhaps very many in whom it is developed. He whose talk is of oxen, will probably dream of oxen: and the condition of human life, which yokes so vast a majority to a daily experience incompatible with much elevation of thought, oftentimes neutralizes the tone of grandeur in the reproductive faculty of dreaming, even for those whose minds are populous with solemn imagery. Habitually to dream magnificently, a man must have a constitutional determination to reverie. This in the first place; and even this, where it exists strongly, is too much liable to disturbance from the gathering agitation of our present English life. Already, in this year 1845, what by the procession through fifty years of mighty revolutions amongst the kingdoms of the earth, what by the continual development of vast physical agencies—steam in all its applications, light getting under harness as a slave for man,★ powers from heaven descending upon education and accelerations of the press, powers of hell (as it might seem, but these also celestial) coming round upon artillery and the forces of destruction—the eye of the calmest observer is troubled; the brain is haunted as if by some jealousy of ghostly beings moving amongst us; and it becomes too evident that, unless this colossal pace of advance can be retarded, (a thing not to be expected,) or, which is happily more probable, can be met by counterforces of corresponding magnitude, forces in the direction of religion or profound philosophy, that shall radiate centrifugally against this storm of life so perilously centripetal towards the vortex of the merely human, left to itself the natural tendency of so chaotic a tumult must be to evil; for some minds to lunacy, for others to a reagency of fleshly torpor. How much this fierce condition of eternal hurry, upon an arena too exclusively human in its interests, is likely to defeat the grandeur which is latent in all men, may be seen in the ordinary effect from living too constantly in varied company. The word *dissipation*, in one of its uses, expresses that effect; the action of thought and feeling is too much dissipated and squandered. To reconcentrate them into meditative habits, a

---

★   Daguerreotype, &c. [Early photographic process, invented in 1839 by Louis Daguerre.]

necessity is felt by all observing persons for sometimes retiring from crowds. No man ever will unfold the capacities of his own intellect who does not at least chequer his life with solitude. How much solitude, so much power. Or, if not true in that rigour of expression, to this formula undoubtedly it is that the wise rule of life must approximate.

Among the powers in man which suffer by this too intense life of the *social* instinct, none suffers more than the power of dreaming. Let no man think this a trifle. The machinery for dreaming planted in the human brain was not planted for nothing. That faculty, in alliance with the mystery of darkness, is the one great tube through which man communicates with the shadowy. And the dreaming organ, in connexion with the heart, the eye, and the ear, compose the magnificent apparatus which forces the infinite into the chambers of a human brain, and throws dark reflections from eternities below all life upon the mirrors of the sleeping mind.

But if this faculty suffers from the decay of solitude, which is becoming a visionary idea in England, on the other hand, it is certain that some merely physical agencies can and so assist the faculty of dreaming almost preternaturally. Amongst these is intense exercise; to some extent at least, and for some persons: but beyond all others is opium, which indeed seems to possess a *specific* power in that direction; not merely for exalting the colours of dream-scenery, but for deepening its shadows; and, above all, for strengthening the sense of its fearful *realities*.

The *Opium Confessions* were written with some slight secondary purpose of exposing this specific power of opium upon the faculty of dreaming, but much more with the purpose of displaying the faculty itself; and the outline of the work travelled in this course. Supposing a reader acquainted with the true object of the Confessions as here stated, viz. the revelation of dreaming, to have put this question:—

"But how came you to dream more splendidly than others?"

The answer would have been:—"Because (*præmissis præmittendis*)[1] I took excessive quantities of opium."

Secondly, suppose him to say, "But how came you to take opium in this excess?"

The answer to *that* would be, "Because some early events in my life had left a weakness in one organ which required (or seemed to require) that stimulant."

Then, because the opium dreams could not always have been understood without a knowledge of these events, it became necessary to relate

---

[1]   "Having made the necessary assumptions."

them. Now, these two questions and answers exhibit the *law* of the work, *i.e.* the principle which determined its form, but precisely in the inverse or regressive order. The work itself opened with the narration of my early adventures. These, in the natural order of succession, led to the opium as a resource for healing their consequences; and the opium as naturally led to the dreams. But in the synthetic order of presenting the facts, what stood last in the succession of development, stood first in the order of my purposes.

At the close of this little work, the reader was instructed to believe—and *truly* instructed—that I had mastered the tyranny of opium. The fact is, that *twice* I mastered it, and by efforts even more prodigious, in the second of these cases, than in the first. But one error I committed in both. I did not connect with the abstinence from opium—so trying to the fortitude under *any* circumstances—that enormity of exercise which (as I have since learned) is the one sole resource for making it endurable. I overlooked, in those days, the one *sine quâ non*[1] for making the triumph permanent. Twice I sank—twice I rose again. A third time I sank; partly from the cause mentioned, (the oversight as to exercise,) partly from other causes, on which it avails not now to trouble the reader. I could moralize if I chose; and perhaps *he* will moralize whether I choose it or not. But, in the mean time, neither of us is acquainted properly with the circumstances of the case; I, from natural bias of judgment, not altogether acquainted; and he (with his permission) not at all.

During this third prostration before the dark idol, and after some years, new and monstrous phenomena began slowly to arise. For a time, these were neglected as accidents, or palliated by such remedies as I knew of. But when I could no longer conceal from myself that these dreadful symptoms were moving forward for ever, by a pace steadily, solemnly, and equably increasing, I endeavoured, with some feeling of panic, for a third time to retrace my steps. But I had not reversed my motions for many weeks, before I became profoundly aware that this was impossible. Or, in the imagery of my dreams, which translated everything into their own language, I saw through vast avenues of gloom those towering gates of ingress which hitherto had always seemed to stand open, now at last barred against my retreat, and hung with funeral crape.

As applicable to this tremendous situation, (the situation of one escaping by some refluent current from the maelstrom roaring for him

---

[1] "Absolute condition."

in the distance, who finds suddenly that this current is but an eddy, wheeling round upon the same maelstrom,) I have since remembered a striking incident in a modern novel. A lady abbess of a convent, herself suspected of Protestant leanings, and in that way already disarmed of all effectual power, finds one of her own nuns (whom she knows to be innocent) accused of an offense leading to the most terrific of punishments. The nun will be immured alive if she is found guilty; and there is no chance that she will not—for the evidence against her is strong—unless something were made known that cannot be made known; and the judges are hostile. All follows in the order of the reader's fears. The witnesses depose; the evidence is without effectual contradiction; the conviction is declared; the judgment is delivered; nothing remains but to see execution done. At this crisis the abbess, alarmed too late for effectual interposition, considers with herself that, according to the regular forms, there will be one single night open during which the prisoner cannot be withdrawn from her own separate jurisdiction. This one night, therefore, she will use, at any hazard to herself, for the salvation of her friend. At midnight, when all is hushed in the convent, the lady traverses the passages which lead to the cells of prisoners. She bears a master-key under her professional habit. As this will open every door in every corridor,—already, by anticipation, she feels the luxury of holding her emancipated friend within her arms. Suddenly she has reached the door; she descries a dusky object; she raises her lamp; and, ranged within the recess of the entrance, she beholds the funeral banner of the Holy Office,[1] and the black robes of its inexorable officials.

I apprehend that, in a situation such as this, supposing it a real one, the lady abbess would not start, would not show any marks externally of consternation or horror. The case was beyond *that*. The sentiment which attends the sudden revelation that *all is lost!* silently is gathered up into the heart; it is too deep for gestures or for words; and no part of it passes to the outside. Were the ruin conditional, or were it in any point doubtful, it would be natural to utter ejaculations, and to seek sympathy. But where the ruin is understood to be absolute, where sympathy cannot be consolation, and counsel cannot be hope, this is otherwise. The voice perishes; the gestures are frozen; and the spirit of man flies back upon its own centre. I, at least, upon seeing those awful gates closed and hung with draperies of woe, as for a death already past,

---

[1]   Roman Inquisition, body of Roman Catholic ecclesiastics established in 1542 to root out Protestant heretics.

spoke not, nor started, nor groaned. One profound sigh ascended from my heart, and I was silent for days.

It is the record of this third, or final stage of opium, as one differing in something more than degree from the others, that I am now undertaking. But a scruple arises as to the true interpretation of these final symptoms. I have elsewhere explained, that it was no particular purpose of mine, and *why* it was no particular purpose, to warn other opium-eaters. Still, as some few persons may use the record in that way, it becomes a matter of interest to ascertain how far it is likely, that, even with the same excesses, other opium-eaters could fall into the same condition. I do not mean to lay a stress upon any supposed idiosyncrasy in myself. Possibly every man has an idiosyncrasy. In some things, undoubtedly, he has. For no man ever yet resembled another man so far, as not to differ from him in features innumerable of his inner nature. But what I point to are not peculiarities of temperament or of organization, so much as peculiar circumstances and incidents through which my own separate experience had revolved. Some of these were of a nature to alter the whole economy of my mind. Great convulsions, from whatever cause, from conscience, from fear, from grief, from struggles of the will, sometimes, in passing away themselves, do not carry off the changes which they have worked. *All* the agitations of this magnitude which a man may have threaded in his life, he neither ought to report, nor *could* report. But one which affected my childhood is a privileged exception. It is privileged as a proper communication for a stranger's ear; because, though relating to a man's proper self, it is a self so far removed from his present self as to wound no feelings of delicacy or just reserve. It is privileged also as a proper subject for the sympathy of the narrator. An adult sympathizes with himself in childhood because he *is* the same, and because (being the same) yet he is *not* the same. He acknowledges the deep, mysterious identity between himself, as adult and as infant, for the ground of his sympathy; and yet, with this general agreement, and necessity of agreement, he feels the differences between his two selves as the main quickeners of his sympathy. He pities the infirmities, as they arise to light in his young forerunner, which now perhaps he does not share; he looks indulgently upon errors of the understanding, or limitations of view which now he has long survived; and sometimes, also, he honours in the infant that rectitude of will which, under *some* temptations, he may since have felt it so difficult to maintain.

The particular case to which I refer in my own childhood, was one of intolerable grief; a trial, in fact, more severe than many people at *any* age are called upon to stand. The relation in which the case stands to my latter opium experiences, is this:—Those vast clouds of gloomy grandeur which overhung my dreams at all stages of opium, but which grew into the darkest of miseries in the last, and that haunting of the human face, which latterly towered into a curse—were they not partly derived from this childish experience? It is certain that, from the essential solitude in which my childhood was passed; from the depth of my sensibility; from the exaltation of this by the resistance of an intellect too prematurely developed, it resulted that the terrific grief which I passed through, drove a shaft for me into the worlds of death and darkness which never again closed, and through which it might be said that I ascended and descended at will, according to the temper of my spirits. Some of the phenomena developed in my dream-scenery, undoubtedly, do but repeat the experiences of childhood; and others seem likely to have been growths and fructifications from seeds at that time sown.

The reasons, therefore, for prefixing some account of a "passage" in childhood, to this record of a dreadful visitation from opium excess, are—1st, That, in colouring, it harmonizes with that record, and, therefore, is related to it at least in point of feeling; 2dly, That possibly it was in part the origin of some features in that record, and so far is related to it in logic; 3dly, That, the final assault of opium being of a nature to challenge the attention of medical men, it is important to clear away all doubts and scruples which can gather about the roots of such a malady. Was it opium, or was it opium in combination with something else, that raised these storms?

Some cynical reader will object—that for this last purpose it would have been sufficient to state the fact, without rehearsing *in extenso*[1] the particulars of that case in childhood. But the reader of more kindness (for a surly reader is always a bad critic) will also have more discernment; and he will perceive that it is not for the mere facts that the case is reported, but because these facts move through a wilderness of natural thoughts or feelings; some in the child who suffers; some in the man who reports; but all so far interesting as they relate to solemn objects. Meantime, the objection of the sullen critic reminds me of a scene sometimes beheld at the English lakes. Figure to yourself an energetic tourist, who protests every where that he comes only to see the lakes. He has no business whatever; he is not searching for any recreant indorser of a bill, but simply in search of the picturesque. Yet this man

---

[1]   "At full length."

adjures every landlord, "by the virtue of his oath," to tell him, and as he hopes for peace in this world to tell him truly, which is the *nearest* road to Keswick. Next, he applies to the postilions[1]—the Westmoreland postilions always fly down hills at full stretch without locking—but nevertheless, in the full career of their fiery race, our picturesque man lets down the glasses, pulls up four horses and two postilions, at the risk of six necks and twenty legs, adjuring them to reveal whether they are taking the *shortest* road. Finally, he descries my unworthy self upon the road; and, instantly stopping his flying equipage, he demands of me (as one whom he believes to be a scholar and a man of honour) whether there is not, in the possibility of things, a *shorter* cut to Keswick. Now, the answer which rises to the lips of landlord, two postilions, and myself, is this—"Most excellent stranger, as you come to the lakes simply to see their loveliness, might it not be as well to ask after the most beautiful road, rather than the shortest? Because, if abstract shortness, if τò brevity[2] is your object, then the shortest of all possible tours would seem, with submission—never to have left London." On the same principle, I tell my critic that the whole course of this narrative resembles, and was meant to resemble, a *caduceus*[3] wreathed about with meandering ornaments, or the shaft of a tree's stem hung round and surmounted with some vagrant parasitical plant. The mere medical subject of the opium answers to the dry withered pole, which shoots all the rings of the flowering plants, and seems to do so by some dexterity of its own; whereas, in fact, the plant and its tendrils have curled round the sullen cylinder by mere luxuriance of *theirs*. Just as in Cheapside, if you look right and left, the streets so narrow, that lead off at right angles, seem quarried and blasted out of some Babylonian brick kiln; bored, not raised artificially by the builder's hand. But, if you enquire of the worthy men who live in that neighbourhood, you will find it unanimously deposed—that not the streets were quarried out of the bricks, but, on the contrary, (most ridiculous as it seems,) that the bricks have supervened upon the streets.

The streets did not intrude amongst the bricks, but those cursed bricks came to imprison the streets. So, also, the ugly pole—hop pole, vine pole, espalier, no matter what—is there only for support. Not the flowers are for the pole, but the pole is for the flowers. Upon the same

---

[1]   Person who rides the left horse of a pair of horses pulling a carriage.
[2]   Brevity itself.
[3]   Winged rod carried by Mercury, messenger of the gods, entwined with serpents; also symbol of the medical profession.

analogy view me, as one (in the words of a true and most impassioned poet⋆) *"viridantem floribus hastas"*—making verdant, and gay with the life of flowers, murderous spears and halberts[1]—things that express death in their origin, (being made from dead substances that had once been made in forests,) things that express ruin in their use. The true object in my "Opium Confessions" is not the naked physiological theme—on the contrary, *that* is the ugly pole, the murderous spear, the halbert—but those wandering musical variations upon the theme— those parasitical thoughts, feelings, digressions, which climb up with bells and blossoms round about the arid stock; ramble away from it at times with perhaps too rank a luxuriance; but at the same time, by the eternal interest attached to the *subjects* of these digressions, no matter what were the execution, spread a glory over incidents that for themselves would be—less than nothing.

⋆ Valerius Flaccus. [Late first-century CE Roman poet; author of epic poem *Argonautica*, on the quest for the Golden Fleece; quotation from VI, 134–36.]

---

[1] Shafted weapons with cutting blade and spike.

SUSPIRIA DE PROFUNDIS. PART I.
THE AFFLICTION OF CHILDHOOD.

It is so painful to a lover of openhearted sincerity, that any indirect traits of vanity should even *seem* to creep into records of profound passion; and yet, on the other hand, it is so impossible, without an unnatural restraint upon the freedom of the narrative, to prevent oblique gleams reaching the reader from such circumstances of luxury or elegance as did really surround my childhood, that on all accounts I think it better to tell him from the first, with the simplicity of truth, in what order of society my family moved at the time from which this preliminary narrative is dated. Otherwise it would happen that, merely by moving truly and faithfully through the circumstances of this early experience, I could hardly prevent the reader from receiving an impression as of some higher rank than did really belong to my family. My father was a merchant; not in the sense of Scotland, where it means a man who sells groceries in a cellar, but in the English sense, a sense severely exclusive—viz. he was a man engaged in *foreign* commerce, and no other; therefore, in *wholesale* commerce, and no other,—which last circumstance it is important to mention, because it brings him within the benefit of Cicero's condescending distinction*—as one to be despised, certainly, but not too intensely to be despised even by a Roman senator. He, this imperfectly despicable man, died at an early age, and very soon after the incidents here recorded, leaving to his family, then consisting of a wife and six children, an unburthened estate producing exactly £1600 a year. Naturally, therefore, at the date of my narrative, if narrative it can be called, he had an income still larger, from the addition of current commercial profits. Now, to any man who is acquainted with commercial life, but above all, with such a life in England, it will readily occur that in an opulent English family of that class—opulent, though not rich in a mercantile estimate—the domestic economy is likely to be upon a scale of liberality altogether unknown amongst the corresponding orders in foreign nations. Whether as to the establishment of servants, or as to the provision made for the comfort of all its members, such a household not uncommonly eclipses the scale of living

---

* Cicero, in a well-known passage of his *Ethics*, speaks of trade as irredeemably base, if petty; but as not so absolutely felonious if wholesale. He gives a *real* merchant (one who is such in the English sense) leave to think himself a shade above small-beer. [Marcus Tullus Cicero (143–106 BCE), or "Tully": Roman statesman, orator, and writer; "small-beer": weak beer; British slang for things of very minor significance.]

even amongst the poorer classes of our nobility, though the most splendid in Europe—a fact which, since the period of my infancy, I have had many personal opportunities for verifying both in England and in Ireland. From this peculiar anomaly affecting the domestic economy of merchants, there arises a disturbance upon the general scale of outward signs by which we measure the relations of rank. The equation, so to speak, between one order of society and another, which usually travels in the natural line of their comparative expenditure, is here interrupted and defeated, so that one rank would be collected from the name of the occupation, and another rank, much higher, from the splendour of the domestic *ménage*.[1] I warn the reader, therefore, (or rather, my explanation has already warned him,) that he is not to infer from any casual gleam of luxury or elegance a corresponding elevation of rank.

We, the children of the house, stood in fact upon the very happiest tier in the scaffolding of society for all good influences. The prayer of Agar—"Give me neither poverty nor riches"[2] was realized for us. That blessing had we, being neither too high nor too low; high enough we were to see models of good manners; obscure enough to be left in the sweetest of solitudes. Amply furnished with the nobler benefits of wealth, *extra* means of health, of intellectual culture, and of elegant enjoyment, on the other hand, we knew nothing of its social distinctions. Not depressed by the consciousness of privations too sordid, not tempted into restlessness by the consciousness of privileges too aspiring, we had no motives for shame, we had none for pride. Grateful also to this hour I am, that, amidst luxuries in all things else, we were trained to a Spartan simplicity of diet—that we fared, in fact, very much less sumptuously than the servants. And if (after the model of the emperor Marcus Aurelius)[3] I should return thanks to Providence for all the separate blessings of my early situation, these four I would single out as chiefly worthy to be commemorated—that I lived in the country; that I lived in solitude; that my infant feelings were moulded by the gentlest of sisters, not by horrid pugilistic brothers; finally, that I and they were dutiful children of a pure, holy, and magnificent church.

---

[1] Household.

[2] Agur, in Proverbs: "Two things I ask of you—do not withhold them in my lifetime: put fraud and lying far from me; give me neither poverty nor wealth, but provide me with the food I need, for if I have too much I shall deny you and say, 'Who is the LORD?' and if I am reduced to poverty I shall steal and besmirch the name of my God" (30:7–9).

[3] Marcus Aurelius (121–180 CE), author of *Meditations*; Book I lists what Aurelius learned from significant figures in his early life.

The earliest incidents in my life which affected me so deeply as to be rememberable at this day, were two, and both before I could have completed my second year, viz. a remarkable dream of terrific grandeur about a favourite nurse, which is interesting for a reason to be noticed hereafter; and secondly, the fact of having connected a profound sense of pathos with the re-appearance, very early in spring, of some crocuses. This I mention as inexplicable, for such annual resurrections of plants and flowers affect us only as memorials, or suggestions of a higher change, and therefore in connexion with the idea of death; but of death I could, at that time, have had no experience whatever.

This, however, I was speedily to acquire. My two eldest sisters—eldest of three *then* living, and also elder than myself—were summoned to an early death. The first who died was Jane[1]—about a year older than myself. She was three and a half, I two and a half, *plus* or *minus* some trifle that I do not recollect. But death was then scarcely intelligible to me, and I could not so properly be said to suffer sorrow as a sad perplexity. There was another death in the house about the same time, viz. of a maternal grandmother; but as she had in a manner come to us for the express purpose of dying in her daughter's society, and from illness had lived perfectly secluded, our nursery party knew her but little, and were certainly more affected by the death (which I witnessed) of a favourite bird, viz. a kingfisher who had been injured by an accident. With my sister Jane's death (though otherwise, as I have said, less sorrowful than unintelligible) there was, however, connected an incident which made a most fearful impression upon myself, deepening my tendencies to thoughtfulness and abstraction beyond what would seem credible for my years. If there was one thing in this world from which, more than any other, nature had forced me to revolt, it was brutality and violence. Now a whisper arose in the family, that a woman-servant, who by acci-dent was drawn off from her proper duties to attend my sister Jane for a day or two, had on one occasion treated her harshly, if not brutally; and as this ill treatment happened within two days of her death—so that the occasion of it must have been some fretfulness in the poor child caused by her sufferings—naturally there was a sense of awe diffused through the family. I believe the story never reached my mother, and possibly it was exaggerated; but upon me the effect was terrific. I did not often see

[1] Jane, aged 3, died in 1790; De Quincey's sister Elizabeth, aged 9, died in 1792.

the person charged with this cruelty; but, when I did, my eyes sought the ground; nor could I have borne to look her in the face—not through anger; and as to vindictive thoughts, how could these lodge in a power-less infant? The feeling which fell upon me was a shuddering awe, as upon a first glimpse of the truth that I was in a world of evil and strife. Though born in a large town, I had passed the whole of my childhood, except for the few earliest weeks, in a rural seclusion. With three inno-cent little sisters for playmates, sleeping always amongst them, and shut up for ever in a silent garden from all knowledge of poverty, or oppres-sion, or outrage, I had not suspected until this moment the true complexion of the world in which myself and my sisters were living. Henceforward the character of my thoughts must have changed greatly; for so *representative* are some acts, that one single case of the class is suffi-cient to throw open before you the whole theatre of possibilities in that direction. I never heard that the woman, accused of this cruelty, took it at all to heart, even after the event, which so immediately succeeded, had reflected upon it a more painful emphasis. On the other hand, I knew of a case, and will pause to mention it, where a mere semblance and shadow of such cruelty, under similar circumstances, inflicted the grief of self-reproach through the remainder of life. A boy, interesting in his appearance, as also from his remarkable docility, was attacked, on a cold day of spring, by a complaint of the trachea—not precisely croup, but like it. He was three years old, and had been ill perhaps for four days; but at intervals had been in high spirits, and capable of playing. This sunshine, gleaming through dark clouds, had continued even on the fourth day; and from nine to eleven o'clock at night, he had showed more animated pleasure than ever. An old servant, hearing of his illness, had called to see him; and her mode of talking with him had excited all the joyousness of his nature. About midnight his mother, fancying that his feet felt cold, was muffling them up in flannels; and, as he seemed to resist her a little, she struck lightly on the sole of one foot as a mode of admonishing him to be quiet. He did not repeat his motion; and in less than a minute his mother had him in her arms with his face looking upwards. "What is the meaning," she exclaimed, in sudden affright, "of this strange repose settling upon his features?" She called loudly to a servant in another room; but before the servant could reach her, the child had drawn two inspirations—deep, yet gentle—and had died in his mother's arms. Upon this the poor afflicted lady made the discovery that those struggles, which she had supposed to be expressions of resistance to herself, were the struggles of departing life. It followed, or seemed to follow, that with these final struggles had blended an expression, on *her* part, of displeasure. Doubtless the child had not distinctly perceived it; but the mother could never look back to the incident without self-reproach. And seven years after, when her own death happened, no progress had been made in reconciling her thoughts to that which only the depth of love could have viewed as any offence.

So passed away from earth one out of those sisters that made up my nursery playmates; and so did my acquaintance (if such it could be called) commence with mortality. Yet, in fact, I knew little more of mortality than that Jane had disappeared. She had gone away; but, perhaps, she would come back. Happy interval of heaven-born ignorance! Gracious immunity of infancy from sorrow disproportioned to its strength! I was sad for Jane's absence. But still in my heart I trusted that she would come again. Summer and winter came again—crocuses and roses; why not little Jane?

Thus easily was healed, then, the first wound in my infant heart. Not so the second. For thou, dear, noble Elizabeth, around whose ample brow, as often as thy sweet countenance rises upon the darkness, I fancy a tiara of light, or a gleaming *aureola*[1] in token of thy premature intellectual grandeur—thou whose head, for its superb developments, was the astonishment of science*—thou next, but after an interval of happy years, thou also wert summoned away from our nursery; and the night

---

* *"The astonishment of science."*—Her medical attendants were Dr Percival, a well-known literary physician, who had been a correspondent of Condorcet, D'Alembert, &c., and Mr Charles White, a very distinguished surgeon. It was he who pronounced her head to be the finest in its structure and development of any that he had ever seen—an assertion which, to my own knowledge, he repeated in after years, and with enthusiasm. That he had some acquaintance with the subject may be presumed from this, that he wrote and published a work on the human skull, supported by many measurements which he had made of heads selected from all varieties of the human species. Meantime, as I would be loth that any trait of what might seem vanity should creep into this record, I will candidly admit that she died of hydrocephalus [accumulation of cerebro-spinal fluid in the brain]; and it has been often supposed that the premature expansion of the intellect in cases of that class, is altogether morbid—forced on, in fact, by the mere stimulation of the disease. I would, however, suggest, as a possibility, the very inverse order of relation between the disease and the intellectual manifestations. Not the disease may always have caused the preternatural growth of the intellect, but, on the contrary, this growth coming on spontaneously, and outrunning the capacities of the physical structure, may have caused the disease. [Thomas Percival (1740–1804) and Charles White (1728–1813), Manchester physicians; Marie Jean Condorcet (1743–94) and Jean D'Alembert (1717–83), French Enlightenment philosophers and mathematicians.]

---

[1]   "Halo."

which, for me, gathered upon that event, ran after my steps far into life; and perhaps at this day I resemble little for good or for ill that which else I should have been. Pillar of fire, that didst go before me to guide and to quicken—pillar of darkness,[1] when thy countenance was turned away to God, that didst too truly shed the shadow of death over my young heart—in what scales should I weigh thee? Was the blessing greater from thy heavenly presence, or the blight which followed thy departure? Can a man weigh off and value the glories of dawn against the darkness of hurricane? Or, if he could, how is it that, when a memorable love has been followed by a memorable bereavement, even suppose that God would replace the sufferer in a point of time anterior to the entire experience, and offer to cancel the woe, but so that the sweet face which had caused the woe should also be obliterated—vehemently would every man shrink from the exchange! In the *Paradise Lost*, this strong instinct of man—to prefer the heavenly, mixed and polluted with the earthly, to a level experience offering neither one nor the other—is divinely commemorated. What worlds of pathos are in that speech of Adam's—"If God should make another Eve,"[2] &c.—that is, if God should replace him in his primitive state, and should condescend to bring again a second Eve, one that would listen to no temptation—still that original partner of his earliest solitude—

> "Creature in whom excell'd
> Whatever can to sight or thought be form'd,
> Holy, divine, good, amiable, or sweet"—[3]

even now, when she appeared in league with an eternity of woe, and ministering to his ruin, could not be displaced for him by any better or happier Eve. "Loss of thee!" he exclaims in this anguish of trial—

> "Loss of thee
> Would never from my heart; no, no, I feel
> The link of nature draw me; flesh of flesh,

---

[1] As the Israelites left Egypt, "all the time the LORD went before them, by day a pillar of cloud to guide them on their journey, by night a pillar of fire to give them light; so they could travel both by day and by night" (Exodus 13:21).

[2] Paraphrase of *Paradise Lost* (9.911); by claiming his devotion to Eve, Adam implicitly displaces his bond with God: "Should God create another *Eve*, and I / Another Rib afford, yet loss of thee / Would never from my heart" (9.911–13).

[3] *Paradise Lost* (9.897–99).

Bone of my bone thou art; and from thy state
Mine never shall be parted, bliss or woe."[1]★

But what was it that drew my heart, by gravitation so strong, to my sister? Could a child, little above six years of age, place any special value upon her intellectual forwardness? Serene and capacious as her mind appeared to me upon after review, was *that* a charm for stealing away the heart of an infant? Oh, no! I think of it *now* with interest, because it lends, in a stranger's ear, some justification to the excess of my fondness. But then it was lost upon me; or, if not lost, was but dimly perceived. Hadst thou been an idiot, my sister, not the less I must have loved thee—having that capacious heart overflowing, even as mine overflowed, with tenderness, and stung, even as mine was stung, by the necessity of being loved. This it was which crowned thee with beauty—

"Love, the holy· sense,
Best gift of God, in thee was most intense."[2]

That lamp lighted in Paradise was kindled for me which shone so steadily in thee; and never but to thee only, never again since thy departure, *durst* I utter the feelings which possessed me. For I was the shiest of children; and a natural sense of personal dignity held me back at all stages of life, from exposing the least ray of feelings which I was not encouraged *wholly* to reveal.

It would be painful, and it is needless, to pursue the course of that

---

★ Amongst the oversights in the *Paradise Lost*, some of which have not yet been perceived, it is certainly *one*—that, by placing in such overpowering light of pathos the sublime sacrifice of Adam to his love for his frail companion, he has too much lowered the guilt of his disobedience to God. All that Milton can say afterwards, does not, and cannot, obscure the beauty of that action: reviewing it calmly, we condemn—but taking the impassioned station of Adam at the moment of temptation, we approve in our hearts. This was certainly an oversight; but it was one very difficult to redress. I remember, amongst the many exquisite thoughts of John Paul, (Richter,) one which strikes me as peculiarly touching upon this subject. He suggests—not as any grave theological comment, but as the wandering fancy of a poetic heart—that, had Adam conquered the anguish of separation as a pure sacrifice of obedience to God, his reward would have been the pardon and reconciliation of Eve, together with her restoration to innocence. [Johann Paul Friedrich Richter (1763–1825), or "Jean Paul," German critic and novelist.]

[1]   *Paradise Lost* 9.912–16.
[2]   Wordsworth, "Tribute to the memory of a favourite dog"; the original reads, "For love, that comes wherever life and sense / Are given by God, in thee was most intense" (27–28).

sickness which carried off my leader and companion. She (according to my recollection at this moment) was just as much above eight years as I above six. And perhaps this natural precedency in authority of judgment, and the tender humility with which she declined to assert it, had been amongst the fascinations of her presence. It was upon a Sunday evening, or so people fancied, that the spark of fatal fire fell upon that train of predispositions to a brain-complaint which had hitherto slumbered within her. She had been permitted to drink tea at the house of a labouring man, the father of an old female servant. The sun had set when she returned in the company of this servant through meadows reeking with exhalations after a fervent day. From that time she sickened. Happily a child in such circumstances feels no anxieties. Looking upon medical men as people whose natural commission it is to heal diseases, since it is their natural function to profess it, knowing them only as *ex-officio*[1] privileged to make war upon pain and sickness—I never had a misgiving about the result. I grieved indeed that my sister should lie in bed: I grieved still more sometimes to hear her moan. But all this appeared to me no more than a night of trouble on which the dawn would soon arise. Oh! moment of darkness and delirium, when a nurse awakened me from that delusion, and launched God's thunderbolt at my heart in the assurance that my sister *must* die. Rightly it is said of utter, utter misery, that it "cannot be *remembered*."[*] Itself, as a remembrable thing, is swallowed up in its own chaos. Mere anarchy and confusion of mind fell upon me. Deaf and blind I was, as I reeled under the revelation. I wish not to recal the circumstances of that time, when *my* agony was at its height, and hers in another sense was approaching. Enough to say—that all was soon over; and the morning of that day had at last arrived which looked down upon her innocent face, sleeping the sleep from which there is no awaking, and upon me sorrowing the sorrow for which there is no consolation.

On the day after my sister's death, whilst the sweet temple of her brain was yet unviolated by human scrutiny, I formed my own scheme for seeing her once more. Not for the world would I have made this known, nor have suffered a witness to accompany me. I had never heard of feelings

---

[*] "I stood in unimaginable trance
And agony, which cannot be remember'd."
     —*Speech of Alhadra in Coleridge's* Remorse.

[Coleridge, *Remorse* (1813), 4.3.76–7; Alhadra expresses the trauma of hearing her husband Isidore's final "death-groan."]

---

[1] "By virtue of [their] office."

that take the name of "sentimental," nor dreamed of such a possibility. But grief even in a child hates the light, and shrinks from human eyes. The house was large; there were two staircases; and by one of these I knew that about noon, when all would be quiet, I could steal up into her chamber. I imagine that it was exactly high noon when I reached the chamber door; it was locked; but the key was not taken away. Entering, I closed the door so softly, that, although it opened upon a hall which ascended through all the stories, no echo ran along the silent walls. Then turning round, I sought my sister's face. But the bed had been moved; and the back was now turned. Nothing met my eyes but one large window wide open, through which the sun of midsummer at noonday was showering down torrents of splendour. The weather was dry, the sky was cloudless, the blue depths seemed the express types of infinity; and it was not possible for eye to behold or for heart to conceive any symbols more pathetic of life and the glory of life.

Let me pause for one instant in approaching a remembrance so affecting and revolutionary for my own mind, and one which (if any earthly remembrance) will survive for me in the hour of death,—to remind some readers, and to inform others, that in the original *Opium Confessions* I endeavoured to explain the reason★ why death, *cæteris paribus*,[1] is more profoundly affecting in summer than in other parts of the year; so far at least as it is liable to any modification at all from accidents of scenery or season. The reason, as I there suggested, lies in the antagonism between the tropical redundancy of life in summer and the dark sterilities of the grave. The summer we see, the grave we haunt with our thoughts; the glory is around us, the darkness is within us. And, the two coming into collision, each exalts the other into stronger relief. But in my case there was even a subtler reason why the summer had this intense power of vivifying the spectacle or the thoughts of death. And, recollecting it, often I have been struck with the important truth—that far more of our deepest thoughts and feelings pass to us through perplexed combinations of *concrete* objects, pass to us as *involutes* (if I may coin that word) in compound experiences incapable of being disentangled, than ever reach us *directly*, and in their own abstract shapes. It had happened that amongst our nursery collection of books was the Bible illustrated with many pictures. And in long dark evenings, as my three sisters with myself sate by the firelight

★ Some readers will question the *fact*, and seek no reason. But did they ever suffer grief at *any* season of the year?

[1] "All things being equal."

round the *guard*[1] of our nursery, no book was so much in request amongst us. It ruled us and swayed us as mysteriously as music. One young nurse, whom we all loved, before any candle was lighted, would often strain her eyes to read it for us; and sometimes, according to her simple powers, would endeavour to explain what we found obscure. We, the children, were all constitutionally touched with pensiveness: the fitful gloom and sudden lambencies of the room by firelight, suited our evening state of feelings; and they suited also the divine revelations of power and mysterious beauty which awed us. Above all, the story of a just man,—man and yet *not* man, real above all things and yet shadowy above all things, who had suffered the passion of death in Palestine, slept upon our minds like early dawn upon the waters. The nurse knew and explained to us the chief differences in Oriental climates; and all these differences (as it happens) express themselves in the great varieties of summer. The cloudless sunlights of Syria—those seemed to argue everlasting summer; the disciples plucking the ears of corn—that *must* be summer; but, above all, the very name of Palm Sunday,[2] (a festival in the English church,) troubled me like an anthem. "Sunday!" what was *that*? That was the day of peace which masqued another peace deeper than the heart of man can comprehend. "Palms!"—what were they? *That* was an equivocal word: palms, in the sense of trophies, expressed the pomps of life: palms, as a product of nature, expressed the pomps of summer. Yet still even this explanation does not suffice: it was not merely by the peace and by the summer, by the deep sound of rest below all rest, and of ascending glory,—that I had been haunted. It was also because Jerusalem stood near to those deep images both in time and in place. The great event of Jerusalem was at hand when Palm Sunday came; and the scene of that Sunday was near in place to Jerusalem. Yet what then was Jerusalem? Did I fancy it to be the *omphalos* (navel) of the earth? That pretension had once been made for Jerusalem, and once for Delphi;[3] and both pretensions had become ridiculous, as the figure of the planet became known. Yes; but if not of the earth, for earth's tenant Jerusalem was the *omphalos* of mortality. Yet how? there on the contrary it was, as we infants understood, that mortality had been trampled under foot. True; but for that very reason there it was that mortality had opened its very gloomiest crater. There it was indeed that the human had risen on wings from the grave; but for that reason there also it was

---

[1]   Fireguard.
[2]   Sunday before Easter, celebrating Christ's entry into Jerusalem.
[3]   Site of the ancient Greek oracle of Apollo.

that the divine had been swallowed up by the abyss: the lesser star could not rise, before the greater would submit to eclipse. Summer, therefore, had connected itself with death not merely as a mode of antagonism, but also through intricate relations to Scriptural scenery and events.

Out of this digression, which was almost necessary for the purpose of showing how inextricably my feelings and images of death were entangled with those of summer, I return to the bedchamber of my sister. From the gorgeous sunlight I turned round to the corpse. There lay the sweet childish figure, there the angel face: and, as people usually fancy, it was said in the house that no features had suffered any change. Had they not? The forehead indeed, the serene and noble forehead, *that* might be the same; but the frozen eyelids, the darkness that seemed to steal from beneath them, the marble lips, the stiffening hands, laid palm to palm, as if repeating the supplications of closing anguish, could these be mistaken for life? Had it been so, wherefore did I not spring to those heavenly lips with tears and never-ending kisses? But so it was *not*. I stood checked for a moment; awe, not fear, fell upon me; and, whilst I stood, a solemn wind began to blow—the most mournful that ear ever heard. Mournful! that is saying nothing. It was a wind that had swept the fields of mortality for a hundred centuries. Many times since, upon a summer day, when the sun is about the hottest, I have remarked the same wind arising and uttering the same hollow, solemn, Memnonian,[1] but saintly swell: it is in this world the one sole *audible* symbol of eternity. And three times in my life I have happened to hear the same sound in the same circumstances, viz. when standing between an open window and a dead body on a summer day.

Instantly, when my ear caught this vast Æolian[2] intonation, when my eye filled with the golden fulness of life, the pomps and glory of the heavens outside, and turning when it settled upon the frost which overspread my sister's face, instantly a trance fell upon me. A vault seemed to open in the zenith of the far blue sky, a shaft which ran up for ever. I in spirit rose as if on billows that also ran up the shaft for ever; and the billows seemed to pursue the throne of God; but *that* also ran before us and fled away continually. The flight and the pursuit seemed to go on for ever and ever. Frost, gathering frost, some Sarsar[3] wind of death, seemed to repel me; I slept—for how long I cannot say; slowly I recovered my self-possession, and found myself standing, as before, close to my sister's bed.

---

[1] When the morning sun shone on the colossus of Memnon, near ancient Thebes, the statue produced musical sounds.
[2] After Aeolus, Greek god of the winds.
[3] From the Arabic "çarçar," a cold wind.

Oh★ flight of the solitary child to the solitary God—flight from the ruined corpse to the throne that could not be ruined!—how rich wert thou in truth for after years. Rapture of grief, that, being too mighty for a child to sustain, foundest a happy oblivion in a heaven-born sleep, and within that sleep didst conceal a dream, whose meanings in after years, when slowly I deciphered, suddenly there flashed upon me new light; and even by the grief of a child, as I will show you reader hereafter, were confounded the falsehoods of philosophers.★★

In the *Opium Confessions* I touched a little upon the extraordinary power connected with opium (after long use) of amplifying the dimensions of time. Space also it amplifies by degrees that are sometimes terrific. But time it is upon which the exalting and multiplying power of opium chiefly spends its operation. Time becomes infinitely elastic, stretching out to such immeasurable and vanishing termini, that it seems ridiculous to compute the sense of it on waking by expressions commensurate to human life. As in starry fields one computes by diameters of the earth's orbit, or of Jupiter's, so in valuing the *virtual* time lived during some dreams, the measurement by generations is ridiculous—by millennia is ridiculous: by æons, I should say, if æons were more determinate, would be also ridiculous. On this single occasion, however, in my life, the very inverse phenomenon occurred. But why speak of it in connexion with opium? Could a child of six years old have been under that influence? No, but simply because it so exactly reversed the operation of opium. Instead of a short interval expanding into a vast one, upon this occasion a long one had contracted into a minute. I have reason to believe that a very long one had elapsed during this wandering or suspension of my perfect mind. When I returned to myself, there was a foot (or I fancied so) on the stairs. I was alarmed. For I believed that, if any body should detect me, means would be taken to prevent my coming again. Hastily, therefore, I kissed the lips that I should kiss no more, and slunk like a guilty thing[1] with stealthy steps

---

★   Φυγὴ μόνῳ πρὸς μόνον.—PLOTINUS. ["Flight of the alone to the alone"; last words of Plotinus, *Enneads* 6.9.11.]

★★   The thoughts referred to will be given in final notes; as at this point they seemed too much to interrupt the course of the narrative. [The final notes were never given.]

---

[1]   Horatio says the Ghost of Hamlet's father "started, like a guilty thing / Upon a fearful summons" (Shakespeare, *Hamlet* 1.1.148–49); and Wordsworth speaks of the "Blank misgivings of a Creature / Moving about in worlds not realised, / High instincts before which our mortal Nature / Did tremble like a guilty Thing surprised" ("Ode: Intimations of Immortality" 148–51).

from the room. Thus perished the vision, loveliest amongst all the shows which earth has revealed to me; thus mutilated was the parting which should have lasted for ever; thus tainted with fear was the farewell sacred to love and grief, to perfect love and perfect grief.

Oh, Ahasuerus, everlasting Jew!★ fable or not a fable, thou when first starting on thy endless pilgrimage of woe, thou when first flying through the gates of Jerusalem, and vainly yearning to leave the pursuing curse behind thee, couldst not more certainly have read thy doom of sorrow in the misgivings of thy troubled brain than I when passing for ever from my sister's room. The worm was at my heart: and, confining myself to that stage of life, I may say—the worm that could not die. For if, when standing upon the threshold of manhood, I had ceased to feel its perpetual gnawings, *that* was because a vast expansion of intellect, it was because new hopes, new necessities, and the frenzy of youthful blood, had translated me into a new creature. Man is doubtless *one* by some subtle *nexus* that we cannot perceive, extending from the newborn infant to the superannuated dotard: but as regards many affections and passions incident to his nature at different stages, he is *not* one; the unity of man in this respect is coextensive only with the particular stage to which the passion belongs. Some passions, as that of sexual love, are celestial by one half of their origin, animal and earthly by the other half. These will not survive their own appropriate stage. But love, which is *altogether* holy, like that between two children, will revisit undoubtedly by glimpses the silence and the darkness of old age: and I repeat my belief—that, unless bodily torment should forbid it, that final experience in my sister's bedroom, or some other in which her innocence was concerned, will rise again for me to illuminate the hour of death.

On the day following this which I have recorded, came a body of medical men to examine the brain, and the particular nature of the complaint, for in some of its symptoms it had shown perplexing anomalies. Such is the sanctity of death, and especially of death alighting on an innocent child, that even gossiping people do not gossip on such a subject. Consequently, I knew nothing of the purpose which drew together these surgeons, nor suspected any thing of the cruel changes which might have been wrought in my sister's head. Long after this I

★ "Everlasting Jew!"—*der ewige Jude*—which is the common German expression for *The Wandering Jew*, and sublimer even than our own. [Ahasuerus refused Christ rest on his way to the Crucifixion and was doomed to roam the earth until the Day of Judgement.]

saw a similar case; I surveyed the corpse (it was that of a beautiful boy, eighteen years old,[1] who had died of the same complaint) one hour *after* the surgeons had laid the skull in ruins; but the dishonours of this scrutiny were hidden by bandages, and had not disturbed the repose of the countenance. So it might have been here; but, if it were *not* so, then I was happy in being spared the shock, from having that marble image of peace, icy and rigid as it was, unsettled by disturbing images. Some hours after the strangers had withdrawn, I crept again to the room, but the door was now locked—the key was taken away—and I was shut out for ever.

Then came the funeral. I, as a point of decorum, was carried thither. I was put into a carriage with some gentlemen whom I did not know. They were kind to me; but naturally they talked of things disconnected with the occasion, and their conversation was a torment. At the church, I was told to hold a white handkerchief to my eyes. Empty hypocrisy! What need had *he* of masques or mockeries, whose heart died within him at every word that was uttered? During that part of the service which passed within the church, I made an effort to attend, but I sank back continually into my own solitary darkness, and I heard little consciously, except some fugitive strains from the sublime chapter of St Paul, which in England is always read at burials. And here I notice a profound error of our present illustrious Laureate.[2] When I heard those dreadful words—for dreadful they were to me—"It is sown in corruption, it is raised in incorruption; it is sown in dishonour, it is raised in glory;"[3] such was the recoil of my feelings, that I could even have shrieked out a protesting—"Oh, no, no!" if I had not been restrained by the publicity of the occasion. In after years, reflecting upon this revolt of my feelings, which, being the voice of nature in a child, must be as true as any mere *opinion* of a child might probably be false, I saw at once the unsoundness of a passage in *The Excursion*.[4] The book is not here, but the substance I remember perfectly. Mr Wordsworth argues, that if it were not for the unsteady faith which people fix upon the beatific condition after death of those whom they deplore, nobody could be

---

[1]   De Quincey's eldest son William died in 1834.

[2]   Wordsworth, Poet Laureate from 1842 to his death in 1849.

[3]   I Corinthians 15:42–43; in this paragraph De Quincey refers in general to Corinthians 15:20–58, basis for the funeral service; De Quincey later refers to verse 51: "Behold, I shew you a mystery; We shall not all sleep, but we shall all be changed."

[4]   "For who could sink and settle to that point / Of selfishness; so senseless who could be / As long and perseveringly to mourn / For any object of his love, removed / From this unstable world, if he could fix / A satisfying view upon that state / Of pure, imperishable, blessedness, / Which reason promises, and holy writ / Ensures to all believers?" (4.153–61).

found so selfish, as even secretly to wish for the restoration to earth of a beloved object. A mother, for instance, could never dream of yearning for her child, and secretly calling it back by her silent aspirations from the arms of God, if she were but reconciled to the belief that really it *was* in those arms. But this I utterly deny. To take my own case, when I heard those dreadful words of St Paul applied to my sister—viz. that she should be raised a spiritual body—nobody can suppose that self-ishness, or any other feeling than that of agonizing love, caused the rebellion of my heart against them. I knew already that she was to come again in beauty and power. I did not now learn this for the first time. And that thought, doubtless, made my sorrow sublimer; but also it made it deeper. For here lay the sting of it, viz. in the fatal words—"We shall be *changed*." How was the unity of my interest in her to be preserved, if she were to be altered, and no longer to reflect in her sweet countenance the traces that were sculptured on my heart? Let a magician ask any woman whether she will permit him to improve her child, to raise it even from deformity to perfect beauty, if that must be done at the cost of its identity, and there is no loving mother but would reject his proposal with horror. Or, to take a case that has actually happened, if a mother were robbed of her child at two years old by gypsies, and the same child were restored to her at twenty, a fine young man, but divided by a sleep as it were of death from all remembrances that could restore the broken links of their once-tender connexion, would she not feel her grief unhealed, and her heart defrauded? Undoubtedly she would. All of us ask not of God for a better thing than that we have lost; we ask for the same, even with its faults and its frailties. It is true that the sorrowing person will also be changed eventually, but that must be by death. And a prospect so remote as that, and so alien from our present nature, cannot console us in an affliction which is not remote but present—which is not spiritual but human.

Lastly came the magnificent service which the English church performs at the side of the grave. There is exposed once again, and for the last time, the coffin. All eyes survey the record of name, of sex, of age, and the day of departure from earth—records how useless! and dropped into darkness as if messages addressed to worms. Almost at the very last comes the symbolic ritual, tearing and shattering the heart with volleying discharges, peal after peal, from the final artillery of woe. The coffin is lowered into its home; it has disappeared from the eye. The sacristan stands ready with his shovel of earth and stones. The priest's voice is heard once more—*earth to earth*, and the dread rattle ascends from the lid of the coffin; *ashes to ashes*, and again the killing sound is heard; *dust to dust*,[1] and the farewell volley announces that the grave— the coffin—the face are sealed up for ever and ever.

Oh, grief! thou art classed amongst the depressing passions. And true it is, that thou humblest to the dust, but also thou exaltest to the clouds. Thou shakest as with ague, but also thou steadiest like frost. Thou sickenest the heart, but also thou healest its infirmities. Among the very foremost of mine was morbid sensibility to shame. And ten years afterwards, I used to reproach myself with this infirmity, by supposing the case, that, if it were thrown upon me to seek aid for a perishing fellow-creature, and that I could obtain that aid only by facing a vast company of critical or sneering faces, I might perhaps shrink basely from the duty. It is true, that no such case had ever actually occurred, so that it was a mere romance of casuistry to tax myself with cowardice so shocking. But to feel a doubt, was to feel condemnation; and the crime which *might* have been, was in my eyes the crime which *had* been. Now, however, all was changed; and for any thing which regarded my sister's memory, in one hour I received a new heart. Once in Westmoreland I saw a case resembling it. I saw a ewe suddenly put off and abjure her own nature, in a service of love—yes, slough it as completely, as ever serpent sloughed his skin. Her lamb had fallen into a deep trench, from which all escape was hopeless without the aid of man. And to a man she advanced boldly, bleating clamorously, until he followed her and rescued her beloved. Not less was the change in myself. Fifty thousand sneering faces would not have troubled me in any office of tenderness to my sister's memory. Ten legions would not have repelled me from seeking her, if there was a chance that she could be found. Mockery! it was lost upon me. Laugh at me, as one or two people did! I valued not their laughter. And when I was told insultingly to cease "my girlish tears," that word "*girlish*" had no sting for me, except as a verbal echo to the one eternal thought of my heart—that a girl was the sweetest thing I, in my short life, had known—that a girl it was who had crowned the earth with beauty, and had opened to my thirst fountains

---

[1] Part of the funeral service: "And Abraham answered [the Lord] and said, Behold now, I have taken upon me to speak unto the Lord, which *am but* dust and ashes" (Genesis 18:27); "He hath cast me into the mire, and I am become like dust and ashes" (Job 30:19).

of pure celestial love, from which, in this world, I was to drink no more.

Interesting it is to observe how certainly all deep feelings agree in this, that they seek for solitude, and are nursed by solitude. Deep grief, deep love, how naturally do these ally themselves with religious feeling; and all three, love, grief, religion, are haunters of solitary places. Love, grief, the passion of reverie, or the mystery of devotion—what were these without solitude? All day long, when it was not impossible for me to do so, I sought the most silent and sequestered nooks in the grounds about the house, or in the neighbouring fields. The awful stillness occasionally of summer noons, when no winds were abroad, the appealing silence of grey or misty afternoons—these were fascinations as of witchcraft. Into the woods or the desert air I gazed as if some comfort lay hid in *them*. I wearied the heavens with my inquest of beseeching looks. I tormented the blue depths with obstinate scrutiny, sweeping them with my eyes and searching them for ever after one angelic face that might perhaps have permission to reveal itself for a moment. The faculty of shaping images in the distance out of slight elements, and grouping them after the yearnings of the heart, aided by a slight defect in my eyes, grew upon me at this time. And I recall at the present moment one instance of that sort, which may show how merely shadows, or a gleam of brightness, or nothing at all, could furnish a sufficient basis for this creative faculty. On Sunday mornings I was always taken to church: it was a church on the old and natural model of England, having aisles, galleries, organ, all things ancient and venerable, and the proportions majestic. Here, whilst the congregation knelt through the long Litany, as often as we came to that passage, so beautiful amongst many that are so, where God is supplicated on behalf of "all sick persons and young children," and that he would "show his pity upon all prisoners and captives"—I wept in secret, and raising my streaming eyes to the windows of the galleries, saw, on days when the sun was shining, a spectacle as affecting as ever prophet can have beheld. The sides of the windows were rich with storied glass; through the deep purples and crimsons streamed the golden light; emblazonries of heavenly illumination mingling with the earthly emblazonries of what is grandest in man. There were the apostles that had trampled upon earth, and the glories of earth, out of celestial love to man. There were the martyrs that had borne witness to the truth through flames, through torments, and through armies of fierce insulting faces. There were the saints who, under intolerable pangs, had glorified God by meek submission to his will. And all the time, whilst this tumult of sublime memorials held on as the deep chords from an accompaniment in the bass, I saw through the wide central field of the window, where the glass was uncoloured, white fleecy clouds sailing over the azure depths of the sky; were it but a fragment or a hint of such a cloud, immediately under the flash of my sorrow-haunted eye, it grew and shaped itself into a vision of beds with white lawny curtains; and in the beds lay sick children, dying children, that were tossing in anguish, and weeping clamorously for death. God, for some mysterious reason, could not suddenly release them from their pain; but he suffered the beds, as it seemed, to rise slowly through the clouds; slowly the beds ascended into the chambers of the air; slowly, also, his arms descended from the heavens, that he and his young children whom in Judea, once and for ever, he had blessed, though they *must* pass slowly through the dreadful chasm of separation, might yet meet the sooner.[1] These visions were self-sustained. These visions needed not that any sound should speak to me, or music mould my feelings. The hint from the Litany, the fragment from the clouds, those and the storied windows were sufficient. But not the less the blare of the tumultuous organ wrought its own separate creations. And oftentimes in anthems, when the mighty instrument threw its vast columns of sound, fierce yet melodious, over the voices of the choir—when it rose high in arches, as might seem, surmounting and overriding the strife of the vocal parts, and gathering by strong coercion the total storm into unity—sometimes I seemed to walk triumphantly upon those clouds which so recently I had looked up to as mementos of prostrate sorrow, and even as ministers of sorrow in its creations; yes, sometimes under the transfigurations of music I felt* of grief itself as a fiery chariot for mounting victoriously above the causes of grief.

I point so often to the feelings, the ideas, or the ceremonies of religion, because there never yet was profound grief nor profound philos-

---

* "*I felt.*"—The reader must not forget, in reading this and other passages, that, though a child's feelings are spoken of, it is not the child who speaks. *I* decipher what the child only felt in cipher. And so far is this distinction or this explanation from pointing to any thing metaphysical or doubtful, that a man must be grossly unobservant who is not aware of what I am here noticing, not as a peculiarity of this child or that, but as a necessity of all children. Whatsoever in a man's mind blossoms and expands to his own consciousness in mature life, must have pre-existed in germ during his infancy. I, for instance, did not, as a child, *consciously* read in my own deep feelings these ideas. No, not at all; nor was it possible for a child to do so. I the child had the feelings, I the man decipher them. In the child lay the handwriting mysterious to *him*; in me the interpretation and the comment.

---

[1] "Verily I say unto you, Except ye be converted, and become as little children, ye shall not enter into the kingdom of heaven" (Matthew 18.3).

ophy which did not inosculate at many points with profound religion. But I request the reader to understand, that of all things I was not, and could not have been, a child trained to *talk* of religion, least of all to talk of it controversially or polemically. Dreadful is the picture, which in books we sometimes find, of children discussing the doctrines of Christianity, and even teaching their seniors the boundaries and distinctions between doctrine and doctrine. And it has often struck me with amazement, that the two things which God made most beautiful among his works, viz. infancy and pure religion, should, by the folly of man, (in yoking them together on erroneous principles,) neutralize each other's beauty, or even form a combination positively hateful. The religion becomes nonsense, and the child becomes a hypocrite. The religion is transfigured into cant, and the innocent child into a dissembling liar.★

God, be assured, takes care for the religion of children wheresoever his Christianity exists. Wheresoever there is a national church established, to which a child sees his friends resorting; wheresoever he beholds all whom he honours periodically prostrate before those illimitable heavens which fill to overflowing his young adoring heart; wheresoever he sees the sleep of death falling at intervals upon men and women whom he knows, depth as confounding to the plummet of his mind as those heavens ascend beyond his power to pursue—*there* take you no thought for the religion of a child, any more than for the lilies how they shall be arrayed, or for the ravens how they shall feed their young.[1]

God speaks to children also in dreams, and by the oracles that lurk in darkness. But in solitude, above all things, when made vocal by the truths and services of a national church, God holds "communion undisturbed" with children. Solitude, though silent as light, is, like light, the mightiest of agencies; for solitude is essential to man. All men come into this world

---

★   I except, however, one case—the case of a child dying of an organic disorder, so therefore as to die slowly, and aware of its own condition. Because such a child is solemnized, and sometimes, in a partial sense, inspired—inspired by the depths of its sufferings, and by the awfulness of its prospect. Such a child having put off the earthly mind in many things, may naturally have put off the childish mind in all things. I therefore, speaking for myself only, acknowledge to have read with emotion a record of a little girl, who, knowing herself for months to be amongst the elect of death, became anxious even to sickness of heart for what she called the *conversion* of her father. Her filial duty and reverence had been swallowed up in filial love.

---

[1]   In Luke Jesus says, "Consider the ravens: for they neither sow nor reap; which neither have storehouse nor barn; and God feedeth them: how much more are ye better than the fowls?"; "Consider the lilies how they grow: they toil not, nor spin not; and yet I say unto you, that Solomon in all his glory was not arrayed like one of these" (12.24, 27).

alone—all leave it *alone*. Even a little child has a dread, whispering consciousness, that if he should be summoned to travel into God's presence, no gentle nurse will be allowed to lead him by the hand, nor mother to carry him in her arms, nor little sister to share his trepidations. King and priest, warrior and maiden, philosopher and child, all must walk those mighty galleries alone. The solitude, therefore, which in this world appals or fascinates a child's heart, is but the echo of a far deeper solitude through which already he has passed, and of another solitude deeper still, through which he *has* to pass: reflex of one solitude—prefiguration of another.

Oh, burthen of solitude, that cleavest to man through every stage of his being—in his birth, which *has* been—in his life, which *is*—in his death, which *shall* be—mighty and essential solitude! that wast, and art, and art to be;—thou broodest, like the spirit of God moving upon the surface of the deeps, over every heart that sleeps in the nurseries of Christendom. Like the vast laboratory of the air, which, seeming to be nothing, or less than the shadow of a shade, hides within itself the principles of all things, solitude for a child is the Agrippa's mirror[1] of the unseen universe. Deep is the solitude in life of millions upon millions who, with hearts welling forth love, have none to love them. Deep is the solitude of those who, with secret griefs, have none to pity them. Deep is the solitude of those who, fighting with doubts or darkness, have none to counsel them. But deeper than the deepest of these solitudes is that which broods over childhood, bringing before it at intervals the final solitude which watches for it, and is waiting for it within the gates of death. Reader, I tell you a truth, and hereafter I will convince you of this truth, that for a Grecian child solitude was nothing, but for a Christian child it has become the power of God and the mystery of God. Oh, mighty and essential solitude, that wast, and art, and art to be—thou, kindling under the torch of Christians' revelations, art now transfigured for ever, and hast passed from a blank negation into a secret hieroglyphic from God, shadowing in the hearts of infancy the very dimmest of his truths!

---

[1] Cornelius Agrippa (1486–1535), *De Occulta philosophia* ["Of Occult Philosophy"]: "[the Air] receives into it self, as it were a divine Looking-glass, the species of all things, as well naturall, as artificiall, as also of all manner of speeches, and retains them; And carrying them with it, and entering into the bodies of Men, and other Animals, through their pores, makes an Impression upon them, as well when they sleep, as when they be awake, and affords matter for divers strange Dreams and Divinations" (1.6).

Part I.—(*Continued from last Number:*)

"*But you forgot her,*" says the Cynic; "*you happened one day to forget this sister of yours?*"—Why not? To cite the beautiful words of Wallenstein,

> "What pang
> Is permanent with man? From the highest
> As from the vilest thing of every day
> He learns to wean himself. For the strong hours
> Conquer him."*

Yes, *there* lies the fountain of human oblivions. It is TIME, the great conqueror, it is the "strong hours" whose batteries storm every passion of men. For, in the fine expression of Schiller, "*Was verschmerzte nicht der mensch?*"[1] What sorrow is it in man that will not finally fret itself to sleep? Conquering, as last, gates of brass, or pyramids of granite, why should it be a marvel to us, or a triumph to Time, that he is able to conquer a frail human heart?

However, for this once my Cynic must submit to be told—that he is wrong. Doubtless, it is presumption in me to suggest that his sneers can ever go awry, any more than the shafts of Apollo.[2] But still, however impossible such a thing is, in this one case it happens that they *have*. And when it happens that they do not, I will tell you, reader, why in my opinion it is; and you will see that it warrants no exultation in the Cynic. Repeatedly I have heard a mother reproaching herself, when the birthday revolved of the little daughter whom so suddenly she had lost, with her own insensibility that could so soon need a remembrancer of the day. But, besides, that the majority of people in this world (as being people called to labour) have no time left for cherishing grief by solitude and meditation, always it is proper to ask whether the memory of the lost person were chiefly dependent upon a visual image. No death

---

* *Death of Wallenstein*, Act v. Scene 1, (Coleridge's Translation,) relating to his remembrances of the younger Piccolomini. [Coleridge translated *Wallenstein* (1800) by Friedrich Schiller (1759–1805) as "The Piccolomini" and "The Death of Wallenstein," both in 1800; here Wallenstein is speaking to his sister-in-law Countess Tertsky about the death of Max Piccolomini.]

---

[1] From Schiller's original German, just before the above lines.
[2] Apollo, Greek and Roman god of music, poetry, prophecy, healing; wielded a bow and arrows.

is usually half so affecting as the death of a young child from two to five years old.

But yet for the same reason which makes the grief more exquisite, generally for such a loss it is likely to be more perishable. Wherever the image, visually or audibly, of the lost person is more essential to the life of the grief, there the grief will be more transitory.

Faces begin soon (in Shakspeare's fine expression) to "dislimn:"[1] features fluctuate: combinations of feature unsettle. Even the expression becomes a mere idea that you can describe to another, but not an image that you can reproduce for yourself. Therefore it is that the faces of infants, though they are divine as flowers in a savanna of Texas, or as the carolling of birds in a forest, are, like flowers in Texas, and the carolling of birds in a forest, soon overtaken by the pursuing darkness that swallows up all things human. All glories of flesh vanish; and this, the glory of infantine beauty seen in the mirror of the memory, soonest of all. But when the departed person worked upon yourself by powers that were intellectual and moral—powers *in* the flesh, though not *of* the flesh—the memorials in your own heart become more steadfast, if less affecting at the first. Now, in my sister were combined for me both graces—the graces of childhood, and the graces of expanding thought. Besides that, as regards merely the *personal* image, always the smooth rotundity of baby features must vanish sooner, as being less individual than the features in a child of eight, touched with a pensive tenderness, and exalted into a characteristic expression by a premature intellect.

Rarely do things perish from my memory that are worth remembering. Rubbish dies instantly. Hence it happens that passages in Latin or English poets which I never could have read but once, (and *that* thirty years ago,) often begin to blossom anew when I am lying awake, unable to sleep. I become a distinguished compositor in the darkness; and, with my aërial composing-stick,[2] sometimes I "set up" half a page of verses, that would be found tolerably correct if collated with the volume that I never had in my hand but once. I mention this in no spirit of boasting. Far from it; for, on the contrary, amongst my mortifications have been compliments to my memory, when, in fact, any compliment that I had merited was due to the higher faculty of an electric aptitude for

---

[1] Shakespeare, *Antony and Cleopatra*: "That which is now a horse, even with a thought / The rack [cloud] dislimns, and makes it indistinct, / As water is in water" (4.14.9–11).

[2] Adjustable, portable, hand-held metal tray in which the compositor assembled individual lines of type for printing.

seizing analogies, and by means of those aërial pontoons passing over like lightning from one topic to another. Still it is a fact, that this pertinacious life of memory for things that simply touch the ear without touching the consciousness, does in fact beset me. Said but once, said but softly, not marked at all, words revive before me in darkness and solitude; and they arrange themselves gradually into sentences, but through an effort sometimes of a distressing kind, to which I am in a manner forced to become a party. This being so, it was no great instance of that power—that three separate passages in the funeral service, all of which but one had escaped my notice at the time, and even that one as to the part I am going to mention, but all of which must have struck on my ear, restored themselves perfectly when I was lying awake in bed; and though struck by their beauty, I was also incensed by what seemed to me the harsh sentiment expressed in two of these passages. I will cite all the three in an abbreviated form, both for my immediate purpose, and for the indirect purpose of giving to those unacquainted with the English funeral service some specimen of its beauty.

The first passage was this, "Forasmuch as it hath pleased Almighty God, of his great mercy, to take unto himself the soul of our dear sister here departed, we therefore commit her body to the ground, earth to earth, ashes to ashes, dust to dust, in sure and certain hope of the resurrection to eternal life." ❖ ❖ ❖

I pause to remark that a sublime effect arises at this point through a sudden rapturous interpolation from the Apocalypse, which, according to the rubric, "shall be said or sung;" but always let it be sung, and by the full choir:—

"I heard a voice from heaven saying unto me, Write, from henceforth blessed are the dead which die in the Lord; even so saith the Spirit; for they rest from their labours."

The second passage, almost immediately succeeding to this awful burst of heavenly trumpets, and the one which more particularly offended me, though otherwise even then, in my seventh year, I could not but be touched by its beauty, was this:—"Almighty God, with whom do live the spirits of them that depart hence in the Lord, and with whom the souls of the faithful, after they are delivered from the burden of the flesh, are in joy and felicity; WE give thee hearty thanks that it hath pleased thee to deliver this our sister out of the miseries of this sinful world; beseeching thee, that it may please thee of thy gracious goodness shortly to accomplish the number of thine elect, and to hasten thy kingdom." ❖ ❖

In what world was I living when a man (calling himself a man of

God) could stand up publicly and give God "hearty thanks" that he had taken away my sister? But, young child, understand—taken her away from the miseries of this sinful world. Oh yes! I hear what you say; I understand *that*; but that makes no difference at all. She being gone, this world doubtless (as you say) is a world of unhappiness. But for me *ubi Cæsar, ibi Roma*[1]— where my sister was, there was paradise; no matter whether in heaven above, or on the earth beneath. And he had taken her away, cruel priest! of his "*great* mercy?" I did not presume, child though I was, to think rebelliously against *that*. The reason was not any hypocritical or canting submission where my heart yielded none, but because already my deep musing intellect had perceived a mystery and a labyrinth in the economies of this world. God, I saw, moved not as *we* moved—walked not as *we* walked—thought not as *we* think. Still I saw no mercy to myself, a poor frail dependent creature—torn away so suddenly from the prop on which altogether it depended. Oh yes! perhaps there was; and many years after I came to suspect it. Nevertheless it was a benignity that pointed far a-head; such as by a child could not have been perceived, because then the great arch had not come round; could not have been recognized if it *had* come round; could not have been valued if it had even been dimly recognized.

Finally, as the closing prayer in the whole service stood, this—which I acknowledged then, and now acknowledge, as equally beautiful and consolatory; for in this was no harsh peremptory challenge to the infirmities of human grief as to a thing not meriting notice in a religious rite. On the contrary, there was a gracious condescension from the great apostle to grief, as to a passion that he might perhaps himself have participated.

"Oh, merciful God! the father of our Lord Jesus Christ, who is the resurrection and the life, in whom whosoever believeth shall live, though he die; who also taught us by his holy apostle St Paul not to be sorry, as men without hope, for them that sleep in *him*; WE meekly beseech thee, O Father! to raise us from the death of sin unto the life of righteousness; that, when we shall depart this life, we may rest in *him* as our hope is—that this our sister doth."

Ah, *that* was beautiful; that was heavenly! We might be sorry, we had leave to be sorry; only not without hope. And we were by hope to rest in *Him*, as this our sister doth. And howsoever a man may think that he is without hope, I, that have read the writing upon these great abysses of grief, and viewed their shadows under the correction of

---

[1] "Wherever Caesar is, Rome is."

mightier shadows from deeper abysses since then, abysses of aboriginal fear and eldest darkness, in which yet I believe that all hope had not absolutely died, know that he is in a natural error. If, for a moment, I and so many others, wallowing in the dust of affliction, could yet rise up suddenly like the dry corpse★ which stood upright in the glory of life when touched by the bones of the prophet; if in those vast choral anthems, heard by my childish ear, the voice of God wrapt itself as in a cloud of music, saying—"Child, that sorrowest, I command thee to rise up and ascend for a season into my heaven of heavens"—then it was plain that despair, that the anguish of darkness, was not *essential* to such sorrow, but might come and go even as light comes and goes upon our troubled earth.

Yes! the light may come and go; grief may wax and wane; grief may sink; and grief again may rise, as in impassioned minds oftentimes it does, even to the heaven of heavens; but there is a necessity—that, if too much left to itself in solitude, finally it will descend into a depth from which there is no re-ascent; into a disease which seems no disease; into a languishing which, from its very sweetness, perplexes the mind and is fancied to be very health. Witchcraft has seized upon you, nympholepsy[1] has struck you. Now you rave no more. You acquiesce; nay, you are passionately delighted in your condition. Sweet becomes the grave, because you also hope immediately to travel thither: luxurious is the separation, because only perhaps for a few weeks shall it exist for you; and it will then prove but the brief summer night that had retarded a little, by a refinement of rapture, the heavenly dawn of reunion. Inevitable sometimes it is in solitude—that this should happen with minds morbidly meditative; that, when we stretch out our arms in darkness, vainly striving to draw back the sweet faces that have vanished, slowly arises a new stratagem of grief, and we say—"Be it that they no more come back to us, yet what hinders but we should go to *them?*"

★ "*Like the dry corpse which stood upright.*"—See the *Second* Book of Kings, chap. xiii. v. 20 and 21. Thirty years ago this impressive incident was made the subject of a large altarpiece by Mr Alston, an interesting American artist, then resident in London. ["Washington Alston (1779–1843), American artist who studied at the Royal Academy in London (1801–09). After a two-year stay in Boston, Massachusetts, he returned to England to pursue his career as artist (1811–18). He exhibited his painting 'The Dead Man Revived by Touching the Bones of the Prophet Elisha' in 1812" (*Works* 15.659).]

---

[1] Ancient belief that the sight of a nymph could cause an uncontrollable ecstasy, hence like "witchcraft."

Perilous is that crisis for the young. In its effect perfectly the same as the ignoble witchcraft of the poor African *Obeah*,⋆ this sublimer witch-craft of grief will, if left to follow its own natural course, terminate in the same catastrophe of death. Poetry, which neglects no phenomena that are interesting to the heart of man, has sometimes touched a little

"On the sublime attractions of the grave."[1]

But you think that these attractions, existing at times for the adult, could not exist for the child. Understand that you are wrong. Understand that these attractions *do* exist for the child; and perhaps as much more strongly than they *can* exist for the adult, by the whole differ-ence between the concentration of a childish love, and the inevitable distraction upon multiplied objects of any love that can affect an adult. There is a German superstition (well-known by a popular translation) of the Erl-king's Daughter,[2] who fixes her love upon some child, and seeks to wile him away into her own shadowy kingdom in forests.

"Who is it that rides through the forest so fast?"

It is a knight, who carries his child before him on the saddle. The Erl-king's Daughter rides on his right hand, and still whispers tempta-tions to the infant audible only to *him*.

⋆ "*African Obeah*."—Thirty years ago it would not have been necessary to say one word of the Obi or Obeah magic; because at that time several distinguished writers (Miss Edgeworth, for instance, in her *Belinda*) had made use of this superstition in fictions, and because the remarkable history of Three-finger'd Jack, a story brought upon the stage, had made the superstition notorious as a fact. Now, however, so long after the case has probably passed out of the public mind, it may be proper to mention—that when an Obeah man, *i.e.,* a professor of this dark collusion with human fears and human credulity, had once woven his dreadful net of ghostly terrors, and had thrown it over his selected victim, vainly did that victim flutter, struggle, languish in the meshes; unless the spells were reversed, he generally perished; and without a wound except from his own too domi-neering fancy. [Obeah: sorcery practised in parts of South American, the West Indies, southern USA, and West Africa; figures in *Belinda* (1801), a novel by Maria Edgeworth (1767–1849); Three-finger'd Jack was a West Indies outlaw who figured in late eighteenth-century melodramas and penny-dreadfuls (pulp fictions).]

---

[1] From Wordsworth, *The Excursion* (4.238).

[2] "A Danish legend of the ellerkong, king of the elves, was the source for the ballad, 'Der Erl-Königs Tochter,' by Johann Gottfried Herder (1744–1803). De Quincey, however, cites the most famous version, 'Der Erlkönig' by Goethe (1749–1832), translated by Matthew Gregory Lewis (1775–1818) in *Tales of Wonder* (1801), 1.51–52" (*Works* 15.659).]

"If thou wilt, dear baby, with me go away,
We will see a fine show, we will play a fine play."

The consent of the baby is essential to her success. And finally she
does succeed. Other charms, other temptations, would have been requi-
site for me. My intellect was too advanced for those fascinations. But
could the Erl-king's Daughter have revealed herself to me, and promised to lead me where my sister was, she might have wiled me by the
hand into the dimmest of forests upon earth. Languishing was my
condition at that time. Still I languished for things "which" (a voice
from heaven seemed to answer through my own heart) "*cannot* be
granted;" and which, when again I languished, again the voice repeated,
"*cannot* be granted."

Well it was for me that, at this crisis, I was summoned to put on the
harness of life, by commencing my classical studies under one of my
guardians,[1] a clergyman of the English Church, and (so far as regarded
Latin) a most accomplished scholar.

At the very commencement of my new studies, there happened an
incident which afflicted me much for a short time, and left behind a
gloomy impression, that suffering and wretchedness were diffused
amongst all creatures that breathe. A person had given me a kitten.
There are three animals which seem, beyond all others, to reflect the
beauty of human infancy in two of its elements—viz. joy, and guileless
innocence, though less in its third element of simplicity, because *that*
requires language for its full expression: these three animals are the
kitten, the lamb, and the fawn. Other creatures may be as happy, but
they do not show it so much. Great was the love which poor silly I had
for this little kitten; but, as I left home at ten in the morning, and did
not return till near five in the afternoon, I was obliged, with some anxiety, to throw it for those seven hours upon its own discretion, as infirm
a basis for reasonable hope as could be imagined. I did not wish the
kitten, indeed, at all less foolish than it was, except just when I was leaving home, and then its exceeding folly gave me a pang. Just about that
time, it happened that we had received, as a present from Leicestershire,
a fine young Newfoundland dog, who was under a cloud of disgrace

---

[1]   Rev. Samuel Hall, vicar of St. Peter's Church, Manchester.

for crimes of his youthful blood committed in that county. One day he had taken too great a liberty with a pretty little cousin of mine, Emma H ——, about four years old. He had, in fact, bitten off her cheek, which, remaining attached by a shred, was, through the energy of a governess, replaced, and subsequently healed without a scar. His name being *Turk*, he was immediately pronounced by the best Greek scholar of that neighbourhood, ἐπώνυμος[1] (*i.e.* named significantly, or reporting his nature in his name). But as Miss Emma confessed to having been engaged in taking away a bone from him, on which subject no dog can be taught to understand a joke, it did not strike our own authorities that he was to be considered in a state of reprobation; and as our gardens (near to a great town) were, on account chiefly of melons, constantly robbed, it was held that a moderate degree of fierceness was rather a favourable trait in his character. My poor kitten, it was supposed, had been engaged in the same playful trespass upon Turk's property as my Leicestershire cousin, and Turk laid her dead on the spot. It is impossible to describe my grief when the case was made known to me at five o'clock in the evening, by a man's holding out the little creature dead: she that I had left so full of glorious life—life which even in a kitten is infinite—was now stretched in motionless repose. I remember that there was a large coal stack in the yard. I dropped my Latin books, sat down upon a huge block of coal, and burst into a passion of tears. The man, struck with my tumultuous grief, hurried into the house; and from the lower regions deployed instantly the women of the laundry and the kitchen. No one subject is so absolutely sacred, and enjoys so *classical* a sanctity among servant girls, as 1. Grief; and 2. Love which is unfortunate. All the young women took me up in their arms and kissed me; and last of all, an elderly woman, who was the cook, not only kissed me, but wept so audibly, from some suggestion doubtless of grief personal to herself, that I threw my arms about her neck and kissed *her* also. It is probable, as I now suppose, that some account of my grief for my sister had reached them. Else I was never allowed to visit *their* region of the house. But, however *that* might be, afterwards it struck me, that if I had met with so much sympathy, or with any sympathy at all, from the servant chiefly connected with myself in the desolating grief I had suffered, possibly I should not have been so profoundly shaken.

But did I in the mean time feel anger towards Turk? Not the least. And the reason was this:—My guardian, who taught me Latin, was in

---

[1] "Eponymous."

the habit of coming over and dining at my mother's table whenever he pleased. On these occasions he, who like myself pitied *dependant* animals, went invariably into the yard of the offices, taking me with him, and unchained the dogs. There were two—*Grim*, a mastiff, and *Turk*, our young friend. My guardian was a bold athletic man, and delighted in dogs. He told me, which also my own heart told me, that these poor dogs languished out their lives under this confinement. The moment that I and my guardian (*ego et rex meus*[1]) appeared in sight of the two kennels, it is impossible to express the joy of the dogs. Turk was usually restless; Grim slept away his life in surliness. But at the sight of us—of my little insignificant self and my six-foot guardian—both dogs yelled with delight. We unfastened their chains with our own hands, they licking our hands; and as to myself, licking my miserable little face; and at one bound they re-entered upon their natural heritage of joy. Always we took them through the fields, where they molested nothing, and closed with giving them a cold bath in the brook which bounded my father's property. What despair must have possessed our dogs when they were taken back to their hateful prisons! and I, for my part, not enduring to see their misery, slunk away when the rechaining commenced. It was in vain to tell me that all people, who had property out of doors to protect, chained up dogs in the same way; *this* only proved the extent of the oppression; for a monstrous oppression it *did* seem, that creatures, boiling with life and the desires of life, should be thus detained in captivity until they were set free by death. That liberation visited poor *Grim* and *Turk* sooner than any of us expected, for they were both poisoned within the year that followed by a party of burglars. At the end of that year I was reading the Æneid; and it struck me, who remembered the howling recusancy of *Turk*, as a peculiarly fine circumstance, introduced amongst the horrors of Tartarus, that sudden gleam of powerful animals, full of life and conscious rights, rebelling against chains: —

"Iræque leonum
Vincla recusantum."★

★   What follows, I think, (for book I have none of any kind where this paper is proceeding,) viz. *et serâ sub nocte rudentum*, is probably a mistake of Virgil's; the lions did not roar because night was approaching, but because night brought with it their principal meal, and consequently the impatience of hunger. [Virgil, *The Aeneid* (7.15–17): "the raging cry of lions resisting their chains and roaring deep into the night."]

---

[1]   "I and my king."

Virgil had doubtless picked up that gem in his visits at feeding-time to the *caveæ*[1] of the Roman amphitheatre. But the rights of brute creatures to a merciful forbearance on the part of man, could not enter into the feeblest conceptions of one belonging to a nation that, (although too noble to be *wantonly* cruel,) yet in the same amphitheatre manifested so little regard even to human rights. Under Christianity, the condition of the brute has improved, and will improve much more. There is ample room. For I am sorry to say, that the commonest vice of Christian children, too often surveyed with careless eyes by mothers, that in their *human* relations are full of kindness, is cruelty to the inferior creatures thrown upon their mercy. For my own part, what had formed the groundwork of my happiness, (since joyous was my nature, though overspread with a cloud of sadness,) had been from the first a heart overflowing with love. And I had drunk in too profoundly the spirit of Christianity from our many nursery readings, not to read also in its divine words the justification of my own tendencies. That which I desired, was the thing which I ought to desire; the mercy that I loved was the mercy that God had blessed. From the sermon on the Mount resounded for ever in my ears— "Blessed are the merciful!" I needed not to add—"For they shall obtain mercy."[2] By lips so holy, and when standing in the atmosphere of truths so divine, simply to have been blessed—*that* was a sufficient ratification; every truth so revealed, and so hallowed by position, starts into sudden life, and becomes to itself its own authentication, needing no proof to convince, needing no promise to allure.

It may well be supposed, therefore, that, having so clearly awakened within me what may be philosophically called the *transcendental* justice of Christianity, I blamed not *Turk* for yielding to the coercion of his nature. He had killed the object of my love. But, besides that he was under the constraint of a primary appetite—Turk was himself the victim of a killing oppression. He was doomed to a fretful existence so long as he should exist at all. Nothing could reconcile this to my benignity, which at that time rested upon two pillars—upon the deep, deep heart which God had given to me at my birth, and upon exquisite health. Up to the age of two, and almost through that entire space of twenty-four months, I had suffered from ague; but when *that* left me, all germs and traces of ill health fled away for ever—except only such

---

[1] "Caves."

[2] Christ's sermon in Matthew 5.3 to 7.27 begins with the beatitudes, including "Blessed *are* the merciful: for they shall obtain mercy" (5.7).

(and those how curable!) as I inherited from my schoolboy distresses in London, or had created by means of opium. Even the long ague was not without ministrations of favour to my prevailing temper; and on the whole, no subject for pity; since naturally it won for me the sweet caresses of female tenderness, both young and old. I was a little petted; but you see by this time, reader, that I must have been too much of a philosopher, even in the year one *ab urbe condita*[1] of my frail earthly tenement, to abuse such indulgence. It also won for me a ride on horseback whenever the weather permitted. I was placed on a pillow, in front of a cankered old man, upon a large white horse, not so young as *I* was, but still showing traces of blood. And even the old man, who was both the oldest and the worst of the three, talked with gentleness to myself, reserving his surliness—for all the rest of the world.

These things pressed with a gracious power of incubation upon my predispositions; and in my overflowing love I did things fitted to make the reader laugh, and sometimes fitted to bring myself into perplexity. One instance from a thousand may illustrate the combinations of both effects. At four years old, I had repeatedly seen the housemaid raising her long broom and pursuing (generally destroying) a vagrant spider. The holiness of all life, in my eyes, forced me to devise plots for saving the poor doomed wretch; and thinking intercession likely to prove useless, my policy was—to draw off the housemaid on pretence of showing her a picture, until the spider, already *en route*, should have had time to escape. Very soon, however, the shrewd housemaid, marking the coincidence of these picture exhibitions with the agonies of fugitive spiders, detected my stratagem; so that, if the reader will pardon an expression borrowed from the street, henceforwards the picture was "no go." However, as she approved of my motive, she told me of the many murders that the spider had committed, and next (which was worse) of the many that he certainly *would* commit if reprieved. This staggered me. I could have gladly forgiven the past; but it *did* seem a false mercy to spare one spider in order to scatter death amongst fifty flies. I thought timidly for a moment, of suggesting that people sometimes repented, and that *he* might repent; but I checked myself, on considering that I had never read any account, and that she might laugh at the idea, of a penitent spider. To desist was a necessity in these circumstances. But the difficulty which the housemaid had suggested, did not depart; it troubled my musing mind to perceive, that

---

[1]   "From the founding of the city" (see *Confessions,* p. 120, n. 3 above), or "from the beginning," Roman method of dating.

the welfare of one creature might stand upon the ruin of another: and the case of the spider remained thenceforwards even more perplexing to my understanding than it was painful to my heart.

The reader is likely to differ from me upon the question, moved by recurring to such experiences of childhood, whether much value attaches to the perceptions and intellectual glimpses of a child. Children, like men, range through a gamut that is infinite, of temperaments and characters, ascending from the very dust below our feet to highest heaven. I have seen children that were sensual, brutal, devilish. But, thanks be to the *vis medicatrix*[1] of human nature, and to the goodness of God, these are as rare exhibitions as all other monsters. People thought, when seeing such odious travesties and burlesques upon lovely human infancy, that perhaps the little wretches might be *kilcrops*.* Yet, possibly, (it has since occurred to me,) even these children of the fiend, as they seemed, might have one chord in their horrible natures that answered to the call of some sublime purpose. There is a mimic instance of this kind, often found amongst ourselves in natures that are not really "horrible," but which *seem* such to persons viewing them from a station not sufficiently central:—Always there are mischievous boys in a neighbourhood, boys who tie canisters to the tails of cats belonging to ladies—a thing which *greatly* I disapprove; and who rob orchards—a thing which *slightly* I disapprove; and behold! the next day, on meeting the injured ladies, they say to me, "Oh, my dear friend, never pretend to argue for him! This boy, we shall all see, will come to be hanged." Well, *that* seems a disagreeable prospect for all parties; so I change the subject; and lo! five years later, there is an English frigate fighting with a frigate of heavier metal, (no matter of what nation). The noble captain has manoeuvred, as only *his* countrymen can manoeuvre; he has delivered his broadsides, as only the proud islanders can deliver them. Suddenly he sees the opening for a *coup-de-main*;[2] through his speaking-trumpet he shouts—"*Where are my boarders?*" And instantly rise upon the deck, with the gaiety of boyhood, in white shirt sleeves bound with black ribands, fifty men, the *elite* of the crew; and behold! at the

---

* "*Kilcrops*."—See, amongst Southey's early poems, one upon this superstition. Southey argues *contra*; but for my part, I should have been more disposed to hold a brief on the other side. ["'Kilcrops' are ever-hungry children, supposed to be fairy changelings. See Southey's poem 'The Killcrop,' which implies that they do not exist" (*Works* 15.660).]

---

[1]   "Healing power."
[2]   "Swift and sudden attack" (French).

very head of them, cutlass in hand, is our friend the tyer of canisters to the tails of ladies' cats—a thing which *greatly* I disapprove, and also the robber of orchards—a thing which *slightly* I disapprove. But here is a man that will not suffer you either greatly or slightly to disapprove him. Fire celestial burns in his eye; his nation, his glorious nation, is in his mind; himself he regards no more than the life of a cat, or the ruin of a canister. On the deck of the enemy he throws himself with rapture; and if *he* is amongst the killed, if he for an object so gloriously unselfish lays down with joy his life and glittering youth, mark this—that, perhaps, he will not be the least in heaven.

But coming back to the case of childhood, I maintain steadfastly— that, into all the *elementary* feelings of man, children look with more searching gaze than adults. My opinion is, that where circumstances favour, where the heart is deep, where humility and tenderness exist in strength, where the situation is favourable as to solitude and as to genial feelings, children have a specific power of contemplating the truth, which departs as they enter the world. It is clear to me, that children, upon elementary paths which require no knowledge of the world to unravel, tread more firmly than men; have a more pathetic sense of the beauty which lies in justice; and, according to the immortal ode of our great laureate, (ode "On the Intimations of Immortality in Childhood,") a far closer communion with God. I, if you observe, do not much inter-meddle with religion, properly so called. My path lies on the interspace between religion and philosophy, that connects them both. Yet here for once I shall trespass on grounds not properly mine, and desire you to observe in St Matthew, chap. xxi., and v. 15,[1] *who* were those that, crying in the temple, made the first public recognition of Christianity. Then, if you say, "Oh, but children echo what they hear, and are no independ-ent authorities!" I must request you to extend your reading into v. 16, where you will find that the testimony of these children, as bearing an *original* value, was ratified by the highest testimony; and the recognition of these children did itself receive a heavenly recognition. And this could *not* have been, unless there were children in Jerusalem who saw into truth with a far sharper eye than Sanhedrims and Rabbis.[2]

It is impossible, with respect to any memorable grief, that it can be

---

[1] "And when the chief priests and scribes saw the wonderful things that he did, and the chil-dren crying in the temple, and saying, Hosanna to the Son of David: they were sore displeased, And said unto him, Hearest thou what these say? And Jesus saith unto them, Yea; have ye never read, Out of the mouth of babes and sucklings thou has perfected praise?"

[2] Supreme legislative, ecclesiastical, and secular council of the ancient Jews.

adequately exhibited so as to indicate the enormity of the convulsion which really it caused, without viewing it under a variety of aspects— a thing which is here almost necessary for the effect of proportion to what follows: 1st, for instance, in its immediate pressure, so stunning and confounding; 2dly, in its oscillations, as in its earlier agitations, frantic with tumults, that borrow the wings of the winds; or in its diseased impulses of sick languishing desire, through which sorrow transforms itself to a sunny angel, that beckons us to a sweet repose. These phases of revolving affection I have already sketched. And I shall also sketch a third, *i.e.* where the affliction, seemingly hushing itself to sleep, suddenly soars upwards again upon combining with *another* mode of sorrow; viz. anxiety without definite limits, and the trouble of a reproaching conscience. As sometimes,* upon the English lakes, waterfowl that have careered in the air until the eye is wearied with the eternal wheel-ings of their inimitable flight—Grecian simplicities of motion, amidst a labyrinthine infinity of curves that would baffle the geometry of Apollonius[1]—seek the water at last, as if with some settled purpose (you imagine) of reposing. Ah, how little have you understood the omnipotence of that life which they inherit! *They* want no rest; they laugh at resting; all is "make believe," as when an infant hides its laugh-ing face behind its mother's shawl. For a moment it is still. Is it mean-ing to rest? Will its impatient heart endure to lurk there for long? Ask rather if a cataract will stop from fatigue. Will a sunbeam sleep on its travels? Or the Atlantic rest from its labours? As little can the infant, as little can the waterfowl of the lakes, suspend their play, except as a variety of play, or rest unless when nature compels them. Suddenly starts off the infant, suddenly ascend the birds, to new evolutions as incalculable as the caprices of a kaleidoscope;[2] and the glory of their motions, from the mixed immortalities of beauty and inexhaustible variety, becomes at least pathetic to survey. So also, and with such life of variation, do the *primary* convulsions of nature—such, perhaps, as

---

*   In this place I derive my feeling partly from a lovely sketch of the appearance, in verse, by Mr Wordsworth; partly from my own experience of the case; and, not having the poems here, I know not how to proportion my acknowledgments. [See Wordsworth, "Waterfowl": "Their jubilant activity evolves / Hundreds of curves and circlets, to and fro, / Upward and downward, progress intricate / Yet unperplexed, as if one spirit swayed / Their indefatigable flight" (10–14).]

[1]   Apollonius of Perga, third-century BCE geometer and mathematician; author of *Conics*.
[2]   Invented by Sir David Brewster (1781–1868), author of *Treatise on the Kaleidoscope* (1819).

only *primary** formations in the human system can experience—come round again and again by reverberating shocks.

The new intercourse with my guardian, and the changes of scene which naturally it led to, were of use in weaning my mind from the mere disease which threatened it in case I had been left any longer to my total solitude. But out of these changes grew an incident which restored my grief, though in a more troubled shape, and now for the first time associated with something like remorse and deadly anxiety. I can safely say that this was my earliest trespass, and perhaps a venial one—all things considered. Nobody ever discovered it; and but for my own frankness it would not be known to this day. But *that* I could not know; and for years, that is from seven or earlier up to ten, such was my simplicity, that I lived in constant terror. This, though it revived my grief, did me probably great service; because it was no longer a state of languishing desire tending to torpor, but of feverish irritation and gnawing care that kept alive the activity of my understanding. The case was this:—It happened that I had now, and commencing with my first introduction to Latin studies, a large weekly allowance of pocket-money, too large for my age, but safely entrusted to myself, who never spent or desired to spend one fraction of it upon any thing but books. But all proved too little for my colossal schemes. Had the Vatican, the Bodleian, and the *Bibliothéque du Roi*[1] been all emptied into one collection for my private gratification, little progress would have been made towards content in this particular craving. Very soon I had run ahead of my allowance, and was about three guineas deep in debt. There I paused; for deep anxiety now began to oppress me as to the course in which this mysterious (and indeed guilty) current of debt would finally flow. For the present it was frozen up; but I had some reason for thinking that Christmas thawed all debts whatsoever, and set them in

---

* "And so, then," the Cynic objects, "you rank your own mind (and you tell us so frankly) amongst the primary formations?" As I love to annoy him, it would give me pleasure to reply—"Perhaps I do." But as I never answer more questions than are necessary, I confine myself to saying, that this is not a necessary construction of the words. Some minds stand nearer to the type of the original nature in man, are truer than others to the great magnet in our dark planet. Minds that are impassioned on a more colossal scale than ordinary, deeper in their vibrations, and more extensive in the scale of their vibrations—whether, in other parts of their intellectual system, they had or had not a corresponding compass— will tremble to greater depths from a fearful convulsion, and will come round by a longer curve of undulations.

---

[1]   The Vatican in Rome, the Bodleian in Oxford, and the Royal Library in Paris, later named the Bibliothèque Nationale; three famous libraries with vast collections.

motion towards innumerable pockets. Now *my* debt would be thawed with all the rest; and in what direction would it flow? There was no river that would carry it off to sea; to somebody's pocket it would beyond a doubt make its way; and who *was* that somebody? This question haunted me for ever. Christmas had come, Christmas had gone, and I heard nothing of the three guineas. But I was not easier for *that*. Far rather I *would* have heard of it; for this indefinite approach of a loitering catastrophe gnawed and fretted my feelings. No Grecian audience ever waited with more shuddering horror for the anagnorisis★ of the Œdipus, than I for the explosion of my debt. Had I been less ignorant, I should have proposed to mortgage my weekly allowance for the debt, or to form a sinking fund for redeeming it; for the *weekly* sum was nearly five per cent on the entire debt. But I had a mysterious awe of ever alluding to it. This arose from my want of some confidential friend; whilst my grief pointed continually to the remembrance—that *so* it had not always been. But was not the bookseller to blame in suffering a child scarcely seven years old to contract such a debt? Not in the least. He was both a rich man, who could not possibly care for my trifling custom, and notoriously an honourable man. Indeed the money which I myself spent every week in books, would reasonably have caused him to presume that so small a sum as three guineas might well be authorized by my family. He stood, however, on plainer ground. For my guardian, who was very indolent, (as people chose to call it,) that is, like his little melancholy ward, spent all his time in reading, often enough would send me to the bookseller's with a written order for books. This was to prevent my forgetting. But when he found that such a thing as "forgetting" in the case of a book, was wholly out of the question for me, the trouble of writing was dismissed. And thus I had become factor-general on the part of my guardian, both for *his* books, and for such as were wanted on my own account in the natural course of my education. My private "little account" had therefore in fact flowed homewards at Christmas, not (as I anticipated) in the shape of an independent current, but as a little tributary rill that was lost in the waters of some more important river. This I now know, but could not then have known with any certainty. So far, however, the affair would

---

★   *i.e.* (As on account of English readers is added,) the recognition of his true identity, which in one moment, and by a horrid flash of revelation, connects him with acts incestuous, murderous, parricidal, in the past, and with a mysterious fatality of woe lurking in the future. [Aristotle, in *Poetics* (XI) uses Sophocles's *Oedipus Rex* to define the *anagnorisis* or moment of recognition in a drama, as when Oedipus realizes that he has fulfilled the prophecy that he will kill his father and marry his mother.]

gradually have sunk out of my anxieties as time wore on. But there was another item in the case, which, from the excess of my ignorance, preyed upon my spirits far more keenly; and this, keeping itself alive, kept also the other incident alive. With respect to the debt, I was not so ignorant as to think it of much danger by the mere amount: my own allowance furnished a scale for preventing *that* mistake: it was the principle, the having presumed to contract debts on my own account, that I feared to have exposed. But this other case was a ground for anxiety even as regarded the amount; not really; but under the jesting representation made to me, which I (as ever before and after) swallowed in perfect faith. Amongst the books which I had bought, all English, was a history of Great Britain, commencing of course with Brutus and a thousand years of impossibilities;[1] these fables being generously thrown in as a little gratuitous *extra* to the mass of truths which were to follow. This was to be completed in sixty or eighty parts, I believe. But there was another work left more indefinite as to its ultimate extent, and which from its nature seemed to imply a far wider range. It was a general history of navigation, supported by a vast body of voyages. Now, when I considered with myself what a huge thing the sea was, and that so many thousands of captains, commodores, admirals, were eternally running up and down it, and scoring lines upon its face so rankly, that in some of the main "streets" and "squares" (as one might call them) their tracks would blend into one undistinguishable blot,—I began to fear that such a work tended to infinity. What was little England to the universal sea? And yet *that* went perhaps to fourscore parts. Not enduring the uncertainty that now besieged my tranquillity, I resolved to know the worst; and on a day ever memorable to me I went down to the bookseller's. He was a mild elderly man, and to myself had always shown a kind indulgent manner. Partly perhaps he had been struck by my extreme gravity; and partly, during the many conversations I had with him, on occasion of my guardian's orders for books, with my laughable simplicity. But there was another reason which had early won for me his paternal regard. For the first three or four months I had found Latin something of a drudgery; and the incident which for ever knocked away the "shores," at that time preventing my launch upon the general bosom of Latin literature, was this:—One day the bookseller took down a Beza's *Latin Testament*;[2] and, opening it, asked

---

[1] A reference to still popular histories of Britain in which the first British kings can be traced to Brutus's mythical great grandson, Aeneas, and thus to the glory of classical Rome.

[2] Protestant scholar Theodore Beza (1519–1605), leading figure of the French Reformation, translated the New Testament into Latin.

me to translate for him the chapter which he pointed to. I was struck by
perceiving that it was the great chapter of St Paul[1] on the grave and resurrection. I had never seen a Latin version: yet from the simplicity of the
scriptural style in *any* translation, (though Beza's is far from good,) I could
not well have failed in construing. But as it happened to be this particular chapter, which in English I had read again and again with so passionate a sense of its grandeur, I read it off with a fluency and effect like some
great opera-singer uttering a rapturous *bravura*.[2] My kind old friend
expressed himself gratified, making me a present of the book as a mark
of his approbation. And it is remarkable, that from this moment, when
the deep memory of the English words had forced me into seeing the
precise correspondence of the two concurrent streams—Latin and
English—never again did any difficulty arise to check the velocity of my
progress in this particular language. At less than eleven years of age, when
as yet I was a very indifferent Grecian, I had become a brilliant master of
Latinity, as my Alcaics and Choriambics[3] remain to testify: and the whole
occasion of a change so memorable to a boy, was this casual summons to
translate a composition with which my heart was filled. Ever after this he
showed me a caressing kindness, and so condescendingly, that generally
he would leave any people for a moment with whom he was engaged,
to come and speak to me. On this fatal day, however, for such it proved
to me, he could not do this. He saw me, indeed, and nodded, but could
not leave a party of elderly strangers. This accident threw me unavoid-
ably upon one of his young people. Now this was a market-day; and there
was a press of country people present, whom I did not wish to hear my
question. Never did human creature, with his heart palpitating at Delphi
for the solution of some killing mystery, stand before the priestess of the
oracle, with lips that moved more sadly than mine, when now advancing
to a smiling young man at a desk. His answer was to decide, though I
could not exactly know *that*, whether for the next two years I was to have
an hour of peace. He was a handsome, good-natured young man, but full
of fun and frolic; and I dare say was amused with what must have seemed
to *him* the absurd anxiety of my features. I described the work to him,
and he understood me at once: how many volumes did he think it would
extend to? There was a whimsical expression perhaps of drollery about
his eyes, but which unhappily, under my preconceptions, I translated into

---

[1]   I Corinthians 15: see p. 156, n. 3 above.
[2]   "Virtuoso performance."
[3]   Metres of Greek or Latin verse.

scorn, as he replied,—"How many volumes? Oh! really I can't say, maybe a matter of 15, 000, be the same more or less." "*More?*" I said in horror, altogether neglecting the contingency of "less." "Why," he said, "we can't settle these things to a nicety. But, considering the subject," (ay, *that* was the very thing which I myself considered,) "I should say, there might be some trifle over, as suppose 400 or 500 volumes, be the same more or less." What, then, here there might be supplements to supplements—the work might positively *never* end. On one pretence or another, if an author or publisher might add 500 volumes, he might add another round 15,000. Indeed it strikes one even now, that by the time all the one-legged commodores and yellow admirals of that generation had exhausted their long yarns, another generation would have grown another crop of the same gallant spinners. I asked no more, but slunk out of the shop, and never again entered it with cheerfulness, or propounded any frank questions as heretofore. For I was now seriously afraid of pointing attention to myself as one that, by having purchased some numbers, and obtained others on credit, had silently contracted an engagement to take all the rest, though they should stretch to the crack of doom.[1] Certainly I had never heard of a work that extended to 15,000 volumes; but still there was no natural impossibility that it should; and, if in any case, in none so reasonably as one upon the inexhaustible sea. Besides, any slight mistake as to the letter of the number, could not affect the horror of the final prospect. I saw by the imprint, and I heard, that this work emanated from London, a vast centre of mystery to me, and the more so, as a thing unseen at any time by my eyes, and nearly 200 miles distant. I felt the fatal truth, that here was a ghostly cobweb radiating into all the provinces from the mighty metropolis. I secretly had trodden upon the outer circumference, had damaged or deranged the fine threads and links,—concealment or reparation there could be none. Slowly perhaps, but surely, the vibration would travel back to London. The ancient spider that sat there at the centre, would rush along the network through all longitudes and latitudes, until he found the responsible caitiff, author of so much mischief. Even, with less ignorance than mine, there *was* something to appal a child's imagination in the vast systematic machinery by which any elaborate work could disperse itself, could levy money, could put questions and get answers—all in profound silence, nay, even in darkness—searching every nook of every town, and of every hamlet in so populous a kingdom. I had some dim terrors, also, connected with the Stationers'

---

[1]   Clap of thunder on the Day of Judgement.

Company.[1] I had often observed them in popular works threatening unknown men with unknown chastisements, for offences equally unknown; nay, to myself, absolutely inconceivable. Could *I* be the mysterious criminal so long pointed out, as it were, in prophecy? I figured the stationers, doubtless all powerful men, pulling at one rope, and my unhappy self hanging at the other end. But an image, which seems now even more ludicrous than the rest, at that time was the one most connected with the revival of my grief. It occurred to my subtlety, that the Stationers' Company, or any other company, could not possibly demand the money until they had delivered the volumes. And, as no man could say that I had ever positively refused to receive them, they would have no pretence for not accomplishing this delivery in a civil manner. Unless I should turn out to be no customer at all, at present it was clear that I had a right to be considered a most excellent customer; one, in fact, who had given an order for fifteen thousand volumes. Then rose up before me this great operahouse "scena" of the delivery. There would be a ring at the front door. A waggoner in the front, with a bland voice, would ask for "a young gentleman who had given an order to *their* house." Looking out, I should perceive a procession of carts and waggons, all advancing in measured movements; each in turn would present its rear, deliver its cargo of volumes, by shooting them, like a load of coals, on the lawn, and wheel off to the rear, by way of clearing the road for its successors. Then the impossibility of even asking the servants to cover with sheets, or counterpanes, or table-cloths, such a mountainous, such a "star-y-pointing"[2] record of my past offences lying in so conspicuous a situation! Men would not know my guilt merely, they would see it. But the reason why this form of the consequences, so much more than any other, stuck by my imagination was, that it connected itself with one of the Arabian nights[3] which had particularly interested myself and my sister. It was that tale, where a young porter, having his ropes about his person, had stumbled into the special "preserve" of some old magician. He finds a beautiful lady imprisoned, to whom (and not without prospects of success) he recommends himself as a suitor, more in harmony with her own years than a withered

---

Trade organization for printers.

[2]   Milton, "On Shakespeare": "What needs my *Shakespeare* for his honor'd Bones / The labor of an age in piled Stones, / Or that his hallow'd relics should be hid / Under a Star-ypointing *Pyramid*" (1.4); reference to the writer's bid for immortality.

[3]   Collection of Arab tales, also called *The Thousand and One Nights*, translated into French in the eighteenth century by Antoine Galland, into English by Edward William Lane in 1839–41.

magician. At this crisis the magician returns. The young man bolts, and for that day successfully; but unluckily he leaves his ropes behind. Next morning he hears the magician, too honest by half, enquiring at the front door, with much expression of condolence, for the unfortunate young man who had lost his ropes in his own zenana.[1] Upon this story I used to amuse my sister, by ventriloquizing to the magician from the lips of the trembling young man—"Oh, Mr Magician, these ropes cannot be mine! They are far too good; and one wouldn't like, you know, to rob some other poor young man. If you please, Mr Magician, I never had money enough to buy so beautiful a set of ropes." But argument is thrown away upon a magician, and off he sets on his travels with the young porter—not forgetting to take the ropes along with him.

Here now was the case, that had once seemed so impressive to me in a mere fiction from a far-distant age and land, literally reproduced in myself. For what did it matter whether a magician dunned one with old ropes for his engines of torture, or Stationers' Hall with 15,000 volumes, (in the rear of which there might also be ropes?). Should *I* have ventriloquized, would my sister have laughed, had either of us but guessed the possibility that I myself, and within one twelve months, and, alas! standing alone in the world as regarded *confidential* counsel, should repeat within my own inner experience the shadowy panic of the young Bagdat intruder upon the privacy of magicians? It appeared, then, that I had been reading a legend concerning myself in the *Arabian Nights*. I had been contemplated in types a thousand years before on the banks of the Tigris. It was horror and grief that prompted that thought.

Oh, heavens! that the misery of a child should by possibility become the laughter of adults!—that even I, the sufferer, should be capable of amusing myself, as if it had been a jest, with what for three years had constituted the secret affliction of my life, and its eternal trepidation— like the ticking of a death-watch[2] to patients lying awake in the plague. I durst ask no counsel; there was no one to ask. Possibly my sister could have given me none in a case which neither of us should have understood, and where to seek for information from others, would have been at once to betray the whole reason for seeking it. But, if no advice, she would have given me her pity, and the expression of her endless love; and, with the relief of sympathy, that heals for a season all distresses, she would have given me that exquisite luxury—the knowledge that,

---

[1]   Harem.
[2]   Beetle whose clicking sounds were supposedly an omen of death.

having parted with my secret, yet also I had *not* parted with it, since it was in the power only of one that could much less betray me than I could betray myself. At this time, that is about the year when I suffered most, I was reading Cæsar. Oh, laurelled scholar—sun-bright intellect—"foremost man of all this world"[1]—how often did I make out of thy immortal volume a pillow to support my wearied brow, as at evening, on my homeward road, I used to turn into some silent field, where I might give way unobserved to the reveries which besieged me! I wondered, and found no end of wondering, at the revolution that one short year had made in my happiness. I wondered that such billows *could* overtake me! At the beginning of that year how radiantly happy! At the end how insupportably alone!

> "Into what depth thou see'st,
> From what height fallen."[2]

For ever I searched the abysses with some wandering thoughts unintelligible to myself. For ever I dallied with some obscure notion, how my sister's love might be made in some dim way available for delivering me from misery; or else how the misery I had suffered and was suffering might be made, in some way equally dim, the ransom for winning back her love.

— — — — — —

Here pause, reader! Imagine yourself seated in some cloud-scaling swing, oscillating under the impulse of lunatic hands; for the strength of lunacy may belong to human dreams, the fearful caprice of lunacy, and the malice of lunacy, whilst the *victim* of those dreams may be all the more certainly removed from lunacy; even as a bridge gathers cohesion and strength from the increasing resistance into which it is forced by increasing pressure. Seated in such a swing, fast as you reach the lowest point of depression, may you rely on racing up to a starry altitude of corresponding ascent. Ups and downs you will see, heights and depths, in our fiery course together, such as will sometimes tempt you to look shyly and suspiciously at me, your guide, and the ruler of the oscillations.

---

[1] Shakespeare, *Julius Caesar* (4.3.22).
[2] Paraphrase of Milton, *Paradise Lost* (1.91–92); Beelzebub says to Satan, "into what Pit thou seest / From what highth fall'n."

Here, at the point where I have called a halt, the reader has reached the lowest depth in my nursery afflictions. From that point, according to the principles of *art* which govern the movement of these Confessions, I had meant to launch him upwards through the whole arch of ascending visions which seemed requisite to balance the sweep downwards, so recently described in his course. But accidents of the press have made it impossible to accomplish this purpose in the present month's journal. There is reason to regret that the advantages of position, which were essential to the full effect of passages planned for equipoise and mutual resistance, have thus been lost. Meantime, upon the principle of the mariner who rigs a *jury*-mast[1] in default of his regular spars, I find my resource in a sort of "jury" peroration—not sufficient in the way of a balance by its *proportions*, but sufficient to indicate the *quality* of the balance which I had contemplated. He who has *really* read the preceding parts of these present Confessions, will be aware that a stricter scrutiny of the past, such as was natural after the whole economy of the dreaming faculty had been convulsed beyond all precedents on record, led me to the conviction that not one agency, but two agencies, had co-operated to the tremendous result. The nursery experience had been the ally and the natural co-efficient of the opium. For that reason it was that the nursery experience has been narrated. Logically, it bears the very same relation to the convulsions of the dreaming faculty as the opium. The idealizing tendency existed in the dream-theatre of my childhood; but the preternatural strength of its action and colouring was first developed after the confluence of the *two* causes. The reader must suppose me at Oxford: twelve years and a half are gone by; I am in the glory of youthful happiness; but I have now first tampered with opium; and now first the agitations of my childhood reopened in strength, now first they swept in upon the brain with power and the grandeur of recovered life, under the separate and the concurring inspirations of opium.

Once again, after twelve years' interval, the nursery of my childhood expanded before me—my sister was moaning in bed—I was beginning to be restless with fears not intelligible to myself. Once again the nurse, but now dilated to colossal proportions, stood as upon some Grecian stage with her uplifted hand, and like the superb Medea standing alone with her children in the nursery at Corinth,* smote me senseless to the

---

* Euripides. [Euripides, *Medea* (1271–78); abandoned by her husband Jason, Medea murders her children in their nursery in Corinth.]

---

[1] Temporary mast hastily erected to replace one that is lost or broken.

ground. Again, I was in the chamber with my sister's corpse—again the pomps of life rose up in silence, the glory of summer, the frost of death. Dream formed itself mysteriously within dream; within these Oxford dreams remoulded itself continually the trance in my sister's chamber,— the blue heavens, the everlasting vault, the soaring billows, the throne steeped in the thought (but not the sight) of "Him that sate thereon;"[1] the flight, the pursuit, the irrecoverable steps of my return to earth. Once more the funeral procession gathered; the priest in his white surplice stood waiting with a book in his hand by the side of an open grave, the sacristan with his shovel; the coffin sank; the *dust to dust* descended. Again I was in the church on a heavenly Sunday morning. The golden sunlight of God slept amongst the heads of his apostles, his martyrs, his saints; the fragment from the litany—the fragment from the clouds—awoke again the lawny beds that went up to scale the heav- ens—awoke again the shadowy arms that moved downwards to meet them. Once again, arose the swell of the anthem—the burst of the Hallelujah chorus—the storm—the trampling movement of the choral passion—the agitation of my own trembling sympathy—the tumult of the choir—the wrath of the organ. Once more I, that wallowed, became he that rose up to the clouds. And now in Oxford, all was bound up into unity; the first state and the last were melted into each other as in some sunny glorifying haze. For high above my own station, hovered a gleaming host of heavenly beings, surrounding the pillows of the dying children. And such beings sympathize equally with sorrow that grovels and with sorrow that soars. Such beings pity alike the children that are languishing in death, and the children that live only to languish in tears.

---

[1] Paraphrase of Milton, "At a Solemn Music."

PART I. CONCLUDED.

THE PALIMPSEST.

YOU know perhaps, masculine reader, better than I can tell you, what is a *Palimpsest*. Possibly you have one in your own library. But yet, for the sake of others who may *not* know, or may have forgotten, suffer me to explain it here: lest any female reader, who honours these papers with her notice, should tax me with explaining it once too seldom; which would be worse to bear than a simultaneous complaint from twelve proud men, that I had explained it three times too often. You therefore, fair reader, understand that for *your* accommodation exclusively, I explain the meaning of this word. It is Greek; and our sex enjoys the office and privilege of standing counsel to yours, in all questions of Greek. We are, under favour, perpetual and hereditary dragomans[1] to you. So that if, by accident, you know the meaning of a Greek word, yet by courtesy to us, your counsel learned in that matter, you will always seem *not* to know it.

A palimpsest, then, is a membrane or roll cleansed of its manuscript by reiterated successions.

What was the reason that the Greeks and the Romans had not the advantage of printed books? The answer will be, from ninety-nine persons in a hundred—Because the mystery of printing was not then discovered. But this is altogether a mistake. The secret of printing must have been discovered many thousands of times before it was used, or *could* be used. The inventive powers of man are divine; and also his stupidity is divine—as Cowper so playfully illustrates in the slow development of the *sofa*[2] through successive generations of immortal dulness. It took centuries of blockheads to raise a joint stool into a chair; and it required something like a miracle of genius, in the estimate of elder generations, to reveal the possibility of lengthening a chair into a *chaise-longue*, or a sofa. Yes, these were inventions that cost mighty throes of intellectual power. But still, as respects printing, and admirable as is the stupidity of man, it was really not quite equal to the task of evading an object which stared him in the face with so broad a gaze. It did not

---

[1]   "Professional interpreters" (Arabic).

[2]   See *The Task* (1784), by William Cowper (1731–1800), the first book of which, "The Sofa," is a mock-Miltonic narrative of the evolution of the sofa.

require an Athenian intellect to read the main secret of printing in many scores of processes which the ordinary uses of life were *daily* repeating. To say nothing of analogous artifices amongst various mechanic artisans, all that is essential in printing must have been known to every nation that struck coins and medals. Not, therefore, any want of a printing art—that is, of an art for multiplying impressions—but the want of a cheap material for *receiving* such impressions, was the obstacle to an introduction of printed books even as early as Pisistratus. The ancients *did* apply printing to records of silver and gold; to marble and many other substances cheaper than gold and silver, they did *not*, since each monument required a *separate* effort of inscription. Simply this defect it was of a cheap material for receiving impresses, which froze in its very fountains the early resources of printing.

Some twenty years ago, this view of the case was luminously expounded by Dr Whately,[1] the present archbishop of Dublin, and with the merit, I believe, of having first suggested it. Since then, this theory has received indirect confirmation. Now, out of that original scarcity affecting all materials proper for durable books, which continued up to times comparatively modern, grew the opening for palimpsests. Naturally, when once a roll of parchment or of vellum had done its office, by propagating through a series of generations what once had possessed an interest for *them*, but which, under changes of opinion or of taste, had faded to their feelings or had become obsolete for their understandings, the whole *membrana* or vellum skin, the twofold product of human skill, costly material, and costly freight of thought, which it carried, drooped in value concurrently—supposing that each were inalienably associated to the other. Once it had been the impress of a human mind which stamped its value upon the vellum; the vellum, though costly, had contributed but a secondary element of value to the total result. At length, however, this relation between the vehicle and its freight has gradually been undermined. The vellum, from having been the setting of the jewel, has risen at length to be the jewel itself; and the burden of thought, from having given the chief value to the vellum, had now become the chief obstacle to its value; nay, has totally extinguished its value, unless it can be dissociated from the connexion. Yet, if this unlinking *can* be effected, then—fast as the inscription upon the

---

[1]   Richard Whately (1787–1863), author of *Elements of Rhetoric* (1828): "the invention of printing is too obvious not to have followed, in a literary nation, the introduction of a paper sufficiently cheap to make the art available" (2).

188   THOMAS DE QUINCEY

membrane is sinking into rubbish—the membrane itself is reviving in its separate importance; and, from bearing a ministerial value, the vellum has come at last to absorb the whole value.

Hence the importance for our ancestors that the separation *should* be effected. Hence it arose in the middle ages, as a considerable object for chemistry, to discharge the writing from the roll, and thus to make it available for a new succession of thoughts. The soil, if cleansed from what once had been hot-house plants, but now were held to be weeds, would be ready to receive a fresh and more appropriate crop. In that object the monkish chemists succeeded; but after a fashion which seems almost incredible; incredible not as regards the extent of their success, but as regards the delicacy of restraints under which it moved; so equally adjusted was their success to the immediate interests of that period, and to the reversionary interests of our own. They did the thing; but not so radically as to prevent us, their posterity, from *un*doing it. They expelled the writing sufficiently to leave a field for the new manuscript, and yet not sufficiently to make the traces of elder manuscript irrecoverable for us. Could magic, could Hermes Trismegistus,[1] have done more? What would you think, fair reader, of a problem such as this—to write a book which should be sense for your own generation, nonsense for the next, should revive into sense for the next after that, but again became nonsense for the fourth; and so on by alternate successions, sinking into night or blazing into day, like the Sicilian river Arethusa, and the English river Mole[2]—or like the undulating motions of a flattened stone which children cause to skim the breast of a river, now diving below the water, now grazing its surface, sinking heavily into darkness, rising buoyantly into light, through a long vista of alternations? Such a problem, you say, is impossible. But really it is a problem not harder apparently than—to bid a generation kill, but so that a subsequent generation may call back into life; bury, but so that posterity may command to rise again. Yet *that* was what the rude chemistry of past ages effected when coming into combination with the reaction from the more refined chemistry of our own. Had *they* been better chemists, had *we* been worse—the mixed result, viz.

---

1   "Thrice-great Hermes," mythical Egyptian teacher of hermeticism, a wedding of high magic and alchemy.

2   Arethusa, underground river that flows into a fountain in Ortygia, Syracuse, Sicily; named after the water nymph, beloved by Alpheus when he saw her bathing in his stream; fled from him to Ortygia, where Artemis changed her into a fountain to protect her virginity; but Alpheus flowed under the sea to unite with Arethusa. Mole is a river that runs into the Thames opposite Hampton Court.

that, dying for *them*, the flower should revive for *us*, could not have been effected: They did the thing proposed to them: they did it effectually; for they founded upon it all that was wanted: and yet ineffectually, since we unravelled their work; effacing all above which they had superscribed; restoring all below which they had effaced.

Here, for instance, is a parchment which contained some Grecian tragedy, the Agamemnon of Æschylus, or the Phœnissæ of Euripides.[1] This had possessed a value almost inappreciable in the eyes of accomplished scholars, continually growing rarer through generations. But four centuries are gone by since the destruction of the Western Empire. Christianity, with towering grandeurs of another class, has founded a different empire; and some bigoted yet perhaps holy monk has washed away (as he persuades himself) the heathen's tragedy, replacing it with a monastic legend; which legend is disfigured with fables in its incidents, and yet, in a higher sense, is true, because interwoven with Christian morals and with the sublimest of Christian revelations. Three, four, five, centuries more find man still devout as ever; but the language has become obsolete, and even for Christian devotion a new era has arisen, throwing it into the channel of crusading zeal or of chivalrous enthusiasm. The *membrana* is wanted now for a knightly romance—for "my Cid," or Cœur de Lion; for Sir Tristrem, or Lybæus Disconus.[2] In this way, by means of the imperfect chemistry known to the mediæval period, the same roll has served as a conservatory for three separate generations of flowers and fruits, all perfectly different, and yet all specially adapted to the wants of the successive possessors. The Greek tragedy, the monkish legend, the knightly romance, each had ruled its own period. One harvest after another had been gathered into the garners of man through ages far apart. And the same hydraulic machinery had distributed, through the same marble fountains, water, milk, or wine, according to the habits and training of the generations that came to quench their thirst.

Such were the achievements of rude monastic chemistry. But the more elaborate chemistry of our own days has reversed all these motions of our simple ancestors, with results in every stage that to *them* would have

---

[1] *Agamemnon*, the first play of the Oresteia trilogy by Aeschylus (525–456 BCE), considered the founder of Greek tragedy, said to have authored over ninety plays, of which only seven survive; *The Phoenissae*, one of Euripides's surviving plays.

[2] Fictional and non-fictional examples of famous knightly or chivalrous figures: The Cid, or *El Cid Campeador* (Cid the Champion), the eleventh-century hero of the Spanish epic, "Song of the Cid," *Poema del Cid* or *Cantar del Mio Cid*; Coeur de Lion, Richard I of England (reigned 1189–99); Sir Tristrem and Lybaeus Disconus, knights of King Arthur's court.

realized the most fantastic amongst the promises of thaumaturgy.[1] Insolent vaunt of Paracelsus,[2] that he would restore the original rose or violet out of the ashes settling from its combustion—*that* is now rivalled in this modern achievement. The traces of each successive handwriting, regularly effaced, as had been imagined, have, in the inverse order, been regularly called back: the footsteps of the game pursued, wolf or stag, in each several chase, have been unlinked, and hunted back through all their doubles; and, as the chorus of the Athenian stage unwove through the antistrophe every step that had been mystically woven through the strophe, so, by our modern conjurations of science, secrets of ages remote from each other have been exorcised★ from the accumulated shadows of centuries. Chemistry, a witch as potent as the Erictho of Lucan,[3] (*Pharsalia*, lib. vi. or vii.,) has extorted by her torments, from the dust and ashes of forgotten centuries, the secrets of a life extinct for the general eye, but still glowing in the embers. Even the fable of the Phœnix[4]—that secular bird, who propagated his solitary existence, and his solitary births, along the line of centuries, through eternal relays of funeral mists—is but a type of what we have done with Palimpsests. We have backed upon each Phœnix in the long *regressus*, and forced him to expose his ancestral Phœnix, sleeping in the ashes below his own ashes. Our good old forefathers would have been aghast at our sorceries; and, if they speculated on the propriety of burning Dr Faustus,[5] *us* they would have burned by acclamation. Trial there would have been none; and they could no otherwise have satisfied their horror of the brazen profligacy marking our modern magic, than by ploughing up the houses of all who had been parties to it, and sowing the ground with salt.

★ Some readers may be apt to suppose, from all English experience, that the word *exorcise* means properly banishment to the shades. Not so. Citation *from* the shades, or sometimes the torturing coercion of mystic adjurations, is more truly the primary sense.

---

[1] The working of miracles.

[2] Paracelsus (1493–1541), Swiss, practised alchemy, astrology, and magic, considered founder of modern chemistry; argued in *De Rerum Natura* (1539) that vegetable life could be regenerated from its own ashes.

[3] Legendary Thessalian witch, figure in the epic poem *Pharsalia* (6.507–830) by Marcus Annaeus Lucanus (39–65 CE), Roman poet; calls upon a spirit to reveal to Pompey the Great's son, Sextus Pompeius, the outcome of the Battle of Pharsalia (48 BCE), in which Julius Caesar beat Pompey to gain control of the Mediterranean.

[4] Mythical creature, said to resurrect itself from its own ashes.

[5] Wandering conjurer who practised black magic, lived in Germany (circa 1488–1541); basis for Christopher Marlowe's *The Tragical History of Doctor Faustus* (probably published in 1604) and Goethe's two parts of *Faust* (1808, 1832).

Fancy not, reader, that this tumult of images, illustrative or allusive, moves under any impulse or purpose of mirth. It is but the coruscation of a restless understanding, often made ten times more so by irritation of the nerves, such as you will first learn to comprehend (its *how* and its *why*) some stage or two ahead. The image, the memorial, the record, which for me is derived from a palimpsest, as to one great fact in our human being, and which immediately I will show you, is but too repellent of laughter; or, even if laughter *had* been possible, it would have been such laughter as oftentimes is thrown off from the fields of ocean★—laughter that hides, or that seems to evade mustering tumult; foam-bells that weave garlands of phosphoric radiance for one moment round the eddies of gleaming abysses; mimicries of earth-born flowers that for the eye raise phantoms of gaiety, as oftentimes for the ear they raise echoes of fugitive laughter, mixing with the ravings and choir-voices of an angry sea.

What else than a natural and mighty palimpsest is the human brain? Such a palimpsest is my brain; such a palimpsest, O reader! is yours. Everlasting layers of ideas, images, feelings, have fallen upon your brain softly as light. Each succession has seemed to bury all that went before. And yet in reality not one has been extinguished. And if, in the vellum palimpsest, lying amongst the other *diplomata*[1] of human archives or libraries, there is any thing fantastic or which moves to laughter, as oftentimes there is in the grotesque collisions of those successive themes, having no natural connexion, which by pure accident have consecutively occupied the roll, yet, on our own heaven-created palimpsest, the deep memorial palimpsest of the brain, there are not and cannot be such incoherencies. The fleeting accidents of a man's life, and its external shows, may indeed be irrelate and incongruous; but the organizing principles which fuse into harmony, and gather about fixed predetermined centres, whatever heterogeneous elements life may have accumulated from without, will not permit the grandeur of human

---

★   "*Laughter from the fields of ocean.*"—Many readers will recall, though at the moment of writing my own thoughts did *not* recall, the well-known passage in the Prometheus—

——'ωαονιον ιεκυματων
'Αμηπιθον ζελασμα.

"Oh multitudinous laughter of the ocean billows." It is not clear whether Æschylus contemplated the laughter as addressing the ear or the eye. [*Prometheus Bound* (89–90), by Aeschylus.]

---

[1]   Historical records.

unity greatly to be violated, or its ultimate repose to be troubled in the retrospect from dying moments, or from other great convulsions.

Such a convulsion is the struggle of gradual suffocation, as in drowning; and, in the original Opium Confessions, I mentioned a case of that nature communicated to me by a lady[1] from her own childish experience. The lady is still living, though now of unusually great age; and I may mention—that amongst her faults never was numbered any levity of principle, or carelessness of the most scrupulous veracity; but, on the contrary, such faults as arise from austerity, too harsh perhaps, and gloomy—indulgent neither to others nor herself. And, at the time of relating this incident, when already very old, she had become religious to asceticism. According to my present belief, she had completed her ninth year, when playing by the side of a solitary brook, she fell into one of its deepest pools. Eventually, but after what lapse of time nobody ever knew, she was saved from death by a farmer, who, riding in some distant lane, had seen her rise to the surface; but not until she had descended within the abyss of death, and looked into its secrets, as far, perhaps, as ever human eye *can* have looked that had permission to return. At a certain stage of this descent, a blow seemed to strike her—phosphoric radiance sprang forth from her eye-balls; and immediately a mighty theatre expanded within her brain. In a moment, in the twinkling of an eye, every act—every design of her past life lived again—arraying themselves not as a succession, but as parts of a coexistence. Such a light fell upon the whole path of her life backwards into the shades of infancy, as the light perhaps which wrapt the destined apostle on his road to Damascus.[2] Yet that light blinded for a season; but hers poured celestial vision upon the brain, so that her consciousness became omnipresent at one moment to every feature in the infinite review.

This anecdote was treated skeptically at the time by some critics. But besides that it has since been confirmed by other experiences essentially the same, reported by other parties in the same circumstances who had never heard of each other; the true point for astonishment is not the *simultaneity* of arrangement under which the past events of life—though in fact successive—had formed their dread line of revelation. This was but a secondary phenomenon; the deeper lay in the resurrection itself, and the possibility of resurrection, for what had so long slept

---

[1]   De Quincey's mother, Elizabeth Penson Quincey (1754–1846).

[2]   Saul of Tarsus, later St. Paul after his conversion on the road to Damascus, when "suddenly there shone from heaven a great light round about [him]" (Acts 22.6).

in the dust. A pall, deep as oblivion, had been thrown by life over every trace of these experiences; and yet suddenly, at a silent command, at the signal of a blazing rocket sent up from the brain, the pall draws up, and the whole depths of the theatre are exposed. Here was the greater mystery: now this mystery is liable to no doubt; for it is reported, and ten thousand times repeated by opium, for those who are its martyrs.

Yes, reader, countless are the mysterious handwritings of grief or joy which have inscribed themselves successively upon the palimpsest of your brain; and, like the annual leaves of aboriginal forests, or the undis-solving snows on the Himalaya, or light falling upon light, the endless strata have covered up each other in forgetfulness. But by the hour of death, but by fever, but by the searchings of opium, all these can revive in strength. They are not dead, but sleeping. In the illustration imag-ined by myself, from the case of some individual palimpsest, the Grecian tragedy had seemed to be displaced, but was *not* displaced, by the monk-ish legend; and the monkish legend had seemed to be displaced, but was *not* displaced, by the knightly romance. In some potent convulsion of the system, all wheels back into its earliest elementary stage. The bewil-dering romance, light tarnished with darkness, the semi-fabulous legend, truth celestial mixed with human falsehoods, these fade even of themselves as life advances. The romance has perished that the young man adored. The legend has gone that deluded the boy. But the deep deep tragedies of infancy, as when the child's hands were unlinked for ever from his mother's neck, or his lips for ever from his sister's kisses, these remain lurking below all, and these lurk to the last. Alchemy there is none of passion or disease that can scorch away these immortal impresses. And the dream which closed the preceding section, together with the succeeding dreams of this, (which may be viewed as in the nature of choruses winding up the overture contained in Part I.,) are but illustrations of this truth, such as every man probably will meet experimentally who passes through similar convulsions of dreaming or delirium from any similar or equal disturbance in his nature.★

★   This, it may be said, requires a corresponding duration of experience; but, as an argument for this mysterious power lurking in our nature, I may remind the reader of one phenom-enon open to the notice of every body, viz. the tendency of very aged persons to throw back and concentrate the light of their memory upon scenes of early childhood, as to which they recall many traces that had faded even to *themselves* in middle life, whilst they often forget altogether the whole intermediate stages of their experience. This shows that naturally, and without violent agencies, the human brain is by tendency a palimpsest.

LEVANA AND OUR LADIES OF SORROW

Oftentimes at Oxford I saw Levana in my dreams. I knew her by her Roman symbols. Who is Levana? Reader, that do not pretend to have leisure for very much scholarship, you will not be angry with me for telling you. Levana was the Roman goddess that performed for the new-born infant the earliest office of ennobling kindness—typical, by its mode, of that grandeur which belongs to man every where, and of that benignity in powers invisible, which even in Pagan worlds sometimes descends to sustain it. At the very moment of birth, just as the infant tasted for the first time the atmosphere of our troubled planet, it was laid on the ground. *That* might bear different interpretations. But immediately, lest so grand a creature should grovel there for more than one instant, either the paternal hand, as proxy for the goddess Levana, or some near kinsman, as proxy for the father, raised it upright, bade it look erect as the king of all this world, and presented its forehead to the stars, saying, perhaps, in his heart— "Behold what is greater than yourselves!" This symbolic act represented the function of Levana. And that mysterious lady, who never revealed her face, (except to me in dreams,) but always acted by delegation, had her name from the Latin verb (as still it is the Italian verb) *levare*, to raise aloft.

This is the explanation of Levana. And hence it has arisen that some people have understood by Levana the tutelary power that controls the education of the nursery. She, that would not suffer at his birth even a prefigurative or mimic degradation for her awful ward, far less could be supposed to suffer the real degradation attaching to the non-development of his powers. She therefore watches over human education. Now, the word *edŭco*, with the penultimate short, was derived (by a process often exemplified in the crystallization of languages) from the word *edūco*, with the penultimate long. Whatsoever *educes* or developes—*educates*. By the education of Levana, therefore, is meant—not the poor machinery that moves by spelling-books and grammars, but that mighty system of central forces hidden in the deep bosom of human life, which by passion, by strife, by temptation, by the energies of resistance, works for ever upon children—resting not day or night, any more than the mighty wheel of day and night themselves, whose moments, like restless spokes, are glimmering★ for ever as they revolve.

★   "*Glimmering.*"—As I have never allowed myself to covet any man's ox nor his ass, nor any thing that is his, still less would it become a philosopher to covet other people's images, or metaphors. Here, therefore, I restore to Mr Wordsworth this fine image of the revolving

If, then, *these* are the ministries by which Levana works, how profoundly must she reverence the agencies of grief! But you, reader! think—that children generally are not liable to grief such as mine. There are two senses in the word *generally*—the sense of Euclid[1] where it means *universally*, (or in the whole extent of the *genus*,) and a foolish sense of this world where it means *usually*. Now I am far from saying that children universally are capable of grief like mine. But there are more than you ever heard of, who die of grief in this island of ours. I will tell you a common case. The rules of Eton require that a boy on the *foundation*[2] should be there twelve years: he is superannuated at eighteen, consequently he must come at six. Children torn away from mothers and sisters at that age not unfrequently die. I speak of what I know. The complaint is not entered by the registrar as grief; but *that* it is. Grief of that sort, and at that age, has killed more than ever have been counted amongst its martyrs.

Therefore it is that Levana often communes with the powers that shake man's heart: therefore it is that she doats upon grief. "These ladies," said I softly to myself, on seeing the ministers with whom Levana was conversing, "these are the Sorrows; and they are three in number, as the *Graces* are three, who dress man's life with beauty; the *Parcæ* are three, who weave the dark arras of man's life in their mysterious loom always with colours sad in part, sometimes angry with tragic crimson and black; the *Furies* are three, who visit with retributions called from the other side of the grave offences that walk upon this; and once even the *Muses*[3] were but three, who fit the harp, the trumpet, or

---

wheel, and the glimmering spokes, as applied by him to the flying successions of day and night. I borrowed it for one moment in order to point my own sentence; which being done, the reader is witness that I now pay it back instantly by a note made for that sole purpose. On the same principle I often borrow their seals from young ladies—when closing my letters. Because there is sure to be some tender sentiment upon them about "memory," or "hope," or "roses," or "reunion:" and my correspondent must be a sad brute who is not touched by the eloquence of the seal, even if his taste is so bad that he remains deaf to mine. [See Wordsworth's "To ——— "("Miscellaneous Sonnets," Part II, "Conclusion"): "now every day / Is but a glimmering spoke in the swift wheel / Of the revolving week" (9–11).]

---

[1]   Greek mathematician (325–265 BCE), author of *The Elements*, which define the principles of geometry.

[2]   Eton, prestigious boys' school founded in 1440 by King Henry VI; "on the foundation," or on scholarship.

[3]   Greek and Roman goddesses; Graces, or Charites: three goddesses who represented beauty, charm, nature, fertility, and creativity; Parcae, Moirae, or Fates: three goddesses who portioned out lives; Furies (also Erinyes or Eumenides; see *Confessions*, p. 86, n. 1 above): three daughters of Earth who represented conscience and punished unnatural crime, especially matricide; Muses: nine goddesses who inspired the arts.

the lute, to the great burdens of man's impassioned creations. These are the Sorrows, all three of whom I know." The last words I say *now*; but in Oxford I said—"one of whom I know, and the others too surely I *shall* know." For already, in my fervent youth, I saw (dimly relieved upon the dark background of my dreams) the imperfect lineaments of the awful sisters. These sisters—by what name shall we call them?

If I say simply—"The Sorrows," there will be a chance of mistaking the term; it might be understood of individual sorrow—separate cases of sorrow,—whereas I want a term expressing the mighty abstractions that incarnate themselves in all individual sufferings of man's heart; and I wish to have these abstractions presented as impersonations, that is, as clothed with human attributes of life, and with functions pointing to flesh. Let us call them, therefore, *Our Ladies of Sorrow*. I know them thoroughly, and have walked in all their kingdoms. Three sisters they are, of one mysterious household; and their paths are wide apart; but of their dominion there is no end. Them I saw often conversing with Levana, and sometimes about myself. Do they talk, then? Oh, no! Mighty phantoms like these disdain the infirmities of language. They may utter voices through the organs of man when they dwell in human hearts, but amongst themselves is no voice nor sound—eternal silence reigns in *their* kingdoms. *They* spoke not as they talked with Levana. *They* whispered not. *They* sang not. Though oftentimes methought they *might* have sung; for I upon earth had heard their mysteries oftentimes deciphered by harp and timbrel, by dulcimer and organ.[1] Like God, whose servants they are, they utter their pleasure, not by sounds that perish, or by words that go astray, but by signs in heaven—by changes on earth—by pulses in secret rivers—heraldries painted on darkness—and hieroglyphics written on the tablets of the brain. *They* wheeled in mazes; *I* spelled the steps. *They* telegraphed from afar; *I* read the signals. *They* conspired together; and on the mirrors of darkness *my* eye traced the plots. *Theirs* were the symbols,—*mine* are the words.

What is it the sisters are? What is it that they do? Let me describe their form, and their presence; if form it were that still fluctuated in its outline; or presence it were that for ever advanced to the front, or for ever receded amongst shades.

The eldest of the three is named *Mater Lachrymarum*, Our Lady of Tears. She it is that night and day raves and moans, calling for vanished

---

[1]   Timbrel: ancient tambourine; dulcimer: stringed instrument with frets, held across the knees, and plucked or strummed.

faces. She stood in Rama, when a voice was heard of lamentation—Rachel weeping for her children, and refusing to be comforted.[1] She it was that stood in Bethlehem on the night when Herod's sword swept its nurseries of Innocents, and the little feet were stiffened for ever, which, heard at times as they tottered along floors overhead, woke pulses of love in household hearts that were not unmarked in heaven.

Her eyes are sweet and subtle, wild and sleepy by turns; oftentimes rising to the clouds; oftentimes challenging the heavens. She wears a diadem round her head. And I knew by childish memories that she could go abroad upon the winds, when she heard the sobbing of litanies or the thundering of organs, and when she beheld the mustering of summer clouds. This sister, the elder, it is that carries keys more than Papal at her girdle, which open every cottage and every palace. She, to my knowledge, sate all last summer by the bedside of the blind beggar, him that so often and so gladly I talked with, whose pious daughter, eight years old, with the sunny countenance, resisted the temptations of play and village mirth to travel all day long on dusty roads with her afflicted father. For this did God send her a great reward. In the spring-time of the year, and whilst yet her own spring was budding, he recalled her to himself. But her blind father mourns for ever over *her*, still he dreams at midnight that the little guiding hand is locked within his own; and still he wakens to a darkness that is *now* within a second and a deeper darkness. This *Mater Lachrymarum* also has been sitting all this winter of 1844–5 within the bedchamber of the Czar,[2] bringing before his eyes a daughter (not less pious) that vanished to God not less suddenly, and left behind her a darkness not less profound. By the power of her keys it is that Our Lady of Tears glides a ghostly intruder into the chambers of sleepless men, sleepless women, sleeping children, from Ganges to the Nile, from Nile to Mississippi. And her, because she is the first-born of her house, and has the widest empire, let us honour with the title of "Madonna."

The second sister is called *Mater Suspiriorum*, Our Lady of Sighs. She never scales the clouds, nor walks abroad upon the winds. She wears no

---

[1] "Then Herod, when he saw that he was mocked of the wise men, was exceeding wroth, and sent forth, and slew all the children that were in Bethlehem, and in all the coasts thereof, from two years old and under, according to the time which he had diligently enquired of the wise men. Then was fulfilled that which was spoken by Jeremy the prophet saying, In Rama was there a voice heard, lamentation, and weeping, and great mourning, Rachel weeping *for* her children, and would not be comforted, because they are not" (Matthew 2.16–18).

[2] The death of Alexandra, daughter of Czar Nicholas I.

diadem. And her eyes, if they were ever seen, would be neither sweet nor subtle; no man could read their story; they would be found filled with perishing dreams, and with wrecks of forgotten delirium. But she raises not her eyes; her head, on which sits a dilapidated turban, droops for ever; for ever fastens on the dust. She weeps not. She groans not. But she sighs inaudibly at intervals. Her sister, Madonna, is oftentimes stormy and frantic; raging in the highest against heaven; and demanding back her darlings. But Our Lady of Sighs never clamours, never defies, dreams not of rebellious aspirations. She is humble to abjectness. Hers is the meekness that belongs to the hopeless. Murmur she may, but it is in her sleep. Whisper she may, but it is to herself in the twilight. Mutter she does at times, but it is in solitary places that are desolate as she is desolate, in ruined cities, and when the sun has gone down to his rest. This sister is the visitor of the Pariah, of the Jew, of the bondsman to the oar in Mediterranean galleys, of the English criminal in Norfolk island,[1] blotted out from the books of remembrance in sweet far-off England, of the baffled penitent reverting his eye for ever upon a solitary grave, which to him seems the altar overthrown of some past and bloody sacrifice, on which altar no oblations can now be availing, whether towards pardon that he might implore, or towards reparation that he might attempt. Every slave that at noonday looks up to the tropical sun with timid reproach, as he points with one hand to the earth, our general mother, but for *him* a stepmother, as he points with the other hand to the Bible, our general teacher, but against *him* sealed and sequestered;*—every woman sitting in darkness, without love to shelter her head, or hope to illumine her solitude, because the heaven-born instincts kindling in her nature germs of holy affections, which God implanted in her womanly bosom, having been stifled by social necessities, now burn sullenly to waste, like sepulchral lamps amongst the ancients;—every nun defrauded of her unreturning May-time by wicked kinsmen, whom God will judge;—every captive in every dungeon;—all that are betrayed, and all that are rejected; outcast by

---

* This, the reader will be aware, applies chiefly to the cotton and tobacco States of North America; but not to them only: on which account I have not scrupled to figure the sun, which looks down upon slavery, as *tropical*—no matter if strictly within the tropics, or simply so near to them as to produce a similar climate.

[1] Island off Australia, occupied and settled in 1788 by the British, who used it as a penal station for convicts from New South Wales and Tasmania from 1825 to 1855, when the station was closed.

traditionary law, and children of *hereditary* disgrace—all these walk with "Our Lady of Sighs." She also carries a key; but she needs it little. For her kingdom is chiefly amongst the tents of Shem,[1] and the houseless vagrant of every clime. Yet in the very highest ranks of man she finds chapels of her own; and even in glorious England there are some that, to the world, carry their heads as proudly as the reindeer, who yet secretly have received her mark upon their foreheads.

But the third sister, who is also the youngest ———! Hush! whisper, whilst we talk of *her*! Her kingdom is not large, or else no flesh should live; but within that kingdom all power is hers. Her head, turreted like that of Cybèle,[2] rises almost beyond the reach of sight. She droops not; and her eyes rising so high, *might* be hidden by distance. But, being what they are, they cannot be hidden; through the treble veil of crape which she wears, the fierce light of a blazing misery, that rests not for matins or for vespers—for noon of day or noon of night—for ebbing or for flowing tide—may be read from the very ground. She is the defier of God. She also is the mother of lunacies, and the suggestress of suicides. Deep lie the roots of her power; but narrow is the nation that she rules. For she can approach only those in whom a profound nature has been upheaved by central convulsions; in whom the heart trembles and the brain rocks under conspiracies of tempest from without and tempest from within. Madonna moves with uncertain steps, fast or slow, but still with tragic grace. Our Lady of Sighs creeps timidly and stealthily. But this youngest sister moves with incalculable motions, bounding, and with a tiger's leaps. She carries no key; for, though coming rarely amongst men, she storms all doors at which she is permitted to enter at all. And *her* name is *Mater Tenebrarum*—Our Lady of Darkness.

These were the *Semnai Theai*, or Sublime Goddesses★—these were the *Eumenides*,[3] or Gracious Ladies, (so called by antiquity in shuddering

---

★   "*Sublime Goddesses.*"—The word σεμνός is usually rendered *venerable* in dictionaries; not a very flattering epithet for females. But by weighing a number of passages in which the word is used pointedly, I am disposed to think that it comes nearest to our idea of the *sublime*; as near as a Greek word *could* come.

---

[1]   "God shall enlarge Japeth, and he shall dwell in the tents of Shem; and Canaan shall be his servant" (Genesis 9:27); Japeth, Shem, and Ham, "the father of Canaan," Noah's three sons; Ham found Noah drunk and naked, and told Japeth and Shem, who covered Noah's nakedness; upon waking, Noah blessed Japeth and Shem, and condemned "Canaan."

[2]   Cybele, or Magna Mater, Mother of the Gods, a Roman goddess associated with nature and fertility, whose crown was in the shape of a city wall; associated with orgiastic cults celebrating the return of spring.

[3]   See p. 196 n. 3 above and *Confessions*, p. 86, n. 1 above.

propitiation)—of my Oxford dreams. MADONNA spoke. She spoke by her mysterious hand. Touching my head, she beckoned to Our Lady of Sighs; and *what* she spoke, translated out of the signs which (except in dreams) no man reads, was this:—

"Lo! here is he, whom in childhood I dedicated to my altars. This is he that once I made my darling. Him I led astray, him I beguiled, and from heaven I stole away his young heart to mine. Through me did he become idolatrous; and through me it was, by languishing desires, that he worshipped the worm, and prayed to the wormy grave. Holy was the grave to him; lovely was its darkness; saintly its corruption. Him, this young idolater, I have seasoned for thee, dear gentle Sister of Sighs! Do thou take him now to *thy* heart, and season him for our dreadful sister. And thou"—turning to the *Mater Tenebrarum*, she said—"wicked sister, that temptest and hatest, do thou take him from *her*. See that thy scepter lie heavy on his head. Suffer not woman and her tenderness to sit near him in his darkness. Banish the frailties of hope—wither the relentings of love—scorch the fountains of tears: curse him as only thou canst curse. So shall he be accomplished in the furnace—so shall he see the things that ought *not* to be seen—sights that are abominable, and secrets that are unutterable. So shall he read elder truths, sad truths, grand truths, fearful truths. So shall he rise again *before* he dies. And so shall our commission be accomplished which from God we had—to plague his heart until we had unfolded the capacities of his spirit."*

---

* The reader, who wishes at all to understand the course of these Confessions, ought not to pass over this dream-legend. There is no great wonder that a vision, which occupied my waking thoughts in those years, should re-appear in my dreams. It was in fact a legend recurring in sleep, most of which I had myself silently written or sculptured in my daylight reveries. But its importance to the present Confessions is this—that it rehearses or prefigures their course. This FIRST part belongs to Madonna. The THIRD belongs to the "Mater Suspiriorum," and will be entitled *The Pariah Worlds*. The FOURTH, which terminates the work, belongs to the "Mater Tenebrarum," and will be entitled *The Kingdom of Darkness*. As to the Second, it is an interpolation requisite to the effect of the others; and will be explained in its proper place. [De Quincey dedicated the first part of *Suspiria* to Mater Lachrymarum; the second part or "interpolation" began with the July 1845 fourth installment; he never completed the third and fourth parts of *Suspiria*.]

THE APPARITION OF THE BROCKEN

Ascend with me on this dazzling Whitsunday★ the Brocken of North Germany.[1] The dawn opened in cloudless beauty; it is a dawn of bridal June; but, as the hours advance, her youngest sister April, that sometimes cares little for racing across both frontiers of May, frets the bridal lady's sunny temper with sallies of wheeling and careering showers—flying and pursuing, opening and closing, hiding and restoring. On such a morning, and reaching the summits of the forest-mountain about sunrise, we shall have one chance the more for seeing the famous Spectre of the Brocken.★★

★   Pentecost Sunday, seventh Sunday after Easter Sunday; celebrates the descent of the Holy Spirit on the Apostles fifty days after Christ's resurrection.

★★ "*Spectre of the Brocken.*" This very striking phenomenon has been continually described by writers, both German and English, for the last fifty years. Many readers, however, will not have met with these descriptions: and on *their* account I add a few words in explanation; referring them for the best scientific comment on the case to Sir David Brewster's "Natural Magic." The spectre takes the shape of a human figure, or, if the visitors are more than one, then the spectres multiply; they arrange themselves on the blue ground of the sky, or the dark ground of any clouds that may be in the right quarter, or perhaps they are strongly relieved against a curtain of rock, at a distance of some miles, and always exhibiting gigantic proportions. At first, from the distance and the colossal size, every spectator supposes the appearance to be quite independent of himself. But very soon he is surprised to observe his own motions and gestures mimicked; and wakens to the conviction that the phantom is but a dilated reflection of himself. This Titan amongst the apparitions of earth is exceedingly capricious, vanishing abruptly for reasons best known to himself, and more coy in coming forward than the Lady Echo of Ovid. One reason why he is seen so seldom must be ascribed to the concurrence of conditions under which only the phenomenon can be manifested: the sun must be near to the horizon, (which of itself implies a time of day inconvenient to a person starting from a station as distant as Elbingerode;) the spectator must have his back to the sun; and the air must contain some vapour—but *partially* distributed. Coleridge ascended the Brocken on the Whitsunday of 1799, with a party of English students from Goettingen, but failed to see the phantom; afterwards in England (and under the same three conditions) he saw a much rarer phenomenon, which he described in the following eight lines. I give them from a corrected copy: (the apostrophe in the beginning must be understood as addressed to an ideal conception): —

> "And art thou nothing? Such thou art as when
> The woodman winding westward up the glen
> At wintry dawn, when o'er the sheep-track's maze
> The viewless snow-mist weaves a glist'ning haze,
> Sees full before him, gliding without tread,
> An image with a glory round its head:
> This shade he worships for its golden hues,
> And *makes* (not knowing) that which he pursues."

---

[1] A peak in the Hartz Mountains; setting of *Walpurgisnacht*, or Walpurgis Night, April 30, a witches' ritual to ward off evil.

Who and what is he? He is a solitary apparition, in the sense of loving solitude; else he is not always solitary in his personal manifestations, but on proper occasions has been known to unmask a strength quite sufficient to alarm those who had been insulting him.

Now, in order to test the nature of this mysterious apparition, we will try two or three experiments upon him. What we fear, and with some reason, is, that as he lived so many ages with foul Pagan sorcerers, and witnessed so many centuries of dark idolatries, his heart may have been corrupted; and that even now his faith may be wavering or impure. We will try.

Make the sign of the cross, and observe whether he repeats it, (as, on Whitsunday,* he surely ought to do.) Look! he does repeat it; but the driving showers perplex the images, and *that*, perhaps, it is which gives him the air of one who acts reluctantly or evasively. Now, again, the sun shines more brightly, and the showers have swept off like squadrons of cavalry to the rear. We will try him again.

Pluck an anemone, one of these many anemones which once was called the sorcerer's flower, and bore a part perhaps in his horrid ritual of fear; carry it to that stone which mimics the outline of a heathen altar, and once was called the sorcerer's altar;** then, bending your

---

[De Quincey draws his account partly from Sir David Brewster (1781–1868), who in *Letters on Natural Magic* (1832) translates the report of M. Haue, who saw it on 23 May 1797, as recorded in J.F. Gmelin's *Göttingische Journal der Wissenschafte* (1798),Vol. 1, part iii. He also draws upon Coleridge's account, though in fact Coleridge climbed the Brocken twice. See Coleridge's *Notebooks* (entries 412 and 447) and *Letters* 1:504. The spectre is an atmospheric phenomenon created when the viewer's shadow is cast upon the surrounding clouds, which constantly shift due to temperature and wind, thus making the apparition appear as a distorted and not always direct reflection of the viewer's shape. Ovid (43 BCE – 17 CE): Roman poet, author of *Metamorphoses* (1 CE); Echo, a nymph who pines for Narcissus; unable to speak except to echo his words back to him, she withers away to just a voice. The quotation from Coleridge at the end of De Quincey's note is from "Constancy to an Ideal Object" (25–32).]

* *"On Whitsunday."*—It is singular, and perhaps owing to the temperature and weather likely to prevail in that early part of summer, that more appearances of the spectre have been witnessed on Whitsunday than on any other day. [The editors of *Works* note that "The sunrise in Spring is at the optimum angle for the light to strike the clouds banked against the mountains to west of the Brocken" (15:663).]

** *"The sorcerer's flower,"* and *"the sorcerer's altar."*—These are names still clinging to the anemone of the Brocken, and to an altar-shaped fragment of granite near one of the summits; and it is not doubted that they both connect themselves through links of ancient tradition with the gloomy realities of Paganism, when the whole Hartz and the Brocken formed for a very long time the last asylum to a ferocious but perishing idolatry. [De Quincey gets these details from Brewster's account.]

knee, and raising your right hand to God, say,—"Father, which art in heaven—this lovely anemone, that once glorified the worship of fear, has travelled back into thy fold; this altar, which once reeked with bloody rites to Cortho, has long been rebaptized into thy holy service. The darkness is gone—the cruelty is gone which the darkness bred; the moans have passed away which the victims uttered; the cloud has vanished which once sate continually upon their graves—cloud of protestation that ascended for ever to thy throne from the tears of the defenceless, and the anger of the just. And lo! I thy servant, with this dark phantom, whom, for one hour on this thy festival of Pentecost, I make *my* servant, render thee untied worship in this thy recovered temple."

Look, now! the apparition plucks an anemone, and places it on an altar; he also bends his knee, he also raises his right hand to God. Dumb he is; but sometimes the dumb serve God acceptably. Yet still it occurs to you, that perhaps on this high festival of the Christian Church, he may be overruled by supernatural influence into confession of his homage, having so often been made to bow and bend his knee at murderous rites. In a service of religion he may be timid. Let us try him, therefore, with an earthly passion, where he will have no bias either from favour or from fear.

If, then, once in childhood you suffered an affliction that was ineffable; If once, when powerless to face such an enemy, you were summoned to fight with the tiger that couches within the separations of the grave; in that case, after the example of Judæa[1] (on the Roman coins)—sitting under her palm-tree to weep, but sitting with her head veiled—do you also veil your head. Many years are passed away since then; and you were a little ignorant thing at that time, hardly above six years old; or perhaps (if you durst tell all the truth) not quite so much. But your heart was deeper than the Danube; and, as was your love, so was your grief. Many years are gone since that darkness settled on your head; many summers, many winters; yet still its shadows wheel round upon you at intervals, like these April showers upon this glory of bridal June. Therefore now, on this dovelike morning of Pentecost,[2] do you veil your head like Judæa, in memory of that transcendant woe, and in testimony that, indeed, it surpassed all utterance of words. Immediately

---

[1] "In 70 CE the Emperor Vespasian struck coins commemorating the conquest of Jerusalem. They showed Judea as a woman sitting sorrowfully under a palm tree (see Paul Mallinson, 'De Quincey's Ann in Judea,' *Notes and Queries* CCV, 1980, 505–7)" [*Works* 15:663].

[2] Whitsunday or Pentecost, "feast of weeks" (Exodus 34:22 and Deuteronomy 16:10); see p. 202, asterisked note on "Whitsunday."

you see that the apparition of the Brocken veils *his* head, after the model of Judæa weeping under her palm-tree, as if he also had a human heart, and that *he* also, in childhood, having suffered an affliction which was ineffable, wished by these mute symbols to breath a sigh towards heaven in memory of that affliction, and by way of record, though many a year after, that it was indeed unutterable by words.

This trial is decisive. You are now satisfied that the apparition is but a reflex of yourself; and, in uttering your secret feelings to *him*, you make this phantom the dark symbolic mirror for reflecting to the daylight what else must be hidden for ever.

Such a relation does the Dark Interpreter, whom immediately the reader will learn to know as an intruder into my dreams, bear to my own mind. He is originally a mere reflex of my inner nature. But as the apparition of the Brocken sometimes is disturbed by storms or by driving showers, so as to dissemble his real origin, in like manner the Interpreter sometimes swerves out of my orbit, and mixes a little with alien natures. I do not always know him in these cases as my own parhelion.[1] What he says, generally is but that which *I* have said in daylight, and in meditation deep enough to sculpture itself on my heart. But sometimes, as his face alters, his words alter; and they do not always seem such as I have used, or *could* use. No man can account for all things that occur in dreams. Generally I believe this—that he is a faithful representative of myself; but he also is at times subject to the action of the god *Phantasus*,[2] who rules in dreams.

Hailstone choruses* besides, and storms, enter my dreams. Hailstones and fire that run along the ground, sleet and blinding hurricanes, revelations of glory insufferable pursued by volleying darkness—these are powers able to disturb any features that originally were but shadow, and to send drifting the anchors of any vessel that rides upon deeps so treacherous as those of dreams. Understand, however, the Interpreter to bear generally the office of a tragic chorus at Athens. The Greek chorus

---

* "*Hailstone choruses.*"—I need not tell any lover of Handel that his oratorio of "Israel in Egypt" contains a chorus familiarly known by this name. The words are—"And he gave them hailstones for rain; fire, mingled with the hail, ran along upon the ground." [*Israel in Egypt*: opera by George Friedrich Handel (1685–1759); premiered in London, April 1739.]

---

[1]   "A bright spot in the sky, often associated with a solar halo and frequently occurring in pairs on either side of the sun (or occasionally above and below it), caused by refraction of sunlight through ice crystals in the atmosphere; a mock sun, a sun-dog" (*OED*).

[2]   Roman god of dreams; son of Somnus, god of sleep.

is perhaps not quite understood by critics, any more than the Dark Interpreter by myself. But the leading function of both must be supposed this—not to tell you any thing absolutely new, *that* was done by the actors in the drama; but to recall you to your own lurking thoughts—hidden for the moment or imperfectly developed, and to place before you, in immediate connexion with groups vanishing too quickly for any effort of meditation on your own part, such commentaries, prophetic or looking back, pointing the moral or deciphering the mystery, justifying Providence, or mitigating the fierceness of anguish, as would or might have occurred to your own meditative heart—had only time been allowed for its motions.

The Interpreter is anchored and stationary in my dreams; but great storms and driving mists cause him to fluctuate uncertainly, or even to retire altogether, like his gloomy counterpart the shy Phantom of the Brocken—and to assume new features or strange features, as in dreams always there is a power not contented with reproduction, but which absolutely creates or transforms. This dark being the reader will see again in a further stage of my opium experience; and I warn him that he will not always be found sitting inside my dreams, but at times outside, and in open daylight.

FINALE TO PART I.
—SAVANNAH-LA-MAR

God smote Savannah-la-Mar,[1] and in one night, by earthquake, removed her, with all her towers standing and population sleeping, from the steadfast foundations of the shore to the coral floors of the ocean. And God said—"Pompeii[2] did I bury and conceal from men through seventeen centuries: this city I will bury, but not conceal. She shall be a monument to men of my mysterious anger; set in azure light through generations to come: for I will enshrine her in a crystal dome of my tropic seas." This city, therefore, like a mighty galleon with all her apparel mounted, streamers flying, and tackling perfect, seems floating along the noiseless depths of ocean: and oftentimes in glassy calms, through the translucid atmosphere of water that now stretches like an air-woven awning above the silent encampment, mariners from every

---

[1]   Jamaican seaport destroyed by a hurricane in 1780.
[2]   Ancient Roman city destroyed by the eruption of Mount Vesuvius on 29 August 79 CE.

clime look down into her courts and terraces, count her gates, and number the spires of her churches. She is one ample cemetery, and *has* been for many a year; but in the mighty calms that brood for weeks over tropic latitudes, she fascinates the eye with a *Fata-Morgana*[1] revelation, as of human life still subsisting in submarine asylums sacred from the storms that torment our upper air.

Thither, lured by the loveliness of cerulean depths, by the peace of human dwellings privileged from molestation, by the gleam of marble altars sleeping in everlasting sanctity, oftentimes in dreams did I and the dark Interpreter cleave the watery veil that divided us from her streets. We looked into the belfries, where the pendulous bells were waiting in vain for the summons which should awaken their marriage peals; together we touched the mighty organ keys, that sang no *jubilates*[2] for the ear of Heaven—that sang no requiems for the ear of human sorrow; together we searched the silent nurseries, where the children were all asleep, and *had* been asleep through five generations. "They are waiting for the heavenly dawn," whispered the Interpreter to himself; "and, when *that* comes, the bells and the organs will utter a *jubilate* repeated by the echoes of Paradise." Then, turning to me, he said—"This is sad: this is piteous: but less would not have sufficed for the purposes of God. Look here: put into a Roman clepsydra[3] one hundred drops of water; let these run out as the sands in an hourglass; every drop measuring the hundredth part of a second, so that each shall represent but the three-hundred-and-sixty-thousandth part of an hour. Now, count the drops as they race along; and, when the fiftieth of the hundred is passing, behold! forty-nine are not, because already they have perished; and fifty are not, because they are yet to come. You see, therefore, how narrow, how incalculably narrow, is the true and actual present. Of that time which we call the present, hardly a hundredth part but belongs either to a past which has fled, or to a future which is still on the wing. It has perished, or it is not born. It was, or it is not. Yet even this approximation to the truth is *infinitely* false. For again subdivide that solitary drop, which only was found to represent the present, into a lower series of similar fractions, and the actual present which you arrest measures now but the thirty-sixth millionth of an hour; and so by infinite declensions

---

[1]   Mirage; Italian for "Morgan le Fay," sorceress of Arthurian legend; also discussed in Brewster's *Letters on Natural Magic*.

[2]   De Quincey pluralizes "jubilate": "A call to rejoice; an outburst of joyous triumph" . (*OED*).

[3]   Water-clock.

the true and very present, in which only we live and enjoy, will vanish into a mote of a mote, distinguishable only by a heavenly vision. Therefore the present, which only man possesses, offers less capacity for his footing than the slenderest film that ever spider twisted from her womb. Therefore, also, even this incalculable shadow from the narrowest pencil of moonlight, is more transitory than geometry can measure, or thought of angel can overtake. The time which *is*, contracts into a mathematic point; and even that point perishes a thousand times before we can utter its birth. All is finite in the present; and even that finite is infinite in its velocity of flight towards death. But in God there is nothing finite; but in God there is nothing transitory; but in God there *can* be nothing that tends to death. Therefore, it follows—that for God there can be no present. The future is the present of God; and to the future it is that he sacrifices the human present. Therefore it is that he works by earthquake. Therefore it is that he works by grief. Oh, deep is the ploughing of earthquake! Oh, deep," (and his voice swelled like a *sanctus*[1] rising from the choir of a cathedral,)—"oh, deep is the ploughing of grief! But oftentimes less would not suffice for the agriculture of God. Upon a night of earthquake he builds a thousand years of pleasant habitations for man. Upon the sorrow of an infant, he raises oftentimes from human intellects glorious vintages that could not else have been. Less than these fierce ploughshares would not have stirred the stubborn soil. The one is needed for earth, our planet—for earth itself as the dwelling-place of man. But the other is needed yet oftener for God's mightiest instrument; yes," (and he looked solemnly at myself,) "is needed for the mysterious children of the earth!"

END OF PART I.

---

[1]   Opening of Holy Communion: "Holy, holy, holy" (Isaiah 6:13).

PART II

The Oxford visions, of which some have been given, were but anticipations necessary to illustrate the glimpse opened of childhood, (as being its reaction.) In this SECOND part, returning from that anticipation, I retrace an abstract of my boyish and youthful days so far as they furnished or exposed the germs of later experiences in worlds more shadowy.

Upon me, as upon others scattered thinly by tens and twenties over every thousand years, fell too powerfully and too early the vision of life. The horror of life mixed itself already in earliest youth with the heavenly sweetness of life; that grief, which one in a hundred has sensibility enough to gather from the sad retrospect of life in its closing stage, for me shed its dews as a prelibation upon the fountains of life whilst yet sparkling to the morning sun. I saw from afar and from before what I was to see from behind. Is this the description of an early youth passed in the shades of gloom? No, but of a youth passed in the divinest happiness. And if the reader has (which so few have) the passion, without which there is no reading of the legend and superscription upon man's brow, if he is not (as most are) deafer than the grave to every *deep* note that sighs upwards from the Delphic caves of human life, he will know that the rapture of life (or any thing which by approach can merit that name) does not arise, unless as perfect music arises—music of Mozart or Beethoven—by the confluence of the mighty and terrific discords with the subtle concords. Not by contrast, or as reciprocal foils do these elements act, which is the feeble conception of many, but by union. They are the sexual forces in music: "male and female created he them;"[1] and these mighty antagonists do not put forth their hostilities by repulsion, but by deepest attraction.

As "in to-day already walks to-morrow,"[2] so in the past experience of a youthful life may be seen dimly the future. The collisions with alien interests or hostile views, of a child, boy, or very young man, so insulated as each of these is sure to be,—those aspects of opposition which such a person *can* occupy, are limited by the exceedingly few and trivial lines of connexion along which he is able to radiate any essential influence

---

[1] "So God created man in his *own* image, in the image of God created he him; male and female created he them" (Genesis 1:27).

[2] Coleridge, *The Death of Wallenstein*; Wallenstein says to the Countess, "As the sun, / Ere it is risen, sometimes paints its image / In the atmosphere, so often do the spirits / Of great events stride on before the events; / And in to-day already walks to-morrow" (5.1.98–102); see p. 163, De Quincey's note above.

whatever upon the fortunes or happiness of others. Circumstances may magnify his importance for the moment; but, after all, any cable which he carries out upon other vessels is easily slipped upon a feud arising. Far otherwise is the state of relations connecting an adult or responsible man with the circles around him as life advances. The network of these relations is a thousand times more intricate, the jarring of these intricate relations a thousand times more frequent, and the vibrations a thousand times harsher which these jarrings diffuse. This truth is felt beforehand misgivingly and in troubled vision, by a young man who stands upon the threshold of manhood. One earliest instinct of fear and horror would darken his spirit if it could be revealed to itself and self-questioned at the moment of birth: a second instinct of the same nature would again pollute that tremulous mirror, if the moment were as punctually marked as physical birth is marked, which dismisses him finally upon the tides of absolute self-controul. A dark ocean would seem the total expanse of life from the first: but far darker and more appalling would seem that interior and second chamber of the ocean which called him away for ever from the direct accountability of others. Dreadful would be the morning which should say—"Be thou a human child incarnate;" but more dreadful the morning which should say—"Bear thou henceforth the sceptre of thy self-dominion through life, and the passion of life!" Yes, dreadful would be both: but without a basis of the dreadful there is no perfect rapture. It is a part through the sorrow of life, growing out of its events, that this basis of awe and solemn darkness slowly accumulates. *That* I have illustrated. But, as life expands, it is more through the *strife* which besets us, strife from conflicting opinions, positions, passions, interests, that the funereal ground settles and deposits itself, which sends upward the dark lustrous brilliancy through the jewel of life—else revealing a pale and superficial glitter. Either the human being must suffer and struggle as the price of a more searching vision, or his gaze must be shallow and without intellectual revelation.

Through accident it was in part, and, where through no accident but my own nature, not through features of it at all painful to recollect, that constantly in early life (that is, from boyish days until eighteen, when by going to Oxford, practically I became my own master) I was engaged in duels of fierce continual struggle, with some person or body of persons, that sought, like the Roman *retiarius*,[1] to throw a net of deadly coercion or constraint over the undoubted rights of my natural freedom. The

---

[1]   Gladiator fighting with a net to ensnare his adversary.

steady rebellion upon my part in one-half, was a mere human reaction of justifiable indignation; but in the other half it was the struggle of a conscientious nature—disdaining to feel it as any mere right or discretional privilege—no, feeling it as the noblest of duties to resist, though it should be mortally, those that would have enslaved me, and to retort scorn upon those that would have put my head below their feet. Too much, even in later life, I have perceived in men that pass for good men, a disposition to degrade (and if possible to degrade through self-degradation) those in whom unwillingly they feel any weight of oppression to themselves, by commanding qualities of intellect or character. They respect you: they are compelled to do so: and they hate to do so. Next, therefore, they seek to throw off the sense of this oppression, and to take vengeance for it, by co-operating with any unhappy accidents in your life, to inflict a sense of humiliation upon you, and (if possible) to force you into becoming a consenting party to that humiliation. Oh, wherefore is it that those who presume to call themselves the "friends" of this man or that woman, are so often those above all others, whom in the hour of death that man or woman is most likely to salute with the valediction—Would God I had never seen your face?

In citing one or two cases of these early struggles, I have chiefly in view the effect of these upon my subsequent visions under the reign of opium. And this indulgent reflection should accompany the mature reader through all such records of boyish inexperience. A goodtempered man, who is also acquainted with the world, will easily evade, without needing any artifice of servile obsequiousness, those quarrels which an upright simplicity, jealous of its own rights, and unpractised in the science of worldly address, cannot always evade without some loss of self-respect. Suavity in this manner may, it is true, be reconciled with firmness in the matter; but not easily by a young person who wants all the appropriate resources of knowledge, of adroit and guarded language, for making his good temper available. Men are protected from insult and wrong, not merely by their own skill, but also in the absence of any skill at all, by the general spirit of forbearance to which society had trained all those whom they are likely to meet. But boys meeting with no such forbearance or training in other boys, must sometimes be thrown upon feuds in the ratio of their own firmness, much more than in the ratio of any natural proneness to quarrel. Such a subject, however, will be best illustrated by a sketch or two of my own principal feuds.

The first, but merely transient and playful, nor worth noticing at all, but for its subsequent resurrection under other and awful colouring in my dreams, grew out of an imaginary slight, as I viewed it, put upon me by one of my guardians. I had four guardians:[1] and the one of these who had the most knowledge and talent of the whole, a banker, living about a hundred miles from my home, had invited me when eleven years old to his house. His eldest daughter, perhaps a year younger than myself, wore at that time upon her very lovely face the most angelic expression of character and temper that I have almost ever seen. Naturally, I fell in love with her. It seems absurd to say so; and the more so, because two children more absolutely innocent than we were cannot be imagined, neither of us having ever been at any school;—but the simple truth is, that in the most chivalrous sense I was in love with her. And the proof that I was so showed itself in three separate modes: I kissed her glove on any rare occasion when I found it lying on a table; secondly, I looked out for some excuse to be jealous of her; and, thirdly, I did my very best to get up a quarrel. What I wanted the quarrel for was the luxury of a reconciliation; a hill cannot be had, you know, without going to the expense of a valley. And though I hated the very thought of a moment's difference with so truly gentle a girl, yet how, but through such a purgatory, could one win the paradise of her returning smiles? All this, however, came to nothing; and simply because she positively would *not* quarrel. And the jealousy fell through, because there was no decent subject for such a passion, unless it had settled upon an old music-master whom lunacy itself could not adopt as a rival. The quarrel meantime, which never prospered with the daughter, silently kindled on my part towards the father. His offence was this. At dinner, I naturally placed myself by the side of M., and it gave me great pleasure to touch her hand at intervals. As M. was my cousin, though twice or even three times removed, I did not feel taking too great a liberty in this little act of tenderness. No matter if three thousand times removed, I said, my cousin is my cousin: nor had I very much designed to conceal the act; or if so, rather on her account than my own. One evening, however, papa observed my manœuvre. Did he seem displeased? Not at all: he even condescended to smile. But the next day he placed M. on the side opposite to myself. In one respect this was really an improvement; because it gave me a better view of my cousin's sweet countenance. But then there was the loss of the hand to be considered, and secondly there was the affront. It was clear that vengeance must be had. Now there was but one thing in this world that I could do even decently: but *that* I could do

---

[1] See *Confessions*, p. 57, n. 3 above.

admirably. This was writing Latin hexameters. Juvenal, though it was not very much of him that I had then read, seemed to me a divine model. The inspiration of wrath spoke through him as through a Hebrew prophet. The same inspiration spoke now in me. *Facit indignatio versum,*[1] said Juvenal. And it must be owned that Indignation has never made such good verses since as she did in that day. But still, even to me this agile passion proved a Muse of genial inspiration for a couple of paragraphs: and one line I will mention as worthy to have taken its place in Juvenal himself. I say this without scruple, having not a shadow of vanity, nor on the other hand a shadow of false modesty connected with such boyish accomplishments. The poem opened thus—

"Te nimis austerum, sacræ qui fœdera mensæ
Diruis, insector Satyræ reboante flagello."[2]

But the line, which I insist upon as of Roman strength, was the closing one of the next sentence. The general effect of the sentiment was—that my clamorous wrath should make its way even into ears that were past hearing:

"——— mea sæva querela
Auribus insidet ceratis, auribus etsi
Non audituris hybernâ nocte procellam."

The power, however, which inflated my verse, soon collapsed; having been soothed from the very first by finding—that except in this one instance at the dinner-table, which probably had been viewed as an indecorum, no further restraint of any kind whatever was meditated upon my intercourse with M. Besides, it was too painful to lock up good verses in one's own solitary breast. Yet how could I shock the sweet filial heart of my cousin by a fierce lampoon or *stylites*[3] against

---

[1] From Juvenal, late first-century to early second-century Roman satiric poet; author of *Satires*: "Indignation will prompt my verse" (*Satires* I.79).

[2] "'You, over-harsh one, who destroy the sacred covenants of the table, I pursue you with the resounding whip of satire.' In 1800, aged fifteen, De Quincey won a prize for his translation of Horace, Ode 22 ... By De Quincey's account, it was in 1796, aged eleven, that he composed this imitation in Latin of Juvenal" (*Works* 2:665); he continues the imitation below: "May my savage complaint fix itself in your waxy ears, even if those ears cannot hear a hurricane on a winter night."

[3] "An ascetic who lived on top of a pillar" (*OED*); De Quincey seems to be conflating the rather absurd posture of the stylite with the idea of a lampoon.

her father, had Latin even figured amongst her accomplishments? Then it occurred to me that the verses might be shown to the father. But was there not something treacherous in gaining a man's approbation under a mask to a satire upon himself? Or would he have always understood me? For one person a year after took the *sacræ mensæ*[1] (by which I had meant the sanctities of hospitality) to mean the sacramental table. And on consideration I began to suspect, that many people would pronounce myself the party who had violated the holy ties of hospitality, which are equally binding on guest as on host. Indolence, which sometimes comes in aid of good impulses as well as bad, favoured these relenting thoughts; the society of M. did still more to wean me from further efforts of satire: and, finally, my Latin poem remained a *torso*. But upon the whole my guardian had a narrow escape of descending to posterity in a disadvantageous light, had he rolled down to it through my hexameters.

Here was a case of merely playful feud. But the same talent of Latin verses soon after connected me with a real feud that harassed my mind more than would be supposed, and precisely by this agency, viz. that it arrayed one set of feelings against another. It divided my mind as by domestic feud against itself. About a year after, returning from the visit to my guardian's, and when I must have been nearly completing my twelfth year, I was sent to a great public school.[2] Every man has reason to rejoice who enjoys so great an advantage. I condemned and *do* condemn the practice of sometimes sending out into such stormy exposures those who are as yet too young, too dependent on female gentleness, and endowed with sensibilities too exquisite. But at nine or ten the masculine energies of the character are beginning to be developed: or, if not, no discipline will better aid in their development than the bracing intercourse of a great English classical school. Even the selfish are forced into accommodating themselves to a public standard of generosity, and the effeminate into conforming to a rule of manliness. I was myself at two public schools; and I think with gratitude of the benefit which I reaped from both; as also I think with gratitude of the upright guardian in whose quiet household I learned Latin so effectually. But the small private schools which I witnessed for brief periods, containing thirty to forty boys, were models of ignoble manners as respected some part of the juniors, and of favouritism amongst the masters. Nowhere is the sublimity of public justice so broadly exemplified as in an English school. There

---

[1] Literally, sacramental tables, or altar.
[2] Spencer's Academy, Winkfield, Wiltshire, which De Quincey entered in 1799 at 14.

is not in the universe such an areopagus[1] for fair play and abhorrence of all crooked ways, as an English mob, or one of the English time-honoured public schools. But my own first introduction to such an establishment was under peculiar and contradictory circumstances. When my "rating," or graduation in the school, was to be settled, naturally my altitude (to speak astronomically) was taken by the proficiency in Greek. But I could then barely construe books so easy as the Greek Testament and the Iliad.[2] This was considered quite well enough for my age; but still it caused me to be placed three steps below the highest rank in the school. Within one week, however, my talent for Latin verses, which had by this time gathered strength and expansion, became known. I was honoured as never was man or boy since Mordecai the Jew.[3] Not properly belonging to the flock of the head master, but to the leading section of the second, I was now weekly paraded for distinction at the supreme tribunal of the school; out of which at first grew nothing but a sunshine of approbation delightful to my heart, still brooding upon solitude. Within six weeks this had changed. The approbation indeed continued, and the public testimony of it. Neither would there, in the ordinary course, have been any painful reaction from jealousy or fretful resistance to the soundness of my pretensions; since it was sufficiently known to some of my schoolfellows, that I, who had no male relatives but military men, and those in India, could not have benefited by any clandestine aid. But, unhappily, the head master was at that time dissatisfied with some points in the progress of his head form; and, as it soon appeared, was continually throwing in their teeth the brilliancy of my verses at twelve, by comparison with theirs at seventeen, eighteen, and nineteen. I had observed him sometimes pointing to myself; and was perplexed at seeing this gesture followed by gloomy looks, and what French reporters call "sensation,"[4] in these young men, whom naturally I viewed with awe as my leaders, boys that were called young men, men that were reading Sophocles[5]—(a name that carried with it the sound of

---

[1] Highest judicial court of Athens.
[2] The New Testament was translated into Greek c. 200 BCE; Homer's *Iliad* was written c. 800 BCE.
[3] See Esther 6:6–11.
[4] De Quincey uses the term to mean "A condition of excited feeling produced in a community by some occurrence; a strong impression (e.g. of horror, admiration, surprise, etc.) produced in an audience or body of spectators, and manifested by their demeanour" (*OED*), yet by way of making this a foreign – i.e. un-English – response, when in fact that idea of sensation as sensibility or heightened, excessive feeling was very much also in the English lexicon.
[5] Greek tragedian (497/6–406 BCE), said to have written approximately 125 plays, of which seven survive.

something seraphic to my ears)—and who never had vouchsafed to waste a word on such a child as myself. The day was come, however, when all that would be changed. One of these leaders strode up to me in the public playgrounds, and delivering a blow on my shoulder, which was not intended to hurt me, but as a mere formula of introduction, asked me, "What the de——l I meant by bolting out of the course, and annoying other people in that manner? Were other people to have no rest for me and my verses, which, after all, were horribly bad?" There might have been some difficulty in returning an answer to this address, but none was required. I was briefly admonished to see that I wrote worse for the future, or else—At this *aposiopesis*[1] I looked enquiringly at the speaker, and he filled up the chasm by saying, that he would "annihilate" me. Could any person fail to be aghast at such a demand? I was to write worse than my own standard, which, by his account of my verses, must be difficult; and I was to write worse than himself, which might be impossible. My feelings revolted, it may be supposed, against so arrogant a demand, unless it had been far otherwise expressed; and on the next occasion for sending up verses, so far from attending to the orders issued, I double-shotted my guns; double applause descended on myself; but I remarked with some awe, though not repenting of what I had done, that double confusion seemed to agitate the ranks of my enemies. Amongst them loomed out in the distance my "annihilating" friend, who shook his huge fist at me, but with something like a grim smile about his eyes. He took an early opportunity of paying his respects to me—saying, "You little devil, do you call this writing your worst?" "No," I replied: "I call it writing my best." The annihilator, as it turned out, was really a good-natured young man; but he soon went off to Cambridge; and with the rest, or some of them, I continued to wage war for nearly a year. And yet, for a word spoken with kindness, I would have resigned the peacock's feather in my cap as the merest of baubles. Undoubtedly, praise sounded sweet in my ears also. But *that* was nothing by comparison with what stood on the other side. I detested distinctions that were connected with mortification to others. And, even if I could have got over *that*, the eternal feud fretted and tormented my nature. Love, that once in childhood had been so mere a necessity to me, *that* had long been a mere reflected ray from a departed sunset. But peace, and freedom from strife, if love were no longer possible, (as so rarely it is in this world,) was the absolute necessity of my heart.

---

[1] "A rhetorical artifice, in which the speaker comes to a sudden halt, as if unable or unwilling to proceed" (*OED*).

To contend with somebody was still my fate; how to escape the contention I could not see; and yet for itself, and the deadly passions into which it forced me, I hated and loathed it more than death. It added to the distraction and internal feud of my own mind—that I could not *altogether* condemn the upper boys. I was made a handle of humiliation to them. And in the mean time, if I had an advantage in one accomplishment, which is all a matter of accident, or peculiar taste and feeling, they, on the other hand, had a great advantage over me in the more elaborate difficulties of Greek, and of choral Greek poetry. I could not altogether wonder at their hatred of myself. Yet still, as they had chosen to adopt this mode of conflict with me, I did not feel that I had any choice but to resist. The contest was terminated for me by my removal from the school, in consequence of a very threatening illness affecting my head; but it lasted nearly a year; and it did not close before several amongst my public enemies had become my private friends. They were much older, but they invited me to the houses of their friends, and showed me a respect which deeply affected me—this respect having more reference, apparently, to the firmness I had exhibited than to the splendour of my verses. And, indeed, these had rather drooped from a natural accident; several persons of my own class had formed the practice of asking me to write verses for *them*. I could not refuse. But, as the subjects given out were the same for all of us, it was not possible to take so many crops off the ground without starving the quality of all.

Two years and a half from this time, I was again at a public school of ancient foundation.[1] Now I was myself one of the three who formed the highest class. Now I myself was familiar with Sophocles, who once had been so shadowy a name in my ear. But, strange to say, now in my sixteenth year, I cared nothing at all for the glory of Latin verse. All the business of school was slight and trivial in my eyes. Costing me not an effort, it could not engage any part of my attention; that was now swallowed up altogether by the literature of my native land. I still reverenced the Grecian drama, as always I must. But else I cared little then for classical pursuits. A deeper spell had mastered me; and I lived only in those bowers where deeper passions spoke.

Here, however, it was that began another and more important struggle. I was drawing near to seventeen, and, in a year after *that*, would arrive the usual time for going to Oxford. To Oxford my guardians made no objection; and they readily agreed to make the allowance then

---

[1]   Manchester Grammar School, which De Quincey entered in 1802 at 16.

universally regarded as the *minimum* for an Oxford student, viz. £200 per annum. But they insisted, as a previous condition, that I should make a positive and definitive choice of a profession. Now I was well aware that, if I *did* make such a choice, no law existed, nor could any obligation be created through deeds or signature, by which I could finally be compelled into keeping my engagement. But this evasion did not suit me. Here, again, I felt indignantly that the principle of the attempt was unjust. The object was certainly to do me service by saving money, since, if I selected the bar as my profession, it was contended by some persons, (misinformed, however,) that not Oxford, but a special pleader's office, would be my proper destination; but I cared not for arguments of that sort. Oxford I was determined to make my home; and also to bear my future course utterly untrammeled by promises that I might repent. Soon came the catastrophe of this struggle. A little before my seventeenth birthday, I walked off one lovely summer morning to North Wales—rambled there for months—and, finally, under some obscure hopes of raising money on my personal security, I went up to London. Now I was in my eighteenth year; and, during this period it was that I passed through that trial of severe distress, of which I gave some account in my former Confessions. Having a motive, however, for glancing backwards briefly at that period in the present series, I will do so at this point.

I saw in one journal an insinuation that the incidents in the *preliminary* narrative were possibly without foundation. To such an expression of mere gratuitous malignity, as it happened to be supported by no one argument except a remark, apparently absurd, but certainly false, I did not condescend to answer. In reality, the possibility had never occurred to me that any person of judgment would seriously suspect me of taking liberties with that part of the work, since, though no one of the parties concerned but myself stood in so central a position to the circumstances as to be acquainted with *all* of them, many were acquainted with each separate section of the memoir. Relays of witnesses might have been summoned to mount guard, as it were, upon the accuracy of each particular in the whole succession of incidents; and some of these people had an interest, more or less strong, in exposing any deviation from the strictest *letter* of the truth, had it been in their power to do so. It is now twenty-two years since I saw the objection here alluded to; and, in saying that I did not condescend to notice it, the reader must not find any reason for taxing me with a blamable haughtiness. But every man is entitled to be haughty when his veracity is impeached; and, still more, when it is impeached by a dishonest objection, or, if not *that*, by an objection which argues a carelessness of attention almost amounting to dishonesty, in a case where it was meant to sustain an imputation of falsehood. Let a man read carelessly if he will, but not where he is meaning to use his reading for a purpose of wounding another man's honour. Having thus, by twenty-two years' silence, sufficiently expressed my contempt for the slander,* I now feel myself at liberty to draw it into notice, for the sake, *inter alia*,[1] of showing in how rash a spirit malignity often works. In the preliminary account of certain boyish adventures which had exposed me to suffering of a kind not commonly incident to persons in my station of life, and leaving behind a temptation to the use of opium under certain arrears of weakness, I had occasion to notice a disreputable attorney in London, who showed me some attentions, partly on my own account as a boy of some expectations, but much more with the purpose of fastening his professional grappling-hooks upon the young Earl of A———t,[2] my former companion, and my present correspondent. This man's house was slightly described, and, with more minuteness, I had exposed some interesting traits in his household economy. A question, therefore, naturally arose in several people's curiosity—Where was this house situated? and the more so because I had pointed a renewed attention to it by saying, that on that very evening, (viz. the evening on which that particular page of the Confessions was written,) I had visited the street, looked up at the windows, and, instead of the gloomy desolation reigning there when myself and a little girl were the sole nightly tenants, sleeping in fact (poor freezing creatures that we both were) on the floor of the attorney's law-chamber, and making a pillow out of his infernal parchments, I had seen with pleasure the evidences of comfort, respectability, and domestic animation, in the lights and stir prevailing through different stories of the house. Upon this the upright critic told his readers that I had described the house as standing in Oxford Street,

---

*   Being constantly almost an absentee from London, and very often from other great cities, so as to command oftentimes no favourable opportunities for overlooking the great mass of public journals, it is possible enough that other slanders of the same tenor may have existed. I speak of what met my own eye, or was accidentally reported to me—but in fact all of us are exposed to this evil of calumnies lurking unseen—for no degree of energy, and no excess of disposable time, would enable any one man to exercise this sort of vigilant police over *all* journals. Better, therefore, tranquilly to leave all such malice to confound itself.

---

[1]   "Amongst other things."
[2]   Earl of Altamont; see *Confessions*, p. 75, n. 4, above.

and then appealed to their own knowledge of that street whether such a house could be *so* situated. Why not—he neglected to tell us. The houses at the east end of Oxford Street are certainly of too small an order to meet my account of the attorney's house; but why should it be at the east end? Oxford Street is a mile and a quarter long, and being built continuously on both sides, finds room for houses of *many* classes. Meantime it happens that, although the true house was most obscurely indicated, *any* house whatever in Oxford Street was most luminously excluded. In all the immensity of London there was but one single street that could be challenged by an attentive reader of the Confessions as peremptorily *not* the street of the attorney's house—and *that* one was Oxford Street; for, in speaking of my own renewed acquaintance with the outside of this house, I used some expression implying that, in order to make such a visit of reconnoissance, I had turned *aside* from Oxford Street. The matter is a perfect trifle in itself, but it is no trifle in a question affecting a writer's accuracy. If in a thing so absolutely impossible to be forgotten as the true situation of a house painfully memorable to a man's feelings, from being the scene of boyish distresses the most exquisite—nights passed in the misery of cold, and hunger preying upon him both night and day, in a degree which very many would not have survived,—he, when retracing his schoolboy annals, could have shown indecision even, far more dreaded inaccuracy, in identifying the house, not one syllable after *that*, which he could have said on any other subject, would have won any confidence, or deserved any, from a judicious reader. I may now mention—the Herod being dead whose persecutions I had reason to fear—that the house in question stands in Greek Street on the west, and is the house on that side nearest to Soho-Square, but without looking into the Square. This it was hardly safe to mention at the date of the published Confessions. It was my private opinion, indeed, that there were probably twenty-five chances to one in favour of my friend the attorney having been by that time hanged. But then this argued inversely; one chance to twenty-five that my friend might be *un*hanged, and knocking about the streets of London; in which case it would have been a perfect god-send to him that here lay an opening (of *my* contrivance, not *his*) for requesting the opinion of a jury on the amount of *solatium*[1] due to his wounded feelings in an action on the passage in the Confessions. To have indicated even the street would have been enough. Because there could surely be but one such Grecian in

---

[1] "Consolation."

Greek Street, or but one that realized the other conditions of the unknown quantity. There was also a separate danger not absolutely so laughable as it sounds. Me there was little chance that the attorney should meet; but my book he might easily have met (supposing always that the warrant of *Sus. per coll.* had not yet on *his* account travelled down to Newgate.)[1] For he was literary; admired literature; and, as a lawyer, he wrote on some subjects fluently; Might he not publish *his* Confessions? Or, which would be worse, a supplement to mine—printed so as exactly to match? In which case I should have had the same affliction that Gibbon the historian dreaded[2] so much; viz. that of seeing a refutation of himself, and his own answer to the refutation, all bound up in one and the same self-combating volume. Besides, he would have cross-examined me before the public in Old Bailey style; no story, the most straightforward that ever was told, could be sure to stand *that*. And my readers might be left in a state of painful doubt whether *he* might not, after all, have been a model of suffering innocence—I (to say the kindest thing possible) plagued with the natural treacheries of a schoolboy's memory. In taking leave of this case and the remembrances connected with it, let me say that, although really believing in the probability of the attorney's having at least found his way to Australia,[3] I had no satisfaction in thinking of that result. I knew my friend to be the very perfection of a scamp. And in the running account between us, (I mean, in the ordinary sense, as to money,) the balance could not be in *his* favour; since I, on receiving a sum of money, (considerable in the eyes of us both,) had transferred pretty nearly the whole of it to *him*, for the purpose ostensibly held out to me (but of course a hoax) of purchasing certain law "stamps;" for he was then pursuing a diplomatic correspondence with various Jews who lent money to young heirs, in some trifling proportion on my own insignificant account, but much more truly on the account of Lord A —t, my young friend. On the other side, he had given to me simply the reliques of his breakfast-table, which itself was hardly more than a relique. But in this he was not to blame. He could

---

[1]   "*Suspendatur per collum*," or "let him be hanged by the neck," an execution sentence; Newgate Prison, notorious prison in Central London, first established in 1188 by Henry II; site of public gallows from 1783 to 1868, when public executions were discontinued; demolished in 1902.

[2]   "Not the same in fact; in his posthumously published *Memoirs* (1796), Edward Gibbon (1737–94) said that he did not wish his own pamphlet, *A Vindication of some Passages in the XVth and XVIth Chapters* (1779) to be bound up with his *History of the Decline and Fall of the Roman Empire*, 6 vols. (1776–1788)" (*Works* 15:665).]

[3]   I.e., criminals were sent to Australia.

not give to me what he had not for himself, nor sometimes for the poor starving child whom I now suppose to have been his illegitimate daughter. So desperate was the running fight, yard-arm to yard-arm, which he maintained with creditors fierce as famine and hungry as the grave; so deep also was his horror (I know not for which of the various reasons supposable) against falling into a prison, that he seldom ventured to sleep twice successively in the same house. That expense of itself must have pressed heavily in London, where you pay half-a-crown at least for a bed that would cost only a shilling in the provinces. In the midst of his knaveries, and what were even more shocking to my remembrance, his confidential discoveries in his rambling conversations of knavish *designs*, (not always pecuniary,) there was a light of wandering misery in his eye at times, which affected me afterwards at intervals when I recalled it in the radiant happiness of nineteen, and amidst the solemn tranquillities of Oxford. That of itself was interesting; the man was worse by far than he had been meant to be; he had not the mind that reconciles itself to evil. Besides, he respected scholarship, which appeared by the deference he generally showed to myself, then about seventeen; he had an interest in literature; *that* argues something good; and was pleased at any time, or even cheerful, when I turned the conversation upon books; nay, he seemed touched with emotion, when I quoted some sentiment noble and impassioned from one of the great poets, and would ask me to repeat it. He would have been a man of memorable energy, and for good purposes, had it not been for his agony of conflict with pecuniary embarrassments. These probably had commenced in some fatal compliance with temptation arising out of funds confided to him by a client. Perhaps he had gained fifty guineas for a moment of necessity, and had sacrificed for that trifle *only* the serenity and the comfort of a life. Feelings of relenting kindness, it was not in my nature to refuse in such a case; and I wished to ★ ★ ★[1] But I never succeeded in tracing his steps through the wilderness of London until some years back, when I ascertained that he was dead. Generally speaking, the few people whom I have disliked in this world were flourishing people of good repute. Whereas the knaves whom I have known, one and all, and by no means few, I think of with pleasure and kindness.

Heavens! when I look back to the sufferings which I have witnessed or heard of even from this one brief London experience, I say if life could throw open its long suits of chambers to our eyes from some

---

[1]   Deleted material not known.

station *beforehand,* if from some secret stand we could look *by anticipa-tion* along its vast corridors, and aside into the recesses opening upon them from either hand, halls of tragedy or chambers of retribution, simply in that small wing and no more of the great caravanserai[1] which we ourselves shall haunt, simply in that narrow tract of time and no more where we ourselves shall range, and confining our gaze to those and no others for whom personally we shall be interested, what a recoil we should suffer of horror in our estimate of life! What if those sudden catastrophes, or those inexpiable afflictions, which *have* already descended upon the people within my own knowledge, and almost below my own eyes, all of them now gone past, and some long past, had been thrown open before me as a secret exhibition when first I and they stood within the vestibule of morning hopes; when the calamities themselves had hardly begun to gather in their elements of possibility, and when some of the parties to them were as yet no more than infants! The past viewed not *as* the past, but by a spectator who steps back ten years deeper into the rear, in order that he may regard it as a future; the calamity of 1840 contemplated from the station of 1830—the doom that rang the knell of happiness viewed from a point of time when as yet it was neither feared nor would even have been intelligible—the name that killed in 1843, which in 1835 would have struck no vibration upon the heart—the portrait that on the day of her Majesty's coronation would have been admired by you with a pure disinterested admiration, but which if seen to-day would draw forth an involuntary groan—cases such as these are strangely moving for all who add deep thoughtfulness to deep sensibility. As the hastiest of improvisations, accept—fair reader, (for you it is that will chiefly feel such an invocation of the past)—three or four illustrations from my own experience.

Who is this distinguished-looking young woman with her eyes drooping, and the shadow of a dreadful shock yet fresh upon every feature? Who is the elderly lady with her eyes flashing fire? Who is the downcast child of sixteen? What is that torn paper lying at their feet? Who is the writer? Whom does the paper concern? Ah! if she, if the central figure in the group—twenty-two at the moment when she is revealed to us—could, on her happy birth-day at sweet seventeen, have seen the image of herself five years onwards, just as *we* see it now, would she have prayed for life as for an absolute blessing? or would she not

---

[1] "A kind of inn in Eastern countries where caravans put up, being a large quadrangle build-ing with a spacious court in the middle" (*OED*).

have prayed to be taken from the evil to come—to be taken away one evening at least before this day's sun arose? It is true, she still wears a look of gentle pride, and a relic of that noble smile which belongs to *her* that suffers an injury which many times over she would have died sooner than inflict. Womanly pride refuses itself before witnesses to the total prostration of the blow; but, for all *that*, you may see that she longs to be left alone, and that her tears will flow without restraint when she is so. This room is her pretty boudoir, in which, till tonight—poor thing!—she has been glad and happy. There stands her miniature conservatory, and there expands her miniature library; as we circum-navigators of literature are apt (you know) to regard all female libraries in the light of miniatures. None of these will ever rekindle a smile on *her* face; and there, beyond, is her music, which only of all that she possesses, will now become dearer to her than ever; but not, as once, to feed a self-mocked pensiveness, or to cheat a half-visionary sadness. She will be sad indeed. But she is one of those that will suffer in silence. Nobody will ever detect *her* failing in any point of duty, or querulously seeking the support in others which she can find for herself in this soli-tary room. Droop she will not in the sight of men; and, for all beyond, nobody has any concern with *that* except God. You shall hear what becomes of her, before we take our departure; but now let me tell you what has happened. In the main outline I am sure you guess already without aid of mine, for we leaden-eyed men, in such cases, see noth-ing by comparison with you our quick-witted sisters. That haughty-looking lady with the Roman cast of features, who must once have been strikingly handsome—an Agrippina,[1] even yet, in a favourable presentation—is the younger lady's aunt. She, it is rumoured, once sustained, in her younger days, some injury of that same cruel nature which has this day assailed her niece, and ever since she has worn an air of disdain, not altogether unsupported by real dignity, towards men. This aunt it was that tore the letter which lies upon the floor. It deserved to be torn; and yet she that had the best right to do so would *not* have torn it. That letter was an elaborate attempt on the part of an accomplished young man to release himself from sacred engagements. What need was there to argue the case of *such* engagements? Could it have been requi-site with pure female dignity to plead any thing, or do more than *look* an indisposition to fulfil them? The aunt is now moving towards the

---

[1] Vipsania Agrippina (36 BCE – 20 CE), daughter of Marcus Vipsanius Agrippa (63–12 BCE), married to Emperor Tiberius (42 BCE – 37 CE), whom he later divorced and assassinated.

door, which I am glad to see; and she is followed by that pale timid girl of sixteen, a cousin, who feels the case profoundly, but is too young and shy to offer an intellectual sympathy.

One only person in this world there is, who *could* to-night have been a supporting friend to our young sufferer, and *that* is her dear loving twin-sister, that for eighteen years read and wrote, thought and sang, slept and breathed, with the dividing-door open for ever between their bedrooms, and never once a separation between their hearts; but she is in a far distant land. Who else is there at her call? Except God, nobody. Her aunt had somewhat sternly admonished her, though still with a relenting in her eye as she glanced aside at the expression in her niece's face, that she must "call pride to her assistance." Ay, true; but pride, though a strong ally in public, is apt in private to turn as treacherous as the worst of those against whom she is invoked. How could it be dreamed by a person of sense, that a brilliant young man of merits, various and eminent, in spite of his baseness, to whom, for nearly two years, this young woman had given her whole confiding love, might be dismissed from a heart like hers on the earliest summons of pride, simply because she herself had been dismissed from *his*, or seemed to have been dismissed, on a summons of mercenary calculation? Look! now that she is relieved from the weight of an unconfidential presence, she has sat for two hours with her head buried in her hands. At last she rises to look for something. A thought has struck her; and, taking a little golden key which hangs by a chain within her bosom, she searches for something locked up amongst her few jewels. What is it? It is a Bible exquisitely illuminated, with a letter attached, by some pretty silken artifice, to the blank leaves at the end. This letter is a beautiful record, wisely and pathetically composed, of maternal anxiety still burning strong in death, and yearning, when all objects beside were fast fading from *her* eyes, after one parting act of communion with the twin darlings of her heart. Both were thirteen years old, within a week or two, as on the night before her death they sat weeping by the bedside of their mother, and hanging on her lips, now for farewell whispers, and now for farewell kisses. They both knew that, as her strength had permitted during the latter month of her life, she had thrown the last anguish of love in her beseeching heart into a letter of counsel to themselves. Through this, of which each sister had a copy, she trusted long to converse with her orphans. And the last promise which she had entreated on this evening from both, was— that in either of two contingencies they would review her counsels, and the passages to which she pointed their attention in the Scriptures;

namely, first, in the event of any calamity, that, for one sister or for both, should overspread their paths with total darkness; and secondly, in the event of life flowing in too profound a stream of prosperity, so as to threaten them with an alienation of interest from all spiritual objects. She had not concealed that, of these two extreme cases, she would prefer for her own children the first. And now had that case arrived indeed, which she in spirit had desired to meet. Nine years ago, just as the silvery voice of a dial in the dying lady's bedroom was striking nine upon a summer evening, had the last visual ray streamed from her seeking eyes upon her orphan twins, after which, throughout the night, she had slept away into heaven. Now again had come a summer evening memorable for unhappiness; now again the daughter thought of those dying lights of love which streamed at sunset from the closing eyes of her mother; again, and just as she went back in thought to this image, the same silvery voice of the dial sounded nine o'clock. Again she remembered her mother's dying request; again her own tear-hallowed promise—and with her heart in her mother's grave she now rose to fulfil it. Here, then, when this solemn recurrence to a testamentary counsel has ceased to be a mere office of duty towards the departed, having taken the shape of a consolation for herself, let us pause.

. . . .

Now, fair companion in this exploring voyage of inquest into hidden scenes, or forgotten scenes of human life—perhaps it might be instructive to direct our glasses upon the false perfidious lover. It might. But do not let us do so. We might like him better, or pity him more, than either of us would desire. His name and memory have long since dropped out of every body's thoughts. Of prosperity, and (what is more important) of internal peace, he is reputed to have had no gleam from the moment when he betrayed his faith, and in one day threw away the jewel of good conscience, and "a pearl richer than all his tribe."[1] But, however that may be, it is certain that, finally, he became a wreck; and of any *hopeless* wreck it is painful to talk—much more so, when through him others also became wrecks.

---

[1] Paraphrase of Shakespeare, *Othello*; Othello, about to die, asks to be remembered as a man obsessed by love, and compares himself to Judas: "... you must speak / Of one that loved not wisely, but too well; / Of one not easily jealous, but, being wrought, / Perplexed in the extreme; of one whose hand, / Like the base Judean, threw a pearl away / Richer than all his tribe" (5.2.343–48).

Shall we, then, after an interval of nearly two years has passed over the young lady in the boudoir, look in again upon *her*? You hesitate, fair friend: and I myself hesitate. For in fact she also has become a wreck; and it would grieve us both to see her altered. At the end of twenty-one months she retains hardly a vestige of resemblance to the fine young woman we saw on that unhappy evening with her aunt and cousin. On consideration, therefore, let us do this. We will direct our glasses to her room, at a point of time about six weeks further on. Suppose this time gone; suppose her now dressed for her grave, and placed in her coffin. The advantage of that is—that, though no change can restore the ravages of the past, yet (as often is found to happen with young persons) the expression has revived from her girlish years. The child-like aspect has revolved, and settled back upon her features. The wasting away of the flesh is less apparent in the face; and one might imagine that, in this sweet marble countenance, was seen the very same upon which, eleven years ago, her mother's darkening eyes had lingered to the last, until clouds had swallowed up the vision of her beloved *twins*. Yet, if that were in part a fancy, this at least is no fancy—that not only much of a child-like truth and simplicity has reinstated itself in the temple of her now reposing features, but also that tranquillity and perfect peace, such as are appropriate to eternity; but which from the *living* countenance had taken their flight for ever, on that memorable evening when we looked in upon the impassioned group—upon the towering and denouncing aunt, the sympathizing but silent cousin, the poor blighted niece, and the wicked letter lying in fragments at their feet.

Cloud, that hast revealed to us this young creature and her blighted hopes, close up again. And now, a few years later, not more than four or five, give back to us the latest arrears of the changes which thou concealest within thy draperies. Once more, "open sesame!" and show us a third generation. Behold a lawn islanded with thickets. How perfect is the verdure—how rich the blossoming shrubberies that screen with verdurous walls from the possibility of intrusion, whilst by their own wandering line of distribution they shape and umbrageously embay, what one might call lawny saloons and vestibules—sylvan galleries and closets. Some of these recesses, which unlink themselves as fluently as snakes, and unexpectedly as the shyest nooks, watery cells, and crypts, amongst the shores of a forest-lake, being formed by the mere caprices and ramblings of the luxuriant shrubs, are so small and so quiet, that one might fancy them meant for *boudoirs*. Here is one that, in a less fickle climate, would make the loveliest of studies for a writer of breathings from some solitary heart, or of *suspiria* from some impassioned memory! And opening from one angle of this embowered study, issues a little narrow corridor, that, after almost wheeling back upon itself, in its playful mazes, finally widens into a little circular chamber; out of which there is no exit, (except back again by the entrance,) small or great; so that, adjacent to his study, the writer would command how sweet a bed-room, permitting him to lie the summer through, gazing all night long at the burning host of heaven. How silent *that* would be at the noon of summer nights, how grave-like in its quiet! And yet, need there be asked a stillness or a silence more profound than is felt at this present noon of day? One reason for such peculiar repose, over and above the tranquil character of the day, and the distance of the place from high-roads, is the outer zone of woods, which almost on every quarter invests the shrubberies—swathing them, (as one may express it,) belting them, and overlooking them, from a varying distance of two and three furlongs, so as oftentimes to keep the winds at a distance. But, however caused and supported, the silence of these fanciful lawns and lawny chambers is oftentimes oppressive in the depth of summer to people unfamiliar with solitudes, either mountainous or sylvan; and many would be apt to suppose that the villa, to which these pretty shrubberies form the chief dependencies, must be untenanted. But that is not the case. The house is inhabited, and by its own legal mistress— the proprietress of the whole domain; and not at all a silent mistress, but as noisy as most little ladies of five years old, for that is her age. Now, and just as we are speaking, you may hear her little joyous clamour as she issues from the house. This way she comes, bounding like a fawn; and soon she rushes into the little recess which I pointed out as a proper study for any man who should be weaving the deep harmonies of memorial *suspiria*. But I fancy that she will soon dispossess it of that character, for her *suspiria* are not many at this stage of her life. Now she comes dancing into sight; and you see that, if she keeps the promise of her infancy, she will be an interesting creature to the eye in after life. In other respects, also, she is an engaging child—loving, natural, and wild as any one of her neighbours for some miles round; viz. leverets, squirrels, and ring-doves. But what will surprise you most is—that, although a child of pure English blood, she speaks very little English; but more Bengalee than perhaps you will find it convenient to construe. That is her Ayah,[1] who comes up from behind at a pace so different from her youthful mistress's. But, if their paces are different, in other things they agree most cordially; and dearly

---

[1] "A native nurse or maidservant, esp. of Europeans in India and other parts of South Asia" (*OED*).

they love each other. In reality, the child has passed her whole life in the arms of this ayah. She remembers nothing elder than *her*, eldest of things is the ayah in her eyes; and, if the ayah should insist on her worshipping herself as the goddess Railroadina or Steamboatina, that made England and the sea and Bengal, it is certain that the little thing would do so, asking no question but this—whether kissing would do for worshipping.

Every evening at nine o'clock, as the ayah sits by the little creature lying awake in bed, the silvery tongue of a dial tolls the hour. Reader, you know who she is. She is the grand-daughter of her that faded away about sunset in gazing at her twin orphans. Her name is Grace. And she is the niece of that elder and once happy Grace, who spent so much of her happiness in this very room, but whom, in her utter desolation, we saw in the boudoir with the torn letter at her feet. She is the daughter of that other sister, wife to a military officer, who died abroad. Little Grace never saw her grand-mamma, nor her lovely aunt that was her namesake, nor consciously her mama. She was born six months after the death of the elder Grace; and her mother saw her only through the mists of mortal suffering, which carried her off three weeks after the birth of her daughter.

This view was taken several years ago; and since then the younger Grace in her turn is under a cloud of affliction. But she is still under eighteen; and of her there may be hopes. Seeing such things in so short a space of years, for the grandmother died at thirty-two, we say—Death we can face: but knowing, as some of us do, what is human life, which of us is it that without shuddering could (if consciously we were summoned) face the hour of birth?

THE ENGLISH MAIL-COACH, OR THE GLORY OF MOTION

SOME twenty or more years before I matriculated at Oxford, Mr Palmer, M.P. for Bath,[1] had accomplished two things, very hard to do on our little planet, the Earth, however cheap they may happen to be held by the eccentric people in comets: he had invented mail-coaches, and he had married the daughter★ of a duke. He was, therefore, just twice as great a man as Galileo, who certainly invented (or *discovered*) the satellites of Jupiter,[2] those very next things extant to mail-coaches in the two capital points of speed and keeping time, but who did *not* marry the daughter of a duke.

These mail-coaches, as organised by Mr Palmer, are entitled to a circumstantial notice from myself—having had so large a share in developing the anarchies of my subsequent dreams, an agency which they accomplished, first, through velocity, at that time unprecedented; they first revealed the glory of motion: suggesting, at the same time, an under-sense, not unpleasurable, of possible though indefinite danger; secondly, through grand effects for the eye between lamp-light and the darkness upon solitary roads; thirdly, through animal beauty and power so often displayed in the class of horses selected for this mail service; fourthly, through the conscious presence of a central intellect, that, in the midst of vast distances,★★ of storms, of darkness, of night, overruled all obstacles into one steady co-operation in a national result. To my own feeling, this Post-office service recalled some mighty orchestra, where a thousand instruments, all disregarding each other, and so far in danger of discord, yet all obedient as slaves to the supreme *baton* of some great leader, terminate in a perfection of harmony like that of heart, veins, and arteries, in a healthy animal organisation. But, finally, that particular element in this whole combination which most impressed myself, and through which it is that to this hour Mr Palmer's mail-coach system tyrannises by terror and terrific beauty over my dreams, lay in

---

★   Lady Madeline Gordon.
★★ One case was familiar to mail-coach travellers, where two mails in opposite directions, north and south, starting at the same minute from points six hundred miles apart, met almost constantly at a particular bridge which exactly bisected the total distance.

---

[1]   John Palmer (1742–1818) instituted the first mail-coach service in 1784. He was Comptroller General of the Post Office in 1786 and became M.P. for Bath in 1801; he never married Lady Madeline Gordon, contrary to De Quincey.
[2]   Galileo (1564–1642), Italian astronomer; in 1610 discovered four of Jupiter's satellites.

the awful political mission which at that time it fulfilled. The mail-coaches it was that distributed over the face of the land, like the opening of apocalyptic vials, the heart-shaking news of Trafalgar, of Salamanca, of Vittoria, of Waterloo.[1] These were the harvests that, in the grandeur of their reaping, redeemed the tears and blood in which they had been sown. Neither was the meanest peasant so much below the grandeur and the sorrow of the times as to confound these battles, which were gradually moulding the destinies of Christendom, with the vulgar conflicts of ordinary warfare, which are oftentimes but gladiatorial trials of national prowess. The victories of England in this stupendous contest rose of themselves as natural *Te Deums*[2] to heaven; and it was felt by the thoughtful that such victories, at such a crisis of general prostration, were not more beneficial to ourselves than finally to France, and to the nations of western and central Europe, through whose pusillanimity it was that the French domination had prospered.

The mail-coach, as the national organ for publishing these mighty events, became itself a spiritualised and glorified object to an impassioned heart; and naturally, in the Oxford of that day, all hearts were awakened. There were, perhaps, of us gownsmen, two thousand *resident** in Oxford, and dispersed through five-and-twenty colleges. In some of these the custom permitted the student to keep what are called "short terms;" that is, the four terms of Michaelmas, Lent, Easter, and Act,[3] were kept severally by a residence, in the aggregate, of ninety-one days, or thirteen weeks. Under this interrupted residence, accordingly, it was possible that a student might have a reason for going down to his home four times in the year. This made eight journeys to and fro. And as these homes lay dispersed through all the shires of the island, and most of us disdained all coaches except his majesty's mail, no city out of London could pretend to so extensive a connexion with

---

* "*Resident.*"—The number on the books was far greater, many of whom kept up an intermitting communication with Oxford. But I speak of those only who were steadily pursuing their academic studies, and of those who resided constantly as *fellows*.

---

[1] British victories in the war against Napoleon; at Trafalgar (1805), the British navy, led by Horatio Nelson (1758–1805), destroyed the French fleet; the Duke of Wellington (1769–1852), and later Prime Minister (1828–30) led the British army at Salamanca (1812), Vittoria (1813), and Waterloo (1815), Napoleon's final defeat.

[2] "Ancient Latin hymn of praise in the form of a psalm, sung as a thanksgiving on special occasions, as after a victory or deliverance; also regularly ... at Morning Prayer in the Church of England" (*OED*).

[3] Michaelmas: the Feast of St. Michael; Act: old name for Trinity (summer) term at Oxford.

Mr Palmer's establishment as Oxford. Naturally, therefore, it became a point of some interest with us, whose journeys revolved every six weeks on an average, to look a little into the executive details of the system. With some of these Mr Palmer had no concern; they rested upon bye-laws not unreasonable, enacted by posting-houses for their own benefit, and upon others equally stern, enacted by the inside passengers for the illustration of their own exclusiveness. These last were of a nature to rouse our scorn, from which the transition was not *very long* to mutiny. Up to this time, it had been the fixed assumption of the four inside people, (as an old tradition of all public carriages from the reign of Charles II.,) that they, the illustrious quaternion, constituted a porcelain variety of the human race, whose dignity would have been compromised by exchanging one word of civility with the three miserable delf ware[1] outsides. Even to have kicked an outsider might have been held to attaint the foot concerned in that operation; so that, perhaps, it would have required an act of parliament to restore its purity of blood. What words, then, could express the horror, and the sense of treason, in that case, which *had* happened, where all three outsides, the trinity of Pariahs, made a vain attempt to sit down at the same breakfast-table or dinner-table with the consecrated four? I myself witnessed such an attempt; and on that occasion a benevolent old gentleman endeavoured to soothe his three holy associates, by suggesting that, if the outsides were indicted for this criminal attempt at the next assizes,[2] the court would regard it as a case of lunacy (or *delirium tremens*)[3] rather than of treason. England owes much of her grandeur to the depth of the aristocratic element in her social composition. I am not the man to laugh at it. But sometimes it expressed itself in extravagant shapes. The course taken with the infatuated outsiders, in the particular attempt which I have noticed, was, that the waiter, beckoning them away from the privileged *salle-à-manger*;[4] sang out, "This way, my good men;" and then enticed them away off to the kitchen. But that plan had not always answered. Sometimes, though very rarely, cases occurred where the intruders, being stronger than usual, or more vicious than usual, resolutely refused to move, and so far carried their point, as to have a separate table arranged for themselves

---

[1] Inexpensive glazed earthenware, originally from Delft in Holland.
[2] "Legislative sitting, statute, statutory measure or manner" (*OED*).
[3] "Species of delirium induced by excessive indulgence in alcoholic liquors" (*OED*).
[4] Dining room.

in a corner of the room. Yet, if an Indian screen could be found ample enough to plant them out from the very eyes of the high table, or *dais,* it then became possible to assume as a fiction of law—that the three delf fellows, after all, were not present. They could be ignored by the porcelain men, under the maxim, that objects not appearing, and not existing, are governed by the same logical construction.

Such now being, at that time, the usages of mail-coaches, what was to be done by us of young Oxford? We, the most aristocratic of people, who were addicted to the practice of looking down superciliously even upon the insides themselves as often very suspicious characters, were we voluntarily to court indignities? If our dress and bearing sheltered us, generally, from the suspicion of being "raff," (the name at that period for snobs,"*) we really *were* such constructively, by the place we assumed. If we did not submit to the deep shadow of eclipse, we entered at least the skirts of its penumbra. And the analogy of theatres was urged against us, where no man can complain of the annoyances incident to the pit or gallery, having his instant remedy in paying the higher price of the boxes. But the soundness of this analogy we disputed. In the case of the theatre, it cannot be pretended that the inferior situations have any separate attractions, unless the pit suits the purpose of the dramatic reporter. But the reporter or critic is a rarity. For most people, the sole benefit is in the price. Whereas, on the contrary, the outside of the mail had its own incommunicable advantages. These we could not forego. The higher price we should willingly have paid, but *that* was connected with the condition of riding inside, which was insufferable. The air, the freedom of prospect, the proximity to the horses, the elevation of seat— these were what we desired; but, above all, the certain anticipation of purchasing occasional opportunities of driving.

Under coercion of this great practical difficulty, we instituted a searching inquiry into the true quality and valuation of the different apartments about the mail. We conducted this inquiry on metaphysical principles; and it was ascertained satisfactorily, that the roof of the coach, which some had affected to call the attics, and some the garrets, was really the drawing-room, and the box was the chief ottoman or sofa in that drawing-room; whilst it appeared that the inside, which had been

---

* "Snobs," and its antithesis, "nobs," arose among the internal factions of shoemakers perhaps ten years later. Possibly enough, the terms may have existed much earlier; but they were then first made known, picturesquely and effectively, by a trial at some assizes which happened to fix public attention. [Raff, or riff-raff: the lower class; snobs: "any one not a gownsman; a townsman" (*OED*); nob: "a person of some wealth or social distinction" (*OED*).]

traditionally regarded as the only room tenantable by gentlemen, was, in fact, the coal-cellar in disguise.

Great wits jump.[1] The very same idea had not long before struck the celestial intellect of China. Amongst the presents carried out by our first embassy to that country was a state-coach. It had been specially selected as a personal gift by George III.; but the exact mode of using it was a mystery to Pekin. The ambassador, indeed, (Lord Macartney,)[2] had made some dim and imperfect explanations upon the point; but as his excellency communicated these in a diplomatic whisper, at the very moment of his departure, the celestial mind was very feebly illuminated; and it became necessary to call a cabinet council on the grand state question—"Where was the emperor to sit?" The hammer-cloth[3] happened to be unusually gorgeous; and partly on that consideration, but partly also because the box offered the most elevated seat, and undeniably went foremost, it was resolved by acclamation that the box was the imperial place, and, *for the scoundrel who drove, he might sit where he could find a perch.* The horses, therefore, being harnessed, under a flourish of music and a salute of guns, solemnly his imperial majesty ascended his new English throne, having the first lord of the treasury on his right hand, and the chief jester on his left. Pekin gloried in the spectacle; and in the whole flowery people, constructively present by representation, there was but one discontented person, which was the coachman. This mutinous individual, looking as blackhearted as he really was, audaciously shouted—"Where am *I* to sit?" But the privy council, incensed by his disloyalty, unanimously opened the door, and kicked him into the inside. He had all the inside places to himself; but such is the rapacity of ambition, that he was still dissatisfied. "I say," he cried out in an extempore petition, addressed to the emperor through a window, "how am I to catch hold of the reins?"—"Any how," was the answer; "don't trouble *me*, man, in my

---

[1]   De Quincey developed the following fictional anecdote from a passage in *An Authentic Account of an Embassy from the King of Great Britain to the Emperor of China*, 3 vols. (London: Nicol, 1797), by Sir George Staunton (1737–1801): "It was a new spectacle to the Chinese, accustomed only to the low, clumsy, two-wheeled carriages. ... When a splendid chariot intended as a present for the Emperor was unpacked and put together, nothing could be more admired; but it was necessary to give directions for taking off the box; for when the mandarines found out that so elevated a seat was destined for the coachman ... they expressed the utmost astonishment that it should be proposed to place any man in a situation *above* the Emperor" (2:343).

[2]   George III (1738–1820), who reigned from 1760–1820, sent George Macartney (1737–1806) as the first British emissary to Peking. The emperor at the time was Qianlong (1711–99), fourth ruler of the Qing dynasty (1735–96).

[3]   "A cloth covering the driver's seat or 'box' in a state or family coach" (*OED*).

glory; through the windows, through the key-holes—how you please."
Finally, this contumacious coachman lengthened the checkstrings into a
sort of jury-reins,[1] communicating with the horses; with these he drove as
steadily as may be supposed. The emperor returned after the briefest of
circuits: he descended in great pomp from his throne, with the severest resolution never to remount it. A public thanksgiving was ordered for his
majesty's prosperous escape from the disease of a broken neck; and the state-
coach was dedicated for ever as a votive offering to the God Fo, Fo—whom
the learned more accurately call Fi, Fi.[2]

A revolution of this same Chinese character did young Oxford of
that era effect in the constitution of mail-coach society. It was a perfect
French revolution; and we had good reason to say, Ca ira.[3] In fact, it
soon became too popular. The "public," a well-known character, particularly disagreeable, though slightly respectable, and notorious for affecting the chief seats in synagogues, had at first loudly opposed this
revolution; but when all opposition showed itself to be ineffectual, our
disagreeable friend went into it with headlong zeal. At first it was a sort
of race between us; and, as the public is usually above 30, (say generally
from 30 to 50 years old,) naturally we of young Oxford, that averaged
about 20, had the advantage. Then the public took to bribing, giving
fees to horse-keepers, &c., who hired out their persons as warming-
pans on the box-seat. That, you know, was shocking to our moral sensibilities. Come to bribery, we observed, and there is an end to all
morality, Aristotle's, Cicero's[4] or anybody's. And, besides, of what use
was it? For we bribed also. And as our bribes to those of the public being
demonstrated out of Euclid[5] to be as five shillings to sixpence, here
again young Oxford had the advantage. But the contest was ruinous to
the principles of the stable-establishment about the mails. The whole
corporation was constantly bribed, rebribed, and often sur-rebribed; so
that a horse-keeper, ostler, or helper, was held by the philosophical at
that time to be the most corrupt character in the nation.

There was an impression upon the public mind, natural enough from
the continually augmenting velocity of the mail, but quite erroneous, that

---

[1] Check-string: "a string by which an occupant of a carriage may signal to the driver to
the stop" (OED); jury-reins: temporary reins.

[2] There are no Chinese gods by these names.

[3] Ca ira, ça ira, ça tiendra, "that will go, that will last," chorus of a popular French
Revolutionary song.

[4] Aristotle (384–322 BCE), ancient Greek philosopher and scientist, author of Nicomachean
Ethics; Cicero, see Suspiria, p. 143, first asterisked note.

[5] See Suspiria, p. 196, n. 1 above.

an outside seat on this class of carriages was a post of danger. On the contrary, I maintained that, if a man had become nervous from some gipsy prediction in his childhood, allocating to a particular moon now approaching some unknown danger, and he should inquire earnestly,—"Whither can I go for shelter? Is a prison the safest retreat? Or a lunatic hospital? Or the British Museum?" I should have replied—"Oh, no; I'll tell you what to do. Take lodgings for the next forty days on the box of his majesty's mail. Nobody can touch you there. If it is by bills at ninety days after date that you are made unhappy—if noters and protesters[1] are the sort of wretches whose astrological shadows darken the house of life—then note you what I vehemently protest, viz., that no matter though the sheriff in every county should be running after you with his *posse,* touch a hair of your head he cannot whilst you keep house, and have your legal domicile, on the box of the mail. It's felony to stop the mail; even the sheriff cannot do that. And an *extra* (no great matter if it grazes the sheriff) touch of the whip to the leaders at any time guarantees your safety." In fact, a bed-room in a quiet house seems a safe enough retreat; yet it is liable to its own notorious nuisances, to robbers by night, to rats, to fire. But the mail laughs at these terrors. To robbers, the answer is packed up and ready for delivery in the barrel of the guard's blunderbuss.[2] Rats again! there *are* none about mail-coaches, any more than snakes in Von Troil's Iceland;[3] except, indeed, now and then a parliamentary rat,[4] who always hides his shame in the "coal-cellar." And, as to fire, I never knew but one in a mail-coach, which was in the Exeter mail, and caused by an obstinate sailor bound to Devonport. Jack, making light of the law and the lawgiver that had set their faces against his offence, insisted on taking up a forbidden seat in the rear of the roof, from which he could exchange his own yarns with those of the guard. No greater offence was then known to mail-coaches; it was treason, it was *læsa majestas,*[5] it was by tendency arson; and the ashes of Jack's pipe, falling amongst the straw of the hinder boot, containing the mail-bags, raised a flame which (aided by the wind of our motion) threatened a revolution in the republic of letters. But even this

[1]   Bills of exchange, such as IOUs for loans.
[2]   "A short gun with a large bore, firing many balls or slugs, and capable of doing execution within a limited range without exact aim" (*OED*).
[3]   De Quincey added a note in 1854: "The allusion is to a well-known chapter in Von Troil's work entitled, "Concerning the Snakes of Iceland." The entire chapter consists of these six words—'There are no snakes in Iceland.'" In fact, the chapter is in Niels Horrebov's *Natural History of Iceland* (1758).
[4]   Member of Parliament who betrays his party's interests to the Opposition.
[5]   "Violated majesty."

left the sanctity of the box unviolated. In dignified repose, the coachman and myself sat on, resting with benign composure upon our knowledge—that the fire would have to burn its way through four inside passengers before it could reach ourselves. With a quotation rather too trite, I remarked to the coachman,—

> —"Jam proximus ardet
> Ucalegon."[1]

But, recollecting that the Virgilian part of his education might have been neglected, I interpreted so far as to say, that perhaps at that moment the flames were catching hold of our worthy brother and next-door neighbour Ucalegon. The coachman said nothing, but by his faint sceptical smile he seemed to be thinking that he knew better; for that in fact, Ucalegon, as it happened, was not in the way-bill.[2]

No dignity is perfect which does not at some point ally itself with the indeterminate and mysterious. The connexion of the mail with the state and the executive government—a connexion obvious, but yet not strictly defined—gave to the whole mail establishment a grandeur and an official authority which did us service on the roads, and invested us with seasonable terrors. But perhaps these terrors were not the less impressive, because their exact legal limits were imperfectly ascertained. Look at those turnpike gates; with what deferential hurry, with what an obedient start, they fly open at our approach! Look at that long line of carts and carters ahead, audaciously usurping the very crest of the road: ah! traitors, they do not hear us as yet, but as soon as the dreadful blast of our horn reaches them with the proclamation of our approach, see with what frenzy of trepidation they fly to their horses' heads, and deprecate our wrath by the precipitation of their crane-neck quarterings.[3] Treason they feel to be their crime; each individual carter feels himself under the ban of confiscation and attainder: his blood is attainted through six generations,[4] and nothing is wanting but the heads-man and his axe, the block and the sawdust, to close up the

---

[1]   From Virgil's *Aeneid* (2.311–12); Aeneas is describing the destruction of Troy to Dido: "Even now Deiphobus' great house has fallen, as the fire-god towers above; even now his neighbour Ucalegon burns."

[2]   List of passengers booked on a coach.

[3]   Quick manoeuvres to move vehicles from the path of oncoming traffic; crane-neck: diagonal shaft connecting front and back axles, which thus pivoted in order to make very sharp turns; quartering: moving a vehicle from the centre of the road for another to pass.

[4]   Attainder: loss of civil rights without trial, usually for crime of treason; said to contaminate the blood of the criminal, who could neither inherit property nor will it to an heir.

vista of his horrors. What! shall it be within benefit of clergy,[1] to delay the king's message on the highroad?—to interrupt the great respirations, ebb or flood, of the national intercourse—to endanger the safety of tidings running day and night between all nations and languages? Or can it be fancied, amongst the weakest of men, that the bodies of the criminals will be given up to their widows for Christian burial? Now, the doubts which were raised as to our powers did more to wrap them in terror, by wrapping them in uncertainty, than could have been effected by the sharpest definitions of the law from the Quarter Sessions.[2] We, on our parts, (we, the collective mail, I mean,) did our utmost to exalt the idea of our privileges by the insolence with which we wielded them. Whether this insolence rested upon law that gave it a sanction, or upon conscious power, haughtily dispensing with that sanction, equally it spoke from a potential station; and the agent in each particular insolence of the moment, was viewed reverentially, as one having authority.

Sometimes after breakfast his majesty's mail would become frisky; and in its difficult wheelings amongst the intricacies of early markets, it would upset an apple-cart, a cart loaded with eggs, &c. Huge was the affliction and dismay, awful was the smash, though, after all, I believe the damage might be levied upon the hundred.[3] I, as far as was possible, endeavoured in such a case to represent the conscience and moral sensibilities of the mail; and, when wildernesses of eggs were lying poached under our horses' hoofs, then would I stretch forth my hands in sorrow, saying (in words too celebrated in those days from the false★ echoes of Marengo)— "Ah! wherefore have we not time to weep over you?" which was quite

---

★ "False echoes"—yes, false! for the words ascribed to Napoleon, as breathed to the memory of Desaix, never were uttered at all. They stand in the same category of theatrical inventions as the cry of the foundering *Vengeur*, as the vaunt of General Cambronne at Waterloo, "*La Garde meurt, mais ne se rend pas*," as the repartees of Talleyrand. [Louis-Charles-Antoine Desaix de Veygoux (1768–1800), French military leader killed at Battle of Marengo (1800), decisive victory in establishing Napoleon's power; upon his death, Napoleon supposedly said the words De Quincey quotes. *Vengeur*: French warship sunk by the British on the 'Glorious First of June,' 1794; Pierre Cambronne (1770–1842): commander of Napoleon's Old Guard, decimated at Waterloo; his 'vaunt' was "The Guard dies, but never surrenders"; Charles-Maurice Talleyrand (1754–1838): French diplomat, politician, and wit.]

---

1 By pleading benefit of clergy, clergy, and all people who could read, could ask to be exempted from punishment in civil court; this right survived until 1827.
2 "In England and Ireland: A court of limited criminal and civil jurisdiction, and of appeal, held quarterly by the justices of peace in the counties (in Ireland by county-court judges), and by the recorder in boroughs" (*OED*).
3 Charged to the hundred, a bureaucratic subdivision of a county almost obsolete by 1800.

impossible, for in fact we had not even time to laugh over them. Tied to post-office time, with an allowance in some cases of fifty minutes for eleven miles, could the royal mail pretend to undertake the offices of sympathy and condolence? Could it be expected to provide tears for the accidents of the road? If even it seemed to trample on humanity, it did so, I contended, in discharge of its own more peremptory duties.

Upholding the morality of the mail, *à fortiori*[1] I upheld its rights, I stretched to the uttermost its privilege of imperial precedency, and astonished weak minds by the feudal powers which I hinted to be lurking constructively in the charters of this proud establishment. Once I remember being on the box of the Holyhead mail, between Shrewsbury and Oswestry, when a tawdry thing from Birmingham, some *Tallyho* or *Highflier*,[2] all flaunting with green and gold, came up alongside of us. What a contrast to our royal simplicity of form and colour is this plebeian wretch! The single ornament on our dark ground of chocolate colour was the mighty shield of the imperial arms, but emblazoned in proportions as modest as a signet-ring bears to a seal of office. Even this was displayed only on a single pannel, whispering, rather than proclaiming, our relations to the state; whilst the beast from Birmingham had as much writing and painting on its sprawling flanks as would have puzzled a decipherer from the tombs of Luxor.[3] For some time this Birmingham machine ran along by our side,—a piece of familiarity that seemed to us sufficiently jacobinical.[4] But all at once a movement of the horses announced a desperate intention of leaving us behind. "Do you see *that*?" I said to the coachman. "I see," was his short answer. He was awake, yet he waited longer than seemed prudent; for the horses of our audacious opponent had a disagreeable air of freshness and power. But his motive was loyal; his wish was that the Birmingham conceit should be full-blown before he froze it. When *that* seemed ripe, he unloosed, or, to speak by a stronger image, he sprang his known resources, he slipped our royal horses like cheetas, or hunting leopards after the affrighted game. How they could retain such a reserve of fiery power after the work they had accomplished, seemed

---

[1] "With stronger reason, still more conclusively" (*OED*).
[2] Tallyho: cry of hunter upon sighting the fox or other prey; Highflier: fast stage-coach.
[3] Luxor, on east bank of the Nile; part of ruins of ancient Thebes; site of numerous tombs.
[4] Jacobin: member of French political society started in 1789 on the site of a Jacobin convent to promote radical principles of equality and democracy; or, a sympathizer with the French revolutionary cause, afterward in England a nearly treasonable practice; in De Quincey's usage, "jacobinical" suggests a too-close foreign intrusion.

hard to explain. But on our side, besides the physical superiority, was a tower of strength, namely, the king's name, "which they upon the adverse faction wanted." Passing them without an effort, as it seemed, we threw them into the rear with so lengthening an interval between us, as proved in itself the bitterest mockery of their presumption; whilst our guard blew back a shattering blast of triumph, that was really too painfully full of derision.

I mention this little incident for its connexion with what followed. A Welshman, sitting behind me, asked if I had not felt my heart burn within me during the continuance of the race? I said—No; because we were not racing with a mail, so that no glory could be gained. In fact, it was sufficiently mortifying that such a Birmingham thing should dare to challenge us. The Welshman replied, that he didn't see *that*; for that a cat might look at a king,[1] and a Brummagem[2] coach might lawfully race the Holyhead mail. "*Race* us perhaps," I replied, "though even *that* has an air of sedition, but not *beat* us. This would have been treason; and for its own sake I am glad that the Tallyho was disappointed." So dissatisfied did the Welshman seem with this opinion, that at last I was obliged to tell him a very fine story from one of our elder dramatists,[3] viz.—that once, in some Oriental region, when the prince of all the land, with his splendid court, were flying their falcons, a hawk suddenly flew at a majestic eagle; and in defiance of the eagle's prodigious advantages, in sight also of all the astonished field-sportsmen, spectators, and followers, killed him on the spot. The prince was struck with amazement at the unequal contest, and with burning admiration for its unparalleled result. He commanded that the hawk should be brought before him; caressed the bird with enthusiasm, and ordered that, for the commemoration of his matchless courage, a crown of gold should be solemnly placed on the hawk's head; but then that, immediately after this coronation, the bird should be led off to execution, as the most valiant indeed of traitors, but not the less a traitor that had dared to rise in rebellion against his liege lord the eagle. "Now," said I to the Welshman, "how painful it would have been to you and me as men of refined feelings, that this poor brute, the Tallyho, in the impossible case of a victory over us, should have been crowned with jewellery, gold, with Birmingham ware, or paste diamonds, and then

---

[1]   Saying from *Proverbs*.
[2]   Insulting form of "Birmingham."
[3]   "Thomas Heywood (1573–1641), actor and playwright, *The Royal King and the Loyal Subject* V.v." (*Works* 16:617).]

led off to instant execution." The Welshman doubted if that could he warranted by law. And when I hinted at the 10th of Edward III. chap. 15,[1] for regulating the precedency of coaches, as being probably the statute relied on for the capital punishment of such offences, he replied drily—That if the attempt to pass a mail was really treasonable, it was a pity that the Tallyho appeared to have so imperfect an acquaintance with law.

These were among the gaieties of my earliest and boyish acquaintance with mails. But alike the gayest and the most terrific of my experiences rose again after years of slumber, armed with preternatural power to shake my dreaming sensibilities; sometimes, as in the slight case of Miss Fanny on the Bath road, (which I will immediately mention,) through some casual or capricious association with images originally gay, yet opening at some stage of evolution into sudden capacities of horror; sometimes through the more natural and fixed alliances with the sense of power so various lodged in the mail system.

The modern modes of travelling cannot compare with the mailcoach system in grandeur and power. They boast of more velocity, but not however as a consciousness, but as a fact of our lifeless knowledge, resting upon *alien* evidence; as, for instance, because somebody *says* that we have gone fifty miles in the hour, or upon the evidence of a result, as that actually we find ourselves in York four hours after leaving London.[2] Apart from such an assertion, or such a result, I am little aware of the pace. But, seated on the old mail-coach, we needed no evidence out of ourselves to indicate the velocity. On this system the word was— *Non magna loquimur,* as upon railways, but *magna vivimus.*[3] The vital experience of the glad animal sensibilities made doubts impossible on the question of our speed; we heard our speed, we saw it, we felt it as a thrilling; and this speed was not the product of blind insensate agencies, that had no sympathy to give, but was incarnated in the fiery eyeballs of an animal, in his dilated nostril, spasmodic muscles, and echoing hoofs. This speed was incarnated in the *visible* contagion amongst brutes of some impulse, that, radiating into *their* natures, had yet its centre and beginning in man. The sensibility of the horse uttering itself in the maniac light of his eye, might be the last vibration in such a movement;

---

[1] Edward III (1312–77), reigned 1327–77; no such statute exists; in a later revision De Quincey named Edward Longshanks or Edward I (1239–1307), who reigned 1272–1307.

[2] Impossible, even by train, in 1849.

[3] Later translated by De Quincey as "we do not make verbal ostentation of our grandeurs, we realise our grandeurs in act, and in the very experience of life."

the glory of Salamanca might be the first—but the intervening link that connected them, that spread the earthquake of the battle into the eyeball of the horse, was the heart of man—kindling in the rapture of the fiery strife, and then propagating its own tumults by motions and gestures to the sympathies, more or less dim, in his servant the horse.

But now, on the new system of travelling, iron tubes and boilers have disconnected man's heart from the ministers of his locomotion. Nile nor Trafalgar[1] has power any more to raise an extra bubble in a steam-kettle. The galvanic cycle is broken up for ever; man's imperial nature no longer sends itself forward through the electric sensibility of the horse; the inter-agencies are gone in the mode of communication between the horse and his master, out of which grew so many aspects of sublimity under accidents of mists that hid, or sudden blazes that revealed, of mobs that agitated, or midnight solitudes that awed. Tidings, fitted to convulse all nations, must henceforwards travel by culinary process; and the trumpet that once announced from afar the laurelled mail, heart-shaking, when heard screaming on the wind, and advancing through the darkness to every village or solitary house on its route, has now given way for ever to the pot-wallopings of the boiler.

Thus have perished multiform openings for sublime effects, for interesting personal communications, for revelations of impressive faces that could not have offered themselves amongst the hurried and fluctuating groups of a railway station. The gatherings of gazers about a mail-coach had one centre, and acknowledged only one interest. But the crowds attending at a railway station have as little unity as running water, and own as many centres as there are separate carriages in the train.

How else, for example, than as a constant watcher for the dawn, and for the London mail that in summer months entered about dawn into the lawny thickets of Marlborough Forest, couldst thou, sweet Fanny of the Bath road, have become known to myself? Yet Fanny, as the loveliest young woman for face and person that perhaps in my whole life I have beheld, merited the station which even *her* I could not willingly have spared; yet (thirty-five years later) she holds in my dreams; and though, by an accident of fanciful caprice, she brought along with her into those dreams a troop of dreadful creatures, fabulous and not fabulous, that were more abominable to a human heart than Fanny and the dawn were delightful.

Miss Fanny of the Bath road, strictly speaking, lived at a mile's

---

[1]   Battle of the Nile (1789), where Nelson routed the French fleet; Battle of Trafalgar, see p. 233, n. 1 above.

distance from that road, but came so continually to meet the mail, that I on my frequent transits rarely missed her, and naturally connected her name with the great thoroughfare where I saw her; I do not exactly know, but I believe with some burthen of commissions to be executed in Bath, her own residence being probably the centre to which these commissions gathered. The mail coachman, who wore the royal livery, being one amongst the privileged few,★ happened to be Fanny's grand-father. A good man he was, that loved his beautiful granddaughter; and, loving her wisely, was vigilant over her deportment in any case where young Oxford might happen to be concerned. Was I then vain enough to imagine that I myself individually could fall within the line of his terrors? Certainly not, as regarded any physical pretensions that I could plead; for Fanny (as a chance passenger from her own neighbourhood once told me) counted in her train a hundred and ninety-nine professed admirers, if not open aspirants to her favour; and probably not one of the whole brigade but excelled myself in personal advantages. Ulysses even, with the unfair advantage of his accursed bow, could hardly have undertaken that amount of suitors.[1] So the danger might have seemed slight—only that woman is universally aristocratic: it is amongst her nobilities of heart that she *is* so. Now, the aristocratic distinctions in my favour might easily with Miss Fanny have compensated my physical deficiencies. Did I then make love to Fanny? Why, yes; *mais oui donc;*[2] as much love as one *can* make whilst the mail is changing horses, a process which ten years later did not occupy above eighty seconds; but *then,* viz. about Waterloo, it occupied five times eighty. Now, four hundred seconds offer a field quite ample enough for whispering into a young woman's ear a great deal of truth; and (by way of parenthesis) some trifle of falsehood. Grandpapa did right, therefore, to watch me. And yet, as happens too often to the grandpapas of earth, in a contest with the admirers of granddaughters, how vainly would he have

---

★ "Privileged few." The general impression was that this splendid costume belonged of right to the mail coachmen as their professional dress. But that was an error. To the guard it *did* belong as a matter of course, and was essential as an official warrant, and a means of instant identification for his person, in the discharge of his important public duties. But the coach-man, and especially if his place in the series did not connect him immediately with London and the General Post Office, obtained the scarlet coat only as an honorary distinc-tion after long or special service.

---

[1] Homer, *Odyssey* (Books 21–22); Ulysses returns home and slays his wife Penelope's suit-ors with his magic bow.

[2] "But of course."

watched me had I meditated any evil whispers to Fanny! She, it is my belief, would have protected herself against any man's evil suggestions. But he, as the result showed, could not have intercepted the opportunities for such suggestions. Yet he was still active; he was still blooming. Blooming he was as Fanny herself.

"Say, all our praises why should lords—"[1]

No, that's not the line:

"Say, all our roses why should girls engross?"

The coachman showed rosy blossoms on his face deeper even than his granddaughter's,—*his* being drawn from the ale-cask, Fanny's from youth and innocence, and from the fountains of the dawn. But, in spite of his blooming face, some infirmities he had; and one particularly, (I am very sure, no *more* than one,) in which he too much resembled a crocodile. This lay in a monstrous inaptitude for turning round. The crocodile, I presume, owes that inaptitude to the absurd *length* of his back; but in our grandpapa it arose rather from the absurd *breadth* of his back, combined, probably, with some growing stiffness in his legs. Now upon this crocodile infirmity of his I planted an easy opportunity for tendering my homage to Miss Fanny. In defiance of all his honourable vigilance, no sooner had he presented to us his mighty Jovian back, (what a field for displaying to mankind his royal scarlet!) whilst inspecting professionally the buckles, the straps, and the silver turrets of his harness, than I raised Miss Fanny's hand to my lips, and, by the mixed tenderness and respectfulness of my manner, caused her easily to understand how happy it would have made me to rank upon her list as No. 10 or 12, in which case a few casualties amongst her lovers (and observe—they *hanged* liberally in those days) might have promoted me speedily to the top of the tree; as, on the other hand, with how much loyalty of submission I acquiesced in her allotment, supposing that she had seen reason to plant me in the very rearward of her favour, as No. 199+1. It must not be supposed that I allowed any trace of jest, or even of playfulness, to mingle with these expressions of my admiration; that would have been insulting to her, and would have been false as regarded my own feelings. In fact, the utter shadowyness of our relations

---

[1]   Pope, "Epistle to Allen Lord Bathurst": "But all our praises why should lords engross?" (249).

to each other, even after our meetings through seven or eight years had been very numerous, but of necessity had been very brief, being entirely on mail-coach allowance—timed, in reality, by the General Post-Office—and watched by a crocodile belonging to the antepenultimate generation, left it easy for me to do a thing which few people ever *can* have done—viz., to make love for seven years, at the same time to be as sincere as ever creature was, and yet never to compromise myself by overtures that might have been foolish as regarded my own interests, or misleading as regarded hers. Most truly I loved this beautiful and ingenuous girl; and had it not been for the Bath and Bristol mail, heaven only knows what might have come of it. People talk of being over head and ears in love—now, the mail was the cause that I sank only over ears in love, which, you know, still left a trifle of brain to overlook the whole conduct of the affair. I have mentioned the case at all for the sake of a dreadful result from it in after years of dreaming. But it seems, *ex abundanti,*[1] to yield this moral—viz. that as, in England, the idiot and the half-wit are held to be under the guardianship of Chancery,[2] so the man making love, who is often but a variety of the same imbecile class, ought to be made a ward of the General Post-Office, whose severe course of *timing* and periodical interruption might intercept many a foolish declaration, such as lays a solid foundation for fifty years' repentance.

Ah, reader! when I look back upon those days, it seems to me that all things change or perish. Even thunder and lightning, it pains me to say, are not the thunder and lightning which I seem to remember about the time of Waterloo. Roses, I fear, are degenerating, and, without a Red revolution, must come to the dust. The Fannies of our island—though this I say with reluctance—are not improving; and the Bath road is notoriously superannuated. Mr Waterton[3] tells me that the crocodile does *not* change—that a cayman, in fact, or an alligator, is just as good for riding upon as he was in the time of the Pharaohs. *That* may be; but the reason is, that the crocodile does not live fast—he is a slow coach. I believe it is generally understood amongst naturalists, that the crocodile is a blockhead. It is my own impression that the Pharaohs were also blockheads. Now, as the Pharaohs and the crocodile domineered over Egyptian society, this accounts for a singular mistake that prevailed on the Nile. The crocodile

---

[1] "Out of an abundance."

[2] Court of Chancery, court of equity under lord high chancellor; abolished in 1873.

[3] Charles Waterton (1782–1865); naturalist, author of *Wanderings in South America* (1825), in which he recounts jumping on a cayman's back and wrestling it onto its back by holding its forelegs, a success he attributes to his experience fox-hunting.

made the ridiculous blunder of supposing man to be meant chiefly for his own eating. Man, taking a different view of the subject, naturally met that mistake by another; he viewed the crocodile as a thing sometimes to worship, but always to run away from. And this continued until Mr Waterton changed the relations between the animals. The mode of escaping from the reptile he showed to be, not by running away, but by leaping on its back, booted and spurred. The two animals had misunderstood each other. The use of the crocodile has now been cleared up—it is to be ridden; and the use of man is, that he may improve the health of the crocodile by riding him a fox-hunting before breakfast. And it is pretty certain that any crocodile, who has been regularly hunted through the season, and is master of the weight he carries, will take a six-barred gate now as well as ever he would have done in the infancy of the Pyramids.

Perhaps, therefore, the crocodile does *not* change, but all things else *do*; even the shadow of the Pyramids grows less. And often the restoration in vision of Fanny and the Bath road, makes me too pathetically sensible of that truth. Out of the darkness, if I happen to call up the image of Fanny from thirty-five years back, arises suddenly a rose in June; or, if I think for an instant of the rose in June, up rises the heavenly face of Fanny. One after the other, like the antiphonies in a choral service, rises Fanny and the rose in June, then back again the rose in June and Fanny. Then come both together, as in a chorus; roses and Fannies, Fannies and roses, without end—thick as blossoms in paradise. Then comes a venerable crocodile, in a royal livery of scarlet and gold, or in a coat with sixteen capes; and the crocodile is driving four-in-hand from the box of the Bath mail. And suddenly we upon the mail are pulled up by a mighty dial, sculptured with the hours, and with the dreadful legend of TOO LATE. Then all at once we are arrived in Marlborough forest, amongst the lovely households★ of the roe-deer: these retire into the dewy thickets; the thickets are rich with roses; the roses call up (as ever) the sweet countenance of Fanny, who, being the granddaughter of a crocodile, awakens a dreadful host of wild semi-legendary animals—griffins, dragons, basilisks, sphinxes—till at length the whole vision of fighting images crowds into one towering armorial shield, a vast emblazonry of human charities and human loveliness that have perished, but quartered heraldically with unutterable horrors of monstrous

---

★ "*Households.*"—Roe-deer do not congregate in herds like the fallow or the red deer, but by separate families, parents, and children; which feature of approximation to the sanctity of human hearths, added to their comparatively miniature and graceful proportions, conciliate to them an interest of a peculiarly tender character, if less dignified by the grandeurs of savage and forest life.

and demoniac natures; whilst over all rises, as a surmounting crest, one fair female hand, with the fore-finger pointing, in sweet, sorrowful admonition, upwards to heaven, and having power (which, without experience, I never could have believed) to awaken the pathos that kills in the very bosom of the horrors that madden the grief that gnaws at the heart, together with the monstrous creations of darkness that shock the belief, and make dizzy the reason of man. This is the peculiarity that I wish the reader to notice, as having first been made known to me for a possibility by this early vision of Fanny on the Bath road. The peculiarity consisted in the confluence of two different keys, though apparently repelling each other, into the music and governing principles of the same dream; horror, such as possesses the maniac, and yet, by momentary transitions, grief, such as may be supposed to possess the dying mother when leaving her infant children to the mercies of the cruel. Usually, and perhaps always, in an unshaken nervous system, these two modes of misery exclude each other—here first they met in horrid reconciliation. There was also a separate peculiarity in the quality of the horror. This was afterwards developed into far more revolting complexities of misery and incomprehensible darkness; and perhaps I am wrong in ascribing any value as a *causative* agency to this particular case on the Bath road—possibly it furnished merely an *occasion* that accidentally introduced a mode of horrors certain, at any rate, to have grown up, with or without the Bath road, from more advanced stages of the nervous derangement. Yet, as the cubs of tigers or leopards, when domesticated, have been observed to suffer a sudden development of their latent ferocity under too eager an appeal to their playfulness—the gaieties of sport in *them* being too closely connected with the fiery brightness of their murderous instincts—so I have remarked that the caprices, the gay arabesques, and the lovely floral luxuriations of dreams, betray a shocking tendency to pass into finer maniacal splendours. That gaiety, for instance, (for such at first it was,) in the dreaming faculty, by which one principal point of resemblance to a crocodile in the mail-coachman was soon made to clothe him with the form of a crocodile, and yet was blended with accessory circumstances derived from his *human* functions, passed rapidly into a further development, no longer gay or playful, but terrific, the most terrific that besieges dreams, viz.—the horrid inoculation upon each other of incompatible natures. This horror has always been secretly felt by man; it was felt even under pagan forms of religion, which offered a very feeble, and also a very limited gamut for giving expression to the human capacities of sublimity or of horror. We read it in the fearful composition of the sphinx. The dragon, again, is the snake inoculated upon the scorpion. The basilisk unites the mysterious malice of the evil eye, unintentional on the part of the unhappy agent, with the intentional venom of some other malignant natures. But these horrid complexities of evil agency are but *objectively* horrid; they inflict the horror suitable to their compound nature; but there is no insinuation that they *feel* that horror. Heraldry is so full of these fantastic creatures, that, in some zoologies, we find a separate chapter or a supplement dedicated to what is denominated heraldic zoology. And why not? For these hideous creatures, however visionary,★ have a real traditionary ground in medieval belief—sincere and partly reasonable, though adulterating with mendacity, blundering, credulity, and intense superstition. But the dream-horror which I speak of is far more frightful. The dreamer finds housed within himself—occupying, as it were, some separate chamber in his brain—holding, perhaps, from that station a secret and detestable commerce with his own heart—some

---

★ "*However visionary.*"—But *are* they always visionary? The unicorn, the kraken [mythical sea monster], the sea-serpent, are all, perhaps, zoological facts. The unicorn, for instance, so far from being a lie, is rather *too* true; for, simply as a *monokeras* [for the Greek "monoceros," or unicorn; perhaps De Quincy is thinking of a rhinoceros], he is found in the Himalaya, in Africa, and elsewhere, rather too often for the peace of what in Scotland would be called the *intending* traveller. That which really *is* a lie in the account of the unicorn—viz., his legendary rivalship with the lion—which lie may God preserve, in preserving the mighty imperial shield that embalms it—cannot be more destructive to the zoological pretensions of the unicorn, than are to the same pretensions in the lion our many popular crazes about his goodness and magnanimity, or the old fancy (adopted by Spenser, and noticed by so many among our elder poets) of his graciousness to maiden innocence. The wretch is the basest and most cowardly among the forest tribes; nor has the sublime courage of the English bull-dog ever been so memorably exhibited as in his hopeless fight at Warwick with the cowardly and cruel lion called Wallace. Another of the traditional creatures, still doubtful, is the mermaid, upon which Southey once remarked to me, that, if it had been differently named, (as, suppose, a mer-ape,) nobody would have questioned its existence any more than that of sea-cows, sea-lions, &c. The mermaid has been discredited by her human name and her legendary human habits. If she would not coquette so much with melancholy sailors, and brush her hair so assiduously upon solitary rocks, she would be carried on our books for as honest a reality, as decent a female, as many that are assessed to the poor-rates. [Edmund Spenser (c1552–1599): poet of *The Faerie Queene* (1590–96), in which a "ramping Lyon rushed suddainly" at Truth, "Hunting full greedie after saluage blood": "Soone as the royall virgin he did spy, / With gaping mouth at her ran greedily, / To have attonce devour'd her tender corse: / But to the pray when as he drew more ny, / His bloudie rage asswaged with remorse, / And with the sight amazed, forgat his furious forse" (1.3.38–45). Concerning Warwick and Wallace: "A menagerie-keeper named Wombwell organized the public baiting of two lions by bulldogs at Warwick on 30 July 1825. The first lion, Nero, refused to fight, but Wallace rose to the occasion and killed two dogs (Thomas Kemp, *A History of Warwick and its People* (Warwick: Cooke, 1905), p. 83)" (*Works* 16:618). Robert Southey (1774–1843): essayist, biographer, historian; Poet Laureate (1813–43). "Poor-rate": "A rate of assessment, for the relief or support of the poor" (*OED*).]

horrid alien nature. What if it were his own nature repeated,—still, if the duality were distinctly perceptible, even *that*—even this mere numerical double of his own consciousness—might be a curse too mighty to be sustained. But how, if the alien nature contradicts his own, fights with it, perplexes, and confounds it? How, again, if not one alien nature, but two, but three, but four, but five, are introduced within what once he thought the inviolable sanctuary of himself? These, however, are horrors from the kingdoms of anarchy and darkness, which, by their very intensity, challenge the sanctity of concealment, and gloomily retire from exposition. Yet it was necessary to mention them, because the first introduction to such appearances (whether causal, or merely casual) lay in the heraldic monsters, which monsters were themselves introduced (though playfully) by the transfigured coachman of the Bath mail.

GOING DOWN WITH VICTORY

But the grandest chapter of our experience, within the whole mail-coach service, was on those occasions when we went down from London with the news of victory. A period of about ten years stretched from Trafalgar to Waterloo: the second and third years of which period (1806 and 1807) were comparatively sterile; but the rest, from 1805 to 1815 inclusively, furnished a long succession of victories; the least of which, in a contest of that portentous nature, had an inappreciable value of position—partly for its absolute interference with the plans of our enemy, but still more from its keeping alive in central Europe the sense of a deep-seated vulnerability in France. Even to tease the coasts of our enemy, to mortify them by continual blockades, to insult them by capturing if it were but a baubling schooner under the eyes of their arrogant armies, repeated from time to time a sullen proclamation of power lodged in a quarter to which the hopes of Christendom turned in secret. How much more loudly must this proclamation have spoken in the audacity* of having bearded the *elite* of their troops, and having

---

* "*Audacity!*" Such the French accounted it; and it has struck me that Soult would not have been so popular in London, at the period of her present Majesty's coronation, or in Manchester, on occasion of his visit to that town, if they had been aware of the insolence with which he spoke of us in notes written at intervals from the field of Waterloo. As though it had been mere felony in our army to look a French one in the face, he said more than once—"Here are the English—we have them: they are caught *en flagrant detit.*" Yet no man should have known us better; no man had drunk deeper from the cup of humiliation than Soult had in the north of Portugal, during his flight from an

beaten them in pitched battles! Five years of life it was worth paying down for the privilege of an outside place on a mail-coach, when carrying down the first tidings of any such event. And it is to be noted that, from our insular situation, and the multitude of our frigates disposable for the rapid transmission of intelligence, rarely did any unauthorised rumour steal away a prelibation from the aroma of the regular despatches. The government official news was generally the first news.

From eight P.M. to fifteen or twenty minutes later, imagine the mails assembled on parade in Lombard Street, where, at that time, was seated the General Post-Office. In what exact strength we mustered I do not remember; but, from the length of each separate *attelage*,[1] we filled the street, though a long one, and though we were drawn up in double file. On *any* night the spectacle was beautiful. The absolute perfection of all the appointments about the carriages and the harness, and the magnificence of the horses, were what might first have fixed the attention. Every carriage, on every morning in the year, was taken down to an inspector for examination—wheels, axles, linchpins, pole, glasses, &c., were all critically probed and tested. Every part of every carriage had been cleaned, every horse had been groomed, with as much rigour as if they belonged to a private gentleman; and that part of the spectacle offered itself always. But the night before us is a night of victory; and behold! to the ordinary display, what a heart-shaking addition!—horses, men, carriages—all are dressed in laurels and flowers, oak leaves and ribbons. The guards, who are his Majesty's servants, and the coachmen, who are within the privilege of the Post-Office, wear the royal liveries of course; and as it is summer (for all the *land* victories were won in summer,) they wear, on this fine evening, these liveries exposed to view, without any covering of upper coats. Such a costume, and the elaborate arrangement of the laurels in their hats, dilated their hearts, by giving to them openly an *official* connection with the great news, in which already they have the general interest of patriotism. That great national sentiment surmounts and quells all sense of ordinary distinctions. Those passengers who happen to be gentlemen are now hardly to

---

English army, and subsequently at Albuera, in the bloodiest of recorded battles. [Nicolas-Jean de Dieu Soult (1769–1851): Marshall of Napoleon's forces in the Peninsula from 1803; defeated disastrously at Battle of Albuera, Portugal (1811); became a royalist after Napoleon's defeat, representing the French government at Victoria's coronation (1834), during which time he was enthusiastically received and visited Manchester. "*En flagrant detit*": from Latin *flagrante delicto*, "in flagrant violation."]

---

[1]   Equipage, team of horses.

be distinguished as such except by dress. The usual reserve of their manner in speaking to the attendants has on this night melted away. One heart, one pride, one glory, connects every man by the transcendant bond of his English blood. The spectators, who are numerous beyond precedent, express their sympathy with these fervent feelings by continual hurrahs. Every moment are shouted aloud by the Post-Office servants the great ancestral names of cities known to history through a thousand years,— Lincoln, Winchester, Portsmouth, Gloucester, Oxford, Bristol, Manchester, York, Newcastle, Edinburgh, Perth, Glasgow—expressing the grandeur of the empire by the antiquity of its towns, and the grandeur of the mail establishment by the diffusive radiation of its separate missions. Every moment you hear the thunder of lids locked down upon the mail-bags. That sound to each individual mail is the signal for drawing off, which process is the finest part of the entire spectacle. Then come the horses into play;—horses! can these be horses that (unless powerfully reined in) would bound off with the action and gestures of leopards? What stir!—what sea-like ferment!—what a thundering of wheels, what a trampling of horses!—what farewell cheers—what redoubling peals of brotherly congratulation, connecting the name of the particular mail—"Liverpool for ever!"—with the name of the particular victory—"Badajoz[1] for ever!" or "Salamanca for ever!" The half-slumbering consciousness that, all night long and all the next day—perhaps for even a longer period—many of these mails, like fire racing along a train of gunpowder, will be kindling at every instant new successions of burning joy, has an obscure effect of multiplying the victory itself, by multiplying to the imagination into infinity the stages of its progressive diffusion. A fiery arrow seems to be let loose, which from that moment is destined to travel, almost without intermission, westwards for three hundred★ miles—northwards for six hundred;

★ "*Three hundred.*" Of necessity this scale of measurement, to an American, if he happens to be a thoughtless man, must sound ludicrous. Accordingly, I remember a case in which an American writer indulges himself in the luxury of a little lying, by ascribing to an Englishman a pompous account of the Thames, constructed entirely upon American ideas of grandeur, and concluding in something like these terms:—"And, sir, arriving at London, this mighty father of rivers attains a breadth of at least two furlongs, having, in its winding course, traversed the astonishing distance of 170 miles." And this the candid American thinks it fair to contrast with the scale of the Mississippi. Now, it is hardly worth while to answer a pure falsehood gravely, else one might say that no Englishman out of Bedlam ever thought of looking in an island for the rivers of a continent; nor, consequently, could have thought of looking for the peculiar grandeur of the Thames in the length of its course, or in the extent of soil which it drains: yet, if he *had* been so absurd,

---

[1] Badajoz, Spain; captured by the British in 1812 from the French by Wellington.

and the sympathy of our Lombard Street friends at parting is exalted a hundredfold by a sort of visionary sympathy with the approaching sympathies, yet unborn, which we were going to evoke.

Liberated from the embarrassments of the city, and issuing into the broad uncrowded avenues of the northern suburbs, we begin to enter upon our natural pace of ten miles an hour. In the broad light of the summer evening, the sun perhaps only just at the point of setting, we are seen from every storey of every house. Heads of every age crowd to the windows—young and old understand the language of our victorious symbols—and rolling volleys of sympathising cheers run along behind and before our course. The beggar, rearing himself against the wall, forgets his lameness—real or assumed—thinks not of his whining trade, but stands erect, with bold exulting smiles, as we pass him. The victory has healed him, and says—Be thou whole! Women and children, from garrets alike and cellars, look down or look up with loving eyes upon our gay ribbons and our martial laurels—sometimes kiss their hands, sometimes hang out, as signals of affection, pocket handkerchiefs, aprons, dusters, anything that lies ready to their hands. On the London side of Barnet, to which we draw near within a few minutes after nine, observe that private carriage which is approaching us. The weather being so warm, the glasses are all down; and one may read, as on the stage of a theatre, everything that goes on within the carriage. It contains three ladies, one likely to be "mama," and two of seventeen or eighteen, who are probably her daughters. What lovely animation, what beautiful unpremeditated pantomime, explaining to us every syllable that passes, in these ingenuous girls! By the sudden start and raising of the hands, on first discovering our laurelled equipage—by the sudden movement and appeal to the elder lady from both of them—and by the heightened colour on their animated countenances, we can

the American might have recollected that a river, not to be compared with the Thames even as to volume of water—viz. the Tiber—has contrived to make itself heard of in this world for twenty-five centuries to an extent not reached, nor likely to be reached very soon, by any river, however corpulent, of his own land. The glory of the Thames is measured by the density of the population to which it ministers, by the commerce which it supports, by the grandeur of the empire in which, though far from the largest, it is the most influential stream. Upon some such scale, and not by a transfer of Columbian standards, is the course of our English mails to be valued. The American may fancy the effect of his own valuations to our English ears, by supposing the case of a Siberian glorifying his country in these terms:—"Those rascals, sir, in France and England, cannot march half a mile in any direction without finding a house where food can be had and lodging: whereas, such is the noble desolation of our magnificent country, that in many a direction for a thousand miles, I will engage a dog shall not find shelter from a snow-storm, nor a wren find an apology for breakfast."

almost hear them saying—"See, see! Look at their laurels. Oh, mama! there has been a great battle in Spain; and it has been a great victory." In a moment we are on the point of passing them. We passengers—I on the box, and the two on the roof behind me—raise our hats, the coachman makes his professional salute with the whip; the guard even, though punctilious on the matter of his dignity as an officer under the crown, touches his hat. The ladies move to us, in return, with a winning graciousness of gesture: all smile on each side in a way that nobody could misunderstand, and that nothing short of a grand national sympathy could so instantaneously prompt. Will these ladies say that we are nothing to *them?* Oh, no; they will not say *that*. They cannot deny—they do not deny—that for this night they are our sisters: gentle or simple, scholar or illiterate servant, for twelve hours to come—we on the outside have the honour to be their brothers. Those poor women again, who stop to gaze upon us with delight at the entrance of Barnet, and seem by their air of weariness to be returning from labour—do you mean to say that they are washerwomen and charwomen? Oh, my poor friend, you are quite mistaken; they are nothing of the kind. I assure you, they stand in a higher rank: for this one night they feel themselves by birthright to be daughters of England, and answer to no humbler title.

Every joy, however, even rapturous joy—such is the sad law of earth—may carry with it grief, or fear of grief, to some. Three miles beyond Barnet, we see approaching us another private carriage, nearly repeating the circumstances of the former case. Here also the glasses are all down—here also is an elderly lady seated; but the two amiable daughters are missing; for the single young person, sitting by the lady's side, seems to be an attendant—so I judge from her dress, and her air of respectful reserve. The lady is in mourning; and her countenance expresses sorrow. At first she does not look up; so that I believe she is not aware of our approach, until she hears the measured beating of our horses' hoofs. Then she raises her eyes to settle them painfully on our triumphal equipage. Our decorations explain the case to her at once; but she beholds them with apparent anxiety, or even with terror. Some time before this, I, finding it difficult to hit a flying mark, when embarrassed by the coachman's person and reins intervening, had given to the guard a *Courier* evening paper, containing the gazette,[1] for the next carriage that might pass. Accordingly he tossed it in

---

[1]   *The Courier.* London evening paper founded in 1792; the gazette is "one of three official journals entitled *The London Gazette, The Edingurgh Gazette,* and *The Dublin Gazette,* issued by authority twice a week, and containing lists of government appointments and promotions ... and other public notices" (*OED*).

so folded that the huge capitals expressing some such legend as—GLORI-OUS VICTORY, might catch the eye at once. To see the paper, however, at all, interpreted as it was by our ensigns of triumph, explained everything; and, if the guard were right in thinking the lady to have received it with a gesture of horror, it could not be doubtful that she had suffered some deep personal affliction in connexion with this Spanish war.

Here now was the case of one who, having formerly suffered, might, erroneously perhaps, be distressing herself with anticipations of another similar suffering. That same night, and hardly three hours later, occurred the reverse case. A poor woman, who too probably would find herself, in a day or two, to have suffered the heaviest of afflictions by the battle, blindly allowed herself to express an exultation so unmeasured in the news, and its details, as gave to her the appearance which amongst Celtic Highlanders is called *fey*.[1] This was at some little town, I forget what, where we happened to change horses near midnight. Some fair or wake had kept the people up out of their beds. We saw many lights moving about as we drew near; and perhaps the most impressive scene on our route was our reception at this place. The flashing of torches and the beautiful radiance of blue lights (technically Bengal lights)[2] upon the heads of our horses; the fine effect of such a showery and ghostly illumination falling upon flowers and glittering laurels, whilst all around the massy darkness seemed to invest us with walls of impenetrable blackness, together with the prodigious enthusiasm of the people, composed a picture at once scenical and affecting. As we staid for three or four minutes, I alighted. And immediately from a dismantled stall in the street, where perhaps she had been presiding at some part of the evening, advanced eagerly a middle-aged woman. The sight of my newspaper it was that had drawn her attention upon myself. The victory which we were carrying down to the provinces on *this* occasion was the imperfect one of Talavera.[3] I told her the main outline of the battle. But her agitation, though not the agitation of fear, but of exultation rather, and enthusiasm, had been so conspicuous when listening, and when first applying for information, that I could not but ask her if she had not some relation in the Peninsular army. Oh! yes: her only son was there. In what regiment? He was a trooper in the 23d Dragoons. My

---

[1] "Fated to die, doomed to death" (*OED*).

[2] Flares or fireworks producing a steady and intense blue light, used for illumination or for signalling.

[3] British commander Wellesley routed the French army at Talavera, Spain on 27–28 July 1809, but heavy losses forced a retreat.

heart sank within me as she made that answer. This sublime regiment, which an Englishman should never mention without raising his hat to their memory, had made the most memorable and effective charge recorded in military annals. They leaped their horses—*over* a trench, where they could *into* it, and with the result of death or mutilation when they could *not*. What proportion cleared the trench is nowhere stated. Those who *did*, closed up and went down upon the enemy with such divinity of fervour—(I use the word *divinity* by design: the inspiration of God must have prompted this movement to those whom even then he was calling to his presence)—that two results followed. As regarded the enemy, this 23d Dragoons, not, I believe, originally 350 strong, paralysed a French column, 6000 strong, then ascending the hill, and fixed the gaze of the whole French army. As regarded themselves, the 23d were supposed at first to have been all but annihilated; but eventually, I believe, not so many as one in four survived. And this, then, was the regiment—a regiment already for some hours known to myself and all London as stretched, by a large majority, upon one bloody aceldama[1]—in which the young trooper served whose mother was now talking with myself in a spirit of such hopeful enthusiasm. Did I tell her the truth? Had I the heart to break up her dream? No. I said to myself, Tomorrow, or the next day, she will hear the worst. For this night, wherefore should she not sleep in peace? After to-morrow, the chances are too many that peace will forsake her pillow. This brief respite, let her owe this to *my* gift and *my* forbearance. But, if I told her not of the bloody price that had been paid, there was no reason for suppressing the contributions from her son's regiment to the service and glory of the day. For the very few words that I had time for speaking, I governed myself accordingly. I showed her not the funeral banners under which the noble regiment was sleeping. I lifted not the overshadowing laurels from the bloody trench in which horse and rider lay mangled together. But I told her how these dear children of England, privates and officers, had leaped their horses over all obstacles as gaily as hunters to the morning's chase. I told her how they rode their horses into the mists of death, (saying to myself, but not saying to *her*,) and laid down their young lives for thee, O mother England! as willingly—poured out their noble blood as cheerfully—as ever, after a long day's sport, when infants, they had rested their wearied heads upon their mothers' knees, or had

---

[1] "And it was known unto all the dwellers at Jerusalem; insomuch as that field is called in their proper tongue, Aceldama, that is to day, The field of blood" (Acts 1:19).

sunk to sleep in her arms. It is singular that she seemed to have no fears, even after this knowledge that the 23d Dragoons had been conspicuously engaged, for her son's safety: but so much was she enraptured by the knowledge that *his* regiment, and therefore *he,* had rendered eminent service in the trying conflict—a service which had actually made them the foremost topic of conversation in London—that in the mere simplicity of her fervent nature, she threw her arms round my neck, and, poor woman, kissed me.

THE VISION OF SUDDEN DEATH

[*Blackwood's* ED.: The reader is to understand this present paper, in its two sections of *The Vision,* & c., and *The Dream-Fugue,* as connected with a previous paper on *The English Mail-Coach,* published in the Magazine for October.[1] The ultimate object was the Dream-Fugue, as an attempt to wrestle with the utmost efforts of music in dealing with a colossal form of impassioned horror. The Vision of Sudden Death contains the mail-coach incident, which did really occur, and did really suggest the variations of the Dream, here taken up by the Fugue, as well as other variations not now recorded. Confluent with these impressions, from the terrific experience on the Manchester and Glasgow mail, were other and more general impressions, derived from long familiarity with the English mail, as developed in the former paper; impressions, for instance, of animal beauty and power, of rapid motion, at the time unprecedented, of connexion with the government and public business of a great nation but, above all, of connexion with the national victories at an unexampled crisis,—the mail being the privileged organ for publishing and dispersing all news of that kind. From this function of the mail, arises naturally the introduction of Waterloo into the fourth variation of the Fugue; for the mail itself having been carried into the dreams by the incident in the Vision, naturally all the accessory circumstances of pomp and grandeur investing this national carriage followed in the train of the principal image.]

   WHAT is to be thought of sudden death? It is remarkable that, in different conditions of society, it has been variously regarded, as the consummation of an earthly career most fervently to be desired, and,

---

[1]   Prefatory note appended to *Blackwood's* publication of "The Vision of Sudden Death"; omitted by De Quincey in later revision.

on the other hand, as that consummation which is most of all to be deprecated. Cæsar the Dictator, at his last dinner party, (*cæna*,) and the very evening before his assassination, being questioned as to the mode of death which, in *his* opinion, might seem the most eligible, replied—"That which should be most sudden."[1] On the other hand, the divine Litany of our English Church,[2] when breathing forth supplications, as if in some representative character for the whole human race prostrate before God, places such a death in the very van of horrors. "From lightning and tempest; from plague, pestilence, and famine; from battle and murder, and from sudden death,—*Good Lord, deliver us.*" Sudden death is here made to crown the climax in a grand ascent of calamities; it is the last of curses; and yet, by the noblest of Romans, it was treated as the first of blessings. In that difference, most readers will see little more than the difference between Christianity and Paganism. But there I hesitate. The Christian church may be right in its estimate of sudden death; and it is a natural feeling, though after all it may also be an infirm one, to wish for a quiet dismissal from life—as that which *seems* most reconcilable with meditation, with penitential retrospects, and with the humilities of farewell prayer. There does not, however, occur to me any direct scriptural warrant for this earnest petition of the English Litany. It seems rather a petition indulged to human infirmity, than exacted from human piety. And, however *that* may be, two remarks suggest themselves as prudent restraints upon a doctrine, which else *may* wander, and *has* wandered, into an uncharitable superstition. The first is this: that many people are likely to exaggerate the horror of a sudden death, (I mean the *objective* horror to him who contemplates such a death, not the *subjective* horror to him who suffers it) from the false disposition to lay a stress upon words or acts, simply because by an accident they have become words or acts. If a man dies, for instance, by some sudden death when he happens to be intoxicated, such a death is falsely regarded with peculiar horror; as though the intoxication were suddenly exalted into a blasphemy. But *that* is unphilosophic. The man was, or he was not, *habitually* a drunkard. If not, if his intoxication were a solitary accident, there can be no reason at all for allowing special emphasis to this act, simply because through misfortune it became his final act. Nor, on the other hand, if it were no accident, but one of his

---

[1] Plutarch (c. 46–127), Greek historian, biographer, and essayist, recounts the story in his life of Julius Caesar in his *Parallel Lives*.
[2] Litany from *The Book of Common Prayer*.

habitual transgressions, will it be the more habitual or the more a transgression, because some sudden calamity, surprising him, has caused this habitual transgression to be also a final one? Could the man have had any reason even dimly to foresee his own sudden death, there would have been a new feature in his act of intemperance—a feature of presumption and irreverence, as in one that by possibility felt himself drawing near to the presence of God. But this is no part of the case supposed. And the only new element in the man's act is not any element of extra immorality, but simply of extra misfortune.

The other remark has reference to the meaning of the word *sudden*. And it is a strong illustration of the duty which for ever calls us to the stern valuation of words—that very possibly Cæsar and the Christian church do not differ in the way supposed; that is, do not differ by any difference of doctrine as between Pagan and Christian views of the moral temper appropriate to death, but that they are contemplating different cases. Both contemplate a violent death; a βιαθανατος—death that is βιαιος:[1] but the difference is—that the Roman by the word "sudden" means an *unlingering* death: whereas the Christian litany by "sudden" means a death *without warning,* consequently without any available summons to religious preparation. The poor mutineer, who kneels down to gather into his heart the bullets from twelve firelocks of his pitying comrades, dies by a most sudden death in Cæsar's sense: one shock, one mighty spasm, one (possibly *not* one) groan, and all is over. But, in the sense of the Litany, his death is far from sudden; his offence originally, his imprisonment, his trial, the interval between his sentence and its execution, having all furnished him with separate warnings of his fate—having all summoned him to meet it with solemn preparation.

Meantime, whatever may be thought of a sudden death as a mere variety in the modes of dying, where death in some shape is inevitable—a question which, equally in the Roman and the Christian sense, will be variously answered according to each man's variety of temperament—certainly, upon one aspect of sudden death there can be no opening for doubt, that of all agonies incident to man it is the most frightful, that of all martyrdoms it is the most freezing to human sensibilities—namely, where it surprises a man under circumstances which offer (or which seem to offer) some hurried and inappreciable chance of evading it. Any effort, by which such an evasion can be accomplished, must be as sudden as the danger which it affronts. Even *that,* even the sickening necessity

---

[1] "Violent death"; "violent."

for hurrying in extremity where all hurry seems destined to be vain, self-baffled, and where the dreadful knell of *too late* is already sounding in the ears by anticipation—even that anguish is liable to a hideous exasperation in one particular case, namely, where the agonising appeal is made not exclusively to the instinct of self-preservation, but to the conscience, on behalf of another life besides your own, accidentally cast upon *your* protection. To fail, to collapse in a service merely your own, might seem comparatively venial; though, in fact, it is far from venial. But to fail in a case where Providence has suddenly thrown into your hands the final interests of another—of a fellow-creature shuddering between the gates of life and death; this, to a man of apprehensive conscience, would mingle the misery of an atrocious criminality with the misery of a bloody calamity. The man is called upon, too probably, to die; but to die at the very moment when, by any momentary collapse, he is self-denounced as a murderer. He had but the twinkling of an eye[1] for his effort, and that effort might, at the best, have been unavailing; but from this shadow of a chance, small or great, how if he has recoiled by a treasonable *lâcheté*?[2] The effort *might* have been without hope; but to have risen to the level of that effort—would have rescued him, though not from dying, yet from dying as a traitor to his duties.

The situation here contemplated exposes a dreadful ulcer, lurking far down in the depths of human nature. It is not that men generally are summoned to face such awful trials. But potentially, and in shadowy outline, such a trial is moving subterraneously in perhaps all men's natures—muttering under ground in one world, to be realised perhaps in some other. Upon the secret mirror of our dreams such a trial is darkly projected at intervals, perhaps, to every one of us. That dream, so familiar to childhood, of meeting a lion, and, from languishing prostration in hope and vital energy, that constant sequel of lying down before him, publishes the secret frailty of human nature—reveals its deep-seated Pariah falsehood to itself—records its abysmal treachery. Perhaps not one of us escapes that dream; perhaps, as by some sorrowful doom of man, that dream repeats for every one of us, through every generation, the original temptation in Eden. Every one of us, in this dream, has a bait offered to the infirm places of his own individual will; once again a snare is made ready for leading him into captivity to a

---

[1] "We will not all die, but we will all be changed, in a moment, in the twinkling of an eye, at the last trumpet. For the trumpet will sound, and the dead will be raised imperishable, and we will be changed" (I Corinthians 15:51–52).

[2] Cowardice.

luxury of ruin; again, as in aboriginal Paradise, the man falls from innocence; once again, by infinite iteration, the ancient Earth groans to God,
through her secret caves, over the weakness of her child; "Nature from
her seat, sighing through all her works," again "gives signs of woe that
all is lost;"[1] and again the counter sigh is repeated to the sorrowing
heavens of the endless rebellion against God. Many people think that
one man, the patriarch of our race, could not in his single person
execute this rebellion for all his race. Perhaps they are wrong. But, even
if not, perhaps in the world of dreams every one of us ratifies for himself
the original act. Our English rite of "Confirmation," by which, in years
of awakened reason, we take upon us the engagements contracted for
us in our slumbering infancy,—how sublime a rite is that! The little
postern gate, through which the baby in its cradle had been silently
placed for a time within the glory of God's countenance, suddenly rises
to the clouds as a triumphal arch, through which, with banners
displayed and martial pomps, we make our second entry as crusading
soldiers militant for God, by personal choice and by sacramental oath.
Each man says in effect—"Lo! I rebaptise myself; and that which once
was sworn on my behalf, now I swear for myself." Even so in dreams,
perhaps, under some secret conflict of the midnight sleeper, lighted up
to the consciousness at the time, but darkened to the memory as soon
as all is finished, each several child of our mysterious race completes for
himself the aboriginal fall.

As I drew near to the Manchester post-office, I found that it was
considerably past midnight; but to my great relief, as it was important
for me to be in Westmorland[2] by the morning, I saw by the huge saucer
eyes of the mail, blazing through the gloom of overhanging houses, that
my chance was not yet lost. Past the time it was; but by some luck, very
unusual in my experience, the mail was not even yet ready to start. I
ascended to my seat on the box, where my cloak was still lying as it had
lain at the Bridgewater Arms. I had left it there in imitation of a nautical discoverer, who leaves a bit of bunting on the shore of his discovery,
by way of warning off the ground the whole human race, and signalis-
ing to the Christian and the heathen worlds, with his best compliments,
that he has planted his throne for ever upon that virgin soil; henceforward

---

[1]   Milton, *Paradise Lost*: "Earth felt the wound, and nature from her seat / Sighing through
      all her works gave signs of woe, / That all was lost" (9.782–4), to indicate the effects of
      the Fall, of Adam and Eve's sin of transgression, upon God's creation.

[2]   De Quincey moved to Dove Cottage, Grasmere in Westmorland in 1809.

claiming the *jus dominii*[1] to the top of the atmosphere above it, and also the right of driving shafts to the centre of the earth below it; so that all people found after this warning, either aloft in the atmosphere, or in the shafts, or squatting on the soil, will be treated as trespassers—that is, decapitated by their very faithful and obedient servant, the owner of the said bunting. Possibly my cloak might not have been respected, and the *jus gentium*[2] might have been cruelly violated in my person—for, in the dark, people commit deeds of darkness, gas being a great ally of morality[3]—but it so happened that, on this night, there was no other outside passenger; and the crime, which else was but too probable, missed fire for want of a criminal. By the way, I may as well mention at this point, since a circumstantial accuracy is essential to the effect of my narrative, that there was no other person of any description whatever about the mail—the guard, the coachman, and myself being allowed for—except only one—a horrid creature of the class known to the world as insiders, but whom young Oxford called sometimes "Trojans," in opposition to our Grecian selves, and sometimes "vermin." A Turkish Effendi,[4] who piques himself on good-breeding, will never mention by name a pig. Yet it is but too often that he has reason to mention this animal; since constantly, in the streets of Stamboul,[5] he has his trousers deranged or polluted by this vile creature running between his legs. But under any excess of hurry he is always careful, out of respect to the company he is dining with, to suppress the odious name, and to call the wretch "that other creature," as though all animal life beside formed one group, and this odious beast (to whom, as Chrysippus observed, salt serves as an apology for a soul)[6] formed another and alien group on the outside of creation. Now I, who am an English Effendi, that think myself to understand good-breeding as well as any son of Othman,[7] beg my reader's

---

[1] "Law of ownership or property."

[2] "Law or right of nations."

[3] Coal-gas lighting was first installed in London in 1814.

[4] "A Turkish title of respect" (*OED*).

[5] Also called Istanbul, largest city and former capital of Turkey; formerly Constantinople, centre of Eastern Roman Empire, then of Byzantine Empire; now seat of Eastern Orthodox Church.

[6] Chrysippus (c. 280–c. 206 BCE), Stoic philosopher; held that animals were created exclusively for human use; De Quincey refers to Cicero in *De Natura deorum*, who held that the soul "is given to the pig as a kind of salt, to keep it from rotting" (2.64.160); De Quincey says that Chrysippus holds the opposite view.

[7] "Son of Othman": any Turk; the Ottoman dynasty ruled Turkey from roughly 1300 to the end of World War I.

pardon for having mentioned an insider by his gross natural name. I shall do so no more: and, if I should have occasion to glance at so painful a subject, I shall always call him "that other creature." Let us hope, however, that no such distressing occasion will arise. But, by the way, an occasion arises at this moment; for the reader will be sure to ask, when we come to the story, "Was this other creature present?" He was *not*; or more correctly, perhaps, *it* was not. We dropped the creature—or the creature, by natural imbecility, dropped itself—within the first ten miles from Manchester. In the latter case, I wish to make a philosophic remark of a moral tendency. When I die, or when the reader dies, and by repute suppose of fever, it will never be known whether we died in reality of the fever or of the doctor. But this other creature, in the case of dropping out of the coach, will enjoy a coroner's inquest; consequently he will enjoy an epitaph. For I insist upon it, that the verdict of a coroner's jury makes the best of epitaphs. It is brief, so that the public all find time to read it; it is pithy, so that the surviving friends (if any *can* survive such a loss) remember it without fatigue; it is upon oath, so that rascals and Dr Johnson cannot pick holes in it.[1] "Died through the visitation of intense stupidity, by impinging on a moonlight night against the off hind wheel of the Glasgow mail! Deodand[2] upon the said wheel—twopence." What a simple lapidary inscription! Nobody much in the wrong but an off-wheel; and with few acquaintances; and if it were but rendered into choice Latin, though there would be a little bother in finding a Ciceronian word for "off-wheel," Morcellus[3] himself, that great master of sepulchral eloquence, could not show a better. Why I call this little remark *moral*, is, from the compensation it points out. Here, by the supposition, is that other creature on the one side, the beast of the world; and he (or it) gets an epitaph. You and I, on the contrary, the pride of our friends, get none.

But why linger on the subject of vermin? Having mounted the box, I took a small quantity of laudanum, having already travelled two hundred and fifty miles—viz., from a point seventy miles beyond London, upon a simple breakfast. In the taking of laudanum there was nothing extraordinary. But by accident it drew upon me the special attention of my assessor on the box, the coachman. And in *that* there was nothing extraordinary.

---

[1]   Samuel Johnson published "Essay on Epitaphs" (1740) and "A Dissertation on Epitaphs Written by Pope" (1756).

[2]   A fine charged against the owner of an object that has caused injury or death.

[3]   Stefano Antonio Morelli (1737–1822), Italian antiquary and expert on Latin inscriptions, *De stilo Inscriptionum Latinarum* (1780).

But by accident, and with great delight, it drew my attention to the fact that this coachman was a monster in point of size, and that he had but one eye. In fact he had been foretold by Virgil as—

"Monstrum horrendum, informe, ingens, cui lumen ademptum."[1]

He answered in every point—a monster he was—dreadful, shapeless, huge, who had lost an eye. But why should *that* delight me? Had he been one of the Calendars in the Arabian Nights,[2] and had paid down his eye as the price of his criminal curiosity, what right had *I* to exult in his misfortune? I did *not* exult: I delighted in no man's punishment, though it were even merited. But these personal distinctions identified in an instant an old friend of mine, whom I had known in the south for some years as the most masterly of mail-coachmen. He was the man in all Europe that could best have undertaken to drive six-in-hand full gallop over *Al Sirat*—that famous bridge of Mahomet[3] across the bottomless gulf, backing himself against the Prophet and twenty such fellows. I used to call him *Cyclops mastigophorus*, Cyclops the whip-bearer, until I observed that his skill made whips useless, except to fetch off an impertinent fly from a leader's head; upon which I changed his Grecian name to Cyclops *diphrélates* (Cyclops the charioter.) I, and others known to me, studied under him the diphrelatic art. Excuse, reader, a word too elegant to be pedantic. And also take this remark from me, as a *gage* d'amitié[4]—that no word ever was or *can* be pedantic which, by supporting a distinction, supports the accuracy of logic; or which fills up a chasm for the understanding. As a pupil, though I paid extra fees, I cannot say that I stood high in his esteem. It showed his dogged honesty, (though, observe, not his discernment,) that he could not see my merits. Perhaps we ought to excuse his absurdity in this particular by remembering his want of an eye. *That* made him blind to my merits. Irritating as this blindness was, (surely it could not be

---

[1] Virgil, *Aeneid*: "a monster terrifying, unformed, without light" (3.658); reference to the Cyclops Polyphemus, which had one eye in the centre of his forehead, which he lost in battle with Odysseus (Homer, *Odyssey*, Book 9).

[2] Calendars belonged to the religious order of Dervishes; in *The Arabian Nights' Entertainment* the three calendars are princes who each tell the story of how he lost his eye, the third of whom "paid down his eye as the price of his criminal curiosity."

[3] In Mahometan tradition a bridge between Earth and Paradise, over Hell, narrower than a hair and sharper than a sword, over which the righteous pass safely while the wicked fall into the abyss.

[4] "Pledge of friendship."

envy?) he always courted my conversation, in which art I certainly had the whip-hand of him. On this occasion, great joy was at our meeting. But what was Cyclops doing here? Had the medical men recommended northern air, or how? I collected, from such explanations as he volunteered, that he had an interest at stake in a suit-at-law pending at Lancaster; so that probably he had got himself transferred to this station, for the purpose of connecting with his professional pursuits an instant readiness for the calls of his law-suit.

Meantime, what are we stopping for? Surely we've been waiting long enough. Oh, this procrastinating mail, and oh this procrastinating post-office! Can't they take a lesson upon that subject from *me*? Some people have called *me* procrastinating. Now you are witness, reader, that I was in time for *them*. But can *they* lay their hands on their hearts, and say that they were in time for me? I, during my life, have often had to wait for the post-office: the post-office never waited a minute for me. What are they about? The guard tells me that there is a large extra accumulation of foreign mails this night, owing to irregularities caused by war and by the packet-service,[1] when as yet nothing is done by steam. For an *extra* hour, it seems, the post-office has been engaged in threshing out the pure, wheaten correspondence of Glasgow, and winnowing it from the chaff of all baser intermediate towns. We can hear the flails going at this moment. But at last all is finished. Sound your horn, guard. Manchester, good bye; we've lost an hour by your criminal conduct at the post-office: which, however, though I do not mean to part with a serviceable ground of complaint, and one which really *is* such for the horses, to me secretly is an advantage, since it compels us to recover this last hour amongst the next eight or nine. Off we are at last, and at eleven miles an hour: and at first I detect no changes in the energy or in the skill of Cyclops.

From Manchester to Kendal, which virtually (though not in law) is the capital of Westmoreland, were at this time seven stages of eleven miles each. The first five of these, dated from Manchester, terminated in Lancaster, which was therefore fifty-five miles north of Manchester, and the same distance exactly from Liverpool. The first three terminated in Preston (called, by way of distinction from other towns of that name, *proud* Preston,) at which place it was that the separate roads from Liverpool and from Manchester to the north became confluent. Within these first three stages lay the foundation, the progress, and termination of our night's adventure. During the first stage, I found out that Cyclops

---

[1] A ship or boat travelling at regular intervals between two ports for mail delivery.

was mortal: he was liable to the shocking affection of sleep—a thing which I had never previously suspected. If a man is addicted to the vicious habit of sleeping, all the skill in aurigation[1] of Apollo himself, with the horses of Aurora[2] to execute the motions of his will, avail him nothing. "Oh, Cyclops!" I exclaimed more than once, "Cyclops, my friend; thou *art* mortal. Thou snorest." Through this first eleven miles, however, he betrayed his infirmity—which I grieve to say he shared with the whole Pagan Pantheon—only by short stretches. On waking up, he made an apology for himself, which, instead of mending the matter, laid an ominous foundation for coming disasters. The summer assizes were now proceeding at Lancaster: in consequence of which, for three nights and three days, he had not lain down in a bed. During the day, he was waiting for his uncertain summons as a witness on the trial in which he was interested; or he was drinking with the other witnesses, under the vigilant surveillance of the attorneys. During the night, or that part of it when the least temptations existed to conviviality, he was driving. Throughout the second stage he grew more and more drowsy. In the second mile of the third stage, he surrendered himself finally and without a struggle to his perilous temptation. All his past resistance had but deepened the weight of this final oppression. Seven atmospheres of sleep seemed resting upon him; and, to consummate the case, our worthy guard, after singing "Love amongst the Roses," for the fiftieth or sixtieth time, without any invitation from Cyclops or myself, and without applause for his poor labours, had moodily resigned himself to slumber—not so deep doubtless as the coachman's, but deep enough for mischief; and having, probably, no similar excuse. And thus at last, about ten miles from Preston, I found myself left in charge of his Majesty's London and Glasgow mail then running about eleven miles an hour.

What made this negligence less criminal than else it must have been thought, was the condition of the roads at night during the assizes. At that time all the law business of populous Liverpool, and of populous Manchester, with its vast cincture of populous rural districts, was called up by ancient usage to the tribunal of Lilliputian Lancaster.[3] To break up this old traditional usage required a conflict with powerful established interests, a large system of new arrangements, and a new parliamentary

---

[1] "The action or art of driving a chariot or coach" (*OED*).
[2] Horses of the Roman goddess of dawn, Aurora, pulled the chariot of the Greek god Apollo.
[3] In Jonathan Swift's *Gulliver's Travels* (1726), the Lilliputians are six inches tall; i.e., Lancaster was much smaller than Manchester or Liverpool.

statute.[1] As things were at present, twice in the year so vast a body of business rolled northwards, from the southern quarter of the county, that a fortnight at least occupied the severe exertions of two judges for its despatch. The consequence of this was—that every horse available for such a service, along the whole line of road, was exhausted in carrying down the multitudes of people who were parties to the different suits. By sunset, therefore, it usually happened that, through utter exhaustion amongst men and horses, the roads were all silent. Except exhaustion in the vast adjacent county of York from a contested election,[2] nothing like it was ordinarily witnessed in England.

On this occasion, the usual silence and solitude prevailed along the road. Not a hoof nor a wheel was to be heard. And to strengthen this false luxurious confidence in the noiseless roads, it happened also that the night was one of peculiar solemnity and peace. I myself, though slightly alive to the possibilities of peril, had so far yielded to the influence of the mighty calm as to sink into a profound reverie. The month was August, in which lay my own birth-day; a festival to every thoughtful man suggesting solemn and often sigh-born thoughts.* The county was my own native county—upon which, in its southern section, more than upon any equal area known to man past or present, had descended the original curse of labour in its heaviest form, not mastering the bodies of men only as of slaves, or criminals in mines, but working through the fiery will. Upon no equal space of earth, was, or ever had been, the same energy of human power put forth daily. At this particular season also of the assizes, that dreadful hurricane of flight and pursuit, as it might have seemed to a stranger, that swept to and from Lancaster all day long, hunting the county up and down, and regularly subsiding about sunset, united with the permanent distinction of Lancashire as the very metropolis and citadel of labour, to point the thoughts pathetically upon that counter vision of rest, of saintly repose from strife and

---

* "Sigh-born:" I owe the suggestion of this word to an obscure remembrance of a beautiful phrase in Giraldus Cambrensis, viz., *suspiriosæ cogitationes.* [Giraldus Cambrensis (c. 1146–c. 1223), Welsh historian, who wrote *Itinerarium Cambriae* or *Itinerary of Wales* (1191) and *De rebus a se gestis*, or *Concerning the Facts of My History* (c. 1204–5).]

---

[1] "In 1798, the Lancashire Sessions Act empowered the Lancashire justices to hold a Court of Annual General Session. In 1838, however, four Lancashire boroughs, including Manchester and Liverpool, secured separate courts of quarter sessions" (*Works* 16:622).

[2] "Prior to the 1832 Reform Bill, the number of constituencies in Yorkshire was small, and for each constituency there was only one voting centre. As there were few borough members, the vast majority of the electors were obliged to flock together from different parts of the county to record their vote" (*Works* 16:622).

sorrow, towards which, as to their secret haven, the profounder aspirations of man's heart are continually travelling. Obliquely we were nearing the sea upon our left, which also must, under the present circumstances, be repeating the general state of halcyon repose. The sea, the atmosphere, the light, bore an orchestral part in this universal lull. Moonlight, and the first timid tremblings of the dawn, were now blending; and the blendings were brought into a still more exquisite state of unity, by a slight silvery mist, motionless and dreamy, that covered the woods and fields, but with a veil of equable transparency. Except the feet of our own horses, which, running on a sandy margin of the road, made little disturbance, there was no sound abroad. In the clouds, and on the earth, prevailed the same majestic peace; and in spite of all that the villain of a schoolmaster has done for the ruin of our sublimer thoughts, which are the thoughts of our infancy, we still believe in no such nonsense as a limited atmosphere. Whatever we may swear with our false feigning lips, in our faithful hearts we still believe, and must for ever believe, in fields of air traversing the total gulf between earth and the central heavens. Still, in the confidence of children that tread without fear *every* chamber in their father's house, and to whom no door is closed, we, in that Sabbatic vision which sometimes is revealed for an hour upon nights like this, ascend with easy steps from the sorrow-stricken fields of earth, upwards to the sandals of God.

Suddenly from thoughts like these, I was awakened to a sullen sound, as of some motion on the distant road. It stole upon the air for a moment; I listened in awe; but then it died away. Once roused, however, I could not but observe with alarm the quickened motion of our horses. Ten years' experience had made my eye learned in the valuing of motion; and I saw that we were now running thirteen miles an hour. I pretend to no presence of mind. On the contrary, my fear is, that I am miserably and shamefully deficient in that quality as regards action. The palsy of doubt and distraction hangs like some guilty weight of dark unfathomed remembrances upon my energies, when the signal is flying for *action*. But, on the other hand, this accursed gift I have, as regards *thought*, that in the first step towards the possibility of a misfortune, I see its total evolution: in the radix,[1] I see too certainly and too instantly its entire expansion; in the first syllable of the dreadful sentence, I read already the last. It was not that I feared for ourselves. What could injure *us?* Our bulk and impetus charmed us against peril in any collision. And I had rode through too many hundreds of perils that were frightful to approach, that were matter

---

[1] Root.

of laughter as we looked back upon them, for any anxiety to rest upon *our* interests. The mail was not built, I felt assured, nor bespoke, that could betray *me* who trusted to its protection. But any carriage that we could meet would be frail and light in comparison of ourselves. And I remarked this ominous accident of our situation. We were on the wrong side of the road. But then the other party, if other there was, might also be on the wrong side; and two wrongs might make a right. *That* was not likely. The same motive which had drawn *us* to the right-hand side of the road, viz., the soft beaten sand, as contrasted with the paved centre, would prove attractive to others. Our lamps, still lighted, would give the impression of vigilance on our part. And every creature that met us, would rely upon us for quartering.★ All this, and if the separate links of the anticipation had been a thousand times more, I saw—not discursively or by effort—but as by one flash of horrid intuition.

Under this steady though rapid anticipation of the evil which *might* be gathering ahead, ah, reader! what a sullen mystery of fear, what a sigh of woe, seemed to steal upon the air as again the far-off sound of a wheel was heard ! A whisper it was—a whisper from, perhaps, four miles off—secretly announcing a ruin that, being foreseen, was not the less inevitable. What could be done—who was it that could do it—to check the storm-flight of these maniacal horses? What! could I not seize the reins from the grasp of the slumbering coachman? You, reader, think that it would have been in *your* power to do so. And I quarrel not with your estimate of yourself. But, from the way in which the coachman's hand was viced between his upper and lower thigh, this was impossible. The guard subsequently found it impossible, after this danger had passed. Not the grasp only, but also the position of this Polyphemus, made the attempt impossible. You still think otherwise. See, then, that bronze equestrian statue. The cruel rider has kept the bit in his horse's mouth for two centuries. Unbridle him, for a minute, if you please, and wash his mouth with water. Or stay, reader, unhorse me that marble emperor: knock me those marble feet from those marble stirrups of Charlemagne.[1]

The sounds ahead strengthened, and were now too clearly the

★ "*Quartering*"—this is the technical word; and, I presume, derived from the French *cartayer*, to evade a rut or any obstacle. [See p. 239, n. 3 above; "De Quincey's etymology is wrong; the 'quarters' were the four parts into which the width of the road was divided by the two wheel ruts and the central track of the horses. 'Quartering' involved moving the vehicle out of the ruts to drive on the 'quarters'" (*Works* 16:623).]

[1]   Charlemagne (742–814 CE), King of the Franks, 764–814.

sounds of wheels. Who and what could it be? Was it industry in a taxed cart?[1]—was it youthful gaiety in a gig? Whoever it was, something must be attempted to warn them. Upon the other party rests the active responsibility, but upon *us*—and, woe is me! that *us* was my single self—rests the responsibility of warning. Yet, how should this be accomplished? Might I not seize the guard's horn? Already, on the first thought, I was making my way over the roof to the guard's seat. But this, from the foreign mails being piled upon the roof, was a difficult, and even dangerous attempt, to one cramped by nearly three hundred miles of outside travelling. And, fortunately, before I had lost much time in the attempt, our frantic horses swept round an angle of the road, which opened upon us the stage where the collision must be accomplished, the parties that seemed summoned to the trial, and the impossibility of saving them by any communication with the guard.

Before us lay an avenue, straight as an arrow, six hundred yards, perhaps, in length; and the umbrageous trees, which rose in a regular line from either side, meeting high overhead, gave to it the character of a cathedral aisle. These trees lent a deeper solemnity to the early light; but there was still light enough to perceive, at the further end of this gothic aisle, a light, reedy gig, in which were seated a young man, and, by his side, a young lady. Ah, young sir! what are you about? If it is necessary that you should whisper your communications to this young lady—though really I see nobody at this hour, and on this solitary road, likely to overhear your conversation—is it, therefore, necessary that you should carry your lips forward to hers? The little carriage is creeping on at one mile an hour; and the parties within it, being thus tenderly engaged, are naturally bending down their heads. Between them and eternity, to all human calculation, there is but a minute and a half. What is it that I shall do? Strange it is, and to a mere auditor of the tale, might seem laughable, that I should need a suggestion from the *Iliad* to prompt the sole recourse that remained. But so it was. Suddenly I remembered the shout of Achilles,[2] and its effect. But could I pretend to shout like the son of Peleus, aided by Pallas? No, certainly: but then I needed not the shout that should alarm all Asia militant; a shout would suffice, such as should carry terror into the hearts of two thoughtless young people, and one

---

[1] Open two-wheeled cart used for trade, taxed for use on the road at a reduced rate.

[2] Reference to Achilles's war-cry in Homer's *Iliad*; Achilles, the son of Peleus, the greatest warrior in Agamemnon's Greek army; Pallas Athene, Greek goddess of war: "Achilles stood and shouted, and Pallas Athene met his cry from afar; but he raised untold confusion among the Trojans" (18.217-19).

gig horse. I shouted—and the young man heard me not. A second time I shouted—and now he heard me, for now he raised his head.

Here, then, all had been done that, by me, *could* be done: more on *my* part was not possible. Mine had been the first step: the second was for the young man: the third was for God. If, said I, the stranger is a brave man, and if, indeed, he loves the young girl at his side—or, loving her not, if he feels the obligation pressing upon every man worthy to be called a man, of doing his utmost for a woman confided to his protection—he will at least make some effort to save her. If *that* fails, he will not perish the more, or by a death more cruel, for having made it; and he will die, as a brave man should, with his face to the danger, and with his arm about the woman that he sought in vain to save. But if he makes no effort, shrinking, without a struggle, from his duty, he himself will not the less certainly perish for this baseness of poltroonery.[1] He will die no less: and why not? Wherefore should we grieve that there is one craven less in the world? No; *let* him perish, without a pitying thought of ours wasted upon him; and, in that case, all our grief will be reserved for the fate of the helpless girl, who, now, upon the least shadow of failure in *him,* must, by the fiercest of translations—must, without time for a prayer—must, within seventy seconds, stand before the judgment-seat of God.

But craven he was not: sudden had been the call upon him, and sudden was his answer to the call. He saw, he heard, he comprehended, the ruin that was coming down: already its gloomy shadow darkened above him; and already he was measuring his strength to deal with it. Ah! what a vulgar thing does courage seem, when we see nations buying it and selling it for a shilling a-day: ah! what a sublime thing does courage seem, when some fearful crisis on the great deeps of life carries a man, as if running before a hurricane, up to the giddy crest of some mountainous wave, from which, accordingly as he chooses his course, he descries two courses, and a voice says to him audibly—"This way lies hope; take the other way and mourn for ever!" Yet, even then, amidst the raving of the seas and the frenzy of the danger, the man is able to confront his situation—is able to retire for a moment into solitude with God, and to seek all his counsel from *him!* For seven seconds, it might be, of his seventy, the stranger settled his countenance steadfastly upon us, as if to search and value every element in the conflict before him. For five seconds more he sate immovably, like one that mused on some great purpose. For five he sate with eyes upraised, like one that prayed in sorrow, under some

---

[1] "The behaviour of a poltroon; laziness; pusillanimity, cowardice" (*OED*).

extremity of doubt, for wisdom to guide him towards the better choice. Then suddenly he rose; stood upright; and, by a sudden strain upon the reins, raising his horse's forefeet from the ground, he slewed him round on the pivot of his hind legs, so as to plant the little equipage in a position nearly at right-angles to ours. Thus far his condition was not improved; except as a first step had been taken towards the possibility of a second. If no more were done, nothing was done; for the little carriage still occupied the very centre of our path, though in an altered direction. Yet even now it may not be too late: fifteen of the twenty seconds may still be unexhausted; and one almighty bound forward may avail to clear the ground. Hurry then, hurry! for the flying moments—*they* hurry! Oh hurry, hurry, my brave young man! for the cruel hoofs of our horses—*they* also hurry! Fast are the flying moments, faster are the hoofs of our horses. Fear not for *him,* if human energy can suffice: faithful was he that drove, to his terrific duty; faithful was the horse to *his* command. One blow, one impulse given with voice and hand by the stranger, one rush from the horse, one bound as if in the act of rising to a fence, landed the docile creature's fore-feet upon the crown or arching centre of the road. The larger half of the little equipage had then cleared our over-towering shadow: *that* was evident even to my own agitated sight. But it mattered little that one wreck should float off in safety, if upon the wreck that perished were embarked the human freightage. The rear part of the carriage—was *that* certainly beyond the line of absolute ruin? What power could answer the question? Glance of eye, thought of man, wing of angel, which of these had speed enough to sweep between the question and the answer, and divide the one from the other? Light does not tread upon the steps of light more indivisibly, than did our all-conquering arrival upon the escaping efforts of the gig. *That* must the young man have felt too plainly. His back was now turned to us; not by sight could he any longer communicate with the peril; but by the dreadful rattle of our harness, too truly had his ear been instructed—that all was finished as regarded any further effort of *his.* Already in resignation he had rested from his struggle; and perhaps, in his heart he was whispering—"Father, which art above, do thou finish in heaven what I on earth have attempted." We ran past them faster than ever mill-race in our inexorable flight. Oh, raving of hurricanes that must have sounded in their young ears at the moment of our transit! Either with the swinglebar,[1] or with the haunch of our near leader, we had struck the

---

[1]   Or swingle-tree: "In a plough, harrow, carriage, etc., a crossbar, pivoted at the middle, to which the traces are fastened, giving freedom of movement to the shoulders of the horse or other draught-animal" (*OED*).

off-wheel of the little gig, which stood rather obliquely and not quite so far advanced as to be accurately parallel with the near wheel. The blow, from the fury of our passage, resounded terrifically. I rose in horror, to look upon the ruins we might have caused. From my elevated station I looked down, and looked back upon the scene, which in a moment told its tale, and wrote all its records on my heart for ever.

The horse was planted immovably, with his fore-feet upon the paved crest of the central road. He of the whole party was alone untouched by the passion of death. The little cany carriage—partly perhaps from the dreadful torsion of the wheels in its recent movement, partly from the thundering blow we had given to it—as if it sympathised with human horror, was all alive with tremblings and shiverings. The young man sat like a rock. He stirred not at all. But *his* was the steadiness of agitation frozen into rest by horror. As yet he dared not to look round; for he knew that, if anything remained to do, by him it could no longer be done. And as yet he knew not for certain if their safety were accomplished. But the lady—

But the lady—! Oh heavens! will that spectacle ever depart from my dreams, as she rose and sank upon her seat, sank and rose, threw up her arms wildly to heaven, clutched at some visionary object in the air, fainting, praying, raving, despairing! Figure to yourself, reader, the elements of the case; suffer me to recal before your mind the circumstances of the unparalleled situation. From the silence and deep peace of this saintly summer night,—from the pathetic blending of this sweet moonlight, dawnlight, dreamlight,—from the manly tenderness of this flattering, whispering, murmuring love,—suddenly as from the woods and fields,—suddenly as from the chambers of the air opening in revelation,—suddenly as from the ground yawning at her feet, leaped upon her, with the flashing of cataracts, Death the crownèd phantom, with all the equipage of his terrors, and the tiger roar of his voice.

The moments were numbered. In the twinkling of an eye our flying horses had carried us to the termination of the umbrageous aisle; at right-angles we wheeled into our former direction; the turn of the road carried the scene out of my eyes in an instant, and swept it into my dreams for ever.

DREAM FUGUE.
ON THE ABOVE THEME OF SUDDEN DEATH.

"Whence the sound
Of instruments, that made melodious chime,
Was heard, of harp and organ; and who mov'd
Their stops and chords, was seen; his volant touch
Instinct through all proportions, low and high,
Fled and pursued transverse the resonant fugue."

Par. Lost, B. xi.[1]
Tumultuosissimamente.[2]

Passion of Sudden Death! that once in youth I read and interpreted by the shadows of thy averted★ signs;—Rapture of panic taking the shape, which amongst tombs in churches I have seen, of woman bursting her sepulchral bonds—of woman's Ionic[3] form bending forward from the ruins of her grave, with arching foot, with eyes upraised, with clasped adoring hands— waiting, watching, trembling, praying, for the trumpet's call to rise from dust for ever;—Ah, vision too fearful of shuddering humanity on the brink of abysses! vision that didst start back—that didst reel away—like a shrivelling scroll from before the wrath of fire racing on the wings of the wind! Epilepsy so brief of horror—wherefore is it that thou canst not die? Passing so suddenly into darkness, wherefore is it that still thou sheddest thy sad funeral blights upon the gorgeous mosaics of dreams? Fragment of music too stern, heard once and heard no more, what aileth thee that thy deep rolling chords come up at intervals through all the worlds of sleep, and after thirty years have lost no element of horror?

★ "*Averted* signs."—I read the course and changes of the lady's agony in the succession of her involuntary gestures; but let it be remembered that I read all this from the rear, never once catching the lady's full face, and even her profile imperfectly.

---

[1]   Milton, *Paradise Lost* (9.558–63).
[2]   "Most tumultuously."
[3]   Order of Classical architecture, using fluted columns with scrolled capitals; "Vitruvius (*fl.* first century BC), Roman architect and engineer, in writing of the origin of the different orders of architecture, observed that the Greeks shaped the Ionic column in 'a new style' of 'feminine slenderness' (*De architectura*, IV.i.7)" (*Works* 16:624).

1

Lo, it is summer, almighty summer! The everlasting gates of life and summer are thrown open wide; and on the ocean, tranquil and verdant as a savannah, the unknown lady from the dreadful vision and I myself are floating: she upon a fairy pinnace, and I upon an English three-decker. But both of us are wooing gales of festal happiness within the domain of our common country—within that ancient watery park—within that pathless chase where England takes her pleasure as a huntress through winter and summer, and which stretches from the rising to the setting sun. Ah! what a wilderness of floral beauty was hidden, or was suddenly revealed, upon the tropic islands through which the pinnace moved. And upon her deck what a bevy of human flowers—young women how lovely, young men how noble, that were dancing together, and slowly drifting towards *us* amidst music and incense, amidst blossoms from forests and gorgeous corymbi[1] from vintages, amidst natural caroling and the echoes of sweet girlish laughter. Slowly the pinnace nears us, gaily she hails us, and slowly she disappears beneath the shadow of our mighty bows. But then, as at some signal from heaven, the music and the carols, and the sweet echoing of girlish laughter—all are hushed. What evil has smitten the pinnace, meeting or overtaking her? Did ruin to our friends couch within our own dreadful shadow? Was our shadow the shadow of death? I looked over the bow for an answer; and, behold! the pinnace was dismantled; the revel and the revellers were found no more; the glory of the vintage was dust; and the forest was left without a witness to its beauty upon the seas. "But where," and I turned to our own crew—"where are the lovely women that danced beneath the awning of flowers and clustering corymbi? Whither have fled the noble young men that danced with *them*?" Answer there was none. But suddenly the man at the masthead, whose countenance darkened with alarm, cried aloud—"Sail on the weather-beam! Down she comes upon us; in seventy seconds she will founder!"

2 .

I looked to the weather-side, and the summer had departed. The sea was rocking, and shaken with gathering wrath. Upon its surface sate mighty mists, which grouped themselves into arches and long cathedral aisles.

---

[1]   Clusters of grapes.

Down one of these, with the fiery pace of a quarrel from a crossbow, ran a frigate right athwart our course. "Are they mad?" some voice exclaimed from our deck. "Are they blind? Do they woo their ruin?" But in a moment, as she was close upon us, some impulse of a heady current or sudden vortex gave a wheeling bias to her course, and off she forged without a shock. As she ran past us, high aloft amongst the shrouds stood the lady of the pinnace. The deeps opened ahead in malice to receive her, towering surges of foam ran after her, the billows were fierce to catch her. But far away she was borne into desert spaces of the sea: whilst still by sight I followed her, as she ran before the howling gale, chased by angry sea-birds and by maddening billows; still I saw her, as at the moment when she ran past us, amongst the shrouds, with her white draperies streaming before the wind. There she stood with hair dishevelled, one hand clutched amongst the tackling—rising, sinking, fluttering, trembling, praying—there for leagues I saw her as she stood, raising at intervals one hand to heaven, amidst the fiery crests of the pursuing waves and the raving of the storm; until at last, upon a sound from afar of malicious laughter and mockery, all was hidden for ever in driving showers; and afterwards, but when I know not, and how I know not,

3 .

Sweet funeral bells from some incalculable distance, wailing over the dead that die before the dawn, awakened me as I slept in a boat moored to some familiar shore. The morning twilight even then was breaking; and, by the dusky revelations which it spread, I saw a girl adorned with a garland of white roses about her head for some great festival, running along the solitary strand with extremity of haste. Her running was the running of panic; and often she looked back as to some dreadful enemy in the rear. But when I leaped ashore, and followed on her steps to warn her of a peril in front, alas! from me she fled as from another peril; and vainly I shouted to her of quicksands that lay ahead. Faster and faster she ran; round a promontory of rock she wheeled out of sight; in an instant I also wheeled round it, but only to see the treacherous sands gathering above her head. Already her person was buried; only the fair young head and the diadem of white roses around it were still visible to the pitying heavens; and, last of all, was visible one marble arm. I saw by the early twilight this fair young head, as it was sinking down to darkness—saw this marble arm, as it rose above her head and her treacherous grave, tossing, faultering, rising, clutching as at some false deceiving hand stretched out from the clouds—saw this marble arm uttering her dying hope, and then her dying despair. The head, the diadem, the arm,—these all had sunk; at last over these also the cruel quicksand had closed; and no memorial of the fair young girl remained on earth, except my own solitary tears, and the funeral bells from the desert seas, that, rising again more softly, sang a requiem over the grave of the buried child, and over her blighted dawn.

I sate, and wept in secret the tears that men have ever given to the memory of those that died before the dawn, and by the treachery of earth, our mother. But the tears and funeral bells were hushed suddenly by a shout as of many nations, and by a roar as from some great king's artillery advancing rapidly along the valleys, and heard afar by its echoes among the mountains. "Hush!" I said, as I bent my ear earthwards to listen—"hush!—this either is the very anarchy of strife, or else"—and then I listened more profoundly, and said as I raised my head—"or else, oh heavens! it is *victory* that swallows up all strife."

4.

Immediately, in trance, I was carried over land and sea to some distant kingdom, and placed upon a triumphal car, amongst companions crowned with laurel. The darkness of gathering midnight, brooding over all the land, hid from us the mighty crowds that were weaving restlessly about our carriage as a centre—we heard them, but we saw them not. Tidings had arrived, within an hour, of a grandeur that measured itself against centuries; too full of pathos they were, too full of joy that acknowledged no fountain but God, to utter themselves by other language than by tears, by restless anthems, by reverberations rising from every choir, of the *Gloria in excelsis.*[1] These tidings we that sate upon the laurelled car had it for our privilege to publish amongst all nations. And already, by signs audible through the darkness, by snortings and tramplings, our angry horses, that knew no fear of fleshly weariness, upbraided us with delay. Wherefore *was* it that we delayed? We waited for a secret word, that should bear witness to the hope of nations, as now accomplished for ever. At midnight the secret word arrived; which word was—Waterloo and Recovered Christendom! The dreadful word shone by its own light; before us it went; high above our leaders' heads it rode, and spread a golden light over the paths which we traversed. Every city, at the presence of the secret word,

---

[1] "Glory in the highest."

threw open its gates to receive us. The rivers were silent as we crossed. All the infinite forests, as we ran along their margins, shivered in homage to the secret word. And the darkness comprehended it.

Two hours after midnight we reached a mighty minster. Its gates, which rose to the clouds, were closed. But when the dreadful word, that rode before us, reached them with its golden light, silently they moved back upon their hinges; and at a flying gallop our equipage entered the grand aisle of the cathedral. Headlong was our pace; and at every altar, in the little chapels and oratories to the right hand and left of our course, the lamps, dying or sickening, kindled anew in sympathy with the secret word that was flying past. Forty leagues we might have run in the cathedral, and as yet no strength of morning light had reached us, when we saw before us the aërial galleries of the organ and the choir. Every pinnacle of the fret-work, every station of advantage amongst the traceries, was crested by white-robed choristers, that sang deliverance; that wept no more tears, as once their fathers had wept; but at intervals that sang together to the generations, saying—

"Chaunt the deliverer's praise in every tongue,"

and receiving answers from afar,

—"such as once in heaven and earth were sung."[1]

And of their chaunting was no end; of our headlong pace was neither pause nor remission.

Thus, as we ran like torrents—thus, as we swept with bridal rapture over the Campo Santo★ of the cathedral graves—suddenly we became

---

★   *Campo Santo.*—It is probable that most of my readers will be acquainted with the history of the Campo Santo at Pisa—composed of earth brought from Jerusalem for a bed of sanctity, as the highest prize which the noble piety of crusaders could ask or imagine. There is another Campo Santo at Naples, formed, however, (I presume,) on the example given by Pisa. Possibly the idea may have been more extensively copied. To readers who are unacquainted with England, or who (being English) are yet unacquainted with the cathedral cities of England, it may be right to mention that the graves within-side the cathedrals often form a flat pavement over which carriages and horses might roll; and perhaps a boyish remembrance of one particular cathedral, across which I had seen passengers walk and burdens carried, may have assisted my dream. [Campo Santo: cemetery; literally "holy field."]

---

[1]   Wordsworth, "Siege of Vienna raised by John Sobieski": "Chant the Deliver's praise in every tongue! / The Cross shall spread, the Crescent hath waxed dim; / He conquering, as in joyful Heaven is sung, / HE CONQUERING THROUGH GOD, AND GOD BY HIM" (11–14).

aware of a vast necropolis rising upon the far-off horizon—a city of sepulchres, built within the saintly cathedral for the warrior dead that rested from their feuds on earth. Of purple granite was the necropolis; yet, in the first minute, it lay like a purple stain upon the horizon—so mighty was the distance. In the second minute it trembled through many changes, growing into terraces and towers of wondrous altitude, so mighty was the pace. In the third minute already, with our dreadful gallop, we were entering its suburbs. Vast sarcophagi rose on every side, having towers and turrets that, upon the limits of the central aisle, strode forward with haughty intrusion, that ran back with mighty shadows into answering recesses. Every sarcophagus showed many bas-reliefs[1]— bas-reliefs of battles—bas-reliefs of battle-fields; of battles from forgotten ages—of battles from yesterday—of battlefields that, long since, nature had healed and reconciled to herself with the sweet oblivion of flowers—of battlefields that were yet angry and crimson with carnage. Where the terraces ran, there did *we* run; where the towers curved, there did *we* curve. With the flight of swallows our horses swept round every angle. Like rivers in flood, wheeling round headlands; like hurricanes that ride into the secrets of forests; faster than ever light unwove the mazes of darkness, our flying equipage carried earthly passions— kindled warrior instincts—amongst the dust that lay around us; dust oftentimes of our noble fathers that had slept in God from Créci to Trafalgar.[2] And now had we reached the last sarcophagus, now were we abreast of the last bas-relief, already had we recovered the arrow-like flight of the illimitable central aisle, when coming up this aisle to meet us we beheld a female infant that rode in a carriage as frail as flowers. The mists, which went before her, hid the fawns that drew her, but could not hide the shells and tropic flowers with which she played— but could not hide the lovely smiles by which she uttered her trust in the mighty cathedral, and in the cherubim that looked down upon her from the topmost shafts of its pillars. Face to face she was meeting us; face to face she rode, as if danger there were none. "Oh baby!" I exclaimed, "shalt thou be the ransom for Waterloo? Must we, that carry tidings of great joy to every people, be messengers of ruin to thee?" In horror I rose at the thought; but then also, in horror at the thought, rose one that was sculptured on the bas-relief—a Dying Trumpeter.

[1] "Low relief; sculpture or carved work in which the figures project less than one half of their true proportions from the surface on which they are carved" (*OED*).

[2] Crécy or Cressy, battle in which Edward III of England defeated the French in 1346; for Trafalgar, see p. 233, n. 1 above.

Solemnly from the field of battle he rose to his feet; and, unslinging his stony trumpet, carried it, in his dying anguish, to his stony lips—sounding once, and yet once again; proclamation that, in *thy* ears, oh baby! must have spoken from the battlements of death. Immediately deep shadows fell between us, and aboriginal silence. The choir had ceased to sing. The hoofs of our horses, the rattling of our harness, alarmed the graves no more. By horror the bas-relief had been unlocked into life. By horror we, that were so full of life, we men and our horses, with their fiery fore-legs rising in mid air to their everlasting gallop, were frozen to a bas-relief. Then a third time the trumpet sounded;[1] the seals were taken off all pulses; life, and the frenzy of life, tore into their channels again; again the choir burst forth in sunny grandeur, as from the muffling of storms and darkness; again the thunderings of our horses carried temptation into the graves. One cry burst from our lips as the clouds, drawing off from the aisle, showed it empty before us— "Whither has the infant fled?—is the young child caught up to God?" Lo! afar off, in a vast recess, rose three mighty windows to the clouds; and on a level with their summits, at height insuperable to man, rose an altar of purest alabaster. On its eastern face was trembling a crimson glory. Whence came *that?* Was it from the reddening dawn that now streamed *through* the windows? Was it from the crimson robes of the martyrs that were painted *on* the windows? Was it from the bloody bas-reliefs of earth? Whencesoever it were—there, within that crimson radiance, suddenly appeared a female head, and then a female figure. It was the child—now grown up to woman's height. Clinging to the horns of the altar,[2] there she stood—sinking, rising, trembling, fainting—raving, despairing; and behind the volume of incense that, night and day, streamed upwards from the altar, was seen the fiery font, and dimly was descried the outline of the dreadful being that should baptise her with the baptism of death. But by her side was kneeling her better angel, that hid his face with wings; that wept and pleaded for *her;* that prayed when *she* could *not;* that fought with heaven by tears for *her* deliverance; which also, as he raised his immortal countenance from his wings, I saw, by the glory in his eye, that he had won at last.

---

[1] "The third angel blew his trumpet, and a great star fell from heaven, blazing like a torch" (Revelation 8:10).

[2] "In the Old Testament, sacrifices were placed upon the horns of the alter (for example, Exodus 29:12); they were also clasped by those seeking sanctuary (for example, 1 Kings 1:50)" (*Works* 16:624).

5

Then rose the agitation, spreading through the infinite cathedral, to its agony; then was completed the passion of the mighty fugue. The golden tubes of the organ, which as yet had but sobbed and muttered at intervals—gleaming amongst clouds and surges of incense—threw up, as from fountains unfathomable, columns of heart-shattering music. Choir and anti-choir were filling fast with unknown voices. Thou also, Dying Trumpeter!—with thy love that was victorious, and thy anguish that was finishing, didst enter the tumult : trumpet and echo—farewell love, and farewell anguish—rang through the dreadful *sanctus*.[1] We, that spread flight before us, heard the tumult, as of flight, mustering behind us. In fear we looked round for the unknown steps that, in flight or in pursuit, were gathering upon our own. Who were these that followed? The faces, which no man could count—whence were *they?* "Oh, darkness of the grave!" I exclaimed, "that from the crimson altar and from the fiery font wert visited with secret light—that wert searched by the effulgence in the angel's eye—were these indeed thy children? Pomps of life, that, from the burials of centuries, rose again to the voice of perfect joy, could it be *ye* that had wrapped me in the reflux of panic?" What ailed me, that I should fear when the triumphs of earth were advancing? Ah! Pariah heart within me, that couldst never hear the sound of joy without sullen whispers of treachery in ambush; that, from six years old, didst never hear the promise of perfect love, without seeing aloft amongst the stars fingers as of a man's hand writing the secret legend—"*ashes to ashes, dust to dust!*"—wherefore shouldst *thou* not fear, though all men should rejoice? Lo! as I looked back for seventy leagues through the mighty cathedral, and saw the quick and the dead that sang together to God, together that sang to the generations of man—ah! raving, as of torrents that opened on every side: trepidation, as of female and infant steps that fled—ah! rushing, as of wings that chased! But I heard a voice from heaven, which said—"Let there be no reflux of panic—let there be no more fear, and no more sudden death! Cover them with joy as the tides cover the shore!" *That* heard the children of the choir, *that* heard the children of the grave. All the hosts of jubilation made ready to move. Like armies that ride in pursuit, they moved with one step. Us, that, with laurelled heads, were passing from the

---

[1] Literally, "holy": "Holy, holy, holy, Lord God Almighty, which was, and is, and is to come". (Revelation 4:8).

cathedral through its eastern gates, they overtook, and, as with a garment, they wrapped us round with thunders that overpowered our own. As brothers we moved together; to the skies we rose—to the dawn that advanced—to the stars that fled: rendering thanks to God in the highest—that, having hid his face through one generation behind thick clouds of War, once again was ascending—was ascending from Waterloo—in the visions of Peace:—rendering thanks for thee, young girl! whom having overshadowed with his ineffable passion of Death— suddenly did God relent; suffered thy angel to turn aside his arm; and even in thee, sister unknown! shown to me for a moment only to be hidden for ever, found an occasion to glorify his goodness. A thousand times, amongst the phantoms of sleep, has he shown thee to me, standing before the golden dawn, and ready to enter its gates—with the dreadful Word going before thee—with the armies of the grave behind thee; shown thee to me, sinking, rising, fluttering, fainting, but then suddenly reconciled, adoring: a thousand times has he followed thee in the worlds of sleep—through storms; through desert seas; through the darkness of quicksands; through fugues and the persecution of fugues; through dreams, and the dreadful resurrections that are in dreams—only that at the last, with one motion of his victorious arm,[1] he might record and emblazon the endless resurrections of his love!

---

[1] Milton, *Paradise Lost*; God foretells Christ's victory over Sin and Death: "At one sling / Of thy victorious arm, well-pleasing Son, / Both Sin, and Death, and yawning grave at last / Through chaos hurled, obstruct the mouth of hell / For ever, and seal up his ravenous jaws" (10.633–37).

Appendix A: Related Texts and Prefaces

1. From Charles Lamb, "Confessions of a Drunkard," in *The Philanthropist: or Repository for Hints and Suggestions Calculated to Promote the Comfort and Happiness of Man*, vol. 3 (London: Richard and Arthur Taylor, 1813), 48–49, 51, 52–54

... I have known [a drunkard] in such state, that when he has tried to abstain but for one evening,—though the poisonous potion had long ceased to bring back its first enchantments, though he was sure it would rather deepen his gloom than brighten it,—in the violence of the struggle, and the necessity he has felt of getting rid of the present sensation at any rate,—I have known him to scream out, to cry aloud, for the anguish and pain of the strife within him.

Why should I hesitate to declare, that the man of whom I speak is myself?

I believe that there are constitutions, robust heads, and iron insides, whom scarce any excesses can hurt; whom brandy, (I have seen them drink it like wine,) at all events whom wine, taken in ever so plentiful measure, can do no worse injury to than just to muddle their faculties, perhaps never very pellucid. On them this discourse is wasted. They would but laugh at a weak brother, who, trying his strength with them, and coming off foiled from the contest, would fain persuade them that such agonistic exercises are dangerous. It is to a very different description of persons I speak. It is to the weak, the nervous, to those who feel the want of some artificial aid to raise their spirits in society to what is no more than the ordinary pitch of all around them without it. This is the secret of our drinking. Such must fly the convivial board in the first instance, if they do not mean to sell themselves for term of life.

... I have seen a print after Corregio,[1] in which three female figures are ministering to a man, who sits fast bound at the root of a tree. Sensuality is soothing him, Evil Habit is nailing him to a branch, and Repugnance at the same instant of time is applying a snake to his side. In his face are feeble delight, the recollection of past rather than perception of present pleasures, languid enjoyment of evil, with utter imbecility to good, a Sybaritic effeminacy,[2] a submission to bondage, the

---

[1] Antonio Allegri da Corregio (1489–1534), Italian Renaissance painter.

[2] Sybaritic, or devoted to luxury and pleasure; after Sybaris, ancient Greek city known for its wealth and luxury.

springs of the will gone down like a broken clock, the sin and the suffering co-instantaneous, or the latter forerunning the former, remorse preceding action—all this represented in one point of time.— When I saw this, I admired the wonderful skill of the painter. But when I went away, I wept, because I thought of my own condition.

Recovering!——O, if a wish could transport me back to those days of youth, when a draught from the next clear spring could slake any heats which summer suns and youthful exercise had power to stir up in the blood, how gladly would I return to thee, pure element, the drink of children, and of child-like holy hermit! In my dreams I can sometimes fancy thy cool refreshment purling over my burning tongue. But my waking stomach rejects it. That which refreshes innocence, only makes me sick and faint.

But is there no middle way betwixt total abstinence, and the excess which kills you?—For your sake, reader, and that you may never attain to my experience, with pain I must utter that there is none, none that I can find. In my stage of habit, (I speak not of habits less confirmed—for some of them I believe the advice to be most prudential,) in the stage which I have reached, to stop short of that measure which is sufficient to draw on torpor and sleep, the benumbing apoplectic sleep of the drunkard, is to have taken none at all. The pain of the self-denial is equal. And what that is, I had rather the reader should believe on my credit, than know from his own trial. He will come to know it, whenever he shall arrive at that state in which, paradoxical as it may appear, *reason shall only visit him through intoxication*. For it is a fearful truth, that the intellectual faculties, by repeated acts of intemperance, may be driven from their orderly sphere of action, their clear daylight ministeries, until they shall be brought at last to depend for the faint manifestation of their departing energies, upon the returning periods of the fatal madness to which they owe their devastation. The drinking man is never less himself than during his sober intervals. Evil is so far his good....

Behold me, then, in the robust period of life, reduced to imbecility and decay. Hear me count my gains and the profits which I have derived from the midnight cup.

Twelve years ago I was possessed of a healthy frame of mind and body. I was never strong: but I think my constitution (for a weak one) was as happily exempt from the tendency to any malady as it was possible to be. I scarce knew what it was to have an ailment. Now, except when I am losing myself in a sea of drink, I am never free from those uneasy sensations, in head and stomach, which are so much worse to bear than any definite pains or aches.

At that time I was seldom in bed after six in the morning, summer and winter. I awoke refreshed, and seldom without some merry thoughts in my head, or some piece of a song to welcome the new-born day. Now, the first feeling which besets me, after stretching out the hours of recumbence to their last possible extent, is a forecast of the wearisome day that lies before me, with a secret wish that I could have lain on still, or never awaked.

Life itself, my waking life, has much of the confusion, the trouble, and obscure perplexity of an ill dream. In the daytime I stumble upon dark mountains.

Business, which though never particularly adapted to my nature, yet as something of necessity to be gone through, and therefore best under-taken with cheerfulness, I used to enter upon with some degree of alacrity, now wearies, affrights, perplexes me; I fancy all sorts of discour-agements, and am ready to give up an occupation which gives me bread, from a harassing conceit of incapacity. The slightest commission given me by a friend, or any small duty which I have to perform for myself, as giving orders to a tradesman, & c. haunts me as a labour impossible to be got through. So much the springs of action are broken.

The same cowardice attends me in all my intercourse with mankind. I dare not promise that a friend's honour, or his cause, would be safe in my keeping, if I were put to the expense of any manly resolution in defend-ing it. So much the springs of moral action are deadened within me.

My favourite occupation in times past now ceases to entertain. I can do nothing readily. Application for ever so short a time kills me. This poor abstract of my condition was penned at long intervals, with scarcely any attempt at connection of thought, which is now difficult to me.

The noble passages which formerly delighted me in history, or poetic fiction, now only draw a few weak tears, allied to dotage. My broken and dispirited nature seems to sink before any thing great and admirable.——

I perpetually catch myself in tears, for any cause, or none. It is inex-pressible how much this infirmity adds to a sense of shame, and a general feeling of deterioration.——

These are some of the instances concerning which I can say with truth, that it was not always so with me.——

Shall I lift up the veil of my weakness any further? Or is this disclo-sure sufficient?——

I am a poor nameless egotist, who have no vanity to consult by these confessions. I know not whether I shall be laughed at, or heard seriously. Such as they are, I commend them to the reader's attention, if he find his own case any way touched. I have told him what I am come to.—Let him stop in time.

2. From Samuel Taylor Coleridge, "Kubla Khan: Or A Vision in a Dream" (1816), in *Christabel; Kubla Khan: A Vision; The Pains of Sleep* (London: John Murray, 1816), 51–58[1]

The following fragment is here published at the request of a poet of great and deserved celebrity,[2] and as far as the Author's own opinions are concerned, rather as a psychological curiosity, than on the ground of any supposed *poetic* merits.

In the summer of the year 1797, the Author, then in ill health, had retired to a lonely farmhouse between Porlock and Linton, on the Exmoor confines of Somerset and Devonshire. In consequence of a slight indisposition, an anodyne had been prescribed, from the effects of which he fell asleep in his chair at the moment that he was reading the following sentence, or words of the same substance, in "Purchas's Pilgrimage":[3] "Here the Khan Kubla commanded a palace to be built, and a stately garden thereunto. And thus ten miles of fertile ground were inclosed with a wall." The author continued for about three hours in a profound sleep, at least of the external senses, during which time he has the most vivid confidence, that he could not have composed less than from two to three hundred lines; if that indeed can be called composition in which all the images rose up before him as *things*, with a parallel production of the correspondent expressions, without any sensation or consciousness of effort. On awaking he appeared to himself to have a distinct recollection of the whole, and taking his pen, ink, and paper, instantly and eagerly wrote down the lines that are here preserved. At this moment he was unfortunately called out by a person

---

1   First written in 1797 and circulated in manuscript in literary circles until its publication in 1816.

2   George Gordon Byron (1788–1824), English poet, dramatist, and erstwhile political activist.

3   Samuel Purchas (1575?–1626), author of *Purchas his pilgrimage. Or Relations of the world and the religions observed in all ages and places discovered, from the Creation unto this present* (1613): "In Xaindu did Cublai Can build a stately pallace, encompassing sixteene miles of plaine ground with a wall, wherein are fertile meddowes, pleasant springs, delightfull streames, and all sorts of beasts of chase and game, and in the middest thereof a sumptuous house of pleasure, which may be removed from place to place" (350).

on business from Porlock, and detained by him above an hour, and on his return to his room, found to his no small surprise and mortification, that though he still retained some vague and dim recollection of the general purpose of the vision, yet, with the exception of some eight or ten scattered lines and images, all the rest had passed away like the images on the surface of a stream into which a stone has been cast, but, alas! without the after restoration of the latter ...

In Xanadu did KUBLA KHAN
A stately pleasure-dome decree:
Where ALPH, the sacred river, ran
Through caverns measureless to man
      Down to a sunless sea.
So twice five miles of fertile ground
With walls and towers were girdled round;
And here were gardens bright with sinuous rills
Where blossom'd many an incense-bearing tree;
And here were forests ancient as the hills,
And folding sunny spots of greenery.

But oh that deep romantic chasm which slanted
Down the green hill athwart a cedarn cover!
A savage place! as holy and inchanted
As e'er beneath a waning moon was haunted
By woman wailing for her demon-lover!
And from this chasm, with ceaseless turmoil seething,
As if this earth in fast thick pants were breathing,
A mighty fountain momently was forced:
Amid whose swift half-intermitted burst
Huge fragments vaulted like rebounding hail,
Or chaffy grain beneath the thresher's flail:
And mid these dancing rocks at once and ever
It flung up momently the sacred river.
Five miles meandering with a mazy motion
Through wood and dale the sacred river ran,
Then reached the caverns measureless to man,
And sank in tumult to a lifeless ocean:
And 'mid this tumult Kubla heard from far
Ancestral voices prophesying war!

The shadow of the dome of pleasure
Floated midway on the waves;
Where was heard the mingled measure
From the fountain and the caves.
It was a miracle of rare device,
A sunny pleasure-dome with caves of ice!

A damsel with a dulcimer
In a vision once I saw:
It was an Abyssinian maid
And on her dulcimer she play'd,
Singing of Mount Abora.
Could I revive within me
Her symphony and song,
To such a deep delight 'twould win me,
That with music loud and long,
I would build that dome in air,
That sunny dome! those caves of ice!
And all who heard should see them there,
And all should cry, Beware! Beware!
His flashing eyes, his floating hair!
Weave a circle round him thrice,
And close your eyes with holy dread:
For he on honey-dew hath fed,
And drank the milk of Paradise.

3. From "Letter from the English Opium Eater," *London Magazine* IV (December 1821): 584–86

To the Editor of the London Magazine.

SIR,

★ ★ ★ ★ ★ ★ ★ ★ ★ ★ ★

... I have seen in the Sheffield Iris a notice[1] of my two papers entitled *Confessions of an English Opium-eater*. Notice of any sort from Mr.
Montgomery[2] could not have failed to gratify me, by proving that I had
so far succeeded in my efforts as to catch the attention of a distinguished
man of genius: a notice so emphatic as this, and introduced by an

---

[1] See Appendix B1, Notice of "Confessions of an English Opium-Eater," *Sheffield Iris*
(December 1821).

[2] James Montgomery (1771–1854), poet and editor of *Sheffield Iris* (1793–1825).

exordium of so much beauty as that contained in the two first paragraphs on the faculty of dreaming, I am bound in gratitude to acknowledge as a more flattering expression and memorial of success than any which I had allowed myself to anticipate.

I am not sorry that a passage in Mr. Montgomery's comments enables me to take notice of a doubt which had reached me before: the passage I mean is this: in the fourth page of the Iris, amongst the remarks with which Mr. Montgomery has introduced the extracts which he has done me the honour to make, it is said—"whether this character," (the character in which the Opium-eater speaks) "be real or imaginary, we know not." The same doubt was reported to me as having been made in another quarter; but, in that instance, as clothed in such discourteous expressions, that I do not think it would have been right for me, or that on a principle of just self-respect, I could have brought myself to answer it at all; which I say in no anger, and I hope with no other pride than that which may reasonably influence any man in refusing an answer to all direct impeachments of his veracity. From Mr. Montgomery, however, this scruple on the question of authenticity comes in the shape which might have been anticipated from his own courteous and honourable nature, and implies no more than a suggestion (in one view perhaps complimentary to myself) that the whole might be professedly and intentionally a fictitious case as respected the incidents—and chosen as a more impressive form for communicating some moral or medical admonitions to the unconfirmed Opium-eater. Thus shaped—I cannot have any right to quarrel with this scruple. But on many accounts I should be sorry that such a view were taken of the narrative by those who may have happened to read it. And therefore, I assure Mr. Montgomery, in this public way, that the entire Confessions were designed to convey a narrative of my own experience as an Opium-eater, drawn up with entire simplicity and fidelity to the facts; from which they can in no respect have deviated, except by such trifling inaccuracies of date, &c. as the memoranda I have with me in London would not, in all cases, enable me to reduce to certainty. Over and above the want of these memoranda, I laboured sometimes (as I will acknowledge) under another, and a graver embarrassment:—To tell nothing *but* the truth—must, in all cases, be an unconditional moral law: to tell the *whole* truth is not equally so: in the earlier narrative I acknowledge that I could not always do this: regards of delicacy towards some who are yet living, and of just tenderness to the memory of others who are dead, obliged me, at various points of my narrative, to suppress what would have added interest to the story, and sometimes, perhaps, have left impressions on the reader favourable to other purposes of an auto-biographer. In cases which touch too closely on their own rights and interests, all men should hesitate to trust their own judgment: thus far I imposed a restraint upon myself, as all just and conscientious men would do: in every thing else I spoke fearlessly, and as if writing private memoirs for my own dearest friends. Events, indeed, in my life, connected with so many remembrances of grief, and sometimes of self-reproach, had become too sacred from habitual contemplation to be altered or distorted for the unworthy purposes of scenical effect and display, without violating those feelings of self-respect which all men should cherish, and giving a lasting wound to my conscience.

Having replied to the question involved in the passage quoted from the Iris, I ought to notice an objection, conveyed to me through many channels, and in too friendly terms to have been overlooked if I had thought it unfounded: whereas, I believe it is a very just one:—it is this: that I have so managed the second narrative, as to leave an overbalance on the side of the *pleasures* of opium; and that the very horrors them-selves, described as connected with the use of opium, do not pass the limit of pleasure.—I know not how to excuse myself on this head, unless by alleging (what is obvious enough) that to describe any pains, of any class, and that at perfect leisure for choosing and rejecting thoughts and expressions, is a most difficult task: in my case I scarcely know whether it is competent to me to allege further, that I was limited, both as to space and time, so long as it appears on the face of my paper, that I did not turn all that I had of either to the best account. It is known to you, however, that I wrote in extreme haste, and under very depressing circumstances in other respects.—On the whole, perhaps, the best way of meeting this objection will be to send you a Third Part of my Confessions★ drawn up with such assistance from fuller memoranda, and the recollections of my only companion during those years, as I shall be

---

★ In the Third Part I will fill up an omission noticed by the *Medical Intelligencer*, (No. 24,) viz.—The omission to record the particular effects of the Opium between 1804–12. This *Medical Intelligencer* is a sort of digest or analytic summary of contemporary medical essays, review, &c. wherever dispersed. Of its general merits I cannot pretend to judge: but, in justice to the writer of the article which respects myself, I ought to say, that it is the most remarkable specimen of skilful abridgement and judicious composition that I remember to have met with.

  [De Quincey never wrote this Third Part; see following Appendix to *Confessions of an English Opium-Eater* (Appendix A4). A review of the two instalments of *Confessions* in *Medical Intelligencer* 24 (October 1821): 613–15; De Quincey's account of the journal is accurate; the review itself consists mostly of a summary and quotation of De Quincey's text.]

able to command on my return to the north: I hope that I shall be able to return thither in the course of next week: and, therefore, by the end of January, or thereabouts, I shall have found leisure from my other employments, to finish it to my own satisfaction....

I remain, Sir,
Your faithful friend and servant,

London, Nov. 27, 1821.   X.Y.Z.

4. From the Appendix to *Confessions of An English Opium-Eater* (London: Taylor and Hessey, 1822). Reprinted in *London Magazine* V (December 1822): 512–14, 516–17

The proprietors of this little work having determined on reprinting it, some explanation seems called for, to account for the non-appearance of a Third Part promised in the London Magazine of December last; and the more so, because the proprietors, under whose guarantee that promise was issued, might otherwise be implicated in the blame—little or much—attached to its non-fulfilment. This blame, in mere justice, the author takes wholly upon himself....

For any purpose of self-excuse, it might be sufficient to say that intolerable bodily suffering had totally disabled him for almost any exertion of mind, more especially for such as demand and presuppose a pleasurable and genial state of feeling: but, as a case that may by possibility contribute a trifle to the medical history of Opium in a further stage of its action than can often have been brought under the notice of professional men, he has judged that it might be acceptable to some readers to have it described more at length. *Fiat experimentum in corpore vili*[1] is a just rule where there is any reasonable presumption of benefit to arise on a large scale; what the benefit may be, will admit of a doubt: but there can be none as to the value of the body: for a more worthless body than his own, the author is free to confess, cannot be: it is his pride to believe—that it is the very ideal of a base, crazy, despicable human system—that hardly ever could have been meant to be seaworthy for two days under the ordinary storms and wear-and-tear of life: and indeed, if that were the creditable way of disposing of human bodies, he must own that he should almost be ashamed to bequeath his wretched structure to any respectable dog....

---

[1] "Try the experiment on a worthless body."

Those who have read the Confessions will have closed them with the impression that I had wholly renounced the use of Opium. This impression I meant to convey: and that for two reasons: first, because the very act of deliberately recording such a state of suffering necessarily presumes in the recorder a power of surveying his own case as a cool spectator, and a degree of spirits for adequately describing it, which it would be inconsistent to suppose in any person speaking from the station of an actual sufferer: secondly, because I, who had descended from so large a quantity as 8,000 drops to so small a one (comparatively speaking) as a quantity ranging between 300 and 160 drops, might well suppose that the victory was in effect achieved. In suffering my readers therefore to think of me as of a reformed opium-eater, I left no impression but what I shared myself; and, as may be seen, even this impression was left to be collected from the general tone of the conclusion, and not from any specific words—which are in no instance at variance with the literal truth.—In no long time after that paper was written, I became sensible that the effort which remained would cost me far more energy than I had anticipated: and the necessity for making it was more apparent every month.... Opium therefore I resolved wholly to abjure, as soon as I should find myself at liberty to lend my undivided attention and energy to this purpose. It was not however until the 24th of June last that any tolerable concurrence of facilities for such an attempt arrived. On that day I began my experiment, having previously settled in my own mind that I would not flinch, but would "stand up to the scratch"—under any possible "punishment." I must premise that about 170 or 180 drops had been my ordinary allowance for many months: occasionally I had run up as high as 500; and once nearly to 700: in repeated preludes to my final experiment I had also gone as low as 100 drops; but had found it impossible to stand it beyond the 4th day—which, by the way, I have always found more difficult to get over than any of the preceding three. I went off under easy sail—130 drops a day for three days: on the 4th I plunged at once to 80: the misery which I now suffered "took the conceit" out of me at once: and for about a month I continued off and on about this mark: then I sunk to 60: and the next day to—none at all. This was the first day for nearly ten years that I had existed without opium. I persevered in my abstinence for 90 hours; i.e. upwards of half a week. Then I took—ask me not how much: say, ye severest, what would ye have done? then I abstained again: then took about 25 drops: then abstained: and so on.

Meantime the symptoms which attended my case for the first six weeks of the experiment were these:—enormous irritability and excitement of the whole system: the stomach in particular restored to a full feeling of vitality and sensibility; but often in great pain: unceasing restlessness night and day: sleep—I scarcely knew what it was: 3 hours out of the 24 was the utmost I had, and that so agitated and shallow that I heard every sound that was near me: lower jaw constantly swelling: mouth ulcerated: and many other distressing symptoms that would be tedious to repeat; amongst which however I must mention one, because it had never failed to accompany any attempt to renounce opium—viz. violent sternutation[1]: this now became exceedingly troublesome: sometimes lasting for 2 hours at once, and recurring at least twice or three times a day.... I protest to you that I have a greater influx of thoughts in one hour at present than in a whole year under the reign of opium. It seems as though all the thoughts which had been frozen up for a decade of years by opium, had now, according to the old fable been thawed at once—such a multitude stream in upon me from all quarters. Yet such is my impatience and hideous irritability—that, for one which I detain and write down, 50 escape me: in spite of my weariness from suffering and want of sleep, I cannot stand still or sit for two minutes together....

... I wished to explain how it had become impossible for me to compose a Third Part in time to accompany this republication: for during the very time of this experiment, the proof sheets of this reprint were sent to me from London: and such was my inability to expand or to improve them, that I could not even bear to read them over with attention enough to notice the press errors, or to correct any verbal inaccuracies. These were my reasons for troubling my reader with any record, long or short, of experiments relating to so truly base a subject as my own body ... No man, I suppose, employs much of his time on the phenomena of his own body without some regard for it; whereas the reader sees that, so far from looking upon mine with any complacency or regard, I hate it and make it the object of my bitter ridicule and contempt: and I should not be displeased to know that the last indignities which the law inflicts upon the bodies of the worst malefactors might hereafter fall upon it. And, in testification of my sincerity in saying this, I shall make the following offer. Like other men, I have particular fancies about the place of my burial: having lived chiefly in a mountainous region, I rather cleave to the conceit that a grave in a

---

[1]   Sneezing.

green church yard amongst the ancient and solitary hills will be a sublimer and more tranquil place of repose for a philosopher than any in the hideous Golgothas[1] of London. Yet if the gentlemen of Surgeons' Hall think that any benefit can redound to their science from inspecting the appearances in the body of an opium-eater, let them speak but a word, and I will take care that mine shall be legally secured to them— i.e. as soon as I have done with it myself. Let them not hesitate to express their wishes upon any scruples of false delicacy, and consideration for my feelings: I assure them they will do me too much honour by 'demonstrating' on such a crazy body as mine: and it will give me pleasure to anticipate this posthumous revenge and insult inflicted upon that which has caused me so much suffering in this life....

Sept. 30th, 1822.

THE END.

5. From 1853 General Preface to *Selections Grave and Gay, from Writings Published and Unpublished*, by Thomas De Quincey (London: James Hogg and Sons, 1853–1860), 1:x–xix

... I will here attempt a rude general classification of all the articles which compose [the American edition].[2] I distribute them grossly into three classes:—*First*, into that class which proposes primarily to amuse the reader; but which, in doing so, may or may not happen occasionally to reach a higher station, at which the amusement passes into an impassioned interest.... Into the second class I throw those papers which address themselves purely to the understanding as an insulated faculty; or do so primarily. Let me call them by the general name of ESSAYS.... Finally, as a third class, and, in virtue of their aim, as a far higher class of compositions included in the American edition, I rank *The Confessions of an Opium-Eater,* and also (but more emphatically) the *Suspiria de Profundis.* On these, as modes of impassioned prose ranging under no precedents that I am aware of in any literature, it is much more difficult to speak justly, whether in a hostile or a friendly character. As yet

---

[1] "Golgotha, that is to say a place of a skull" (Matthew 27:33), the site of Christ's crucifixion. Until the implementation of legislation for burial grounds, cemeteries in nineteenth-century London were infamously overcrowded and unsanitary.

[2] Ticknor, Reed, and Fields of Boston began publishing *De Quincey's Writings* in 1851, which ran to 20 volumes by 1859 and was the impetus for De Quincey to undertake editing his collected works in Britain as *Selections Grave and Gay* (1853–60); the first Boston volume was *Confessions of an English Opium-Eater; and Suspiria de Profundis* (1851).

neither of these two works has ever received the least degree of that correction and pruning which both require so extensively; and of the *Suspiria*, not more than perhaps one-third has yet been printed. When both have been fully revised, I shall feel myself entitled to ask for a more determinate adjudication on their claims as works of art. At present I feel authorised to make haughtier pretensions in right of their *conception* than I shall venture to do, under the peril of being supposed to characterise their *execution*. Two remarks only I shall address to the equity of my reader. First, I desire to remind him of the perilous difficulty besieging all attempts to clothe in words the visionary scenes derived from the world of dreams, where a single false note, a single word in a wrong key, ruins the whole music; and, secondly, I desire him to consider the utter sterility of universal literature in this one department of impassioned prose; which certainly argues some singular difficulty suggesting a singular duty of indulgence in criticising any attempt that even imperfectly succeeds. The sole Confessions, belonging to past times, that have at all succeeded in engaging the attention of men, are those of St. Augustine and of Rousseau.[1] The very idea of breathing a record of human passion, not into the ear of the random crowd, but of the saintly confessional, argues an impassioned theme. Impassioned, therefore, should be the tenor of the compositions. Now, in St. Augustine's Confessions, is found one most impassioned passage, viz. the lamentation for the death of his youthful friend in the 4th Book; one, and no more. Further there is nothing. In Rousseau there is not even so much. In the whole work there is nothing grandly affecting but the character and the inexplicable misery of the writer.

6. From the Explanatory Notice to Volume Four (1854) of *Selections Grave and Gay*, from *Writings Published and Unpublished*, by Thomas De Quincey (London: James Hogg and Sons, 1853–1860), xii–xiv

This little paper [*The English Mail-Coach*], according to my original intentions, formed part of the "Suspiria de Profundis," from which, for a momentary purpose, I did not scruple to detach it, and to publish it apart, as sufficiently intelligible even when dislocated from its place in a larger whole. To my surprise, however, one or two critics, not carelessly

---

[1]. Augustine of Hippo (345–430), rhetorician and theologian, author of *Confessions* (c. 400 CE); for Jean-Jacques Rousseau, see *Confessions*, p. 50, n. 3, above.

in conversation, but deliberately in print, professed their inability to apprehend the meaning of the whole, or to follow the links of the connection between its several parts.... Thirty-seven years ago, or rather more, accident made me, in the dead of night, and of a night memorably solemn, the solitary witness to an appalling scene, which threatened instant death in a shape the most terrific to two young people, whom I had no means of assisting, except in so far as I was able to give them a most hurried warning of their danger; but even *that* not until they stood within the very shadow the catastrophe, being divided from the most frightful of deaths by scarcely more, if more at all, than seventy seconds.

Such was the scene, such in its outline, from which the whole of this paper radiates as a natural expansion. This scene is circumstantially narrated in Section the Second, entitled, "The Vision of Sudden Death."

But a movement of horror, and of spontaneous recoil from this dreadful scene, naturally carried the whole of that scene, raised and idealised, into my dreams, and very soon into a rolling succession of dreams. The actual scene, as looked down upon from the box of the mail, was transformed into a dream, as tumultuous and changing as a musical fugue. This troubled Dream is circumstantially reported in Section the Third, entitled, "Dream-Fugue upon the Theme of Sudden Death." What I had beheld from my seat upon the mail; the scenical strife of action and passion, of anguish and fear, as I had there witnessed them moving in ghostly silence; this duel between life and death narrowing itself to a point of such exquisite evanescence as the collision neared; all these elements of the scene blended, under the law of association, with the previous and permanent features at that time lay—1st, in velocity unprecedented; 2dly, in the power and beauty of the horses; 3dly, in the official connection with the government of a great nation; and, 4thly, in the function, almost a consecrated function, of publishing and diffusing through the land the great political events, and especially the great battles during a conflict of unparalleled grandeur. These honorary distinctions are all described circumstantially in the FIRST or introductory section ("The Glory of Motion"). The three first were distinctions maintained at all times; but the fourth and grandest belonged exclusively to the war with Napoleon; and this it was which most naturally introduced Waterloo into the dream. Waterloo, I understood, was the particular feature of the "Dream-Fugue" which my censors were least able to account for. Yet surely Waterloo, which, in common with every other great battle, it had been our special privilege to publish over all the land, most naturally entered the Dream under the license of our privilege. If not—if there be anything amiss—let the Dream be responsible. The Dream is a law to itself: and as well quarrel with a rainbow for showing, or for *not* showing, a secondary arch. So far as I know, every element in the shifting movements of the Dream derived itself either primarily from the incidents of the actual scene, or from secondary features associated with the mail.... But the Dream knows best; and the Dream, I say again, is the responsible party.

7. From the Prefatory Notice to *Confessions of an English Opium-Eater* **(1856), in** *Selections Grave and Gay,* **from** *Writings Published and Unpublished,* **by Thomas De Quincey (London: James Hogg and Sons, 1853–1860), 5:xi–xv**

When it had been settled that, in the general series of these republications, the "Confessions of an English Opium-Eater" should occupy the Fifth Volume, I resolved to avail myself most carefully of the opening thus made for a revision of the entire work. By accident, a considerable part of the Confessions (all, in short, except the Dreams) had originally been written hastily; and, from various causes, had never received any strict revision, or, *virtually,* so much as an ordinary verbal correction. But a great deal more was wanted than this. The main narrative should naturally have moved through a succession of secondary incidents; and with leisure for recalling these, it might have been greatly inspired. Wanting all opportunity for such advantages, this narrative had been needlessly impoverished. And thus it had happened, that not so properly correction and retrenchment were called for, as integration of what had been left imperfect, or amplification of what, from the first, had been insufficiently expanded.

... Compared with its own former self, the book must certainly tend, by its very principle of change, whatever should be the *execution* of that change, to become better: and in my own opinion, after all drawbacks and allowances for the faulty exemplification of a good principle, it *is* better. This should be a matter of mere logical or inferential necessity; since, in pure addition to everything previously approved, there would now be a clear surplus of extra matter—all that might be good in the old work, and a great deal beside that was new. Meantime this improvement has been won at a price of labour and suffering that, if they could be truly stated, would seem incredible. A nervous malady, of very peculiar character, which has attacked me intermittingly for the last eleven years, came on in May last, almost concurrently with the commencement of this revision; and so obstinately has this malady pursued its noiseless, and what I may call subterraneous, siege, since none of the symptoms are externally manifested, that, although pretty nearly dedicating myself to this one solitary labour, and not intermitting or relaxing it for a single day, I have yet spent, within a very few days, six calendar months upon the re-cast of this one small volume.

The consequences have been distressing to all concerned. The press has groaned under the chronic visitation; the compositors shudder at the sight of my handwriting, though not objectionable on the score of legibility; and I have much reason to fear that, on days when the pressure of my complaint has been heaviest, I may have so far given way to it, as to have suffered greatly in clearness of critical vision.... To fight up against the wearing siege of an abiding sickness, imposes a fiery combat. I attempt no description of this combat, knowing the unintelligibility and the repulsiveness of all attempts to communicate the Incommunicable.

I have thus made the reader acquainted with one out of two cross currents that tended to thwart my efforts for improving this little work. There was, meantime, another, less open to remedy from my own uttermost efforts. All along I had relied upon a crowning grace, which I had reserved for the final pages of this volume, in a succession of some twenty or twenty-five dreams and noon-day visions, which had arisen under the latter stages of opium influence. These have disappeared: under some circumstances which allow me a reasonable prospect of recovering them; some unaccountably; and some dishonourably. Five or six, I believe, were burned in a sudden conflagration which arose from the spark of a candle falling unobserved amongst a very large pile of papers in a bedroom, when I was alone and reading.... Amongst the papers burned partially, but not burned as to be absolutely irretrievable, was the "Daughter of Lebanon;" and this I have printed, and have intentionally placed it at the end, as appropriately closing a record in which the case of poor Ann the Outcast formed not only the most memorable and the most suggestively pathetic incident, but also *that* which, more than any other, coloured—or (more truly I should say) shaped, moulded and remoulded, composed and decomposed—the great body of opium dreams. The search after the lost features of Ann, which I spoke of as pursued in the crowds of London, was in a more proper sense pursued through many a year in dreams. The general idea of a search and a chase reproduced itself in many shapes. The person, the rank, the age, the scenical position, all varied themselves for ever; but the same leading traits more or less faintly remained of a lost

Pariah[1] woman, and of some shadowy malice which withdrew her, or attempted to withdraw her, from restoration and from hope....

8. From "The Dark Interpreter," in Alexander H. Japp, *The Posthumous Works of Thomas De Quincey*, 2 vols. (London: William Heinemann, 1891), 7–12[2]

"Oh, eternity with outstretched wings, that broodest over the secret truths in whose roots lie the mysteries of man—his whence, his whither—have I searched thee, and struck a right key on thy dreadful organ!"

Suffering is a mightier agency in the hands of nature, as a Demiurgus[3] creating the intellect, than most people are aware of.

The truth I heard often in sleep from the lips of the Dark Interpreter. Who is he? He is a shadow, reader, but a shadow with whom you must suffer me to make you acquainted. You need not be afraid of him, for when I explain his nature and origin you will see that he is essentially inoffensive; or if sometimes he menaces with his countenance, that is but seldom: and then, as his features in those moods shift as rapidly as clouds in a gale of wind, you may always look for the terrific aspects to vanish as fast as they have gathered. As to his origin—what it is, I know exactly, but cannot without a little circuit of preparation make you understand. Perhaps you are aware of that power in the eye of many children by which in darkness they project a vast theatre of phantasmagorical figures moving forwards or backwards between their bed-curtains and the chamber walls. In some children this power is semi-voluntary—they can control or perhaps suspend the shows; but in others it is altogether automatic. I myself, at the date of my last confessions, had seen in this way

---

1. A member of a low caste in southern India; social outcast.

2. The following three excerpts are taken from Alexander H. Japp's late nineteenth-century editing of De Quincey's further writings for *Suspiria de Profundis* (see p. 303, n. 1 below). As the editors of *Works of Thomas De Quincey* indicate, Japp was often creative in reconstructing these working texts from De Quincey's manuscripts, or was working from manuscripts that no longer exist or have gone missing (see editorial apparatus for *Suspiria de Profundis* in *Works*, vol. 15). Nonetheless, the three following texts, apart from having been well recognized as part of De Quincey's oeuvre since the late nineteenth century, are a sufficiently accurate and telling indication of his intentions for the further expansion of *Suspiria* as to warrant their inclusion here. "The Dark Interpreter," probably written in 1845, especially makes fuller sense of that figure's importance in "The Apparition of the Brocken."

3. A Platonic deity who fashions the sensible world according to eternal ideas; a Gnostic deity who creates the material world; an autonomous creative force.

more processions—generally solemn, mournful, belonging to eternity, but also at times glad, triumphal pomps, that seemed to enter the gates of Time—than all the religions of paganism, fierce or gay, ever witnessed. Now, there is in the dark places of the human spirit—in grief, in fear, in vindicative wrath—a power of self-projection not unlike to this. Thirty years ago, it may be, a man called Symons committed several murders in a sudden epilepsy of planet-struck fury. According to my recollection, this case happened at Hoddesdon, which is in Middlesex. "Revenge is sweet!" was his hellish motto on that occasion, and that motto itself records the abysses which a human will can open. Revenge is *not* sweet, unless by the mighty charm of a charity that seeketh not her own it has become benignant. And what he had to revenge was woman's scorn. He had been a plain farm-servant; and, in fact, he was executed, as such men often are, on a proper point of professional respect to their calling, in a smock-frock, or blouse, to render so ugly a clash of syllables. His young mistress was every way and by much his superior, as well in prospects as in education. But the man, by nature arrogant, and little acquainted with the world, presumptuously raised his eyes to one of his young mistresses. Great was the scorn with which she repulsed his audacity, and her sisters participated in her disdain. Upon this affront he brooded night and day; and, after the term of his service was over, and he, in effect, forgotten by the family, one day he suddenly descended amongst the women of the family like an Avatar[1] of vengeance. Right and left he threw out his murderous knife without distinction of person, leaving the room and the passage floating in blood.

The final result of this carnage was not so terrific as it threatened to be. Some, I think, recovered; but, also, one, who did not recover, was unhappily a stranger to the whole cause of his fury. Now, this murderer always maintained, in conversation with the prison chaplain, that, as he rushed on in his hellish career, he perceived distinctly a dark figure on his right hand, keeping pace with himself. Upon *that* the superstitious, of course, supposed that some fiend had revealed himself, and associated *his* superfluous presence with the dark atrocity.... The fact is, in point of awe a fiend would be a poor, trivial *bagatelle*[2] compared to the shadowy projections, *umbras* and *penumbras*,[3] which the unsearchable depths of

---

[1] In Hindu mythology, the incarnation of a deity; an incarnation in human form.
[2] Short literary or musical piece; a trifle.
[3] "Umbra": the central dark core of a sunspot; the part of a shadow from which all light from the source is excluded; "penumbra": the partly shaded region around the dark core of a sunspot, or the partly shaded region of the shadow.

man's nature is capable, under adequate excitement, of throwing off, and even into stationary forms. I shall have occasion to notice this point again. There are creative agencies in every part of human nature, of which the thousandth part could never be revealed in one life....

In after-life, from twenty to twenty-four, on looking back to those struggles of my childhood, I used to wonder exceedingly that a child could be exposed to struggles on such a scale. But two views unfolded upon me as my experience widened, which took away that wonder. The first was the vast scale upon which the sufferings of children are found everywhere expanded in the realities of life. The generation of infants which you see is but part of those who belong to it; were born in it; and make, the world over, not one half of it. The missing half, more than an equal number to those of any age that are now living, have perished by every kind of torments.... And of those who survive to reach maturity what multitudes have fought with fierce pangs of hunger, cold, and nakedness! When I came to know all this, then reverting my eye to *my* struggles, I said oftentimes it was nothing! Secondly, in watching the infancy of my own children, I made another discovery—it is well known to mothers, to nurses, and also to philosophers—that the tears and lamentations of infants during the year or so when they have no *other* language of complaint run through a gamut that is as inexhaustible as the cremona of Paganini.[1] An ear but moderately learned in that language cannot be deceived as to the rate and *modulus*[2] of the suffering which it indicates. A fretful or peevish cry cannot by any efforts make itself impassioned. The cry of impatience, of hunger, of irritation, of reproach, of alarm, are all different—different as a chorus of Beethoven from a chorus of Mozart. But if ever you saw an infant suffering for an hour, as sometimes the healthiest does, under some attack of the stomach, which has the tiger-grasp of the Oriental cholera,[3] then you will hear moans that address to their mothers an anguish of supplication for aid such as might storm the heart of Moloch.[4] Once hearing it, you will not forget it. How, it was a constant

---

[1] The violin of Italian composer and violinist Niccolo Paganini (1782–1840).

[2] The coefficient by which the logarithms in one system are multiplied to ascertain the logarithms in another.

[3] "The most devastating epidemics of cholera in the nineteenth century occurred in southeast Asia" [*Works* 15:730].

[4] Semitic deity associated with the sacrifice of children; Milton, *Paradise Lost*, named him first among the rebel angels: "First *Moloch*, horrid King besmear'd with blood / Of human sacrifice, and parents' tears, / Though for the noise of Drums and Timbrels loud / Their children's cries unheard, that pass'd through fire / To his grim Idol" (1.392–96).

remark of mine, after any storm of that nature (occurring, suppose, once in two months), that always on the following day, when a long, long sleep had chased away the darkness and the memory of the darkness from the little creature's brain, a sensible expansion had taken place in the intellectual faculties of attention, observation, and animation.... Pain driven to agony, or grief driven to frenzy, is essential to the ventilation of profound natures.... A nature which is profound in excess, but also introverted and abstracted in excess, so as to be in peril of wasting itself in interminable reverie, cannot be awakened sometimes without afflictions that go to the very foundations, heaving, stirring, yet finally harmonizing; and it is in such cases that the Dark Interpreter does his work, revealing the worlds of pain and agony and woe possible to man—possible even to the innocent spirit of a child.

9. Manuscript list for proposed plan of *Suspiria de Profundis*, in Alexander H. Japp, *The Posthumous Works of Thomas De Quincey*, 2 vols. (London: William Heinemann, 1891), 4–5[1]

1. Dreaming. †
2. The Affliction of Childhood. †
   Dream Echoes. †
3. The English Mail Coach. †
   (1) The Glory of Motion.
   (2) Vision of Sudden Death.
   (3) Dream-fugue.
4. The Palimpsest of the Human Brain. †
5. Vision of Life. †
6. Memorial Suspiria. †

---

[1]   In reconstructing this plan, Japp writes: "From a list found among [De Quincey's] MSS. we are able to give the arrangement of the whole as it would have appeared had no accident occurred, and all the papers been at hand. Those followed by a cross are those which are now recovered, and those with a dagger what were reprinted either as 'Suspiria' or otherwise in Messrs. Black's editions....Thus of the thirty-two 'Suspiria' intended by the author, we have only nine that received his final corrections, and even with those now recovered, we have only about one half of the whole, presuming that those which are lost or remained unwritten would have averaged about the same length as those we have" (4–5). The editors of *Works* question Japp's conjectural schema (for one thing, he was working from only partial information of the Suspiria that had appeared in print to that point), and provide a list of sixteen proposed Suspiria from a manuscript in De Quincey's hand in the Berg Collection (New York Public Library; see *Works* 15:567). See the discussion of *Suspiria* in the Introduction to the present edition.

7. Levana and our Ladies of Sorrow.
8. Solitude of Childhood. ✠
9. The Dark Interpreter. ✠
10. The Apparition of the Brocken. †
11. Savannah-la-Mar.
12. The Dreadful Infant. (There was the glory of innocence made perfect; there was the dreadful beauty of infancy that had seen God.)
13. Foundering Ships.
14. The Archbishop and the Controller of Fire.
15. God that didst Promise.
16. Count the Leaves in Vallombrosa.
17. But if I submitted with Resignation, not the less I searched for the Unsearchable—sometimes in Arab Deserts, sometimes in the Sea.
18. That ran before us in Malice.
19. Morning of Execution.
20. Daughter of Lebanon. †
21. Kyrie Eleison.
22. The Princess that lost a Single Seed of a Pomegranate. ✠
23. The Nursery in Arabian Deserts.
24. The Halcyon Calm and the Coffin.
25. Faces! Angels' Faces!
26. At that Word.
27. Oh, Apothanate! that hatest Death, and cleansest from the Pollution of Sorrow.
28. Who is this Woman that for some Months has followed me up and down? Her face I cannot see, for she keeps for ever behind me.
29. Who is this Woman that beckoneth and warneth me from the Place where she is, and in whose Eyes is Woeful remembrance? I guess who she is. ✠
30. Cagot and Cressida.
31. Lethe and Anapaula.
32. Oh, sweep away, Angel, with Angelic Scorn, the Dogs that come with Curious Eyes to gaze.

10. From Book Five of William Wordsworth, *The Prelude, or Growth of a Poet's Mind; An Autobiographical Poem* (London: Edward Moxon, 1850), ll. 65-98, 110-52

> On poetry and geometric truth,
> And their high privilege of lasting life

From all internal injury exempt,
I mused, upon these chiefly: and at length,
My senses yielding to the sultry air,
Sleep seized me, and I passed into a dream.
I saw before me stretched a boundless plain
Of sandy wilderness, all black and void,
And as I looked around, distress and fear
Came creeping over me, when at my side,
Close at my side, an uncouth shape appeared
Upon a dromedary, mounted high.
He seemed an Arab of the Bedouin tribes:
A lance he bore, and underneath one arm
A stone, and in the opposite hand a shell
Of a surpassing brightness. At the sight
Much I rejoiced, not doubting but a guide
Was present, one who with unerring skill
Would through the desert lead me; and while yet
I looked and looked, self-questioned what this freight
Which the new-comer carried through the waste
Could mean, the Arab told me that the stone
(To give it in the language of the dream)
Was "Euclid's Elements;" and "This," said he,
"Is something of more worth;" and at the word
Stretched forth the shell, so beautiful in shape,
In colour so resplendent, with command
That I should hold it to my ear. I did so,
And heard that instant in an unknown tongue,
Which yet I understood, articulate sounds,
A loud prophetic blast of harmony;
An Ode, in passion uttered, which foretold
Destruction to the children of the earth
By deluge, now at hand....
....
While this was uttering, strange as it may seem,
I wondered not, although I plainly saw
The one to be a stone, the other a shell;
Nor doubted once but that they both were books,
Having a perfect faith in all that passed.
Far stronger, now, grew the desire I felt
To cleave unto this man; but when I prayed

To share his enterprise, he hurried on
Reckless of me: I followed, not unseen,
For oftentimes he cast a backward look,
Grasping his twofold treasure.—Lance in rest,
He rode, I keeping pace with him; and now
He, to my fancy, had become the knight
Whose tale Cervantes tells; yet not the knight,
But was an Arab of the desert too;
Of these was neither, and was both at once.
His countenance, meanwhile, grew more disturbed;
And, looking backwards when he looked, mine eyes
Saw, over half the wilderness diffused,
A bed of glittering light: I asked the cause:
"It is," said he, "the waters of the deep
Gathering upon us;" quickening then the pace
Of the unwieldly creature he bestrode,
He left me: I called after him aloud;
He heeded not; but, with his twofold charge
Still in his grasp, before me, full in view,
Went hurrying o'er the illimitable waste,
With the fleet waters of a drowning world
In chase of him; whereat I waked in terror,
And saw the sea before me, and the book,
In which I had been reading, at my side.[1]

Full often, taking from the world of sleep
This Arab phantom, which I thus beheld,
This semi-Quixote, I to him have given
A substance, fancied him a living man,
A gentle dweller in the desert, crazed
By love and feeling, and internal thought
Protracted among endless solitudes;
Have shaped him wandering upon this quest!
Nor have I pitied him; but rather felt
Reverence was due to a being thus employed;
And thought that, in the blind and awful lair
Of such a madness, reason did lie couched.

---

[1]   *Don Quixote* (1605), by Miguel de Cervantes Saavedra (1547–1616), Spanish novelist and
dramatist. As a prelude to the dream, Wordsworth notes that he was reading *Don Quixote*.

Appendix B: Reviews, Letters, Notes

1. From James Montgomery, Notice of "Confessions of an English Opium-Eater," *Sheffield Iris* (December 1821): 3–4; in Alexander H. Japp, *Thomas De Quincey: His Life and Writings* (London: James Hogg, 1877), 1:240–46

Man leads a double life on earth: he inhabits a world of reality by day, and world of imagination by night. A third of human existence would be lost if the blank space of sleep were not filled up with pictured fancies that amuse the brain in dreams; and these, how grotesque and extravagant soever they be, yet bear such analogy to truth, that, were all the actions of an individual recorded on one hand, and his dreams brought to light on the other, it would puzzle Duns Scotus and Thomas Aquinas[1] themselves to say, whether his character might not be less equivocally determined by the latter than the former. One thing is clear, that more of the secrets of his heart would be betrayed from the completion of that life which he leads in sleep than that which he leads before the world. Awake, and among his fellow-creatures, whose eyes are at all times upon him, man acts, even when he is least conscious of it, under habitual restraint; but the scene of his dreams is the sanctuary of his own mind, into which none beside himself can intrude. The miscreated shapes that people them are the offspring of his peculiar phantasy, and no eye but his can see them; nor, unless he chooses to divulge his invisible adventures in that *terra incognita*, is there one breathing that can track his footsteps thither, or by felicity of apprehension catch a glimpse of its frontier, any more than a spirit can be followed in its flight through the valley of the shadow of death, or the region in the eternal world that receives it be described by mortal optics from this side of the grave. When man enters the cave of Morpheus, he disappears from the multitude, and remains inaccessible till his involuntary return.

In such retirement, under cover of night more impenetrable than that which envelops the universe—in a little world of his own where all is light and life and liberty to him and to him only, the slumberer is thoroughly and purely himself; he acts, he speaks, he thinks, he feels, without disguise and without reserve. He cannot help being honest here in the

---

[1] Joannes Duns Scotus (1265?–1308?), Scottish philosopher, theologian, and Franciscan; St. Thomas Aquinas (c. 1225–74), Italian philosopher, theologian, and Dominican friar, author of *Summa Theologiae*.

exercise of his virtues, or the exposure of his vices; there is no hypocrisy beyond that ineffable point, which we all may pass thousands of times, yet never *recollect*, passing it once—the point of falling asleep. We shall be told, and we admit, that there are innumerable fallacies in dreams—"the stuff that dreams are made of" is proverbial for that which is most puerile, incongruous, and inane. It is not, however, what they are, but what they represent, that deserves attention, and will repay it. The images of which they are composed may be hieroglyphics, more undecipherable than those of Egypt, without the key that unlocks their mysteries; that key every man possesses for his own use, and employing it he may learn, from apparently unintelligible jargon, lessons of self-knowledge whereby to regulate his waking-hours; for to these all his night visions have a reference, and are as surely reflections, however misshapen of their forms, as the Spectre of the Alps, towering from the valley to the firmament, at sunrise, is only an ærial image of the beholder himself, dilated by mist through immensity. But it may be prudent to draw in here; perhaps we have already said more than we can prove—which is the easiest thing in the world to do, as the reader will soon see, if he tries his knack of assertion on any paradoxical topic;—be it understood then, that it is the moral and not the fable of dreams into which we must look for the interpretation of life and character; that fable, like the fictions of poetry, is often distorted with strange and irrelevant associations, which have either no meaning at all, or no meaning worth unravelling. But, that the phantoms and changes that occur in dreams, while they are mere repetitions, cross-readings, and exaggerations of matters of fact, at the same time exemplify the habits, pursuits, understandings, affections, and antipathies of the dreamers, may be ascertained by anybody who will take the trouble to retrace and compare the remembrances of his own nocturnal vagaries. There may be persons of such adamant frames and imperturbable spirits, that these echoes of life are silent with them; the night answers not to the day while they repose, nor does slumber do more for them than it does for plants which are said to sleep, but were never yet known to dream. These may think that we rave, when we give so much importance to *unrealities*; but could one of these phlegmatic gentry catch his neighbour napping, and walk into his dreams, he would probably make such discoveries there as might cause him to love or hate, fear or despise, that neighbour, not only more than he had formerly done, but more than he would otherwise ever have had occasion to do.

We have been led into this rhapsody by reading the "Confessions of an Opium-Eater," lately published ... Opium-eating is not a very common taste in this country, nor is there much fear that any reader will be tempted to contract it, for the sake of being tortured and transported, as this marvellous sufferer has been, in the process of recovery from the perdition into which the fell drug had absorbed him. He, indeed, is evidently a man of fiery temperament, and vulgar beings, even if they do learn to swallow with delight as much crude abomination in a day as would "poison six dragoons and their horses," must not hope to have their darkness illumined by visions so tremendously magnificent and exquisitely agonising as his were....

But, if nobody in his senses is likely to be allured to the practice of eating this insane drug "that takes the reason prisoner," by reading the "Confessions of an Opium-Eater," many might be profited by the resolute perusal of them with self-application; for it may be safely affirmed, that every habitual indulgence of appetite or intellect, beyond what nature requires, or will endure, for the health of body or mind, is a species of opium-eating.... The novel-reader, in this sense, is an opium-eater. How the mind is teased and pleased, bewildered and weakened, fatigued and tormented—while the heart is unconsciously experiencing a process by which its honest sensibilities are blunted, and its affections disordered, if not absolutely vitiated, thousands and tens of thousands of the loveliest and most pitiable of our fair country-women can tell—to say nothing of the multitudes of our own sex, who read themselves into dandies and coxcombs, and bloods and bullies, by inordinate doses of these mawkish exhibitions of the inspissated juice of poppies, that grow on the banks of Lethe, making people forget everything but what ought not to be remembered. And are not newspaper readers opium-eaters too? We grant that they are, and yet we shall not say a word about the maddening potions of radicalism, or the bewitching philtres of loyalty, administered by the most notorious of our empirical brethren, lest we should be reminded of the "sleeping draughts" (opiates with a vengeance), prepared at the office of the "Iris." Poets are also opium-eaters, (inveterate ones) in the sentimental acceptation of the term.

2. From "Opiologia; or Confessions of an English Opium-Eater: being an Extract from the Life of a Scholar," *Medico-Chirurgical Review 2* (March 1822): 881–901

... When we first glanced at this production, we considered the title as a mere vehicle, through which some romantic or satirical tale was to be conveyed. On reading a little farther, we soon perceived that this first impression was erroneous, and that these confessions bore intrinsic marks of authenticity. We have since been satisfied, by proofs the most unequivocal, of the respectability of the personage, and the truth of the narrative. The perusal of this interesting paper, recalled to our memories many images and sensations of early life, now nearly obliterated by time, though stamped, at the period of occurrence, with more than common force of impression. We too, were opium-eaters—but on a very limited scale, and for a very short time, compared with the author now under consideration. We well recollect, however, the inexpressible delight produced by opium, when prostrate on the bed of suffering, on a far distant shore! To say that it soothed or removed pain, would be doing great injustice to the effects of this astonishing medicine. The positive pleasure superinduced, the beatific visions engendered, and the dreams of ideal happiness, spread in gorgeous profusion before the mind's eye, far exceeded all that thought can imagine, much more language pourtray! Our personal experience does not coincide, in all respects, with that of our author—a circumstance not to be wondered at, when we consider the varieties of constitution and mental susceptibility, from nature, habit, and education. Our author, drawing, with great fidelity no doubt, from his own personal feelings, grows sceptical as to the feelings and representations of others, and dogmatical as to the physical effects of opium on the human mind and body. A more extended circle of observation would have shewn him, that the analogy between opium and alcohol, in their effects and consequences, is far greater than he is disposed to allow—and the same observation would have presented to him, the various, and, sometimes, opposite effects of the latter substance upon different constitutions. The agency of opium too, on this frame of ours, is very different in health and in disease. Every medical man has had abundant opportunities of seeing opium produce sleep at one time, and unconquerable waking at another; when the patient knew nothing of the nature of the medicine taken. In our own persons, and in others, we have often observed that, sleep is by no means a general consequence of a full dose of opium, in painful and irritable states of the system.... In many constitutions, although it blunts the acuteness, and mitigates the severity of pain, it raises such a tumultuous and chaotic imagery before the mind of the patient, as induces him to beg, that the same medicine may not again be administered. But as we shall have several occasional remarks to make on some portions of the narrative—if narrative it can be called—we shall proceed, at once, to give a sketch of these very curious and interesting confessions to our medical brethren.

... [T]he main part of our author's suffering, and the principal subject of these confessions, were his DREAMS. The first intimation he had of any important change going on [in] this part of his physical economy, was in the middle of 1817, when a kind of waking faculty of conjuring up all sorts of phantoms in the dark, became truly distressing to him.... We would, in the first place, beg leave to surmise that these perturbed dreams of our author were not the *direct* nor the *necessary* effects of opium. We grant, *indeed*, that the inordinate usage of this potent drug produced two effects of contributory or preparatory to the dreaming process described above. It heightened and rendered more vivid the trains of waking thought—and, in fact, the whole operations of the intellect; while it gradually, though slowly, deteriorated the functions of the digestive organs. But we do maintain that any other cause or combination of causes, capable of producing the same effects, mental and corporeal; whether wine, excessive study, sedentary habits, or even disease itself, would produce, to a greater or less extent, according to individual idiosyncrasy, the same phenomena, during sleep, which our author has described with so much spirit and feeling....

What then is the plain and obvious operation of opium (always meaning a moderate dose) which we see and feel, in others or in ourselves? The most constant and important effect is that of lessening the sensibility of the nervous system, and thus checking the transmission of sensations (or more strictly speaking *impressions*) to the sensorium, whether painful or pleasant. This reduction of *sensation* in the brain and nervous system does not appear to reduce the activity of *reflection*—on the contrary, the intellectual operations are quickened under the influence of opium—a proof that the action of the drug is not uniformly sedative or stimulant on all parts of the system....

3. From Review of *Confessions of an English Opium-Eater* (London: Taylor and Hessey, 1822), *The British Critic* 18 (November 1822): 531–32

The author of this little volume is a smart, clever person, but is so extremely anxious that the world should think him a *genius*, that it is really very difficult to distinguish, that part of his book which consists of sober truth, from that which is, perhaps, merely the effect of the large quantities of opium which he had, at one time of his life, been in the habit of taking. Whether the operation of this drug has produced any disease in the more solid parts of the understanding, it may be difficult to determine, from these "Confessions"; though from the strong tendency which all "opium eaters" exhibit, as we are told, to mystify their minds in the fumes of German metaphysics, we imagine that such a conclusion would not be unwarrantable. It is, however clear, if we take this work as the datum of our opinions, that the effects of opium are very fatal to those organs in which the propensity to "self-admiration resides"; converting that pardonable degree of vanity, which is necessary in order to keep a man upon tolerable terms with himself, into a morbid affection, which leads him not merely to exaggerate the importance and extent of the good qualities which he possesses, but to pride himself even upon what Mr. Burke calls "the shameful parts of his constitution"; making him believe, for example, that the dirtiness of his nails, or the holes in his small clothes, are as interesting in his case, as cleanliness and decency, in the case of others....

The long and short of these "Confessions" is, that the subject of them is a person, who in all other respects, is pretty much like many of his neighbours, except that from long habit he had brought himself to such an unnatural state as to be able to take, without any sensible inconvenience, 8000 drops of laudanum in a day; and that by painful and persevering efforts, he has detached himself from the horrible chain in which he was bound. The history which he gives of the progress of the diseased appetite which he had created, and of the symptoms attendant upon his cure, are however detailed with so much genius, and fancy, and poetry, and metaphysics—which things our author seems to consider as the basis of his character,—that we shall forbear from producing any extracts from this part of the work....

4. From Review of *Confessions of an English Opium-Eater* (London: Taylor and Hessey, 1822), *The British Review, and London Critical Journal* 20 (December 1822): 474–75, 488–89

A brain morbidly affected by long excess of indulgence in opium cannot reasonably be expected to display a very consistent or connected series of thoughts and impressions. The work before us is accordingly a performance without any intelligible drift or design. It is, however, a sort of kaleidoscope, presenting to the eye a great variety of dazzling forms and colours, symmetrically and harmoniously disposed and blended, and yet expressing nothing, and resembling nothing. It is not easy to say what the author intends by his book, except its sale and circulation; whether he means what he says, or if not all, how much;

whether he is serious, and if not always, when; whether he designs to deal in fact, or in fiction; whether he intends to praise, or to ridicule; to reverence, or to scoff; to laugh, or to cry; whether he is learned or unlearned; gloomy, or gay; busy, or idle; married, or single. After all, however, the scene spread before us is a very elegant tissue of confusion, a rich piece of mosaic, on which the eye of fancy, if not of intelligence, reposes with delight; and upon the whole without much danger; though we cannot say more for its morality, than that where it is lax or indecorous, it seems to be rather the effect of absence of thought, than want of principle.

Desultory and rambling as the thoughts of the opium-eater must be admitted to be, there is much evidence, throughout the volume, of a great kindness of disposition, and of what we should call good-heartedness; and he must be but little alive to the impressions of genuine humour, who does not often, in going through the work, feel its subtle agency upon his spirits, provoking him to laugh, without knowing, why or at what. There are also touches of pathos in these pages which show the author to be no stranger to the avenues that conduct to the interior of the bosom. Whether we are to attribute it to his opium, or to faculties original and improved which opium has not been able to overcome, we pretend not to say; but it is evident that the writer of this little book rules despotically an imaginative empire, which he can at any time lay under the largest contribution to his wants. If his opium is to have the credit of all this, and the sublime pictures of ideal combinations which have been drawn upon his fancy, and engraved upon his pages, are the literal products of his dreams while under the fascination of his celestial drug, we must take the account as altogether the most extraordinary of man, that has hitherto been authenticated; and that the author was well warranted in saying that opium, and not the opium-eater, is the hero of the tale.

... No book, we will venture to say, has ever so energetically depicted the pleasures and pains of opium. The balance is certainly very much on the side of the pains, looking only to its influence on the mind. The effects of this baneful drug, however, on the body, when taken for any but pure medicinal purposes, under the controul and discretion of professional experience, are exhibited in sundry forms of disease, in squalid enervation, and in accelerated old age. We trust our author has had enough of it; and as he probably has done dreaming, except according to the usage of his ancestors, we may hope for some useful products of his intelligent and active mind, without any things of Messrs.

Kant or Ricardo mingled in their substance; who, as they have been the companions of his morbid existence, may not safely be associated with his sound waking, and sober creations. If he can resolve to turn his future thoughts to what is useful, in this age of abused intellect, we heartily wish him long to live in all "sober certainty of waking bliss."[1]

5. From Review of *Confessions of an English Opium-Eater* (London: Taylor and Hessey, 1822), *The Monthly Review* 100 (March 1823): 288–89

The bare announcement of *Confessions* has in it something of a popular and attractive nature, not very easy for ordinary or indeed for *any* readers to resist. It would seem to imply the communication of matters which, for private and particular reasons, have hitherto been withholden from the public eye, yet are in some way so connected with individuals or with society as to be interesting to the community. To the usual attractions of auto-biography, this species of writing adds the novelty of obviously implied self-accusation; and we see the accuser and the accused standing forth in the same character, pleading guilty, and preparing to take their trial before the tribunal of their country. It would, then, be requiring too much from human curiosity to demand that it should be silent or affect indifference on such an occasion; and we thus find that, from the time of Jean-Jacques up to the present Opium-Eater, the world has been fond of assuming the character of a father-confessor, listening to the sins and errors of its votaries, and perhaps giving absolution with a kind and merciful spirit, provided that the detail be sufficiently instructive and amusing. We may add, also, that it is an infirmity of our common nature to be eager in receiving what was not exactly intended for its ears, whether this desire arises from a love of the marvellous, or of scandal, or of pure knowledge.

It is not, however, in this view only that the *Opium-Eater's Confessions* will be found intitled to a share of public regard; for the manner in which they are delivered, and their style of execution, confer on them a separate interest of their own. They have an air of reality and life; and they exhibit such strong graphic powers as to throw an interest and even a dignity round a subject which, in less able hands, might have been rendered a tissue of trifles and absurdities. They are, indeed, very picturesque and vivid

---

[1] From Milton, *Comus*. Comus says, upon hearing the Lady, "Such sober certainty of waking bliss, / I never heard till now" (263–64).

sketches of individual character and feelings; drawn with a boldness yet an exactness of pencil, that is to be found only in one or two prominent geniuses of our day. They have consequently met with a degree of attention and applause that is seldom accorded to auto-biographies even of a more important and laborious kind: but this is the privilege of genius; for, though they are not very instructive and edifying to a large portion of society, and can apply perhaps only to *a very select company* of *Opium-Eaters,* they are not therefore the less original and amusing. They combine strong sense with wild and somewhat fantastic inventions, accuracy of detail with poetic illustration, and analytical reasoning and metaphysical research with uncommon pathos and refinement of ideas. From the variety of opposite but good qualities which they exhibit, as well as from a ceratin *enjouement* and raciness of expression, we are inclined to suspect that they were poured forth under the operation of the *pleasures* rather than of the *pains* of opium; and we are the more confirmed in this opinion by the reasons which the writer assigns for not fulfilling his promise of giving us a third part: viz. the being subjected to such pangs from the want of the alluring drug as appear to have unfitted him for farther exertion.

6. From Review of *Confessions of an English Opium-Eater* (London: Taylor and Hessey, 1822), *The Eclectic Review* 19 (April 1823): 366, 371

We have for some time hesitated whether or not to notice this strange production. As a biographical romance, it contains so much that is objectionable and positively disgusting, that we should have not thought it advisable to give it a place in our pages. But as it aspires to the character of a medical document, we cannot altogether pass it over. An unauthenticated statement like the present, could not, indeed, be safely assumed as *data* for any conclusion of a scientific kind. The veracity and the competency of the witness, would require to be first ascertained; and in the present case, superadded to the usual fallaciousness of the accounts furnished by patients of themselves, we have the uncertainty arising from the patient's being an opium drunkard, and his discovering, notwithstanding his experience in the use of the article, great ignorance of his subject....

As to the unhappy Author of this production, although his flippancy and dogmatism might justify severity, his situation disarms us. Had he not painted the pleasures of opium in such glowing colours, we should have disposed to give him credit for intending, by this volume, to make

some atonement for the misspent and irrevocable past. But the seductive picture he presents is but too likely to tempt some of his readers to
begin a practice, in favour of which he cites so many illustrious and
noble precedents, and to outweigh the remote evils of what he represents as but an abuse of the habit. The work is written throughout in
the tone of apology for a secret, selfish, suicidal debauchery: it is the
physical suffering consequent upon it, that alone excites in the Writer
a moment's regret. In a medical point of view, the work is quite worthless: in a moral point of view, it is truly affecting. Its literary merits we
leave others to canvass.

7. From Review of *Confessions of an English Opium-Eater* (London: Taylor and Hessey, 1822), *The North American Review* 18 (January 1824): 91–92

Pain is, according to the doctrine of some wise men, the only motive
to action; and in their opinion, therefore, all this throng of men that we
see crowding and justling each other in the world, and crossing each
others' paths in all directions, is made up of so many *patients*, each in the
eager search of some particular remedy for the evil he feels or fears. But
of all the modes of assuaging present pain, or seeking present pleasure,
the most preposterous is that of sacrificing the means of future comfort;
and the habits least worthy of a thinking being, are those which make
the mind depend for its solaces and enjoyments, on physical sensations
and affections. The impulse of excited passions or appetite is allowed
by the world to be some apology for many acts, that would not otherwise be excusable; but it should seem incredible, that any person would
cooly, and with deliberate purpose, choose a substance to put into his
stomach, which, though it may dispel present anxiety, or call up a train
of agreeable images and sensations, is yet certain to remain in his system
a future poison, inducing pain, weakness, melancholy, and early decrepi-
tude. This is however done, more or less frequently, by many persons,
and most flagrantly of all, by those who resort to opium as a luxury. A
case of this description makes the subject of this book, of which we are
treating, and which the author professes to write to illustrate the moral
and physical decay and destruction consequent upon such a practice.
We believe that very few persons, if any, in this country, abandon themselves to the use of opium as a luxury; nor does there appear to be any
great danger of the introduction of this species of intemperance. The
history of a case is, therefore, the less important, as an illustration of the

fatal effects of this habit; and we accordingly notice this work, more as an object of taste and literary curiosity, than by way of warning persons against a pernicious practice.

8. From George Gilfillan, "Thomas De Quincey," *The Eclectic Review* 27 (April 1850): 399–401, 402, 405–6, 407

... Had the public, twenty years ago, feeling Mr. De Quincey to be one of the master spirits of the age, and, therefore, potentially, one of its greatest benefactors, inquired deliberately into his case, sought him out, put him beyond the reach of want, encouraged thus his heart, and strengthened his hand, rescued him from the mean miseries into which he was plunged, smiled approvingly upon the struggles he was making to conquer an evil habit—in one word, *recognised* him, what a different man had he been now, and over what magnificent wholes had we been rejoicing, in the shape of his works, instead of deploring powers and acquirements thrown away, in rearing towers of Babel, tantalizing in proportion to the magnitude of their design, and the beauty of their execution. Neglected and left alone as a corpse in the shroud of his own genius, a fugitive, though not a vagabond, compelled day after day to fight absolute starvation at the point of his pen, the marvel is, that he has written so much which the world may not willingly let die. *But*, it is the world's fault that the writings it now recognises, and may henceforth preserve on a high shelf, are rather the sublime ravings of De Quincey drunk, than the calm, profound cogitations of De Quincey sober.... He was never intoxicated with [opium] in his life; nay, he denies its power to intoxicate. Nor did it at all weaken his intellectual faculties, any more than it strengthened them. We have heard poor creatures consoling themselves for their inferiority by saying, "Coleridge would not have written so well but for opium." "No thanks to De Quincey for his subtlety—he owes it to opium." Let such persons swallow the drug, and try to write the "Suspiria," or the "Aids to Reflection."[1]
Coleridge and De Quincey were great in spite of their habits....
We pass gladly to the subject of his genius. That is certainly one of

---

[1] Coleridge, *Aids to Reflection, in the formation of a manly character, on the several grounds of prudence, morality, and religion* (1825). Along with Coleridge's *On the Constitution of Church and State according to the idea of each* (1830), *Aids* redeemed Coleridge's public image as failed poet and opium addict and cemented his influence on later Victorian notions of statehood, morality, and civic and cultural education. By comparing *Aids* to *Suspiria*, however, Gilfillan also suggests the work's philosophical brilliance.

the most singular in its power, variety, culture, and eccentricity, our age
has witnessed. His intellect is at once solid and subtle, reminding you
of veined and figured marble, so beautiful and evasive in aspect, that you
must touch ere you are certain of its firmness. The motion of his mind
is like that of dancing, but it is the dance of an elephant, or of a
Polyphemus,[1] with his heavy steps, thundering down the music to
which it moves. Hence his humour often seems forced in motion, while
always fine in spirit. The contrast between the slow march of his
sentences, the frequent gravity of his spirit, the recondite masses of his
lore, the logical severity of his diction, and his determination, at times,
to be desperately witty, produces a ludicrous effect, but somewhat different from what he had intended. It is "Laughter" lame, and only able to
hold one of his sides, so that you laugh at, as well as with him. But few,
we think, would have been hypercritical in judging of Columbus' first
attitudes as he stepped down upon his new world. And thus, let a great
intellectual explorer be permitted to occupy his own region, in whatever way, and with whatever ceremonies, may seem best to himself....

De Quincey's works, if collected, would certainly possess sufficient
bulk; they lie scattered, in prodigal profusion, through the thousand and
one volumes of our periodical literature: and we are certain, that a selection of their better portions would fill ten admirable octavos.[2] Mr. De
Quincey himself was lately urged to collect them. His reply was, "Sir,
the thing is absolutely, insuperably and for ever impossible. Not the
arch-angel Gabriel, nor his multipotent adversary,[3] durst attempt any
such thing!" We suspect, at least, that death must seal the lips of the "old
man eloquent," ere such a selection shall be made. And yet, in those
unsounded abysses, what treasures might be found—of criticism, of
logic, of wit, of metaphysical acumen, of research, of burning eloquence,
and essential poetry! ... As it is, his place in the future gallery of ages is
somewhat uncertain. For all he has hitherto done, or for all the impression he has made upon the world, his course may be marked as that of
a brilliant, but timid, meteor, shooting athwart the midnight, watched
by but few eyes, but accompanied by the keenest interest and admiration of those who did watch it. Passages of his writings may be

---

1 Odysseus blinded the Cyclops Polyphemus in order to escape from his cave.
2 Size of pieces of paper (about 6" x 9") cut from a sheet to form 8 pieces or 16 pages.
3 In *Paradise Lost* the arch-angel Gabriel stands charge at the Gate of Paradise to defend
   Eden's borders against Satan's entry; in Books 5 and 6, Raphael recounts to Adam how
   Michael and Gabriel fought Satan and his rebel armies; "multipotent" thus refers both to
   Satan's considerable power and to his various allies.

preserved in collections; and, among natural curiosities in the museum of man, his memory must assuredly be included as the greatest consumer of laudanum and learning—as possessing the most potent of brains, and the weakest of wills, of almost all men who ever lived.... De Quincey has never ceased to believe in Christianity. In an age when most men of letters have gone over to the sceptical side, and too often treat with insolent scorn, as sciolistic and shallow, those who still cling to the gospel, it is refreshing to find one who stands confessedly at the head of them all, in point of talent and learning, so intimately acquainted with the tenets, so profoundly impressed by the evidences, and so ready to do battle for the cause, of the blessed faith of Jesus....

9. From David Masson, Review of *Selections Grave and Gay,* from *Writings Published and Unpublished,* by Thomas De Quincey, Vols. I. and II.; containing "Autobiographic Sketches" (Edinburgh: James Hogg, 1853–54), in *British Quarterly Review* 20 (1854): 166–70, 184–87

By the established customs of all languages, there is an immense interval between the mental state accounted proper in prose composition, and that allowed, and even required, in verse. A man, for the most part, would be ashamed of permitting himself in prose the same freedom of intellectual whimsy, the same arbitrariness of combination, the same riot of imagery, the same care for the exquisite in sound and form, perhaps even the same depth and fervour of feeling, that he would exhibit unabashed in verse. There is an idea, as it were, that if the matter lying in the mind waiting for expression is of a very select and rare kind, or if the mood is peculiarly fine and elevated, a writer must quit the platform of prose, and ascend into the region of metre.... In short, we allow all ordinary business of a literary kind—plain statement, equable narrative, profound investigation, strong direct appeal—to be transacted in prose; we even permit a moderate amount of beauty, of enthusiasm, and of imaginative play to intermingle with the current of prose-composition; but there is a point, marked either by the unusual fineness of the matter of thought, its unusual arbitrariness and luxuriance, its unusual grandeur, or its unusually impassioned character, at which, by a sort of law of custom, a man must either consent to be silent, or must lift himself into verse. On such occasions it is as when a speaker is expected to leave his ordinary place in the body of the house and mount the tribune.... A man who writes in prose is, by the fact that he does so, kept within the bounds of prose in the character of his mental combinations. Those peculiar finenesses and flights of intellectual activity which are native to verse, are then simply not developed. His thoughts stop short precisely at that point of richness, quaintness, or luxuriance where prose ceases to be prose.... Where *is* that ideal point at which a man must either smother what is brewing in him, or ascend the tribune and speak in verse? What are the limits and capabilities of prose; and through what series of grada-tions does prose pass into technical and completed verse? If a man refuses to be whirled past the extreme prose point, what amount of farther intel-lectual possibility, and of what precise kind, does he thus forego? Is the ulterior region into which verse admits co-extensive with that which it leaves behind: and, if not, what is its measure? Does it overhang the realm of prose like superior ether, nearer the empyrean, or does it only softly round it to a small measurable distance? Is the relation of prose to verse that of absolute inferiority, or of inferiority in some respects counter-balanced by superiority in others? In short, what is it that verse can do that prose cannot, and what is the value of this special kind of intellec-tual work which only verse can transact?

... [T]here are passages in Mr. De Quincey's writings, whose power as specimens of impassioned and imaginative prose would be felt as something new. His *Confessions*, his *Suspiria de Profundis*, and even his present volumes of *Autobiographic Sketches*, contain passages which, for weird and sublime beauty, and for power of embodying the impalpable and the phantasmic, are not surpassed anywhere in poetry.... [N]o one can fail to remark, in exact accordance with what we have advanced in the course of this article, that precisely as the passion gains in force and intensity, and the pure process of poetic combination transacts itself with ease and a vigour, the language acquires and sustains a more decided metrical cadence. It would not be difficult to arrange parts of the passages so that what has been printed as prose should present to the eye the appearance of irregular verse. And so generally, a peculiar rhythm or music will always be found in highly impassioned or imaginative prose. The voice swells with its burthen; the hand rises and falls; and the foot beats time. And thus, as we have more than once said, prose passes into verse by visible gradations. Still, there is a clear line of separation between the most metrical prose, and what is conventionally recognised as verse; and with all the great effects that may be produced on this side of the line of separation, Prose, as such, is entitled to be credited. And why should not prose do its utmost? ... All speed, then, to the prose invasion of the peculiar realm of verse; and the farther the conquest can proceed, perhaps the better in the end for both parties. The time is perhaps coming when the best prose shall be more like verse than it now is, and the best verse shall not disdain a certain resemblance to prose.

10. Review of *Selections Grave and Gay*, from *Works Published and Unpublished*, by Thomas De Quincey, Vols. I, II, and III (London and Edinburgh: James Hogg & Sons, 1853–60), in *The Eclectic Review* ns. 8 (1854): 385–86, 387–88

... If genius be defined as originality of thought and style, we challenge this for De Quincey, in a degree as large, perhaps, as appertains to any man of the age. Connected with, and, in some respects, less than some of the Lakers, he is no more an imitator of theirs than Vesuvius is an imitator of Etna. If genius be defined to be a combination of imagination, passion, and constructive power, then, even in this sense, we maintain De Quincey's claim to its possession. All his earnest writings, especially his "Suspiria de Profundis," are as full of passion as of imagination; and what more exquisite than the construction of some of his dreams, and of all his sentences. The constructive power discovered in them might, in happier circumstances, and had it been attended by a sterner will, have reared the shapeliest and largest fabrics of intellectual masonry. Or if genius be identified with growth, and if that growth be most wonderful, which has taken place under difficulties, how marvellous above that of most men must be De Quincey's genius, which has grown under a self-imposed pressure as great as though a tree were to surmount the weight of the Sphynx, or the Pyramid of Cheops! ...

[De Quincey's *Works*] may be considered to constitute an irregular autobiography. This adds greatly to the charm of De Quincey's writings. You never long lose sight of himself. Even as in dreams, we become centrical to each shadowy scene, and pass with the swiftness of thought through a thousand shifting adventures, and, however fast the pageants sweep along, they never leave us behind; so with the writings of this marvellous magician. He is everywhere—not as if protruded by conceit—but as if he were a necessary part of every spectacle. In a nature so peculiar as his, egotism ceases to be egotism, and assumes a certain catholic air; you feel you cannot spare a single I—since each personal pronoun is an algebraic symbol of great and general truths. The littleness of ordinary egotism departs, and you feel, as it were, standing beside a great mountain which is speaking of itself in all its voices, in the torrents talking at its feet, in the pines moaning on its sides, in the notes of bees and birds, ravens and eagles, flitting over its herbless granite, or hovering in the air around, and in the thunder with which it has enwrapped its brow, all of which voices seem parts in one vast soliloquy, sounding through the eternal solitudes. Thus a man of genius may be represented when his demon has moved him to discourse of himself, and such is the sublime egotism of Rousseau, Wordsworth, Byron, and De Quincey.

The mind which can expect thus to interest the world in itself, must possess not merely great powers, but great peculiarities; much weakness as well as strength; many faults as well as virtues; must have struggled and suffered severely. The autobiography of a pure and passionless spirit, of a holy and happy angel, would be an insipid affair. It would possess little to commend it to the hearts of men. There must be vicissitude, anxiety, humanity, even folly and sin, united with moral resistance and virtue, great powers struggling with great difficulties of some kind, ere you can listen with an entire surrender of your spirit to a man speaking of himself.... Now, De Quincey's nature and powers are so peculiar, his history has been so diversified, and his errors and sufferings have been so considerable, that we feel he is entitled always to use the first person, and that he never writes so gracefully as when he does. A brain of such potency united to a bodily presence so "weak and contemptible," and to a will weaker still—an intellect so subtle, connected with an imagination so grand and massive—a temper so gentle and woman-like coupled with so much quick and searching misery—a mind so splendid, and yet, which has always shone through clouds, and sometimes been swathed in the "dunnest smoke of hell"[1]—the union of powers so commanding, so varied, and so highly cultivated, and of abject slavery to one unhappy habit—such are some of the contradictory materials out of which De Quincey has piled up his graven image of himself, an image resembling somewhat that which appeared to Nebuchadnezzar in dream[2]—its head of gold, breast of silver, legs of brass, and feet of iron, *mingled with miry clay.*

---

[1] Shakespeare, *Macbeth*; Lady Macbeth, anticipating the murder of Duncan, says: "Come, thick night, / And pall thee in the dunnest smoke of hell, / That my keen knife see not the wound it makes" (1.5.48–50).

[2] In Daniel 2:27–45, Daniel interprets King Nebuchadnezzar's dream of a "great image" whose "head *was* of fine gold, his breast and his arms of silver, his belly and his thighs of brass, his legs of iron, his feet part of iron and part of [miry] clay" (2:31–33).

11. From 1855 Letter from De Quincey to his daughter Emily about the expansion of *Confessions* for vol. 5 of *De Quincey's Works*, in Alexander H. Japp, *Thomas de Quincey: His Life and Writings. With Unpublished Correspondence*, 2 vols. (London: John Hogg, 1877), 2:109–10

Volume v. is on the point of closing, viz., "THE CONFESSIONS." It is almost rewritten; and there cannot be much doubt that here and there it is enlivened, and so far improved. To justify the enormous labour it has cost me, most certainly it *ought* to be improved. And yet, reviewing the volume as a *whole*, now that I can look back from nearly the end to the beginning, greatly I doubt whether many readers will not prefer it in its original fragmentary state to its present full-blown development. But if so, why could I not have felt this objection many weeks since, when it would have come in time to save me what has proved an exhausting labour. The truth is, I *did* feel it; but what countervailed that objection was secretly the following awkward dilemma:—A doubt had arisen whether, with my own horrible recoil from the labour of converging and unpacking all hoards of MSS., I could count upon bringing together enough of the "Suspiria" (yet unpublished) materially to enlarge the volume. If not, this volume (standing amongst sister volumes of 320 to 360 pp.) would present only a beggarly amount of 120 pp. upon which arose this dilemma—Either the volume must be strengthened by the addition of papers altogether alien, which to me was eminently disagreeable, as breaking up the unity of the volume— or else, if left in the slenderness of figure, would really to *my* feeling involve us in an act that looked very like swindling.... Such being the case, no remedy remained but that I should *doctor* the book, and expand it into a portliness that might countenance its price. I should, however, be misleading you if any impression were left upon your mind that I had eked out the volume by any wire-drawing[1] process: on the contrary, nothing has been added which did not originally belong to my outline of the work, having been left out chiefly through hurry at the period of first, *i.e.*, original, publication in the autumn of 1821....

---

[1]   To draw or stretch out forcibly to a rarefied point; to attenuate.

12. From "Thomas De Quincey," *The Athenæum* No. 1677 (December 1859): 814–15

... There is little that Charity would mention or be silent about with regard to Thomas De Quincey's life with which the public are not already familiar. Those of his writings which are of any value or interest contain the story of his friendships and quarrels, the dreams of his youth, the error of his manhood, and the disappointments of his riper age. In them he held up to public observation his moral infirmities, the pathetic secrets of his home, and the weaknesses of those friends who had cherished him in periods of mental distress and external trouble. As a writer he was an egotist, even more than a mystic. He could never take his pen in his hand without digressing from the subject immediately under consideration to personal feelings and individual experiences. Unfortunately for his reputation and his friends, with a mind so constituted he lived almost entirely in domestic retirement, and in following the bent of his genius, was guilty of betraying confidences that, as a man of honour, he ought to have held sacred. "The Confessions," the "Suspiria de Profundis," and his other autobiographical sketches, are at once the materials of his literary fame and the memorials of his life....

Of his writings, and all of them are steeped in egotism, "The Confessions" are the most characteristic. In their elegance of diction, playfulness of style, subdued pedantry, and utter shamelessness, the entire man is made known to the reader. The assurance with which he holds himself up to inspection as an instance of human misery—and not of guilt, at the very time that he explains with analytical exactness how indulgence in opium had robbed him of the energy to use his talents for his own good or that of others, is a marvellous instance of how a mind may by a habit of diseased introspection become so tolerant of its own deformities as to lose all sensitiveness about them. Surely his was the most unhealthy and abnormal mind to be found amongst modern writers. In many respects he resembled Coleridge,—in his love of classic literature and metaphysical inquiry, in the diversity of his intellectual sympathies, and in his habit of minutely dissecting his own emotions; but he lacked the philosophic breadth and genuine Christian goodness of the poet. Coleridge could not reflect without agonies of remorse on the moral infirmities,—which De Quincey, with as much flippancy as wit, wrote of as a condition bordering on jest....

13. Review of *The Works of Thomas De Quincey*, 15 vols. (Edinburgh: Adam & Charles Black, 1862–63), in *British Quarterly Review* 38 (1863): 14–16, 28–29

If we turn to the "Works," which so well fill these fifteen handsome volumes, we note that the longest of them are the "Confessions," the "Recollections of the English Lakes," and the "Autobiographic Sketches," each limited to a single volume; the first having been much increased by foot-notes and various addenda, and the last coming down only to 1814. The twelve remaining volumes are made up of eighty-four separate papers ... They treat, as we need hardly say, a vast variety of topics. But among them all is there, in our own judgment, not one great work, not a single essay, discussion, or treatise, or tale, on which a lasting literary reputation can be built. As it has been these last thirty years and more, so it will continue to be in the future: De Quincey will be the synonym of the Opium-eater, and the "Opium Confessions" will be their author's chief memorial. That several of the essays are of notable excellence, and show the presence of a master's hand, we most fully and heartily recognise; but this suffices not. He could have done and ought to have done more. He produced "studies" rather than works ...

In what sense De Quincey possessed genius we have several times thought would be a question not very easy to answer. Nay, presumptuous as it may seem, we very much doubt whether he ever set himself clearly to consider and resolve the question as to what genius *is*. He appears to us to speak of it either with sheer carelessness and haste, or under a settled and complete misconception. Certainly the word is one which we almost all use carelessly. For genius is the highest form in which the spiritual becomes incarnate for us, and were we to limit this name to the highest incarnations alone, it is manifest we should take away some of the grounds of our boasting and self-glorifying, and should have greatly to curtail the list of our declared greatest men. Yet the popular misuse of the word is attended with real inconveniences.... [S]omehow, genius and distinguished talent are being perpetually confounded, and that not only in merely popular usage and by the vulgar, but by our public writers, by our best speakers, and in the best society.... Shakespeare and Bacon had genius, if you like; but Thomas De Quincey had, according to our thinking, simply a fine, brilliant, and unusual talent, and of genius none at all....

... There is one word that never comes near [De Quincey's writings], and apparently never troubled the author of them: that word is Duty.

We say it with extreme regret, but the truth is, we do not see how a man with any sense of this could either have written what Mr. De Quincey has written, or have done, under like conditions of time and faculty, so little as Mr. De Quincey has done. He took opium at first to mitigate pain: he continued to take it as a merely sensational gratification. It made him, as we fear, little better than an artist, and, in his own degraded sense of the word, little better than a rhetorician. In a life of nearly seventy-five years, dedicated from childhood to the pursuits of the scholar and the man of letters, he achieved and secured for himself neither the respect and affection of his contemporaries, nor the making of his fame with posterity, but simply a by-name which we trust may never be challenged by another, THE ENGLISH OPIUM-EATER.

Appendix C: The Opium Question: History and Politics

1. From Jean-Baptiste Tavernier, *The Six Voyages of John Baptista Tavernier, Baron of Aubonne; through Turkey, into Persia and the East-Indies, for the Space of Forty Years* (London: Robert Littlebury and Moses Pitt, 1677), 1:242

Besides their Tobacco [the Turks] have also *Opium* made of Poppies, cut as they grow, out of which they draw the juice and make it into Pills. They take no more at first than the head of a pin, increasing their dose by degrees, till they come to take the quantity of half a wall-nut. When they are come to that pitch they dare not give over, for fear of endangering their lives, or addicting themselves to drink wine. In their youth you shall see these *Theriakis* or *takers of Opium*, with pale pensive and dejected countenances, and the use of their speech almost lost: If they omit to take for a day together this ill-continued drug that heats their brains, and causes them to act ridiculously and to talk idly, when it has done working, they are as cold and stupid as before, which obliges 'em to take it again. For this reason they are short liv'd: or if they do live till forty, they complain heavily of the pains that proceed from the cold venome of the herb. They that have a mind to kill themselves, swallow a large piece, and drink Vinegar after it, to prevent the relief of any other Counterpoyson, and so they dye smiling. They have another sort of drink to make themselves merry, which they call *Kokemaar*, composed of boyld Poppy seed. They take it in broth, and there are particular houses call'd *Kokemaar Krone*, where people meet to divertise those that see the ridiculous postures which that intoxicating drink causes them to shew. Before it works they quarrel with one another, and call one at other all to naught, but never fight. When the drug begins to work, they grow friends, and some are for making complements, others for telling a long tedious story, which renders them very vain.

2. From Sir John Chardin, *The Travels of Sir John Chardin into Persia and the East-Indies* (London: Moses Pitt, 1686), 243–45

As for Grave Men, that abstain from Wine, as forbidden and unlawful of it self, they warm and elivate themselves with Seed of Poppies, tho' it be more inebriating, and more fatal than Wine ... That Drug is pretty well known in our Country to be a Narcotick in the highest Degree, and a true Poison. The *Persians* find that it entertains their Fancies with pleasant Visions, and a kind of Rapture; those who take it, begin to feel the Effects of it an Hour after; ... After the Operation is over, the Body grows Cold, Pensive and Heavy, and remains in that Manner, Indolent and Drowsy, till the Pill is repeated.... But as little soever as one Accustoms himself to those Poppy Pills, one must constantly use them, and if one misses taking them but one Day, it is discern'd in one's Face and Body, which is cast into such a languishing State, as would move any one to Pity. It fares a great deal worse with those, in whom is rooted the Habit of taking that Poison, for if they forbear it, they endanger their Lives by it.... The Government has endeavour'd several times to prevent the Use of that Drug, upon the Account of the fatal Effects it has throughout the whole Kingdom, but it could never Compass it, for it is general a Disease, that out of ten Persons, you shall not find one clear from that ill Habit....

There is a Decoction of the Shell, and of the Seed of Poppies, which they call, *Locguenor*, and sell Publickly in all their Cities, as they do Coffee. 'Tis good Sport to be in those Decoction houses, among those that drink of them, and to observe them before the Operation, and after, during the Time of the Operation. When they come into the Decoction house, they are Dull, Pale, and Languishing, and soon after they have drunk two or three Cups of that Liquor, they are Peevish, and like Mad-Men, nothing Pleases them; they find Fault with any thing, and Quarrel together, but afterwards they are Friends again, and every Man giving up himself to his Predominant Inclination, the Amorous entertains with Love-stories to his Angel; another between Sleeping and Waking, laughs in his Sleeve; another Swaggers like a Hector; another tells a Story of a Cock and a Bull, in a Word, you would think you are really in a Madhouse. A sort of Drowsiness and Lethargy succeeds that uneven and immoderate Mirth: But the *Persians*, instead of calling it by its deserv'd Name, call it a Rapture, and maintain, that there is a Supernatural, and a Divine Impulse, in that Frame of Mind.

3. From William Marsden, *The History of Sumatra, Containing An Account of the Government, Laws, Customs, and Manners of the Native Inhabitants, with a Description of the Natural Productions, and a Relation of the Ancient Political State of that Island* (London: Thomas Payne and Son, 1783), 239–42

The Sumatrans, and more particularly the Malays, are much attached, in common with many other eastern people, to the custom of smoking *opium*. The poppy which produces it, not growing on the island, it is annually imported from Bengal in considerable quantities, in chests containing an hundred and forty pounds each. It is made up in cakes of five or six pound weight, and packed with dried leaves; in which situation it will continue good and valuable for two years, but after that period grows hard, and diminishes considerably in value. It is of a darker color, and has less strength than the Turkey opium. About an hundred and fifty chests are consumed annually on the West coast, where it is purchased, on an average, at three hundred dollars the chest, and sold again at five or six. But on occasion of extraordinary scarcity I have known it to sell for it's weight in silver, and a single chest to fetch upwards of three thousand dollars.

The method of preparing it for use is as follows. The raw opium is first boiled or seethed in a copper vessel; then strained through a cloth, to free it from impurities; and then a second time boiled. The leaf of the *bacoo*, shred fine, is mixed with it, in a quantity sufficient to absorb the whole; and it is afterwards made up into small pills, about the size of a pea, for smoking. One of these being put into the small tube that projects from the side of the opium pipe, that tube is applied to a lamp, and the pill being lighted, is consumed at one whiff, or inflation of the lungs....

The use of opium among these people, as that of intoxicating liquors among other nations, is a species of luxury, which all ranks adopt according to their ability, and which, when once become habitual, it is almost impossible to shake off. Being however, like other luxuries, expensive, few only, among the lower class of people, can compass the regular enjoyment of it; even where it's use is not restrained, as it is among the pepper planters, to the times of their festivals. That the practice of opium smoking must be some degree prejudicial to the health, is highly probable; yet I am inclined to think that effects have been attributed to it, much more pernicious to the constitution, than it is in reality the cause of.... It has been usual also to attribute to the practice, destructive consequences of another nature; from the frenzy it has been supposed to excite in those who take it in quantities. But this should probably rank with the many errors that mankind have been led into, by travellers addicted to the marvellous; and there is every reason to believe, that the furious quarrels, desperate assassinations, and sanguinary attacks, which the use of opium is said to give birth to, are idle notions, originally adopted through ignorance, and since maintained, from the mere want of investigation, without having any solid foundation. That those desperate acts of indiscriminate murder, called by us, *mucks*, and by the natives, *mongamo*, do actually take place, and in some parts of the east, frequently, (on Java in particular) is not to be controverted; but it is not equally evident that they proceed from any intoxication, except that of their unruly passions. Too often they are occasioned by excess of cruelty and injustice in their oppressors....

It is true that the Malays, when, in a state of war, they are bent on any daring enterprize, fortify themselves with a few whiffs of opium, to render them insensible to danger; as the people of another nation are said to take a dram; but it must be observed that, the resolution for this act, precedes, and is not the effect of the intoxication. They take the same precaution, previous to being led to public execution, but on these occasions shew greater signs of stupidity, than frenzy. Upon the whole, it may be reasonably concluded, that the sanguinary achievements, for which the Malays have been famous, or infamous rather, in history, are more justly derived from the natural ferocity of their disposition, than from the qualities of the drug whatever. The pretext of the soldiers of the country guard, for using opium, is, that it may render them watchful on their nightly posts: we, on the contrary, administer it to procure sleep; and according to the quantity it has either effect. The delirium it produces is known to be so very pleasing, that Pope has supposed this to have been designed by Homer, when he describes the delicious draught prepared by Helen, called *Nepenthe*, which exhilarated the spirits, and banished from the mind the recollection of woe.

4. From Thomas Robert Malthus, *An essay on the principle of population, or, A view of its past and present effects on human happiness: with an inquiry into our prospects respecting the future removal or migration of the evils which it occasions.* **2nd ed. (London: J. Johnson, 1806), 11–17, 356–59**

[T]he power of population is indefinitely greater than the power in the earth to produce subsistence for man. Population, when unchecked, increases in a geometrical ratio. Subsistence increases only in an arithmetical ratio. A slight acquaintance with numbers will shew the immensity of the first power in comparison of the second. By that law of our nature which makes food necessary to the life of man, the effects of these two unequal powers must be kept equal. This implies a strong and constantly operating check on population from the difficulty of subsistence. This difficulty must fall some where; and must necessarily be severely felt by a large portion of mankind. Through the animal and vegetable kingdoms, nature has scattered the seeds of life abroad with the most profuse and liberal hand. She has been comparatively sparing in the room, and the nourishment necessary to rear them. The germs of existence contained in this spot of earth, with ample food, and ample room to expand in, would fill millions of worlds in the course of a few thousand years. Necessity, that imperious all pervading law of nature, restrains them within the prescribed bounds. The race of plants, and the race of animals shrink under this great restrictive law. And the race of man cannot, by any efforts of reason, escape from it. Among plants and animals its effects are waste of feed, sickness, and premature death. Among mankind, misery and vice....

This natural inequality of the two powers of population, and of production in the earth, and that great law of our nature which must constantly keep their effects equal, form the great difficulty that to me appears insurmountable in the way to the perfectibility of society. All other arguments are slight and subordinate consideration in comparison of this. I see no way by which man can escape from the weight of this law which pervades all animated nature. No fancied inequality, no agrarian regulations in their utmost extent, could remove the pressure of it even for a single century. And it appears, therefore, to be decisive against the possible existence of a society, all members of which should live in ease, happiness, and comparative leisure; and feel no anxiety about providing the means of subsistence for themselves and families....

The first great awakeners of the mind seem to be the wants of the body. They are the first stimulants that rouse the brain of infant man into sentient activity: and such seems to be the sluggishness of original matter, that unless, by a peculiar course of excitements, other wants, equally powerful, are generated, these stimulants seem, even afterwards, to be necessary, to continue that activity which they first awakened. The savage would slumber for ever under his tree, unless he were roused from his torpor by the cravings of hunger, or the pinchings of cold; and the exertions that he makes to avoid these evils, by procuring food, and building himself a covering, are the exercises which form and keep in motion his faculties, which otherwise would sink into listless inactivity. From all that experience has taught us concerning the structure of the human mind, if those stimulants to exertion, which arise from the wants of the body, were removed from the mass of mankind, we have much more reason to think, that they would be sunk to the level of brutes, from a deficiency of excitements, than that they would be raised to the rank of philosophers by the possession of leisure. In those countries, where nature is the most redundant in spontaneous produce, the inhabitants will not be found the most remarkable for acuteness of intellect. Necessity has been with great truth called the mother of invention. Some of the noblest exertions of the human mind have been set in motion by the necessity of satisfying the wants of the body. Want has not unfrequently given wings to the imagination of the poet; pointed the flowing periods of the historian; and added acuteness to the researches of the philosopher: and though there are undoubtedly many minds at present, so far improved by the various excitements of knowledge, or of social sympathy, that they would not relapse into listlessness, if their bodily stimulants were removed; yet, it can scarcely be doubted, that these stimulants could not be withdrawn from the mass of mankind, without producing a general and fatal torpor, destructive of all the germs of future improvement.

5. From David Ricardo, *The Principles of Political Economy and Taxation* (London: J. Murray, 1817), 93–95

In those countries where there is an abundance of fertile land, but where, from the ignorance, indolence, and barbarism of the inhabitants, they are exposed to all the evils of want and famine, and where it has been said that population presses against the means of subsistence, a very different remedy should be applied from that which is necessary in long settled countries, where, from the diminishing rate of the supply of raw produce, all the evils of a crowded population are experienced. In the one case, the evil proceeds from a want of education in all ranks of the people. To be made happier they require only to be better governed and instructed, as the augmentation of capital, beyond the augmentation of people, would be the inevitable result. No increase in the population can be too great, as the powers of production are still greater. In the other case, the population increases faster than the funds required for its support. Every exertion of industry, unless accompanied by a diminished rate of increase in the population, will add to the evil, for production cannot keep pace with it.

With a population pressing against the means of subsistence, the only remedies are either a reduction of people or a more rapid accumulation of capital. In rich countries, where all the fertile land is already cultivated, the latter remedy is neither very practicable nor very desirable, because its effort would be, if pushed very far, to render all classes equally poor. But in poor countries, where there are abundant means of production in store, from fertile land not yet brought into cultivation, it is the only safe and efficacious means of removing the evil, particularly as its effect would be to elevate all classes of the people.

The friends of humanity cannot but wish that in all countries the labouring classes should have a taste for comforts and enjoyments, and that they should be stimulated by all legal means in their exertions to procure them. There cannot be a better security against a superabundant population. In those countries where the labouring classes have the fewest wants, and are contented with the cheapest food, the people are exposed to the greatest vicissitudes and miseries. They have no place of refuge from calamity; they cannot seek safety in a lower station; they are already so low that they can fall no lower. On any deficiency of the chief article of their subsistence there are few substitutes of which they can avail themselves and dearth to them is attended with almost all the evils of famine.

6. From R.R. Madden, *Travels in Turkey, Egypt, Nubia, and Palestine, in 1824, 1825, 1826, & 1827*, 2 vols., 2nd ed. (London: Whittaker, Treacher, and Co., 1833), 1:18–21

I had heard so many contradictory reports of the sensations produced by this drug, that I resolved to know the truth, and, accordingly, took my seat in the coffeehouse, with half a dozen *Theriakis*. Their gestures were frightful; those who were completely under the influence of the opium talked incoherently, their features were flushed, their eyes had an unnatural brilliancy, and the general expression of their countenances was horribly wild. The effect is usually produced in two hours, and last four or five: the dose varies from three grains to a drachm. I saw one old man take four pills, of five or six grains each, in the course of two hours; I was told he had been using opium for five and twenty years; but this is a very rare example of an opium eater passing thirty years of age, if he commence the practice early. The debility, both moral and physical, attendant on its excitement, is terrible; the appetite is soon destroyed, every fibre of the body trembles, the nervous system becomes disordered, but still they cannot abandon the custom: they are miserable till the hour arrives for taking their daily dose; and when its delightful influence begins, they are all fire and animation. Some of them compose excellent verses, and others address the bystanders in the most eloquent discourses, imagining themselves emperors, and owners of all the harems in the world. I commenced with one grain; in the course of an hour and a half it produced no perceptible effect ... After two hours and a half from the first dose, I took two grains more; and shortly after this dose, my spirits became sensibly excited: the pleasure of the sensation seemed to depend on an universal expansion of mind and matter. My faculties appeared enlarged: every thing I looked on seemed increased in volume; I had no longer the same pleasure when I closed my eyes which I had when they were open; it appeared to me as if it was only external objects, which were acted on by the imagination, and magnified into images of pleasure ... I made my way home as fast as possible, dreading, at every step, that I should commit some extravagance. In walking, I was hardly sensible of my feet touching the ground, it seemed as if I slid along the street, impelled by some invisible agent, and that my blood was composed of some etherial fluid, which rendered my body lighter than air. I got to bed the moment I reached home. The most extraordinary visions filled my brain all night. In the morning I rose, pale and dispirited: my head ached; my body was so debilitated that I was obliged to remain on the sofa all the day, dearly paying for my first essay at opium eating.

7. From John Francis Davis, *The Chinese: A General Description of The Empire of China and Its Inhabitants*, 2 vols. (London: Charles Knight and Co., 1836), 2:432–36

The engrossing taste of all ranks and degrees in China for *opium*, a drug whose importation has of late years exceeded the aggregate value of every other English import combined, deserves some particular notice, especially in connection with the revenues of British India, of which it forms an important item. The use of this pernicious narcotic has become as extensive as the increasing demand for it was rapid from the first. The contraband trade (for opium has always been prohibited as hurtful to the health and morals of the people) was originally at Macao; but we have already seen that the Portugese of that place, by their short-sighted rapacity, drove it to the island of Lintin,[1] where the opium is kept stored in armed ships, and delivered to the Chinese smugglers by written orders from Canton, on the sales being concluded, and the money paid, at that place.... This had, at length, the effect of drawing the serious attention of the Peking government to the growing evil, and it seems certain that the aggregate value of the importation, which in 1832 exceeded the enormous amount of 15,000,000 dollars, or between three and four millions sterling, has since diminished....

It seems that opium is almost entirely imported from abroad; worthless subordinates in offices, and nefarious traders, first introduced the abuse; young persons of family, wealthy citizens and merchants, adopted the custom, until at last it reached the common people. I have learned on inquiry, from scholars and official persons, that opium-smokers exist in all the provinces, but the larger proportion of these are to be found in the government offices; and that it would be a fallacy to suppose that there are not smokers among all ranks of civil and military officers, below the station of provincial governors and their deputies. The magistrates of districts issue proclamations, interdicting the clandestine sale of opium, at the same time that their kindred, and clerks, and servants smoke it as before. Then the nefarious traders make a pretext of the interdict for raising the price. The police, influenced by the people in the public offices, become the secret purchasers of opium, instead of labouring for its suppression; and thus all interdicts and regulations become vain.... The amount of the opium, imported by us, has thus been greater than that of tea exported. The pernicious drug, sold to the Chinese, has exceeded in market-value the wholesome leaf that has been purchased from them; and the balance of the trade has been paid to us in silver. The opium of late certainly exhibits a decrease in sale-amount, compared with some former years; but the effect of the new law against it in China remains yet to be fully ascertained. Its consumption, at least until that law was passed, pervaded all classes, and had spread with astonishing rapidity through the country.

---

[1]   Lintin and Macao, above: ports of entry for British ships in Southeast China.

8. From Samuel Morewood, *A Philosophical and Statistical History of the Inventions and Customs of Ancient and Modern Nations in the Manufacture and Use of Inebriating Liquors*. 2nd ed. (Dublin and London, 1838), 107–8, 113–14, 130–34

The people of Java indulge to excess in the use of [opium]. Upon such of them, as well natives as slaves, who have become desperate by the pressure of misfortune or disappointment, it operates in a frightful manner, giving them an artificial courage, and rendering them frantic, in which state they sally forth, in all the horrors of despair, to attack the object of their hatred, crying *amok! amok!* which signifies kill! kill! Thus infuriated, they indiscriminately stab every person they meet, till self-preservation at length renders it necessary to destroy them. This is what is termed *running a muck*.

An English ambassador, lately sent to a Mahometan prince, was conducted, upon his arrival at the palace, through several richly-decorated and spacious apartments, crowded with officers arrayed in superb dresses, to a room, small in dimensions, but ornamented with the most splendid and costly furniture. The attendants withdrew. After a short interval, two persons, of superior mien, entered the saloon, followed by state-bearers, carrying under a lofty canopy a litter covered with delicate silks, and the richest Cashmere shawls, upon which lay a human form to all appearance dead, except that its head was dangling loosely from side to side, as the bearers moved into the room. Two officers, holding rich fillagree salvers, carried each a chalice, and a vial containing a black fluid. The ambassador, considering the spectacle to be connected with some court ceremony of mourning, endeavoured to retire; but he was soon undeceived by seeing the officers holding up the head of the apparent corpse, and, after gently chafing the throat and returning the tongue, which hung from a mouth relaxed and gaping, pouring some of the black liquor into the throat, and closing the jaws until it sank down the passage. After six or seven times repeating the ceremony, the figure opened its eyes, and shut its mouth voluntarily; it then swallowed a large portion of the black fluid, and, within an hour, an animated being sat on the couch, with blood returning into his lips, and a feeble power of articulation. In the Persian language he addressed his visiter [sic], and inquired the particulars of his mission. Within two hours this extraordinary person became alert, and his mind capable of arduous business. The ambassador, after apologizing for the liberty, ventured to inquire into the cause of the scene which he had just witnessed. "Sir," said he, "I am an inveterate opium-taker; I have by slow degrees fallen into this melancholy process. Out of the diurnal twenty-four periods of time, I continually pass eighteen in this reverie.— Unable to move, or to speak, I am yet conscious, and the time passes away amid pleasing phantasies; nor should I ever awake from the wanderings of this state, had I not the most faithful and attached servants, whose regard and religious duty impel them to watch my pulse. As soon as my heart begins to falter, and my breathing is imperceptible, except on a mirror, they immediately pour the solution of opium into my throat, and restore me as you have seen.—Within four hours I shall have swallowed many ounces, and much time will not pass away, ere I relapse into my ordinary torpor."

In Great Britain, opium has been more used as a medicine than as an exciter of the spirits, although its infatuating influence is not altogether unknown in those countries, since the reveries of Asiatic luxury and effeminacy have in too many instances infected the manners and habits of the British people. To what extent an Englishman may be brought to take this opiate, is exemplified in the admirable and well-written "Confessions of an Opium Eater," first published in the London Magazine for October, 1821, and since in a separate volume.... The power of this drug affects the imagination with visions of substantial delights, which no other narcotic has ever yet been found to produce; and man under its influence associates, with his own station in life, those pleasurable images which he is led to believe would render him happy. But it may be said, that the usual effects of opium are to raise the spirits and elevate the mind, and when the body is not labouring under disease, it raises the moral affections to a state of cloudless serenity, over which the diviner spirit of our nature is paramount. This effect of the drug continues so long as the constitution is able to bear the ravages of its influence, for its fascinations are such, that, like the wand of a magician, it creates a visionary temple round its victim, and leads him through the mazes of delights, till at length he falls a sacrifice at the altar of his own imagination....

9. From W.H. Medhurst, *China: Its State and Prospects, with Especial Reference to the Spread of the Gospel: Containing Allusions to the Antiquity, Extent, Population, Civilization, Literature, and Religion of the Chinese* (London: John Snow, 1838), 56–57, 83–84

From 1792 to 1812, a period of twenty years, the increase [in the population of the Chinese] has been inconsiderable compared with former years, being only one-sixth of the whole, and scarcely an addition of one percent per annum. This diminution in the rate of increase, during the last twenty years, previous to 1812, may be accounted for, partially by the growth of emigration, and, more fully, by the *introduction of opium*, which since the latter part of the last century, has been smuggled into the country, at an enormous rate. Those who have not seen the effects of opium smoking, in the eastern world, can hardly form any conception of its injurious results on the health, energies, and lives of those who indulge in it. The debilitating of the constitution, and the shortening of life, are sure to follow, in a few years, after the practice has been commenced; as soon and as certainly, if not much more so, than is seen to be the case with those unhappy persons, who are addicted to the use of ardent spirits. The dealers in opium are little aware how much harm they are the instruments of doing, by carrying on this demoralizing and destructive traffic; but, the difference between the increase of the Chinese people, before and after the introduction of opium, ought to open their eyes, and lead them to ask themselves whether they are not accountable for the diseases and deaths of all those, who have suffered by its introduction. And if it be true that the Chinese increased at the rate of three per cent. per annum, before the commencement of the traffic, and at the rate of one per cent. per annum, since, it would be well for them to consider, whether the deficiency is not to be attributed, in some degree, to opium, and the guilt to be laid at the door of those who are instrumental in introducing it. They may flatter themselves, that if the growth of population were not thus checked by the introduction of opium, its increase would be curtailed by wars or pestilences; or the superabundant populace would perish by famine, and starvation effect what opium would not accomplish. Still, whatever cause might contribute to the balancing of the population with the means of subsistence, human life could not be sacrificed, without blame being attached somewhere; and blame, in proportion to the greatness of the evil which might result from the measure.

... When the habit is once formed, it grows till it becomes inveterate; discontinuance is more and more difficult, until at length, the sudden deprivation of the accustomed indulgence produces certain death. In proportion as the wretched victim comes under the power of the infatuating drug, so is his ability to resist temptation less strong; and debilitated in body as well as mind, he is unable to earn his usual pittance, and not unfrequently sinks under the cravings of an appetite, which he is unable to gratify. Thus they may be seen, hanging their heads by the doors of the opium shops, which the hard hearted keepers, having fleeced them out of their all, will not permit them to enter; and shut out from their own dwellings, either by angry relatives or ruthless creditors, they die in the streets unpitied and despised. It would be well, if the rich opium merchant, were sometimes present to witness such scenes as these, that he might be aware how his wretched customers terminate their course, and see where his speculations, in thousands of instances, end. When the issue of this pernicious habit is not fatal, its tendencies are to weaken the strength, and to undermine the constitution; while the time and property spent in this voluptuous indulgence, constitute so much detracted from the wealth and industry of the country, and tend to plunge into deeper distress those weak and dependent members of society, who are already scarcely able to subsist at all.

10. From Rev. Algernon S. Thelwall, *The Iniquities of the Opium Trade with China; being a Development of the Main Causes which exclude The Merchants of Great Britain from the advantages of an Unrestricted commercial intercourse with that vast empire* (London: Wm. H. Allen and Co., 1839), 134–36, 139–45, 158, 172–74

Ruling an empire upon which the sun never sets—possessed of an extent of dominion, such as Rome in her greatest glory never saw—and containing a population, with which no empire upon earth but that of China can compare,—Great Britain, in regard to all the elements of earthly glory,—in regard to power, dominion, and wealth,—seems indeed to be lifted up as an object of admiration and envy to the whole world. And great in proportion to the glory and exaltation of our country, must be her responsibility in the sight of Him, before whom all nations are counted as the drop on the bucket, and as the small dust of the balance. And the consideration of this responsibility becomes more solemn, when we consider the vast multitudes of *Heathen* that are subject to the British sceptre. It has been calculated that the Heathen and Mohammedan subjects of Queen Victoria are not less in number than 130,000,000! and if to this number, directly under the dominion of Great Britain, should be added the population of the allied and tributary states of India, which are under British influence and protection, it seems probable that 230,000,000 would be much nearer the mark.

Then—as if the mere extent of earthly glory and dominion were not abundantly sufficient to provoke the envy, and, with the envy, the secret hatred of all other nations—how much has there been beside, arising out of various circumstances of our past history, to excite still deeper feelings of hostility! Insomuch that, be the causes what they may, is it not the fact, that we have not *now* a true and trustworthy friend among all the nations of the earth?—that there is not one people under heaven, that would not, openly or secretly, rejoice and triumph at the humiliation of Great Britain? Yet, if we compare the state of our defences with the vast extent of our possessions—the measureless line of coast and frontier which is obvious to attacks that would most seriously affect us—was ever a great nation in such a defenceless position? Or do we find, within our own narrow boundaries, that union which is strength?

... Must we not conceive it a very possible thing, yea, highly probable, that Chinese statesmen and patriots will say respecting us—"Shall we open our ports *to wholesale smugglers,* and *to wholesale dealers in poison?* Shall we put these foreign smugglers and murderers upon an equal footing with our own peaceable and injured subjects? Shall we deal with them, or communicate with them, as if they were honest men, or worthy of any respect? Have they not reason to be well content, that we suffer them to live? and to marvel at our forbearance, that we have not long since expelled them from our boundaries, never to return, or put them to death without mercy?"

The very thought of their using such language respecting us may be very humiliating—very galling to our national pride: but is it not *natural* that *they* should use it? Let us put ourselves in their place, and think with ourselves, how *we* should judge concerning a people, whose very name we could not dissociate in our minds from the constant, determined practice of smuggling poison into our country, that was ruining and destroying thousands of our population every year?

I desire—I call for—calm consideration of the facts of the case. Nor do I wish any one to take these facts upon my word. I have never been in China, nor in the East-Indies; I therefore cannot speak as an eye and ear witness of these facts; but I fairly and faithfully laid before you the whole of the evidence that has reached me. I have submitted the statement to those who have been in India and China, and they assure me that my statement is correct....

Is it self-evident, that we hold our Eastern Empire by *moral power,* and not by *physical strength?* And do we acknowledge the vast importance of that *moral power,* which is greater than fleets and armies?

Is it, indeed, one of the foremost elements of national strength and greatness, and one of the strongest bulwarks of national security? If so, how stands our national character in the East, with reference hereunto?

How *is* this affected?—How *must* this be affected—by the fact, that, while we profess and call ourselves Christians, in opposition to the poor idolatrous Heathen,—enlightened and civilized, in opposition to a dark and ignorant, and (at best) semi-barbarous people,—we are seen continually implicated in iniquities, which the natives of India and of China have discernment enough to look upon with detestation? The heathen government of China has long regarded opium smoking, and the opium trade, with such just and merited abhorence [sic], that it utterly refuses to grow rich, and to increase its resources, by the sanction of one or the other! Shall *we*, then, consent, as Christians and as Britons, to lend ourselves to this traffic? to amass wealth by dealing in poison? to be judged in the eyes of half the population of the world—to have our national character estimated among five hundred millions of our fellow-creatures, mainly by the obvious, well-known fact, that *thus* it is that we grow rich? ...

... I have called attention to facts and documents: and documents and facts are stubborn things. *If* these documents be authentic, and *if* those facts be proved, I ask of every considerate and reflecting man, Can it be doubted but that the name and profession of Christianity is grossly dishonoured by the fact (well known throughout Eastern Asia), that those who profess and call themselves Christians are systematically and perseveringly engaged in this iniquitous and poisonous traffic? that our national character is degraded, and covered with infamy too well deserved, among the nations of the East? that, in connexion herewith, and as an inevitable consequence, the sinews of our strength are enervated, and the very foundations of our power in India perilled and endangered? that the greatest market in the world is comparatively closed—and that justly—against the productions of our national industry? that we are deservedly excluded from all honourable and comfortable intercourse—commercial or diplomatic—with the most populous Empire upon earth? that the cause of the glorious Gospel of Christ itself is compromised, and the progress of Christian missions among half the population of the globe is effectually impeded? and that among three hundred, or rather five hundred, millions of our fellow-men, we are justly branded as wholesale corrupters and murderers of an unoffending people? And all this for the sordid lust of gain!!

11. From Thomas De Quincey, "The Opium and the China Question," *Blackwood's Edinburgh Magazine* 47 (June 1840): 717–38

The power of gravitation is the greatest we know of; yet it is nothing at all if you would apply it to the sending up of rockets. The English navy might as reasonably throw bomb-shells into the crater of Vesuvius, by way of bidding it be quiet, or into the Kingdom of the Birds above us, as seek to make any deep impression upon such a vast callous hulk as the Chinese empire. It is defended by its essential non-irritability, arising out of the intense non-development of its resources; were it better developed, China would become an *organized* state, a *power* like Britain: at present it is an inorganic mass—something to be kicked, but which cannot kick again—having no commerce worth counting—no vast establishments of maritime industry—no arsenals—no shipbuilding towns—no Portsmouths, Deals, Deptfords, Woolwiches, Sunderlands, Newcastles, Liverpools, Bristols, Glasgows; in short, no vital parts–no organs–no heart–no lungs. As well deliver you broadsides against the impassive air; or, Prospero's words, "Stab the still closing waters / With all-bemock'd-at wounds."[1] ... China is, like Russia, defensible, without effort of her men, by her own immeasurable extent, combined with the fact of having no vulnerable organs—no local concentrations of the national power in which a mortal wound can be planted. There lay the mistake of Napoleon in his desperate anabasis to Moscow: in the whole area of interminable Muscovy, which centuries could not effectually traverse with armies, there was but one weak or vulnerable place, and that was the heart of the Czar. But it was too deadly a stake to throw upon that single chance the fate of so vast an army, and the future *préstige* of the French military name.... [A]ll had perished that *could* perish for Russia, after which every loss must be a French loss. Even without the winter, the French army was a condemned body after that. *There* surely was a deadly miscalculation. And such a miscalculation is ours in meditating the retrieval of our losses by war upon this inert and most lubberly of masses.

... War, as a measure of finance—as a mere resource of a delinquent and failing exchequer, is certainly less likely to succeed with an empire like China, so compact, so continental, so remote—and, beyond all

---

[1] *"stab ... wounds"*: misquotation of Shakespeare, *The Tempest* (3.3.63-4); the speech is Ariel's: "The elements, / Of whom your swords are tempered, may as well / Wound the loud winds, or with bemocked-at stabs / Kill the still-closing waters ... " (3.3.61-4).

other disqualifying circumstances, so inorganic—than with any other in the known world. The French have an expression for a man who is much mixed up in social relations—that he is *repandu dans le monde*; or, as Lord Bolingbroke once said of Pope, by translating that phrase, *scattered and diffused in society*. Now this is the very description of our own English condition as a people; and, above all other facts, it proclaims our indomitable energy, and our courageous self-dependence. Of all nations that ever have been heard of, we are the most scattered and exposed: we are to be reached by a thousand wounds in thousands of outlying extremities; the very outposts of civilisation are held by Englishmen, every where maintaining a reserve of reliance upon the mighty mother in Europe—every where looking to her in the last extremities for aid, or for summary vengeance, in the case of her aid coming too late; but all alike, in the ordinary state of things, relying upon themselves against all enemies; and thinking it sufficient matter of gratitude to England that she has sent them out with stout arms—with a reverence for laws—with constitutional energy, and, above all, with a pure religion. Such are we English people—such is the English condition. Now, what we are in the very supreme degree, that is China in the lowest. We are the least defended by massy concentration—she the most so. WE have the colonial instinct in the strongest degree—China in the lowest. With us the impulses of expatriation are almost morbid in their activity—in China they are undoubtedly morbid in their torpor.

Appendix D: The Opium Question: Medicine and Psychology

1. From Andrew Baxter, *An Enquiry into the Nature of the Human Soul*, 2nd ed., 2 vols. (London, 1737), 2:47–48, 145–46, 155–56

... [T]hus by easy steps we see, *that dreaming may degenerate into possession*; and that the cause and nature of both is the same, differing only in degree; for *dreaming* is but *possession in sleep*, from which we are relieved again when we awake, and external objects being to solicit the perceptivity through the senses: but the other possession is more stubborn, and not to be displaced so easily. We may conceive, when such a being is allowed the ascendant over our ordinary sensations and ideas, it will keep up that power as long as possible.... Now it is not easy to conceive what can be meant by not *letting our imaginations loose upon us*, unless it be understood of restraining the power of these invisible beings, which would otherwise incessantly distress the soul with such unpleasing sights....

Let us consider the disease called the *Incubus*, or *night-mare*, which many persons are tormented with in their sleep. It is generally accompanied with frightful, ghastly apparitions, which are then obtruded on the imagination; so that the *party* is made to fancy that the distemper itself proceeds from *their* pressing him down with a weight like to stifle him.... And this, I believe, is allowed to be a casual distemper of the brain, by which the animal spirits are obstructed. But now the bodily indisposition here, and the disagreeable vision made to accompany it, are *two very different things*: and as it would be absurd to make the *disorder* of the material organ the *efficient cause* of the apparitions that are exhibited along with it; for these are often *ugly phantoms*, which to fright us the more, appear to have bad designs upon us, threaten us, wrestle with us, get us down, all which infer a designing, intelligent cause: so, their being exhibited along with it, and adapted to it, shews us, I think, that these beings wait for, and catch the opportunity of the indisposition of the body, to represent at the same time something terrifying also to the mind.

2. From George Young, *A Treatise on Opium, Founded upon Practical Observations* (London, 1753), v–ix, 110–11

... [O]pium is a poison by which great numbers are daily destroyed; not, indeed, by such doses as kill suddenly, for that happens very seldom, but by its being given unseasonably in such diseases and to such constitutions for which it is not proper. Everybody knows that a large dose of laudanum will kill, and, therefore, they need not be cautioned on that head; but there are few who consider it as a slow poison, though it certainly is so, when improperly given. Here it is, that cautions are necessary, and the rather, because its operation is sometimes so slow and gradual, that the true cause of the patient's death is not suspected, even by the prescriber himself, who, therefore, persist in this fatal error. The danger of opium, as a slow poison, flows often from two sources, which I will just mention here: One of them is, that it is often the best palliative, and gives present ease, even in diseases, which it either confirms or increases: by this temporary relief, we are often decoyed into mistakes about its effects, and, indeed, it is no great wonder.... Another considerable source of the mischiefs done by this drug, is, the commonly received notion, that opium should be given at any time, when watching or pain is excessive; I am so much of the contrary opinion, that, with me, it is almost a rule not to give it when either of the two is immoderate, ... and if it happens to force some disturbed slumbers, they prove more intolerable than the watching, and are commonly succeeded by a greater excess of pain. I hope this caution will be of use to such as think opium serves only to abate pain and procure sleep, without considering when it is that it increases the cause of the pain.

3. From John Awsiter, *An Essay on the Effects of Opium, Considered as A Poison*, 2nd ed. (London: G. Kearsly, 1767), 4–5, 7–8

The great Doctor *Mead*,[1] in his Tract upon Poisons, gives an Example of such a Power being in Opium, by pouring it, dissolved in warm Water, into a Dog. Had that able Genius, adequate to the Task, pursued his Experiments with that Spirit wherewith he abounded, it would have yet added to the Obligation the World owes him; but over the Means necessary to be used to counteract this Poison, and the Effects of it upon *human* Bodies, he has drawn a Veil ... Far be it from me to comment

---

[1] See p. 53, n. 3.

upon the Principles of this Doctrine; he was too just not to be sensible of what he wrote; perhaps he thought the Subject of too delicate a Nature to be made common, and as many People might then indiscriminately use it, it would take from that necessary Fear and Caution, which should prevent their experiencing the extensive Power of this Drug: for there are many Properties in it, if universally known, that would habituate the Use, and make it more in Request with us than the *Turks* themselves, the Result of which Knowledge must prove a general Misfortune....

Though it is a received Opinion, that Opium, with us, and other Countries where not manufactured, has not near the Strength of that used by the People where it grows; yet in *Turkey* they can venture to take it in larger Quantities; and hence it is manifest, that the Effects would be more pernicious amongst them, if they did not use it in a most pure State; and though Habit might conduce to the Constitution bearing it in much larger Doses, than we in *England* dare give it, yet certainly the constant Use of it, unless when of a most fine Texture of Parts, must sooner prove hurtful, than the immoderate and constant Drinking of Wines, and Spirits; and by this Means, the Lives of the major Part of the Eastern Countries, where it is so much requested, would drop in the Flower of their Youth, and which Nations, in the Space of a Century, be depopulated.

4. From Samuel Crumpe, *An Inquiry Into the Nature and Properties of Opium* (London: G.G. and J. Robinson, 1793), 43–48

In the animal functions, the principal alterations occasioned by Opium are the following:
The hilarity of mind is by degrees augmented, and continues to increase, if the dose has been considerable, until the delirium of intoxication is produced; which, as when resulting from spirituous liquors, is attended in different constitutions with different symptoms. It is, however, more generally productive of a pleasant and joyous state of mind than the contrary; and it, in many, occasions an increased disposition to venery. After these effects have continued for some time, they are succeeded by others of a very opposite nature; the mind becomes gradually dull and languid, the body averse to motion, little affected by customary impressions, and inclined to sleep. If the dose has been considerable, all these symptoms continue to increase; and tremors, convulsions, vertigo, stupor, insensibility, and deprivation of muscular

action appear variously complicated, and in various degrees, proportioned to the excess in the dose, and peculiarity of constitution in the sufferer.... In the eastern countries, where Opium is taken in very large quantities, its enlivening and exhilarating effects are universally known and acknowledged. The Turks, and other nations, swallow it in large quantities, when marching to battle, or under any other circumstances, which require a mind void of depressing fears, and inspired with fortitude. If oppressed by cares or misfortunes, they have recourse to the same assistance, and from its exhilarating powers experience a temporary suspension of melancholy and anxiety. In short, like wine and spirituous liquors in civilized Europe, it is in these countries the support of the coward, the solace of the wretched, and the daily source of intoxication to the debauchee.

5. From "Dreams" in *Encyclopædia Britannica*, 3rd ed. (Edinburgh, A. Bell and C. MacFarquhar, 1797), 6:120, 121–22

It appears, then, that in dreaming we are not conscious of being asleep: that to a person dreaming, his dreams seem realities: that though it be uncertain whether mankind are all liable to dreams, yet it is well known that they are not all *equally* liable to dream: that the nature of a person's dreams depends in some measure on his habits of action, and on the circumstances of his life: that the state of the health too, and the manner in which the vital functions are carried on, have a powerful influence in determining the character of a person's dreams: that in sleep and in dreaming, the senses are either absolutely inactive, or nearly so: that such concerns as we have been very deeply interested in during the preceding day, are very likely to return upon our minds in dreams in the hours of rest: that dreams may be rendered prophetic of future events; and therefore, wherever we have such evidence of their having been prophetic as we would accept on any other occasion, we cannot reasonably reject the fact on account of its absurdity; but that they do not appear to have been actually such, in those instances in which the superstition of nations, ignorant of true religion, has represented them as referring to futurity, nor in those instances in which they are viewed in the same light by the vulgar among ourselves: and, lastly, that dreaming is not a phenomenon peculiar to human nature, but common to mankind with the brutes.

The ingenious Mr. Baxter, in his Treatise on the Immateriality of the Human Soul, endeavours to prove that dreams are produced by the agency of some spiritual beings, who either amuse or employ themselves seriously in engaging mankind in all those imaginary transactions with which they are employed in dreaming.... Wolfius, and after him M. Formey, have supposed, that dreams never arise in the mind, except in consequent of some of the organs of sensation having been previously excited.... But what passes in dreams is so very different from all that we do when awake, that it is impossible for the dreamer himself to distinguish, whether his powers of sensation *perform* any part on the occasion.... Other physiologists tell us, that the mind, when we dream, is in a state of *delirium*. Sleep, they say, is attended with what is called a *collapse* of the brain; during which either the whole or a part of the nerves of which it consists, are in a state in which they cannot carry on the usual intercourse between the mind and the organs of sensation. When the whole of the brain is in this state, we become entirely unconscious of existence, and the mind sinks into inactivity: when only a part of the brain is *collapsed*, as they term it, we are then neither asleep nor awake, but in a sort of delirium between the two.... In the last edition of this work, a theory somewhat different from any of the foregoing was advanced on this subject. It was observed, that the nervous fluid, which is allowed to be secreted from the blood by the brain, appears to be likewise absorbed from the blood by the extremities of the nerves. It was farther advanced, that as this fluid was to be considered as the principle of sensibility: therefore, in all cases in which a sufficient supply of it was not absorbed from the blood by the extremities of the nerves, the parts of the body to which those nerves belonged, must be, in some degree, deprived of sensation.... It followed of consequence, that, in sleep, the nervous fluid between the extreme parts of the nerves and the brain must either be at rest, or be deficient, or be prevented by some means from passing into the brain: and it was concluded, that whenever irregular motions of this fluid were occasioned by an internal cause, *dreaming* was produced.—In this manner it appeared that we might be deceived with regard to the operation of any of the senses;—so as to fancy that we saw objects not actually before us,—to hear imaginary sounds,—to taste,—to feel, and to smell in imagination.... Amid this uncertainty with respect to the manner in which our powers of mind and body perform their functions in dreaming; it is pleasing to find that we can, however, apply to useful purposes the imperfect knowledge which we have been able to acquire concerning this series of phenomena. Our dreams are affected by the state of our health, by the manner in which we have passed the preceding day, by our general habits of life, by the hopes which we most fondly indulge, and the fears which prevail most over our fortitude when we are awake. From recollecting our dreams, therefore, we may learn to correct many improprieties in our conduct; to refrain from bodily exercises, or from meats and drinks that have unfavourable effects on our constitution; to resist, in due time, evil habits that are stealing upon us; and to guard against hopes and fears which detach us from our proper concerns, and unfit us for the duties of life. Instead of thinking what our dreams may forebode, we may with much better reason reflect by what they have been occasioned, and look back to those circumstances in our past life to which they are owing. The sleep of innocence and health is sound and refreshing; their dreams delightful and pleasing. A distempered body, and a polluted or perturbed mind, are haunted in sleep with frightful, impure, and unpleasing dreams.

6. From Thomas Trotter, *A View of the Nervous Temperament* (London: Longman, Hurst, Rees, and Orme, 1807), xv–xviii, 133–38

The last century has been remarkable for the increase of a class of diseases, but little known in former times, and what had slightly engaged the study of physicians prior to that period. They have been designated in common language, by the terms, NERVOUS; SPASMODIC; BILIOUS; INDIGESTION; STOMACH COMPLAINTS; LOW SPIRITS; VAPOURS, & c. A generic definition of them, from their protean shapes and multiform appearance, is almost impracticable. They vary in every constitution; and assume in the same person, at different times of life, an inconstant assemblage of symptoms.... But from causes, to be hereafter investigated, we shall find, that nervous ailments are no longer confined to the better ranks of life, but rapidly extending to the poorer classes. In this neighbourhood, as far I am able to judge from my own experience, they are by no means limited to the rich: and it affords a melancholy picture of the healthy of the community, to observe this proportion so very large. It is probable the other countries of Europe do not exhibit such general examples of these diseases; as many of their causes are to be traced to the peculiar situation of Britain; its insular varieties of climate and atmosphere; its political institutions and free government; and above every thing, its vast wealth, so diffused among all ranks of people.

[Narcotics] include ardent spirits, opium, and all those articles commonly called anodynes, hypnotics, paregorics, & c.... All the articles now enumerated, act very much alike on the human body. In small quantities, they induce vigour, activity, and strength, and an increase of muscular power throughout the frame; at the same time are felt serenity, pleasure and courage of mind. In larger doses they bring on sleep, stupor and delirium; and when carried to the utmost quantity, insensibility, apoplexy and death.... When long continued, they are known to weaken the nervous system in a surprizing degree; disposing to amentia, epilepsy, palsy, tremors, convulsions, melancholy, madness, & c. No substances in nature more certainly injure the powers of digestion, and bring on all severe symptoms of nervous infirmity.... The bodily complaints of the human race, when enervated by luxury and refinement, seem to produce more acute pain, at least the temperate man is observed to bear sickness with more patience and resignation, than those accustomed to indulgence. The spirits are apt to flag, as if the mind had no resting place. Opium alone gives relief, though it must feed the disease. Such persons seem to compound with their physician for sound nights and days of ease; and if he does not comply, he must be changed. Hard is the talk imposed on the medical attendant; he must obey, or starve. The *night draught* thus becomes familiar in the family: the servant goes to the apothecary for it with as little ceremony as he buys kitchen salt. He sees the shop boy count the drops into the phial, and when he gets home, narrates the composition of the placebo to the cook and the nursemaid. Not a domestic in the house but soon learns what a fine thing laudanum is; and master swears he can get no rest without it.... [T]here is reason to believe, that even medical men themselves, have of late, entered too easily into the indiscriminate use of opium. He must be a short-sighted physician that does not calculate upon the ultimate effects of his prescription: it is a weak excuse for getting quit of the importunities of a patient, by complying with an improper request, that may afford temporary ease, at the expence of permanent health. In the nervous temperament it is particularly hurtful. I am acquainted with numbers of ladies that feel such horror at taking it, as nothing can equal; and in every illness they may labour under, constantly warn the medical visitor about giving it, as no disguise can make it agreeable to them. But, when opium happens to be soothing to weak nerved people, from their quick sensations, it is apt to be the more craved for, and converted into habit. The langour and dejection which follow its operation pave the way for the repetition of the dose, till general debility succeeds. In such constitutions, the exhibition of opium ought never to take place on slight occasions.

7. From Robert Macnish, *The Anatomy of Drunkenness* (Glasgow: W.R. McPhun, 1827), 21–23

The drunkenness produced by opium has also some characteristics which it is necessary to mention. This drug is principally employed by the Mahommetans. By their religion these people are forbidden the use of wine, and use opium as a substitute. And a delightful substitute it is while the first excitation continues; for the images it occasions in the mind are more exquisite than any produced even by wine. There is reason to believe that the use of this medicine has, of late years, gained ground in Great Britain. We are told by the "English Opium-Eater," whose powerful and interesting "Confessions" have excited so deep an interest, that the practice exists among the work people at Manchester. Many of our fashionable ladies have recourse to it when troubled with vapours, or low spirits: some of them carry it even about with them for the purpose. This practice is most pernicious, and no way different from that of drunkards, who swallow wine and other liquors to drive away care. While the first effects continue, the intended purpose is sufficiently gained, but the melancholy which follows is infinitely greater than can be compensated by the previous exhilaration. In this country opium is much used, but seldom with the view of producing intoxication. Some, indeed, deny that it can do so, strictly speaking. If by intoxication is meant a state precisely similar to that from over-indulgence in vinous or spiritous liquors, they are undoubtedly right; but drunkenness merits a wider latitude of significance. The ecstasies of opium are much more entrancing than those of wine. There is more poetry in its visions, more mental aggrandizement, more range of imagination. Wine invigorates the animal powers and propensities chiefly, but opium strengthens those peculiar to man, and gives for a period amounting to hours, a higher tone to the thinking faculties. Then the dreams of the opium-eater— they are the creations of a highly excited fancy, rich and unspeakably delightful. But when the medicine has been continued too long, or operates on a diseased constitution, these feelings wear away. The sleep is no longer cheered with its former visions of happiness. Frightful dreams usurp their place, and the person becomes the victim of an almost perpetual misery. Opium resembles the other agents of intoxication in this, that the fondness for it increases with use, and that, at last, it becomes nearly essential for bodily comfort and peace of mind. Some will take to the extent of from one to two drachms daily. There are many persons who make a practice of swallowing half an ounce of laudanum night and morning. The "English Opium-Eater" himself, furnishes the most extraordinary instance on record of the power of habit in bringing the body to withstand the drug.

8. From "The Narcotics We Indulge In–Part II," *Blackwood's Edinburgh Magazine* (November 1853): 605–20

The effects of opium upon the system of the healthy are generally esteemed to be eminently prejudicial. Not only is an indulgence in the use of opium held to be criminal in itself, because of the evil consequences which are supposed to follow it, but it is esteemed a criminal act to make the procuring of it easy, and thus indirectly to minister to its more extensive consumption. The opinion is now, however, beginning to prevail among medical men, that opium taken in moderation, even for a serious [sic] of years, is not necessarily injurious to health. Like spiritous liquors and tobacco, it acts as a sure poison when taken immoderately, but the moderate enjoyment of any of the three has not been proved to be either generally or necessarily, and upon all constitutions, attended by ill effects. It may be that the temptation to excess in the case of opium is greater, and that the habitual users of it are less frequently able to resist its seductive influence. But even this, as a physiological question, has by no means been satisfactorily established, and we must be cautious in pushing our conclusions farther than known facts will carry us.... The use of this drug, as a narcotic indulgence, appears to be on the increase upon the European population generally. Among the less provident, especially of the working classes in our own large manufacturing towns, the use of laudanum as a care-dispelling, happiness-giving potion—often as a dispeller of hunger—is said to be greatly extending. If so, we should expect that among us, as among the Turks and Chinese, opium will find many who are unable to resist its seductive allurements, and whom it will drag into the extreme of mental and bodily misery. Of its powers of seduction, indeed, even over the less delicate and susceptible organisation of our northern European races, and of the absolute slavery to which it can reduce even the strongest minds among us, we have two remarkable examples in the celebrated Coleridge, and in the author of the *English Opium-Eater*.

9. From Mordecai C. Cooke, *The Seven Sisters of Sleep. Popular History of the Seven Prevailing Narcotics of the World* (London: James Blackwood, 1860), 150–51, 164–65

What are the true effects of opium are best described by an eminent physician, who has studied well the results produced by all such influences upon the brain. The imagination appears to be acted upon, independent of the peculiar torpor, accompanied by sensations of gratification, and the absence of all communication with the external world. The senses convey no false impressions to the brain; all that is seen, heard, or felt, is faithfully delineated, but the imagination clothes each object in its own fanciful garb. It exaggerates, it multiplies, it colours, it gives fantastic shapes; there is a new condition arising out of ordinary perception, and the reason, abandoning itself to the imagination, does not resist the delight of the indulging in visions. If the eyes are closed, and nothing presented to excite the external senses, a whole train of vivid dreams are presented. A theatre is lighted up in the brain—graceful dancers perform the most captivating evolutions—music of an unearthly character floats along—poesy, whose harmonious numbers, and whose exciting themes, are far beyond the power of the human mind, is unceasingly poured forth. Memory is, however, generally asleep—all the passions, affections, and motions have lost their sway. It is all an exquisite indolence, during which dreams spontaneously arise, brilliant, beautiful, and exhilarating. There is order, harmony, tranquillity. If a single object has been vividly impressed upon the eye, it is multiplied a thousand times by the imagination–vast processions pass him in his reveries in mournful pomp.

But the worst Pandemonium which those who indulge in opium suffer, is that of the mind. Opium retains at all times its power of exciting the imagination, provided sufficient doses are taken; but when it has been continued so long as to bring disease upon the constitution, the pleasurable feelings wear away, and are succeeded by others of a very different kind. Instead of disposing the mind to be happy, it acts upon it like the spell of a demon, and calls up phantoms of horror and disgust. The fancy, still as powerful, changes its direction. Formerly it clothed all objects with the light of heaven—now it invests them with the attributes of hell. Goblins, specters, and every kind of distempered vision haunt the mind, peopling it with dreary and revolting imagery. The sleep is no longer cheered with its former sights of happiness. Frightful

dreams usurp their place, till at least the person becomes the victim of
an almost perpetual misery.

10. From Henry Havelock Ellis, *The Dance of Life* (New York: Houghton Mifflin, 1923), 51–53

... [Decadence] is generally used ... to express the literary methods of a
society which has reached its limits of expansion and maturity—"the
state of society ... which produces too large a number of individuals
who are unsuited to the labours of the common life. A society should
be like an organism. Like an organism, in fact, it may be resolved into
a federation of smaller organisms, which may themselves be resolved
into a federation of cells. The individual is the social cell. In order that
the organism should perform its functions with energy it is necessary
that the organisms composing it should perform their functions with
energy, but with a subordinated energy, and in order that these lesser
organisms should themselves perform their functions with energy, it is
necessary that the cells comprising them should perform their functions with energy, but with a subordinated energy. If the energy of the
cells becomes independent, the lesser organisms will likewise cease to
subordinate their energy to the total energy and the anarchy which is
established constitutes the *decadence* of the whole. The social organism
does not escape this law and enters into decadence as soon as the individual life becomes exaggerated beneath the influence of acquired well-
being, and of heredity. A similar law governs the development and
decadence of that other organism which we call language. A style of
decadence is one in which the unity of the book is decomposed to give
place to the independence of the page, in which the page is decomposed to give place to the independence of the phrase, and the phrase
to give place to the independence of the word." A decadent style, in
short, is an anarchistic style in which everything is sacrificed to the
development of the individual parts. Apuleius, Petronius, St. Augustine,
Tertullian, are examples of this *decadence* in ancient literature; Gautier
and Baudelaire in French literature; Poe and especially Whitman (in so
far as he can be said to have a style) in America; in English literature Sir
Thomas Browne is probably the most conspicuous instance; later De
Quincey, and, in part of their work, Coleridge and Rossetti.

Select Bibliography

Editions of De Quincey (listed in chronological order by date of publication)

De Quincey, Thomas. *Confessions of an English Opium-Eater*. London: Taylor & Hessey, 1822.

———. *Confessions of an English Opium-Eater and Suspiria de Profundis*. Boston: Ticknor & Fields, 1850.

———. *De Quincey's Writings*. Ed. James Thomas Fields. 20 vols. Boston: Ticknor, Reed, & Fields, 1851.

———. *The Works of Thomas De Quincey*. 3rd ed. 16 vols. Edinburgh: A. and C. Black, 1871.

———. *The Collected Writings of Thomas De Quincey*. Ed. David Masson. 14 vols. Edinburgh: Adam and Charles Black, 1890.

———. *The Posthumous Works of Thomas De Quincey*. Ed. Alexander H. Japp. London: William Heinemann, 1891.

———. *The Confessions of an English Opium-Eater, and Other Essays*. London: Macmillan, 1901.

———. *Selected Writings of Thomas de Quincey*. Ed. Phillip Van Doren Stern, London: Nonesuch Press; New York: Random House, 1939.

———. *Confessions of an English Opium-Eater, together with selections from the Autobiography of Thomas de Quincey*. Ed. Edward Sackville-West. London: Cresset Press, 1950.

———. *Confessions of an English Opium-Eater*. Ed. Malcolm Elwin. London: Macdonald, 1956.

———. *Confessions of an English Opium-Eater*. Ed. John E. Jordan. London: Dent, 1960.

———. *Confessions of an English Opium-Eater, and Other Writings*. Ed. Aileen Ward. New York: New American Library, 1966.

———. *Confessions of an English Opium-Eater and Other Writings*. Ed. Grevel Lindop. Oxford: Oxford UP, 1985; rev. ed. 1998.

———. *Confessions of an English Opium Eater*. Ed. Alethea Hayter. New York: Penguin, 1986.

———. *The Works of Thomas De Quincey*. Ed. Grevel Lindop et al. 21 vols. London: Pickering & Chatto, 2000–04.

Other materials

Abrams, M.H. *The Milk of Paradise: The Effect of Opium Visions on the Works of De Quincey, Crabbe, Francis Thompson, and Coleridge*. New York: Octagon Books, 1971.

Augustine, *Confessions*. Trans. John K. Ryan. New York: Doubleday, 1960.

Awsiter, John. *An Essay on the Effects of Opium, Considered as A Poison*. 2nd ed. London: G. Kearsly, 1767.

Barine, Arvede. *Névrosés: Hoffmann, Quincey, Edgar Poe, G. De Nerval*. Paris: Hachette, 1898.

———. *Névrosés: Thomas De Quincey, Gérard de Nerval*. Paris: Hachette, 1936.

Barrell, John. *The Infection of Thomas De Quincey: A Psychopathology of Imperialism*. New Haven: Yale UP, 1991.

Baudelaire, Charles. *Les Paradis Artificiels* (1860). Trans. Stacy Diamond. New York: Citadel, 1996.

Baxter, Andrew. *An Enquiry into the Nature of the Human Soul*. 2nd ed. 2 vols. London, 1737.

Baxter, Edmund. *De Quincey's Art of Autobiography*. Edinburgh: Edinburgh UP, 1990.

Beer, John. "De Quincey and the Dark Sublime: The Wordsworth-Coleridge Ethos." *Thomas De Quincey: Bicentenary Studies*. Ed. Robert Lance Snyder. Norman: U of Oklahoma P, 1985. 164–98.

Berridge, Virginia, and Griffith Edwards. *Opium and the People: Opiate Use in Nineteenth-Century England*. 2nd ed. New Haven: Yale UP, 1987.

Bilsland, John W. "De Quincey's Critical Dilations." *University of Toronto Quarterly* 52.2 (Fall 1982): 79–83.

———. "De Quincey's Opium Experiences." *Dalhousie Review* 55 (1975): 419–30.

———. "On De Quincey's Theory of Literary Power." *University of Toronto Quarterly* 26 (1957): 469–80.

Black, Joel D. "Confession, Digression, Gravitation: Thomas De Quincey's German Connection." *Thomas De Quincey: Bicentenary Studies*. 308–37. Ed. and intro. Robert Lance Snyder. Norman: U of Oklahoma P, 1985.

Blake, Kathleen. "The Whispering Gallery and Structural Coherence in De Quincey's Revised *Confessions of an English Opium-Eater*." *Studies in English Literature, 1500–1900* 13.4 (Fall 1973): 632–42.

Brewster, David. *Letters on Natural Magic, Addressed to Sir Walter Scott*. London: John Murray, 1832.

Brown, John. *The Elements of Medicine; or, A Translation of the Elementa Medicinæ Brunonis*. 2 vols. London: J. Johnson, 1788.

Bruss, Elizabeth. *Autobiographical Acts: The Changing Situation of a Literary Genre*. Baltimore: Johns Hopkins UP, 1976.

Burwick, Frederick. "De Quincey and the Aesthetics of Violence." *The Wordsworth Circle* 37.2 (Spring 1996): 78–86.

———. "The Dream Visions of Jean Paul and Thomas De Quincey." *Comparative Literature* 20.1 (Winter 1968): 1–26.

———. *Thomas De Quincey: Knowledge and Power*. Basingstoke: Palgrave, 2001.

Cafarelli, Annette Wheeler. "De Quincey and Wordsworthian Narrative." *Studies in Romanticism* 28 (1989): 121–47.

Caseby, Richard. *The Opium-Eating Editor: Thomas De Quincey and the Westmorland Gazette*. Kendal: The Westmorland Gazette, 1985.

Chardin, Sir John. *The Travels of Sir John Chardin into Persia and the East-Indies*. London: Moses Pitt, 1686.

Clark, David. "We 'Other Prussians': Bodies and Pleasures in De Quincey and Late Kant." *European Romantic Review* 14.2 (Summer 2003): 265–91.

Clej, Alina. *A Genealogy of the Modern Self: Thomas De Quincey and the Intoxication of Writing*. Stanford: Stanford UP, 1995.

Coleridge, Samuel Taylor. *Christabel; Kubla Khan: A Vision; The Pains of Sleep*. London: John Murray, 1816.

———. *Collected Letters of Samuel Taylor Coleridge*. Ed. Earle Leslie Griggs. 6 vols. Oxford: Clarendon, 1956-1971.

———. *The Collected Notebooks of Samuel Taylor Coleridge*. Ed. Kathleen Coburn and Merton Christensen. 4 vols. New York: Bollingen Series: Pantheon Books, 1957-90.

Cooke, Michael G. "De Quincey, Coleridge, and the Formal Uses of Intoxication." *Yale French Studies* 50 (1974): 26–40.

Cooke, Mordecai C. *The Seven Sisters of Sleep. Popular History of the Seven Prevailing Narcotics of the World*. London: James Blackwood, 1860.

Corrigan, Timothy. "Interpreting the Uncitable Text: The Literary Criticism of Thomas De Quincey." *Ineffability: Naming the Unnamable from Dante to Beckett*. Ed. Peter S. Hawkins and Anne Howland Schotter. New York: AMS, 1984. 131–46.

Crumpe, Samuel. *An Inquiry Into the Nature and Properties of Opium*. London: G.G. and J. Robinson, 1793.

Davis, John Francis. *The Chinese: A General Description of The Empire of China and Its Inhabitants*. 2 vols. London: Charles Knight and Co., 1836.

De Luca, V.A. *Thomas De Quincey: The Prose of Vision*. Toronto: U of Toronto P, 1980.

De Quincey, Thomas. "On the Temperance Movement of Modern Times." *Tait's Edinburgh Magazine* (October 1845): 658–65.

———. "The Opium and the China Question." *Blackwood's Edinburgh Magazine* 47 (June 1840): 717–38.

Derrida, Jacques. "The Rhetoric of Drugs: An Interview with Jacques Derrida." Interview by Jacques Herpieu. *differences* 5.1 (1993): 1–25.

Devlin, D.D. *De Quincey, Wordsworth and the Art of Prose.* London: MacMillan, 1983.

"Dreams." *Encyclopædia Britannica.* 3rd ed. Edinburgh: A. Bell and C. MacFarquhar, 1797. 120–22.

Eaton, Horace Ainsworth. *Thomas De Quincey: A Biography.* New York: Oxford UP, 1936.

Ellis, Henry Havelock. *The Dance of Life.* New York: Houghton Mifflin, 1923.

Faflak, Joel. "De Quincey Collects Himself." *Nervous Reactions: Victorian Recollections of Romanticism.* Ed. Joel Faflak and Julia Wright. Albany, NY: State U of New York P, 2004.

———. "Romanticism and the Pornography of Talking." *Nineteenth-Century Contexts* 27 (March 2005): 77–97.

Foucault, Michel. *The History of Sexuality. Vol 1: An Introduction.* Trans. Robert Hurley. New York: Vintage Books, 1990.

Frye, Northrop. "The Drunken Boat: The Revolutionary Element in Romanticism." *Romanticism Reconsidered: Selected Papers from the English Institute.* Ed. Northrop Frye. New York: Columbia UP, 1963.

Gilfillan, George. "Thomas De Quincey." *The Eclectic Review* 27 (April 1850): 397–408.

Goethe, Johann Wolfgang von. *The Sorrows of Young Werther* (1774). Trans. Michael Hulse. New York: Penguin, 1989.

Groves, David. "Thomas De Quincey and the *Edinburgh Literary Gazette,* and the *Affinity of Languages.*" *English Language Notes* 26.3 (1989): 55–69.

Haltresht, Michael. "The Meaning of De Quincey's 'Dream Fugue on ... Sudden Death.'" *Literature and Psychology* 26 (1976): 31–36.

Harding, Geoffrey. *Opiate Addiction, Morality and Medicine: From Moral Illness to Pathological Disease.* New York: St. Martin's, 1988.

Hayter, Alethea. *Opium and the Romantic Imagination: Addiction and Creativity in De Quincey, Coleridge, Baudelaire and Others.* Wellingborough, England: Crucible, 1988.

Hendricks, C.. "Thomas De Quincey, Symptomatologist." *PMLA* 60 (1945): 828–40.

Holstein, Michael. "'An Apocalypse of the World Within': Autobiographical Exegesis in De Quincey's *Confessions of an English Opium-Eater* (1822)." *Prose Studies* 2 (1979): 88–102.

Inglis, Brian. *The Opium War.* London: Hodder, 1976.

Jack, Ian. "De Quincey Reviews His Confessions." *PMLA* 72 (1957): 122–46.

Jacobus, Mary. "The Art of Managing Books: Romantic Prose and the Writing of the Past." *Romanticism and Language*. Ed. Arden Reed. London: Methuen & Co., 1984. 215–46.

Japp, Alexander H., ed. *Thomas De Quincey: His Life and Writings*. 2 vols. London: John Hogg, 1877.

———. *Posthumous Works of Thomas De Quincey*. London: William Heinemann, 1891.

Jones, John. *The Mysteries of Opium Reveal'd*. London, 1700.

Jordan, John Emory. *De Quincey to Wordsworth: A Biography of a Relationship*. Berkeley: U of California P, 1962.

———. *Thomas De Quincey, Literary Critic: His Method and Achievement*. Berkeley: U of California P, 1952.

———, ed. *De Quincey as Critic*. London: Routledge, 1973.

Kant, Immanuel. *Anthropology from a Pragmatic Point of View*. Trans. Victor Lyle Dowdell. Carbondale, IL: Southern Illinois UP, 1996.

Klancher, Jon. *The Making of English Reading Audiences, 1790–1832*. Madison: U of Wisconsin P, 1987.

Lamb, Charles. "Confessions of a Drunkard." *The Philanthropist: or Repository for Hints and Suggestions Calculated to Promote the Comfort and Happiness of Man*. Vol. 3. London: Richard and Arthur Taylor, 1813.

Leask, Nigel. *British Romantic Writers and the East: Anxieties of Empire*. Cambridge: Cambridge UP, 1992.

Leighton, Angela. "De Quincey and Women." *Beyond Romanticism: New Approaches to Texts and Contexts, 1780–1832*. Ed. Stephen Copley and John Whale. London: Routledge, 1992. 160–77.

Lever, Karen M. "De Quincey as Gothic Hero: A Perspective on *Confessions of an English Opium-Eater* and *Suspira de Profundis*." *Texas Studies in Literature and Language* 21 (1979): 332–46.

Levin, Susan M. *The Romantic Art of Confession: De Quincey, Musset, Sand, Lamb, Hogg, Frémy, Soulié, Janin*. Columbia, SC: Camden House, 1998.

Lindop, Grevel. *The Opium-Eater: A Life of Thomas De Quincey*. London: Dent, 1981.

Logan, Peter Melville. *Nerves and Narratives: A Cultural History of Hysteria in 19th-Century British Prose*. Berkeley: U of California P, 1997.

Macnish, Robert. *The Anatomy of Drunkenness*. Glasgow: W.R. McPhun, 1827.

Madden, R.R. *Travels in Turkey, Egypt, Nubia, and Palestine, in 1824, 1825, 1826, & 1827*. 2 vols. 2nd ed. London: Whittaker, Treacher, and Co., 1833.

Malthus, Thomas Robert. *An essay on the principle of population, or, A view of its past and present effects on human happiness: with an inquiry into our prospects respecting the future removal or migration of the evils which it occasions.* 2nd ed. London: J. Johnson, 1806.

Maniquis, Robert M. "The Dark Interpreter and the Palimpsest of Violence: De Quincey and the Unconscious." *Thomas De Quincey: Bicentenary Studies.* 109–39. Ed. and intro. Robert Lance Snyder. Norman: U of Oklahoma P, 1985.

Marsden, William. *A History of Sumatra, Containing An Account of the Government, Laws, Customs, and Manners of the Native Inhabitants, with a Description of the Natural Productions, and a Relation of the Ancient Political State of that Island.* London: Thomas Payne and Son, 1783.

Masson, David. Rev. of *Selections Grave and Gay, from Writings Published and Unpublished*, by Thomas De Quincey. *British Quarterly Review* 20 (1854): 163–88.

———. *De Quincey*. London: Macmillan, 1881.

May, Claire B. "From Dream to Text: The Collective Unconscious in the Aesthetic Theory of Thomas De Quincey." *Journal of Evolutionary Psychology* 16.1–2 (1995): 75–83.

McDonagh, Josephine. *De Quincey's Disciplines*. Oxford: Clarendon, 1994.

McFarland, Thomas. *Romantic Cruxes: The English Essayists and the Spirit of the Age*. Oxford: Clarendon, 1987.

Medhurst, W.H. *China: Its State and Prospects, with Especial Reference to the Spread of the Gospel: Containing Allusions to the Antiquity, Extent, Population, Civilization, Literature, and Religion of the Chinese.* London: John Snow, 1838.

Miller, Joseph Hillis. *The Disappearance of God: Five Nineteenth-Century Writers*. Cambridge, MA: Harvard UP, 1963.

Milligan, Barry. *Pleasures and Pains: Opium and the Orient in Nineteenth-Century British Culture*. Charlottesville: U of Virginia P, 1995.

Milner, Max. *L'imaginaire des drogues: de Thomas De Quincey à Henri Michaux.* Paris: Gallimard, 2000.

Morewood, Samuel. *A Philosophical and Statistical History of the Inventions and Customs of Ancient and Modern Nations in the Manufacture and Use of Inebriating Liquors.* 2nd ed. Dublin and London, 1838.

Morrison, Robert. "De Quincey and the Opium-Eater's Other Selves." *Romanticism* 5.1 (1999): 87–103.

———. "Opium Eaters and Magazine Wars: De Quincey and Coleridge in 1821." *Victorian Periodicals Review* 30 (1997): 27–40.

———. "Red De Quincey." *The Wordsworth Circle* 29 (1988): 131–36.

"The Narcotics we indulge in — Part II." *Blackwoods Edinburgh Magazine* (November 1853): 605–20.

Notice of *Confessions of an English Opium-Eater*. *The Monthly Magazine* 54 (December 1822): 450.

"Opiologia; or *Confessions of an English Opium-Eater*: being an Extract from the Life of a Scholar." *Medico-Chirurgical Review* 2 (March 1822): 881–901.

O'Quinn, Daniel. "The Gog and Magog of Hunnish Desolation: De Quincey, Kant, and the Practice of Death." *Nineteenth-Century Contexts* 20 (1997): 261–86.

——."Murder, Hospitality, Philosophy: De Quincey and the Complicitous Grounds of National Identity." *Studies in Romanticism* 38 (1999): 135–70.

——."Ravishment Twice Weekly: De Quincey's Opera Pleasures." *Romanticism on the Net* 34–35 (May–August 2004).

——."Who Owns What: Slavery, Property and Eschatological Compensation in Thomas De Quincey's Opium Writings." *Texas Studies in Language and Literature* 45.3 (Fall 2003): 362–92.

Platzner, Robert L. "De Quincey and the Dilemma of Romantic Autobiography." *Dalhousie Review* 61 (1981): 605–17.

Plotz, Judith. *Romanticism and the Vocation of Childhood*. New York; Houndmills, Basingstoke, Hampshire: Palgrave, 2001.

Porter, Roger J. "The Demon Past: De Quincey and the Autobiographer's Dilemma." *Studies in English Literature* 20.4 (Fall 1980): 591–609.

Proudfit, Charles L. "Thomas De Quincey and Sigmund Freud: Sons, Fathers, Dreamers—Precursors of Psychoanalytic Developmental Psychology." *Thomas De Quincey: Bicentenary Studies*. 88–107. Ed. and intro. Robert Lance Snyder. Norman: U of Oklahoma P, 1985.

Ramsey, Roger. "The Structure of De Quincey's *Confessions of an English Opium-Eater*." *Prose Studies 1800–1900* 1.2 (1978): 21–29.

Ready, Robert. "De Quincey's Magnificent Apparatus." *Interspace and the Inward Sphere: Essays on Romantic and Victorian Self*. Ed. Norman A. Anderson and Margene E. Weiss. Macomb: Western Illinois UP, 1978.

Rev. of *Confessions of an English Opium-Eater*. *The British Critic* 18 (November 1822): 531–34.

Rev. of *Confessions of an English Opium-Eater*. *The British Review, and London Critical Journal* 20 (December 1822): 474–89.

Rev. of *Confessions of an English Opium-Eater*. *The Monthly Review* 100 (March 1823): 288–96.

Rev. of *Confessions of an English Opium-Eater*. *The Eclectic Review* 19 (April 1823): 366–71.

Rev. of *Confessions of an English Opium-Eater*. *The North American Review* 18 (January 1824): 91–98.

Rev. of *Selections Grave and Gay, from Works Published and Unpublished, by Thomas De Quincey*. *The Eclectic Review* ns. 8 (1854): 385–88.

Rev. of *The Works of Thomas De Quincey*. *British Quarterly Review* 38 (1863): 1–29.

Ricardo, David. *The Principles of Political Economy and Taxation*. London: J. Murray, 1817.

Roberts, Daniel Sanjiv. *Revisionary Gleam: De Quincey, Coleridge, and the High Romantic Argument*. Liverpool: Liverpool UP, 2000.

Ronell, Avita. *Crack Wars: Literature, Addiction, Mania*. Lincoln: U of Nebraska P, 1992.

Rousseau, Jean-Jacques. *Confessions* (1782). Trans. Angela Scholar. Ed. Patrick Coleman. London: Oxford UP, 2000.

Russett, Margaret. "De Quincey, Nerves, and Narration." *Review* 22 (2000): 191–97.

———. *De Quincey's Romanticism: Canonical Minority and the Forms of Transmission*. Cambridge: Cambridge UP, 1997.

Rzepka, Charles. Letter to Forum. *PMLA* 115 (January 2000): 93–94.

———. *Sacramental Commodities: Gift, Text, and the Sublime in De Quincey*. Amherst: U of Massachusetts P, 1995.

Sackville-West, Edward. *A Flame in Sunlight: The Life and Works of Thomas De Quincey*. London: Cassell and Co., 1936.

———. *Thomas De Quincey, his Life and Work*. New Haven: Yale UP, 1936.

Schneider, Elisabeth. *Coleridge, Opium and "Kubla Khan."* Chicago: U of Chicago P, 1953.

Schmitt, Cannon. *Alien Nation: Nineteenth-Century Gothic Fictions and English Nationality*. Philadelphia: U of Pennsylvania P, 1997.

Sedgewick, Eve Kosoksy. *The Coherence of Gothic Conventions*. New York: Arno Press, 1980.

———. "Epidemics of the Will." *Tendencies*. Durham: Duke UP, 1993. 130–42.

Snyder, Robert Lance, ed. *Thomas De Quincey: Bicentenary Studies*. Norman: U of Oklahoma P, 1985.

———. "'The Loom of *Palingenesis*': De Quincey's Cosmology in 'System of Heavens.'" *Thomas De Quincey: Bicentenary Studies*. 338–60.

Spector, Stephen J. "Thomas De Quincey: Self-Effacing Autobiographer." *Studies in Romanticism* 18 (1979): 501–20.

Sudan, Rajani. "Englishness 'A'muck': De Quincey's Confessions." *Genre* 27.4 (Winter 1994): 377–94.

Tavernier, Jean-Baptiste. *The Six Voyages of John Baptista Tavernier, Baron of Aubonne; through Turkey, into Persia and the East-Indies, for the Space of Forty Years.* London: Robert Littlebury and Moses Pitt, 1677.

Thelwall, Algernon S. *The Iniquities of the Opium Trade with China; being a Development of the Main Causes which exclude The Merchants of Great Britain from the advantages of an Unrestricted commercial intercourse with that vast empire.* London: Wm. H. Allen and Co., 1839.

"Thomas De Quincey." *The Athenæum* No. 1677 (December 1859): 814–15.

Thomas, Ronald R. *Dreams of Authority: Freud and the Fictions of the Unconscious.* Ithaca: Cornell UP, 1990.

Thron, E.M. "Speed, Steam, Self, and Thomas De Quincey." *Interspace and the Inward Sphere: Essays on Romantic and Victorian Self.* Ed. Norman A. Anderson and Margene E. Weiss. Macomb: Western Illinois U P, 1978. 51–58.

Tomkinson, Neil. *The Christian Faith and Practice of Samuel Johnson, Thomas De Quincey, and Thomas Love Peacock.* Lewiston, NY: E. Mellen Press, 1992.

Travernier, Jean-Baptiste. *The Six Voyages of John Baptista Tavernier, Baron of Aubonne; through Turkey, into Persia and the East-Indies, for the Space of Forty Years.* London: Robert Littlebury and Moses Pitt, 1677.

Trotter, Thomas. *An Essay, Medical, Philosophical, and Chemical, on Drunkenness.* London: Longman, Hurst, Rees, and Orme, 1803.

——. *A View of the Nervous Temperament.* London: Longman, Hurst, Rees, and Orme, 1807.

Vrettos, Athena. *Somatic Fictions: Imagining Illness in Victorian Culture.* Stanford: Stanford UP, 1995.

Wallen, Martin. "Body Linguistics in Schreber's *Memoirs* and De Quincey's *Confessions.*" *Mosaic* 24 (1991): 93–108.

Wellek, Rene. "De Quincey's Status in the History of Ideas." *Philological Quarterly* 23 (1944): 248–75.

Whale, John. "De Quincey's Anarchic Moments." *Essays in Criticism* 33 (1983): 273–93.

——. *Thomas De Quincey's Reluctant Autobiography.* London: Croom Helm, 1984.

Wilner, Joshua. "The Stewed Muse of Prose." *Comparative Literature* 104.5 (1989): 1085–98.

——. "Autobiography and Addiction: The Case of De Quincey." *Genre* 14 (1981): 493–503.

Wohl, Anthony S. *Endangered Lives: Public Health in Victorian Britain.* Cambridge, MA: Harvard UP, 1983.

Woof, Robert. *Thomas De Quincey: An English Opium-Eater, 1785–1859: Exhibitions at the Grasmere and Wordsworth Museum, 24 June–31 October 1985 and at the National Library of Scotland, 16 November 1985–31 January 1986.* Cumbria: Trustees of Dove Cottage, 1985.

Wordsworth, William. *The Prelude: 1799, 1805, 1850.* Ed. Jonathan Wordsworth, M.H. Abrams, and Stephen Gill. New York: W.W. Norton and Co., 1979.

Wright, David, ed. *Recollections of the Lakes and Lake Poets.* By Thomas De Quincey. Toronto: Penguin, 1985.

Young, George. *A Treatise on Opium, Founded upon Practical Observations.* London, 1753.

Young, Michael Cochise. "'The True Hero of the Tale': De Quincey's *Confessions* and Affective Autobiographical Theory." *Thomas De Quincey: Bicentenary Studies.* 54–71. Ed. and intro. Robert Lance Snyder. Norman: U of Oklahoma P, 1985.

Youngquist, Paul. "De Quincey's Crazy Body." *PMLA* 114 (May 1999): 346–58.